ARIADNE'S WEB

TOR BOOKS BY FRED SABERHAGEN

The Berserker® Series
The Berserker Wars ∘ *Berserker Base* (with Poul Anderson, Ed Bryant, Stephen Donaldson, Larry Niven, Connie Willis, and Roger Zelazny) ∘ *Berserker: Blue Death* ∘ *The Berserker Throne* ∘ *Berserker's Planet* ∘ *Berserker Kill* ∘ *Berserker Fury*

The Dracula Series
The Dracula Tapes ∘ *The Holmes-Dracula Files* ∘ *An Old Friend of the Family* ∘ *Thorn* ∘ *Dominion* ∘ *A Matter of Taste* ∘ *A Question of Time* ∘ *Séance for a Vampire* ∘ *A Sharpness on the Neck*

The Swords Series
The First Book of Swords
The Second Book of Swords
The Third Book of Swords
The First Book of Lost Swords: Woundhealer's Story
The Second Book of Lost Swords: Sightblinder's Story
The Third Book of Lost Swords: Stonecutter's Story
The Fourth Book of Lost Swords: Farslayer's Story
The Fifth Book of Lost Swords: Coinspinner's Story
The Sixth Book of Lost Swords: Mindsword's Story
The Seventh Book of Lost Swords: Wayfinder's Story
The Last Book of Swords: Shieldbreaker's Story
An Armory of Swords (editor)

The Books of the Gods
The Face of Apollo

Other Books
A Century of Progress ∘ *Coils* (with Roger Zelazny) ∘ *Dancing Bears* ∘ *Earth Descended* ∘ *The Mask of the Sun* ∘ *Merlin's Bones* ∘ *The Veils of Azlaroc* ∘ *The Water of Thought*

ARIADNE'S

WEB

THE · SECOND · BOOK · OF · THE · GODS

FRED SABERHAGEN

TOR®

° A TOM DOHERTY ASSOCIATES BOOK °
NEW YORK

ARIADNE'S WEB

Copyright © 2000 by Fred Saberhagen

A Tor Book
Published by Tom Doherty Associates, LLC
175 Fifth Avenue
New York, NY 10010

www.tor.com

Tor® is a registered trademark of Tom Doherty Associates, LLC.

Library of Congress Cataloging-in-Publication Data

Saberhagen, Fred.
    Ariadne's web / Fred Saberhagen.
        p.   cm.—(the second Book of the gods)
    "A Tom Doherty Associates book."
    ISBN 0-312-86629-1
    1. Ariadne (Greek mythology)—Fiction. 2. Minotaur (Greek mythology)
—Fiction. 3. Theseus (Greek mythology)—Fiction. 4. Crete (Greek)—
Fiction. I. Title.
PS3569.A215 A75 2000
813'54—dc21   99-051784

First Edition: January 2000

Printed in the United States of America

0 9 8 7 6 5 4 3 2 1

ARIADNE'S
WEB

o *O n e* o

All through the hours of darkness there had been a howling of the wind, and perhaps of livelier things than wind, in the chimneys and around the parapets of the sprawling palace in the elder city of Kandak. A scud of low clouds kept driving in from the empty reaches of the Great Sea, across the island kingdom of Corycus. Outside the stone walls of the palace, winter's offensive from the northland seemed at last about to conquer the territory that had been occupied for several pleasant months by autumn. Inside the palace walls, a frightened king, driven to desperate steps in his efforts to cling to his throne, had spent the night attending to the efforts of his chief magician, a wrinkled and shriveled man named Creon.

For long hours a young soldier called Alex the Half-Nameless had watched them both, the king and Creon, as they went through the recitation of spells, and the bloody sacrifice of animals, all seemingly without producing the least result. The mess of the sacrifice had been cleared away, and king and magician, conferring together in low voices, had seemed on the point of abandoning the effort, when suddenly the god they had been trying to summon stood towering over them, bleary-eyed and swaying like a drunk.

With the first light of morning, Alex the Half-Nameless was shivering, mostly with excitement, though with the fires ignored and untended a damp cold had begun to dominate the great hall of the palace.

Except for the business going on in front of him, it had been a night of routine guard duty, interrupted only by a couple of short latrine breaks. With his short spear in hand, Alex had spent the hours of the night standing more or less at attention with three of his comrades in arms. All four, like soldiers everywhere, were waiting to be told what to do next. A fair amount of effort had gone into trying not to think. For tonight's duty all had been ordered to wear full battle dress, including light helmet and breast-plate. Greaves armored their shins above their sandaled feet, while chain mail reinforced the kilts of their uniforms. They were accustomed to the weight of their formal arms and armor, but it had been a long night, and the hardware was becoming burdensome.

Much earlier in the night, when the king's magician had begun his efforts to evoke the god, a fire had been roaring in each of the huge hearths, one at each end of the hall, flames surging and bending as the wind drove down the chimneys. But by now the light and heat had dimmed to mere ghosts of their full selves. The only visible flame was in the north hearth, small and wispy, in the heart of a section sawn from a great log. Meanwhile, half of the torches burning in sconces on the high walls had guttered and gone out.

Gripping his short spear, tensing and relaxing youthful muscles in an effort to generate some bodily heat, Alex, like most of the handful of other people present, was looking at King Minos on his throne at the moment when the god arrived. Two other men were standing near the throne, and naturally none of the three, not even the seated king, was more than merely human mortal. There came a moment of silence in which Alex happened to blink. At that same instant, a fierce gust of autumn wind rattled the closed shutters defending all the windows, and jostled the doors of the hall's two entrances against the latches that held them shut. And in the next moment, in the time consumed by a mere flicker of a young man's eyelids, there were four figures in his field of vision. So it seemed to the young soldier that the new arrival must have ridden the very wind to appear where he was.

The fourth figure was no mere human being. A god was standing in front of Alex the Half-Nameless now, and a single glance was enough to tell him that this god was Dionysus.

Like the great majority of humans anywhere in the world, Alex had never seen a god. But unlike many of his fellow mortals, he had never doubted the existence of such beings. Tonight he and the handful of others gathered in the great hall had been waiting through the hours of darkness for this amazing thing to happen—

and now at last the wonder had occurred, a real deity had manifested himself.

A swirl of mist, and a stale odor as of wet, dark, dead leaves had entered with the visitor. There sounded also, in the four corners of the hall, a murmuring of soft voices, snatches of song from invisible throats, accompanied by the music of invisible flutes. Alex could recognize details from many of the stories. By all these signs it was obvious that the being who stood before them was an avatar of Dionysus, the Twice-Born.

But a silence had fallen over the humans gathered in the great hall. This was not quite the appearance which Alex, at least, had been expecting. The realization forced itself upon them all that the visitor was no greater in stature than humanity—there was of course no reason why he should be—and at the moment he appeared less impressive than many merely mortal men.

The shocking and ugly fact was that Dionysus was fat. Not only fat, bloated, his once-fair skin blotched red and gray. At a closer look, Alex could see that there was gray in the god's hair and beard, and patches of both had fallen out. There were still remnants of a once-considerable beauty in that face, a comeliness now all but erased by the all-too-human ravages of age and dissipation. The cloak of the Twice-Born, which he kept tightly wrapped around his massive body, was stained and frayed.

Judging by the strange newcomer's appearance alone, Alex might have dared to suspect that he was an impostor. But no impostor, unless he were a god himself, could have contrived such an entrance.

As a child and youth, Alex the Half-Nameless had been fascinated by stories of the gods, and had eagerly gathered every scrap of knowledge that he could regarding them. Now it crossed his mind to wonder that the Twice-Born had not arrived in a chariot drawn by panthers, bedecked with vine branches and ivy.

But what had actually occurred so far was quite marvelous enough to keep the young soldier staring, open-mouthed.

Now and then, mingled with the continued wind, there was a rapid, light clopping sound, suggesting to Alex's active imagination the hooves of invisible satyrs on the paved floor.

Greener leaves, conveying no hint of wet or darkness, were garlanded around the brow of the newcomer, entangled with the flow of his brown hair, and his right hand clutched a golden wine cup. His laughter boomed. But the longer Alex watched, the more he was convinced that there was something wrong with this divine visitor. Besides the look of bloated shabbiness, there seemed an attitude of desperation.

King Minos was an unimpressive monarch, well into middle age. He still sat staring silently at the new arrival, and the expression on the king's face was one that Alex had seen there before, that of a man accustomed to dealing with disappointment. Tonight Minos wore a gloriously brocaded robe, of scarlet interwoven with the blue of the sea, and a light gold circlet of a crown. He carried no arms, nor did anyone in the great hall, except for the small detail of soldiers.

"Welcome, my Lord Dionysus." It was Creon, the cadaverous magician-priest, who broke the silence at last. In his sepulchral voice there was more wonder than heartiness, as he extended his hand in a ritual movement toward the god. "In the king's name, welcome."

Dionysus did not move forward the two or three steps that would have allowed him to touch the magician's outstretched hand. The Twice-Born gave no sign that he was impressed by his welcome, or by the king's magician who claimed to be his priest, or, for that matter, by the king himself. Silently the visitor directed his world-weary gaze, in turn, at each of the humans who had been anticipating his arrival. To judge by his reaction, what he saw was no better or worse than he had expected. When the god's gray-eyed gaze fell on Alex, the main impression the young soldier received was one of exhaustion.

"What do you know of the gods?" The voice of Dionysus was a kind of parody of a conspiratorial whisper, but still it had a resonance, and was so far the most impressive thing about his person. Again the god glanced from one human to another, as if he hoped for answers to his question not only from the king and his magician, but from their soldiers too, and even from their menial servants.

But it was only the king who answered. After exchanging looks with his priest-adviser, Minos evidently decided that this was a time when protocol and ceremony should be minimized. In a tone and manner that seemed to claim his equality with the one he addressed, Minos said, "I know what it is necessary to know, Twice-Born Lord. That all of you who are now gods began your lives as mortal men and women."

Perhaps the royal manner and tone sounded simply impertinent to Dionysus. The pudgy chin lifted. "Oh?"

"Yes." Minos persisted bravely. "That each god or goddess whom we see on earth has attained divinity by somehow coming into possession of a Face. Yours is of course the Face of Dionysus—or do you prefer to be called Twice-Born, or by the name of Bacchus?"

"It does not matter."

The king nodded. Now his hands, bejeweled and soft with years of luxury, sketched a flat, small object in the air. "Each Face is a thing as clear as fine glass, they say, but with a suggestion of flow, of movement, visible inside it—is that not correct?"

But the visitor seemed tired of the subject. He made an impatient gesture. "Why me, Minos? Of all the deities you might have tried to summon, why did you choose me?"

The king paused, as if to consider. Then he said: "We have long worshipped you, great Dionysus. From one end of my kingdom to the other, my people have long sought your favor, with prayer, and sacrifice, and—"

"Yes, yes. And the real reason?"

There was a pause, in which Minos exchanged looks with his magician before answering. "The truth is, Lord Dionysus, that we chose to summon you because, of all the mighty powers who could be helpful, we thought you most likely to respond."

"Because you thought that I was weakened, I suppose."

There was a rustling sound, sharp but not loud, almost at the king's elbow, running up along the massive column that stood there supporting stone arches that curved above. The young soldier Alex, gaping like everyone else, began to notice a process that was already well under way, the greening of the great hall, the writhing of vines up through the stone-and-timber floor, wrapping the columns that held up the roof.

Alex thought he heard a faint birdsong, and felt a welcome ghost of summerlike warmth. And now there was more evidence that the god had not come unattended, for some of those who had accompanied him were now taking on half-visible form, in the far corners of the great chamber, where the light was faintest. The little that Alex could see and hear of them suggested they were less human than the one who'd brought them. The soldier glimpsed what had to be a kind of satyr darting by, the upper body small, like that of a naked child, but that appearance belied by the beard that curled around the chin, and by the hairy nether parts. The creature, whatever it was, moved with great nimbleness upon two shaggy goat-legs. Now the faint voices from invisible throats, some of them sounding too high-pitched to be human, were crooning a drinking song, to the accompanying music of unseen flutes. Any suspicion that the visitor could be an impostor had long since vanished into the realm of fairy tales.

For a moment Alex had been distracted from what Dionysus was saying. But he caught the end of it: "—right enough. Right enough, so far, as far as you go."

And then without warning the god fell into a paroxysm of coughing that almost bent him double, a racking noise that sounded as if it might be damaging his lungs.

The king politely ignored his guest's spasm. But, magical vines and satyrs notwithstanding, Minos gave the impression of being less and less impressed by his visitor as the interview went on. The king's own voice was gradually reverting more and more to its accustomed royal tone.

"One day," said the king, now almost lecturing, "when you were still only a mortal man, you somehow found, or were given—or perhaps seized by force—the Face of Dionysus. That might have happened a year ago, perhaps a hundred years—"

"Sometimes it feels a thousand," the other wheezed, when he had done with coughing.

The monarch pressed bravely on. "—and at that time you were brave enough, or perhaps frightened enough, to put it on. The Face melted into your head, as Faces always do when people wear them. And there yours still rests at this moment, somewhere behind your eyes, as invisible as your soul. And like your soul, your spirit, it will remain with you until you . . . for the rest of your life. And as long as it is with you, you enjoy all the powers of a god."

The Twice-Born did not seem to have been bothered by the casual suggestion that he might once have been frightened. Indeed, it did not seem impossible that he could even now be well acquainted with fear. He only nodded his head gently.

" 'Enjoy.' Oh, I enjoy them, yes." *Cough* again, and *cough*. "You have said nothing," he observed hoarsely, "about all the pain."

Then the visitor gestured negligently toward Creon. "Tell me, King Minos—did this adviser of yours, this self-anointed priest of mine who stands beside you—did any of your wise informants, your magicians, or perhaps they call themselves odylic experts—did even one of them tell you anything about the pain?"

The gaunt magician frowned, but held his peace. The king said, "I am sorry if you are currently experiencing any kind of discomfort, Lord Dionysus, but I suppose it will get better. All authorities agree that gods are very hard to kill."

"And so we are." In the left hand of Dionysus there suddenly appeared, clean out of nowhere, a sturdy wooden staff, perhaps seven feet long and thick as a man's wrist. *That is the* thyrsus, Alex told himself, in silent awe, recognizing an element from the stories. The shaft was ivy-covered, and tipped with a pine cone, just as in the legends and the tales.

Dionysus was now leaning part of his considerable weight upon his staff, as if he really needed its support.

"You should remember that," the god continued. Once more he turned his head to look around the hall. "So, this is the welcome you've arranged. Lucky for you that I place little value upon ceremony. But you're right, for now my wants are simple, I desire only a few months of peace. I must rest until the spring. As you say, things'll be better then."

"Would you care to sit down, Lord Dionysus?" The monarch gestured courteously toward one of the empty chairs, of which there were a few nearby.

"I'll sit when I'm ready."

Now Alex was having a hard time taking his eyes off the *thyrsus*, as if with some part of his mind he could sense that power was centered there. All the mortals in the room, except for the king and his chief magician, had been impressed by the sudden appearance of the ornate staff. Alex thought there was something written on it, thin lines of small, graven characters going up and down the wooden shaft. The writing was too small for him to read, even supposing that it had all been in the only language that he knew. Certainly no more than one of the sets of characters was in that tongue.

Minos was speaking again. "There is nothing in this world that I want more than to provide my Lord Dionysus with a secure place to rest during the tiresome winter that is only now beginning. All the comforts, magical and, um, otherwise." The king paused for a deep breath. He seemed to have finally found the tone, the manner, that he wanted to use; one that might have been appropriate speaking to an important ambassador, a human from one of the kingdoms ringing the shore of the Great Sea.

"But," the king continued, "there is a certain problem that must first be solved, before any of us will be able to rest in safety."

"Ah, hum. Yes, I supposed there would be. Everyone has problems. What is yours?"

"My brother," said Minos simply. "He wishes to take the throne away from me."

"Oh he does, hey?" Dionysus drew himself up a little taller, straightening his shoulders. "Seems a damned unbrotherly thing to do."

In the privacy of his own mind, where as a private soldier he entertained nearly all of his important thoughts, Alex was coming to the conclusion that what his early quest for knowledge had taught him about the nature of the gods, and what the king's brief speech had just confirmed, was very probably the truth. The one who stood before them, staff in hand, gave the impression of possessing a dual nature. The man, who was one component of that nature, was terrified, feeling that death was near, even if the god was not.

Alex stared, with a mixture of fear and fascination, at what a great god had become—at the evidence that those who were called immortal were not, after all, immune to damage and to failure. Only the Faces were immortal, indestructible, while their wearers came and went. He remembered all the stories that were told, of all the marvels wrought by the one some called the God of Many Names. Dionysus, Bacchus, Twice-Born . . . there were indeed a host of other titles, most of which the young soldier could not now recall.

Three or four of the ordinary household servants of the palace had also spent the night in the great hall, standing by to serve the king and his magician, though so far the servants had had little to do. Now, somewhere in the background, at least two of these people were being drawn into interaction with some of the entourage of inhuman attendants who had come with the great visitor. Alex could hear a man and a woman in low-voiced talk, but he did not want to spare a moment to see what they were up to.

Almost since the moment of his entry, Dionysus had been standing in one place, swaying a little on his feet. But now he suddenly lurched forward, so that the king on his throne involuntarily recoiled. But the tottering god had suddenly decided that he did, after all, need a place to sit down. He threw himself not into the chair Minos had indicated, but another, taller, not quite a throne, that had once been occupied by the queen on state occasions, and had now been practically unused for almost two decades. There seemed no special significance in this choice of a resting place. Rather it was as if the distinguished visitor had simply made the handiest selection, to keep himself from falling.

As soon as the god's substantial bottom was firmly supported by the chair, he rapped the floor sharply with his ornate staff. His resonant voice boomed out, more loudly than before: "Let's settle your little problem now. Where is this treasonous brother? Let him be brought here, so I can warn him—do you think, Minos, that a warning will be sufficient?"

"Regrettably," said King Minos, clasping his soft hands together, "I have grave doubts about that. And at this moment I am not even sure exactly where my brother is."

Suddenly he looked sharply at the soldier standing nearest to Alex, who happened to be the corporal in command of the small contingent. "And the commander of the guard still has not appeared. Where is he?"

The corporal saluted awkwardly. "I don't know where either of them are, majesty."

At that point, everyone was distracted by Dionysus sliding out of the seat he had just taken, a movement quite obviously involuntary, that left his divine form sprawled on the rush-strewn floor, his *thyrsus* clattering down beside him. In the next moment he was grabbing at the breasts of a kitchen wench, a poor and simple girl, but not unattractive, who for the last minute had been approaching him slowly from across the room, as if drawn by some invisible thread of fascination. Only a moment ago this girl had been engaged in murmured conversation with the sprites and satyrs halfway across the room, and now she was lying with their god on the floor. Dionysus pawed at her bosom without even turning his head to look at her. It seemed a purely reflex action, as joyless and even hopeless as his booming laughter.

And over in a far corner of the great room, one of the household's male servants, who had also somehow become involved with the inhuman Dionysian entourage, had evidently just taken something to drink that did not agree with him. The servant was suddenly vomiting, abandoned to helpless, hopeless retching.

And now the god himself, forcing himself to sit up straight on the floor, appeared to be struggling to regain some shreds of dignity. Absently he let go of the girl, and tried to straighten the garland of vines that now perched crookedly on his head.

It was growing more and more obvious to the onlookers that this specimen of divinity was hopelessly drunk.

But again his impressive voice filled the hall. "Must reassure the rightful heir—who's that, by the way? Your son, I s'pose? Is it any one of these wretches here?" And Dionysus squinted at the handful of people present, again taking them one at a time, as if he suspected them of trying to hide their true identities.

Minos, who had been rubbing his forehead wearily, raised his head. "I have no son, Lord Dionysus. In fact there is no undisputed heir; a matter that I have not yet had the time to rectify."

You have had almost eighteen years, thought Alex, in silent accusation. Everyone knew it was that long since the true, respected queen had died; since then there had been only royal concubines, and no offspring worth mentioning. *You have delayed shamefully, oh king, and in doing so you were unfair to your two marvelous and deserving daughters.* His grip tightened on his spear. *And some would even say that it is not true that you have no son.*

To judge from the expression on the king's face, it seemed that the royal thoughts might possibly be running along similar lines. Minos did not seem drunk, despite the formidable amount of wine he had consumed during the night, a little at a time. But he did seem very bitter.

"My late wife . . ." the king began to say, then let his words rest there, as if he could see no point in going on with them. He looked around him, at the small gathering of his fellow humans in the great hall, and their disgraceful visitor, and it was as if he were asking himself, *how have I come to this?*

Abruptly the god rolled over on his side, turning his back on all three of the people who had so far been most affected by his presence—the lamenting monarch, the feebly vomiting varlet in the far corner, and the dazed serving wench. As Dionysus rolled, the folds of his cloak came open. Scanty and wretched undergarments hung loose, revealing gross nakedness, including a flabby paunch that the deity swung around only with some difficulty.

The move had brought the Twice-Born into a position

directly facing Alex. Now, thrusting with one elbow on the floor to raise himself a little, squinting at the lithe form of the young soldier, who was standing only about ten feet away, Dionysus addressed him in a low voice: "Once I . . . I was . . . like you."

Being spoken to directly by a god, any god, was something of a shock for Alex—though not quite the shock it would have been an hour ago. Still, he was flustered and did not know what to think, let alone what he ought to say if he should be required to answer. The note of envy in the god's voice was staggering.

Alex had never had cause to consider himself particularly handsome. He was of average size, generally healthy, and perhaps physically a little stronger than most young men, at least when his anger was aroused. His brown beard was at last starting to grow in with a reasonable thickness. But no one had ever found any god-like qualities in either his mind or body. Vaguely he could foresee humorous taunting in the barracks when it became known there what the god had said.

To Alex's relief, he was not required to respond. Already Dionysus had turned his back on him, and was groping for a wine-skin, obviously looking for a drink. When he found what he sought and held it up, the skin hung flat and empty on his hand. Whatever magical sources of wine he might possess, they seemed to be running dry.

Alex could only stare at the divine visitor sitting helplessly on the floor. In the young man's mind, fear, disillusion verging on embarrassment, and a great curiosity were struggling for dominance.

The king had fallen silent after his own small outburst, and was evidently making an effort to collect himself. As an awkward silence grew in the great hall, Alex noticed that the general transformation which had been wrought by the entrance of Dionysus was already fading, as if the power that had brought it into being was waning fast. The vines that had begun to climb the pillars in the hall were dying, the luxuriant growth of leaves turned dry and dead and falling. The drafty air was distributing them in little swirls around the floor. The thicker stems were turning to stone, so that they now seemed to have been carved as part of the pillars by some master artisan. The lesser sprites and powers, all but invisible presences that had accompanied the entrance of the god, were dying too, or perhaps only silently taking their departure, one by one. Fading with the flute music into nothingness.

Minos started to speak again, then stopped. He cocked his head, turning it slightly as if trying to listen to some faint, unwelcome noise.

Now Alex could hear it too. There were at least two men, it seemed, making no particular effort to be quiet, for he could hear their voices just outside the closed door of the main entrance to the hall.

---

*Y*ou sent for me, my brother?" The last two words were spoken in a tone of mockery, by the man who was standing just outside the door when it swung open. It was a harsh voice, one that Alex immediately recognized, though he had seldom heard it before.

In through the open door strode a tall man garbed in a robe of royal splendor, wearing a sword and a bronze breastplate. His head was bare. He advanced with a confidence that did not seem at all shaken when his gaze fell upon the immortal visitor. It was as if Prince Perses, the king's younger brother, had expected nothing less.

A step behind the prince came a military officer, General Scamander, commander of the Palace Guard, fully armed and armored, younger than the prince, and much more massively built. The commander swung the large door shut behind him, and in a few clipped words ordered Alex and his three comrades to see that it remained that way. There were only two exits from the great hall, the second being a small door commonly used only by servants. The soldiers of the guard were to prevent anyone from going in or out by either way.

"I did not send for you, no," said Minos, who appeared suddenly diminished upon his throne.

"I see you have summoned another." Perses nodded, unsurprised. "Well, so be it. I, too, have decided that my affairs might prosper better with an ally."

"And you are not to interfere," Scamander added, speaking in a low voice, but certainly not a whisper, to his men.

"Yes sir," responded Alex, in ragged chorus with his comrades. And like them, he wondered silently: *Interfere in what?*

General Scamander, informally known among his troops and behind his back as the Butcher, for some feat of pacification accomplished on the mainland many years ago, turned and stood with his hands behind his back, smiling benevolently in the general direction of Minos on his throne.

The corporal was now hastily giving orders, and Alex and the other two privates instantly obeyed. Two men were now stationed at each door, Alex being assigned to the main entrance, and all of them were now slightly farther from the throne than they had been.

Alex understood the confidence of the new arrivals, their casual attitude about the presence of Dionysus, when he observed the next figure to appear in the great hall.

All ordinary portals were closed, but this newcomer minded that no more than Dionysus had. It was a truly impressive form which now materialized just behind the prince; and at his first glimpse of it, Alex understood that after a lifetime without ever seeing a single god, he had encountered two in the space of a few minutes.

This second divinity was physically somewhat smaller than the Twice-Born. Not a bulky shape, hardly more than half the size of the commander of the guard; but beside it, even the Butcher seemed to have shrunk to insignificance. A male body, thin to the point of emaciation, wearing almost nothing but a necklace of small round objects. When Alex looked more closely, he could see that they were human skulls, somehow shrunken or miniaturized to the size of oranges. The skin was grayish overall, mottled here and there with shades of blue. Matted locks of almost colorless hair fell in coils on either side of the thin, beardless face, and at first the young soldier thought there was something wrong with the high brow. But then Alex realized that what he was looking at was not exactly a defect. There was a third eye, browless, no trick of decoration but a real organ, centered in the forehead, perhaps an inch above the usual two.

Not everyone at first recognized the newcomer. The soldier standing beside Alex asked him a question, in a whisper so low that it was barely audible an arm's length away: "Who?—What—?"

And Alex, with the hair standing up on the back of his neck, mouthed one soft word in reply: "Shiva."

Shiva the Destroyer.

A movement at the far end of the hall caught Alex's eye. Looking in that direction he saw the figure of a bull, a little larger than life size. In the faint light of dying fires the hide of the animal (that was of course not really an animal at all) looked the gray of dead wood ashes. Nandi, the bull, was wingless, but capable of the swiftest flight . . . a creature as inseparable from Shiva as the leopards and chariot were from Dionysus.

Alex, who from childhood had been fascinated with the stories of the gods, saw the bluish neck—legend said that Shiva was thus marked as a result of holding in his throat the poison thrown up at the churning of the cosmic ocean, near the time of the creation of the world, and thus saving humanity from its effects.

The Third Eye of Shiva now winked briefly, partially open, just long enough to afford an anxious onlooker a hint of destructive fire somehow impounded.

If the king had been right in his earlier claim, about the Faces of the Gods—and Alex knew nothing to suggest that Minos had been wrong—then even this dark god, like all the other gods, was only a transformed human.

But somehow that thought made the presence of the Destroyer no easier to bear.

At his first sight of Shiva, Dionysus had frozen momentarily, as if turned to stone. A moment later the Twice-Born one let out a hoarse yell, half of terror, half of challenge, then grabbed up his *thyrsus* staff and struggled to his feet.

Ignoring both gods for the moment, Prince Perses strode straight forward toward his brother, drawing his sword as he advanced. Minos, still looking weary as well as frightened, stood up unarmed from the throne and barked an order to the commander of his guard—

Alex did not hear the words of the command clearly. But whatever they were, they were ignored. And by that the king knew his fate.

Minos spoke a few words to his brother, in so low a tone that Alex could not hear them. Prince Perses, grinning mirthlessly, said nothing, but only continued his advance without pause, and when he came within reach of the throne used his sword, once, twice, in a thorough and workmanlike way.

Minos met his death with stoic dignity.

The slain man fell, his blood leaked out. Royalty had been reduced in a moment to a mere object. Alex had seen killing before—such matters were all in a day's work for a soldier—but never had he seen a human life ended quite as cold-bloodedly as this.

Any of the handful of other humans in the hall who might have been inclined to fight for Minos were held motionless by a combination of fear and habitual obedience. The soldiers all stood frozen under the Butcher's glare.

"Hold your posts," the general advised them, in a hard but yet not unfatherly tone. "That's it. Good men."

And Dionysus, after that one blustering moment in which he had seemed to challenge the intruders, was suddenly no more to be seen. The Third Eye of Shiva had opened fully for a flicker of time, emitting a dazzling narrow lance of light, and the dropped and abandoned staff fell clattering on the floor. At a touch of the ray from Shiva's forehead, the stout wood smoked and flared and disappeared.

When the surviving people, Alex and his fellow soldiers among them, had the chance to look around again through eyes that were no longer dazzled by reflections of the Third Eye's beam, no trace of the terrified Dionysus was to be seen. His entourage of satyrs and invisible, discordant singers had vanished with him, leaving only a residue of vomit, and grape leaves, and crumbling, dying vines. The servants who had taken part in his last celebration went crawling and slinking away, as well as they were able. The man who had been retching was silent now, perhaps terrified into a semblance of self-control.

The smell of wet leaves had been covered, smothered, by the sharper smell of blood.

"I am now Minos," said the old king's brother, speaking clearly into the sudden silence. He who had been Prince Perses was standing now with the empty throne just behind him, as if very nearly ready to sit down on it. His sword was back in its scabbard on his belt. Alex could not remember seeing him wipe the blade on anything.

"You are Minos, majesty," acknowledged the Butcher, and offered a sharp military salute. Then the general shot a quick glare at his soldiers, to make sure that they were following his lead. Alex's right arm shot up obediently. Behind the general, Shiva was standing like a statue, and said nothing.

The new Minos stood looking down with satisfaction at the dead body of his brother, lying almost at his feet. Behind him, the priest-magician Creon had been standing with folded arms during the violence, obviously not much perturbed and perhaps not surprised.

"You are now Minos," Creon echoed quickly. Then he added, "I do not know the fate of Dionysus, majesty."

The usurper, now bending over the body of his brother, shook his head, as if to say that he did not know either, nor much care, where the defeated god had gone.

General Scamander stepped forward suddenly, picked up from the stone floor the slender golden circlet that was the traditional crown of Corycus, and with a humble gesture offered it toward the throne. With steady fingers Perses accepted the emblem of authority, and casually put it on his own head.

The commander of the guard, who had drawn his own sword only to salute with it, now slammed it back into its scabbard. Turning around again, he began in his harsh voice to tell the simple soldiers what they had just seen.

Alex's own eyes and ears had told him a wildly different story, but now was certainly not the time to suggest that there might be some discrepancy, or even think about it. Alex found that his eyes kept returning to the dead body of the old king on the floor.

Having concluded his narration, the general immediately began to go over it again, repeating his explanation in short simple words, as if to children. Anyone who had been too shocked or stupid to understand the business the first time had better get it now. The main point to be grasped was how Dionysus, the treacherous god who had just fled the hall, had slain the old king before departing.

"You saw that, did you not?" His glare swung from one soldier to another, making sure to get the reaction that he wanted from each one before moving to the next. Now it was Alex's turn. "You?" the officer demanded.

"Yes. Yes, sir." And at the same time Alex remained perfectly aware that that was not at all what he had seen. But that knowledge must be suppressed. And anyway, with true gods and great magic involved in these events, could a simple man trust his own senses, his own thoughts, in anything?

"Good lad," said the Butcher, heartily, and turned away to begin the same process with the servants.

"Enough," said Shiva, speaking for the first time. Every head in the great hall—excepting only that of the dead king—turned to look at him. All who had not heard Shiva's light, smooth voice before were surprised at how it sounded.

"Enough," the god concluded. "It matters not, what any of them saw."

And, with no more fuss than that, the bloody business had been finished.

General Scamander, who was still commander of the guard, assured the new king that troops who could be depended on to support him were now holding the palace.

He who had been Prince Perses, who now formally repeated his announcement that he was taking the name of Minos, exchanged a few words with his two close human supporters, while Shiva stood in the background, his arms folded. Whether the god was presiding over the scene or simply attending would have been hard to judge by looking at him.

Then the new king raised his voice, speaking to all the humans within earshot. "Rouse the household, there is news that everyone must hear. And a terrible sight that all must see."

Within a few minutes, a small, excited group of newcomers had gathered, and was growing by the minute. Alex heard someone remarking, in a low, cautious voice, on the fact that the old king had left no legitimate son—there were two daughters, and in the normal course of events the elder, Phaedra, might have expected to assume the throne upon her father's death.

"And no son," someone else observed, whispering. As if that might have any bearing on the legitimacy of succession, which according to the traditional rules it did not.

"His only son is—Asterion," murmured another. And there was muttered laughter, accompanied by looking over shoulders. It was the way common folk behaved when one of their number dared to tell a sexual joke about someone far above them.

And only moments after that, the younger of the old king's two daughters, Princess Ariadne, came bursting into the hall before anyone there had begun to expect her. Alex and his partner at the main entrance each took a hesitant step in her direction, but then hung back. Not even the Butcher would expect anyone to hold back the princesses from their father's body. This was the woman Alex had come to worship, helplessly, beginning on the first day he had seen her, long months ago, on his first day in the palace.

Ariadne fell on her knees beside the corpse, and for a long moment only crouched there, stunned, her white hands spread like a dancer's on outflung arms. From the moment she entered the great hall, Alex was unable to tear his gaze away from her, and his grip tightened on the shaft of his spear.

Oh Princess, I swear to you that I could do nothing. Had you been here, I would have gladly died for you. Not even a god would have touched you, not while I was alive. Alex with a pang could imagine the princess demanding of him: "Then why did you not die for my father?" To which his only answer must have been: *Then I would have been unable to ever serve you again in any way.*

Ariadne was nineteen, light brown hair hanging loose in long ringlets about her shoulders, her slender body wrapped in a white robe that she would ordinarily have worn only in her chamber. Her feet were bare on the stone floor, as were those of her personal servant, a slave girl who had swept in beside her, almost unnoticed. The slave girl's name, as Alex remembered, was Clara.

Ariadne's first loud cry of grief was still hanging in the air, when Princess Phaedra, some two years older than her sister, came bursting in, completely unattended.

Phaedra was the shorter of the two sisters, her hair dark, her body compact and womanly. Her cries of grief were not as loud as Ariadne's, but Alex had no doubt that they were every bit as sincere.

"Father! They have killed you!" The scream seemed torn from the bottom of Ariadne's heart.

And in that moment Alex, though he still did not stir an inch from the post where he had been commanded to stand guard, knew in his own heart that he was ready to cheerfully give up his own life, if by doing so he might spare the woman he worshipped even one minute of such horror and sorrow. *If he were now to dart quickly across the room, and thrust with his spear for the usurper's throat . . .*

But it was almost certain that the other soldiers would be quick enough to stop him before he could kill Perses. Also, Alex thought that Shiva was watching him, from the far side of the room, and the Third Eye could dart death as quickly as thought.

And even if, by some miracle of skill and endurance, he succeeded in cutting down the usurper, what then? Ariadne would be spared nothing in the bloody turmoil that would be sure to follow.

All good reasons for holding back. But perhaps not the real reason. The truth was that in this matter he was not the master of his own will. He had been ordered not to interfere.

When the first spasms of grief had subsided, the princesses confronted their uncle, who affected an air of great sympathy, told them the tale of murderous Dionysus, and strongly suggested that now it was time for them to return to their respective rooms.

Phaedra, on regaining control of herself, dared to raise her eyes and confront Perses. In a low voice she asserted, "Many will say that on my father's death I should be queen."

The new king was gentle and tolerant. "My dear niece, your grief has naturally unsettled you. Your dear father with his dying breath insisted that I take the throne. All these witnesses will confirm the fact. Is it not so?"

And so it was.

Gradually the sorrowing princesses allowed themselves to be led away by their own attendants, and what was left of the assembly broke up. Alex was soon free to confirm the official version of events among his wondering barrack-mates, who had already heard a formal announcement from an officer.

Soon the body of old Minos was removed, at the orders of his brother the new king, to another room, where it would lie in state. The new Minos was announcing plans, so well organized that they might almost have been prepared ahead of time, for a public display of Dionysus's victim, in the plaza before the palace.

Then the new king said to the last of his remaining attendants, "Leave us alone. The Lord Shiva and I have certain matters to discuss between us."

He had to tell the Butcher twice; then the big man saluted briskly and withdrew.

At last there were only two figures left in the great hall.

"Certain matters . . ." the former Prince Perses began, and had to stop and clear his throat, and make a new beginning. "There are certain matters, Lord Shiva, that ought to be spelled out clearly between us. So there will be no chance of later misunderstanding."

The light was brighter in the great hall now. Before the last servants retired, more torches had been brought, and fires rekindled. The figure that had assumed the throne was grayish-blue, in a way that suggested the residue of fire. Facial features sharp and thin, almost to the point of caricature. The rest of the body seemed hardly more robust, essentially little more than a skeleton. The Third Eye, lid closed as if in sleep, made no more than a modest bulge in the middle of the forehead. In the changed light the necklace of skulls took on a deceptively artificial look. But for all that, it was a body, a solid human body, not any mere apparition.

The god's two normal eyes were fully open. In his light and somehow metallic voice he replied, "Let there be understanding between us. You will kneel when you address me." And he extended an arm, to point with a skeletal forefinger to the floor.

For a long moment Perses observed a frozen silence. Then: "I am the king!"

Shiva was unmoved. "Only because I have made you so. I can unmake you just as easily. I am a god, and you will kneel. Or you will learn what it means to incur the anger of a god." A pause. "Don't be concerned, our agreement stands. Later, I will let you have your throne back. I do not plan to spend much time with toys."

Muttering under his breath, he who was determined to be Minos looked around to make sure that they were still alone in the great hall. Then he rose from the throne and moved two hesitant steps forward. Then he lowered his heavy body to one knee.

Few of the scores of people making up the household had ever seen a god before. Now as they all came trickling into the great hall, murmuring and whispering their astonishment, they found themselves also confronting the awesome presence of Shiva, not enthroned but standing behind the throne.

A first search for the divine fugitive had already been made, through the palace and its immediate grounds. But of the god Dionysus there was not a trace to be seen. There was no thought of looking for a secret passage. Gods, even failing gods, could be expected to have the power to vanish when they willed.

And already the dark god was demanding sacrifice, and of no ordinary kind.

The man who had now assumed the name of Minos turned to his soldiers and exhorted them, "We are going to discover those responsible for my brother's death, and punish them."

And the wind howled mournfully, around the parapets and down the chimneys. The first clear sunlight on that morning seemed woefully slow in coming.

"sterion?"

I did not answer the call at once, but stood in silence, looking out through leaves. Spring sunshine striking through the fresh leaves of the tangled vines made patches of bright translucent green, leaving caves of shadow within the roofed-over sections of the endless, intertwining passageways that comprised the great bulk of the Labyrinth. Somewhere just out of sight, perhaps in the next open courtyard, or maybe in the one after that, water was trickling musically from one of the Maze's many fountains into an adjoining pool. In the years of my youth, the sound of running water, far or near, was almost never absent. The curving walls and tunnels, most of their surfaces hard stone, sometimes played games with sound.

"Asterion, where are you?"

The young, clear voice was of course that of Ariadne, the younger of my two sisters, both older than myself. (Phaedra, the eldest of our sibling trio, was by the test of flesh and blood only my half-sister—more on that subject later.)

Even at Ariadne's second call I did not answer. First I wanted to make quite sure she was alone.

To find me today she had come more than half a mile out of the palace, which stood right at one edge of the great Maze. Most people would have been utterly lost before they walked five minutes in the Labyrinth, but I had no fear that that would ever happen to Ariadne, who had been coming to visit me since both of us were only children. I had not seen her for more than a week, an unusually long time between her visits.

But I was not at all surprised that she had come today. On the previous night I had dreamt of encountering her in this small courtyard, and in such matters my dreams are seldom wrong.

When Ariadne called my name a third time, and still I could perceive no sign that anyone else was with her, or had followed her in stealth, I advanced out of deep blue shadow, and came pacing on my two very human legs across the small sunlit plaza. On its far side my sister stood, looking up at me in trusting welcome. I am seven feet tall, almost exactly. A little more if the horns are counted, curving up as they do, one on each side of my inhuman skull, in rather graceful symmetry, to a level about an inch higher than the top of my head. (My ears sometimes rise higher too, but they are so mobile that I don't count them.)

Ariadne was two years older than my seventeen, and by most human standards she was beautiful. Her light brown hair fell in long curling coils on both sides of her heart-shaped face. On that day she was wearing, as typical day-to-day costume, gold-painted sandals, and a linen shift. It was not her custom to wear much jewelry, and today she had on none at all, save for a medallion Daedalus had given her. (He had given Minos and Phaedra their own, equivalent gifts at the same time—and I had mine a month later, after the Artisan had become acquainted with me.) Ariadne's bright disk of gold and silver was tucked inside her dress and out of sight, but I could see the silvery chain that held it round her neck. On the island of Corycus, women of the upper class exposed their breasts only on formal, dress-up occasions.

Her face lit up at the sight of my advancing form, clad in a kilt and large, plebeian sandals. (My feet, like my legs, are very human, comparatively hairless, and no bigger than those of many normal men.)

"There you are!" she cried, and burst out at once with an announcement that could not wait. "Oh, I have so much to tell!" My sister was in a fever that seemed half anxiety, half joy.

"Some of it at least must be good news," I observed, accepting a joyful hug. For most of my life I have been aware that my voice does not sound quite like those of other men. There is no way that it possibly could, given the inhuman shape of my throat and head. But to my sister the tones of my speech were quite familiar, and she had no difficulty understanding.

It was almost the first time in half a year that I had seen Ariadne smiling, that I had been able to catch sight in her of any happiness at all.

"You are right," she told me, nodding her head for emphasis. "But some of it is not." And her smile faded rapidly, as she considered some problem that I was certainly going to hear about within the next few minutes.

My stomach like my limbs is very nearly human. Extending an arm to a mutant tree nearby, I plucked an early fruit that hung within reach, and ate it while we talked. Still a trifle green, but that was only to be expected so early in the season. Each day I grew wearier of the dried stuff that had largely seen me through the winter. It was something like an apple, and a little like a peach, but not that much like either, and a thing for which I had no name. Names sometimes bewilder me. Each spring the fruit of this tree, like that of many others growing in my home, was something different. The ashes in the little hearth nearby were long dead. The nearby vines that had looked dead a week before were springing forth with fresh new green.

Much vegetation grows wild inside my home, and in several places there are even groves of trees. In very many places grass has started up in the cracks between paving stones, especially in the hundreds of miles of passages where almost no one ever walks. But some strong protection, odylic magic perhaps, or only a dearth of moisture, has so far kept the place from being entirely overgrown.

I had been rather expecting Ariadne to bring me some news on this day, probably details of the long-expected arrival of the Tribute people, whose black-sailed ship had entered the harbor of Kandak at least a week ago. And she began to do just that, but in fact I was listening with only half an ear, because I had an announcement of my own that I wished to make.

The idea had been growing for some time in my monstrous head that I was long overdue to venture once more out of the Labyrinth. I wanted to see for myself what the world out there was truly like, not just how it looked when reflected in my dreams and those of other folk; I had been so young when I was immured in the great Maze that I could remember very little else. For some months now, ever since midwinter when the days began to lengthen, dreams had been urging me to go on an excursion.

My sister paused, and out of habit glanced back briefly, first over one shoulder and then the other, before she went on speaking, even though in the remote fastnesses of the Labyrinth we had no real worry about being overheard. Now, I thought, she had come to her real news.

She said, "Our uncle's god grows stronger day by day— stronger and more demanding. Now they are killing slaves, almost daily, in one of the courtyards of the palace. At least it isn't under my window. Slaves and prisoners, for no good reason but to feed Shiva's joy in killing." She paused. "Have you dreamt about him yet?"

"About Shiva?" I shook my horned head, no. "But of late I have seen our father more than once in dreams, and heard his voice."

"Our father?"

"I mean Minos," I said, and Ariadne relaxed slightly. I went on, "It is as if he calls me from a great distance. I can't tell what he's saying."

"From the realm of Hades?" Now my sister shivered.

"I—don't know." I didn't think the communication came from the Underworld, but it had always been difficult for me to try to explain to her my adventures in the realm of Oneiros, god of dreams.

I did not and do not remember, of course, how I came to be born in the shape I have. There were occasional dreams—and I was certain that these particular visions were no more than ordinary dreams—in which the monstrous transformation had happened to me only after birth. In these dreams, my mother might still have died in childbirth, but it would not have been because of the horns I bore on my inhuman head.

Why had anyone suffered such a monstrous child to live? My old nurse, the first of a short succession of folk who had cared for me in childhood, and whom I only dimly remembered now, had sometimes whispered fiercely to me that I was, must be, the offspring of Father Zeus himself. "They say that the Thunderer will sometimes take the form of a bull—and it is in that form that he came to your mother!"

My memories of what had happened to me in dreams became confabulated with what I could recall of reality, and I was by no means always certain which were really the most real. Once, so long ago that I could not remember details, I, Asterion, had looked into a mirror, a real mirror of fine smooth glass. And more than once I had lain on my belly on the pavement, somewhere in the endless cool recesses of the Labyrinth, gazing into one or another of the many quiet pools. In those reflecting surfaces I always saw something very different than what I beheld when I looked at the faces of other people. The most unpleasant of my dreams were those that had to do with mirrors.

One part of my spotty education had to do with the gods— how those strange and awesome beings had played a vital role in human affairs some generations ago, but then had faded from sight, so effectively that many people had begun to doubt their very existence.

Not that I, Asterion, could remember ever seeing a god myself. Not with my waking eyes.

On that spring day in the Labyrinth, Ariadne brought as one item of news certain details that had only recently reached the island of Corycus, from a certain place on the mainland hundreds of miles away. The details elaborated on a story that was already somewhat old, telling how the great gods Apollo and Hades, and the comparatively trivial human forces that supported each of them, had within the past year fought a tremendous battle. And how Apollo had established his Oracle upon the site, and how on that mountain, on whose summit some said Olympus lay, the great Sun-God had forbidden human sacrifice.

"Much of that is old news," I remarked.

"Of course." My sister jutted her fine chin at me. "But wouldn't it be a good thing if the people of Corycus served Apollo too?"

"Probably—but they no longer have much chance to do so. I doubt that there is any longer even one active shrine or temple of

Apollo, anywhere on the island. Our noble uncle remains devoted to a very different god."

"I have just been talking with some of the people of the Tribute." That was not changing the subject, at least not the way Ariadne thought.

"Nine youths and nine maidens, just as Uncle demanded of his tributaries?"

My sister nodded.

"And now that these people of the Tribute are here, what is Uncle really going to do with them? I understood that they were not to become slaves."

"No, several of them are even of noble blood. The official word that Uncle has announced to the people is that . . ."

Ariadne hesitated at that point and had to start over. "There are several things that I am anxious to tell you, my brother, and one of them is painful."

"So you said. Well, let me hear the painful message first." But though I asked so boldly, I was afraid of what my sister might be going to tell me. Afraid of hearing in real life a frightening message which had already been given to me in some dream, and which I had then mercifully forgotten. But there would be no forgetting it this time.

Ariadne said, "Our noble uncle, and all the priests of Shiva that are now coming to our island, like flies gathering on a dead body . . ."

"Yes?"

". . . they are telling everyone that the nine youths and nine maidens are going to be sacrificed to the Minotaur. To you."

I knew that people called me by that name sometimes, gave me the appellation of a monster, as if to remind themselves never to think of me as human. But there was nothing to be done about it. " 'Sacrificed,' " I said. "You mean killed. Like the slaves and prisoners you mentioned earlier."

"Yes."

Some time passed in which I endeavored to make sense of this latest announcement. "And sacrificed to me? To *me*?"

"I know that the idea must sound foolish—"

Suddenly angry, I turned away and went stalking about the little plaza, clenching and unclenching my fists. " 'Foolish'? That doesn't begin to describe it! Do they think me some kind of demon, demanding human sacrifice? What am I supposed to do with youths and maidens? Eat them? I don't even eat meat. Drink their blood? Or maybe love them to death, go rutting on them like—but you know I don't even . . ."

"I know! I know, dear Asterion." Gently my sister tried to soothe me. Grabbed one finger of one of my enormous though manlike hands, and tugged me to a halt, when my pacing would have carried me away from her. "Zeus has made you different. And I love you, and understand you as you are. But the world does not know you as I do. People are always ready to hear tales of a monster, and I fear the official story is going to be believed."

"And of course the people of the Tribute *are* really going to be slain in sacrifice."

"Shiva is demanding it. Or so his priests are whispering. We seldom see the god himself. The whispers are that he spends much of his time worrying about assassination plots."

I thought that human sacrifice had not been the original intention of the usurper, when he claimed the Tribute. He had wanted the young folk as hostages, perhaps. As a way of encouraging our enemies to discover ways that they could live with us. Part of the justification given when the Tribute was first announced was that the new Minos, emboldened by the god-power of Shiva at his back, was more than ever determined to assert his authority over those poor fools and weaklings in their disunited kingdoms on the mainland. Send tribute, or my matchless navy will attack your ports, destroy your shipping!

In a little while I had talked the sharpest edge of my anger away. "But something else has happened to you, sister. Something good, it must have been, for despite our uncle's wickedness you are beginning to be happy."

Immediately she brightened. "Oh, yes! I don't doubt that you can see in me the effects of what has happened."

"Describe this happy miracle to me."

She jumped up lightly and walked about, unable to sit still. "His name is Theseus."

"Ah."

"I am in love, desperately in love!"

"Somehow I suspected as much."

"His name is Theseus!" This time Ariadne almost sang the word.

I was happy for my sister, but also already beginning to be jealous, in a way. "Yes, I understood that the first time. So, who is Theseus, where does he come from? What is he like?"

"He is one of the youths of the Tribute. What is he like? How can I tell you? Like a god, strong and handsome beyond my powers of description. He is really a prince, who was taken prisoner in one of those foolish mainland wars, and then . . ."

"Stop. Wait." Finally I managed to break in upon the rhapsody. "Back up a moment. You seem to be telling me he's one of the eighteen—? Ariadne, you can't be serious!"

"Asterion, I've never been so serious in all my life."

I stared at her. "Perhaps you haven't. This is the first time you have ever told me that you were in love."

"Yes, it is . . . Of course I am going to arrange it somehow that his life will be spared." To Ariadne, an effective sentence of death hanging over her newly beloved was only an awkward detail that had to be managed somehow, on the order of a conflict of dates when a party was being organized. My sister, being who she was, had no doubt at all that she would be able to accomplish that. Confidently she added, "I know that I can count on you to do whatever may be necessary to help."

"Of course, my sister." I took her small hand in both of mine, and patted it. "Tell me more."

"Have you seen Prince Theseus in your dreams, Asterion? Tell me what you have seen!"

Thinking the matter over, I realized that I very well might have seen this supposed paragon, some night when my eyes were closed and my senses absent from my body, without knowing his name. Lately I had dreamt of bad things happening to several people I could not identify. From my sister's description I began to understand just who that stalwart youth might be, what role he had played in those dreams.

What I had seen would only alarm my sister to no purpose, and so I lied to her. "I have seen a great many things as usual, a great many people. And in my dreams people do not always look like themselves in real life. It will take time for me to sort them out."

She accepted the lie happily.

"But look here, Ariadne, surely all these people of the Tribute —nine youths and nine maidens—are being held as prisoners?"

"They are."

"Then how is it you are able to talk with this Theseus at all?"

Before answering, my sister once more cast worried glances over both shoulders. "Their confinement is quite mild. Actually they are not in the cells under the palace, but are only being held aside, apart, in a section of the Labyrinth close by." She supplied a few details of the local topography, from which I was able to visualize the area.

"But surely they are guarded."

"Yes. But I have many friends in the palace, and I even still have a few among the soldiers. So it wasn't too difficult for him to get a message out to me." She paused, sobering. "The message said that he was the son of a sea lord, from somewhere in the Out-flung Islands, and he had information of great importance, that he wanted to give to me in person. It concerned our father's death."

I thought that over for a while. "If your Theseus is telling the truth about his parentage, then his father must be in some way a rival of our respected and noble uncle."

"Yes, I suppose that's true."

"But he didn't actually give his father's name."

"No."

Several names suggested themselves to me, of powerful men active in current affairs around the world, but I saw no reason to prefer any of them to the others. Later I would try to narrow down the field. "So, you naturally thought it necessary to meet with a prisoner who sent you such a message. And when you met, did he actually have anything new to say, about what happened to our Father Minos?"

Ariadne frowned slightly. "No, not really. Slightly different versions of the rumors we have already heard. But more and more I am coming to believe that Uncle must have had something to do with killing him."

"Very likely," I agreed in a quiet voice. Lately there had been revelatory dreams.

When I had listened to all that Ariadne had to tell me, I cut short her glowing descriptions of her lover, in which she was beginning to repeat herself, to make an announcement of my own. "Sister, I am determined to go out into the city. I want to see and hear for myself something of what is going on."

She looked concerned, perhaps because my project might delay one of hers. "Is this because of something I have just told you?"

"No, it's nothing to do with you or Theseus. I've been thinking about it for a while."

"But is it wise?"

"Are you the one to counsel me on wisdom? But no, lately I have very often dreamed about such an outing. So much, that I take it as something I must do."

Immediately Ariadne had something new to worry about. But as usual my sister was (and I had counted on the fact) more than half ready for a prank, for almost any adventure. There was a new eagerness in her voice as she said, "If you're determined to go out, maybe I can help. When do you want to go? Tonight?"

"That was my thought."

Briefly she was serious again. "Of course Uncle will be very angry—if he finds out."

"Let him be angry if he wants."

"You're not afraid he'll kill you, as he did our Father Minos?" I shook my head.

My sister nodded slowly. "Of course if he got rid of you, he could hardly claim that you were demanding sacrifices."

"But why not? I suppose I would live on in legend. No, I doubt very much that dear Uncle will try to inflict any serious punishment on me. Not for such a minor offense. Not for one so obviously a child of Zeus—unless he thinks that sending eighteen hostages to live with me in the Labyrinth will be my punishment—I can see how that might work."

I paused. "Of course your situation and Phaedra's is quite different, living in the palace as you do. How is Phaedra, by the way?"

"I see little of her, as usual." Then Ariadne tossed her head defiantly. "As for punishment, I'll take my chances. Even if Uncle learns you've gone on an excursion out of the Labyrinth, he needn't know that I had anything to do with it. And the less Phaedra knows about it the better. Not that she would ever betray us willingly, but . . ."

"Yes," I said. Our elder sister generally tended to keep to the rules, until they became totally unendurable. And she had never been able to conceal her thoughts and feelings with any degree of success. "Have you told her about Theseus?"

"No. Asterion, you *will* help me, won't you? His life must be saved, whatever else happens."

"Whatever else?"

"I mean it."

"Then I promise. I'll do whatever may be necessary. But I don't know anything about him. The next time I go to sleep, I will try to find out what I can, about him and about what Uncle may be planning. Then we can devise some stratagem of our own."

"You will find out nothing bad about Theseus." Tossing her head again, Ariadne turned and started away. "Excuse me, but there are many things that I must do."

"Wait. Just how do you mean to help me, in the matter of my visiting the city?" Knowing my sister as I did, I was certain she would not forget the matter, and I thought it prudent to know as soon as possible what scheme she was concocting. Ariadne meant well, but any recipient of her aid could count himself lucky not to be involved in new perils.

"You'll see!" Already at the nearest branching of the passageway, she waved goodbye vivaciously. "Meet me in the courtyard of the three statues, one hour before sunset!"

---

*T*o pass the time before the appointed hour of my next meeting with my sister, I decided to go and talk to Daedalus, who I considered by far the wisest counselor among the few I had available.

Impractical as I was in many matters, it seemed to me that saving the life of Theseus was likely to be a far more difficult problem than Ariadne was willing to admit. But my personal search for a solution would have to wait until I could sleep and dream again. In the meantime, possibly Daedalus could help.

Headed toward the place where I expected to find him, I gave little conscious attention to the course my feet were taking, yet I made good time.

I suppose that you who have never walked those convoluted pathways cannot really conceive what they are like. Passages within the Labyrinth transform themselves from wide to narrow to wide again, according to no pattern that the sole permanent inhabitant, myself, has ever been able to ascertain. Stairways appear, seemingly at random, never any more than eight or ten steps in any one flight. When a passage is elevated it is quite likely that another one, or two or three, will cross beneath the high place, out of sight.

But most of the Maze, as you may know, is roofless, and walls in those uncovered portions are generally about fifteen feet high. They also display a notable lack of useful projections, so climbing them is very hard work at best. One person standing on another's shoulders gains no real advantage. And the top of each wall, more often than not, is an almost blade-sharp edge, impossible to walk on, difficult even to grasp. In keeping with this theme, the roofs of the covered sections of passageway tend to be steeply sloping, and precarious. There are also some low-level roofs, easily climbable but useless for getting out, or even seeing over the adjoining walls. What flat and solid covering there is, is thin, and at the time of which I write it was badly rotted in places, so people tended to fall through when they tried to walk on it.

At frequent intervals a passageway will widen a little, doubling or tripling its breadth to create a space that could be called a room, if it happens to be covered, as it sometimes is. Occasionally such a room contains a fireplace or open hearth, and the vines that in summer grow so long make good fuel when they are dead and dry in winter. Not that Corycus ever experiences a real winter, by the standards of the northern mainland, with persistent snow and ice. Instead we have shorter days, gray skies, dull rain.

There are a few spots within the Labyrinth from which it is actually possible, when one stands up high enough, to see, at a distance of ten or twelve miles, the sometimes snowy peaks of the low ridge that the inhabitants of Corycus call a range of mountains. But the points from which such an observation is possible are hard to find.

The center of the Maze was less than a mile, as a bird might fly, from the place where I had spoken with my sister. But to get from one point to the other through the passages required a minimum walk of almost three times that distance; and one who did not know the Labyrinth might easily have walked a hundred times as far to arrive at the same destination. Assuming (and it is a large assumption) that he or she would be able to find the way at all. Many are incredulous when they first hear that a square of the earth's surface, only two miles by two, might, without the use of magic or any special cleverness, contain a thousand miles of passageways, each broad enough for human traffic. But so it is.

Here and there I managed to subtract miles from my journey, by climbing over a wall, or walking briefly atop one of the roofed segments of a passage, the narrow supports bending under my weight.

Still, to reach a portion of the Maze where I might reasonably begin to look for Daedalus took me the better part of an hour. I knew that I had almost reached my goal when I entered the central region, which was more ancient and stranger than any of the rest. Here the possibility of confusion was even greater, and the walls and floors were made of panels and blocks formed from a different material, some product of the era when the gods were born, not readily identifiable as either stone or wood or metal.

The central part of the Labyrinth, an area about a quarter of a mile square, had the look and feel of being older than any of the rest. The style in which it was built, and the materials, did not match those of the surrounding work. Where there had obviously once been buildings, now there were only rooms, many of them roofless and half-overgrown with the same kinds of vegetation that sprouted in the endless miles of the surrounding passageways. Patches that once were garden had now gone wild, but continued to produce some edible stuff. There were conflicting stories, legends, regarding this construction, which must have taken place back in the ancient epoch, at the time when the gods were born— or created. This portion of the Labyrinth included endless rooms, some roofed, some open, filled with complex, incomprehensible apparatus. All of this, or almost all, had fallen into ruin decades or even centuries before I was born. Following that notable event, another seventeen years passed before Daedalus arrived, and was assigned by our noble uncle the task of trying to unravel the truth of ancient mysteries.

Gradually, over the centuries since this center portion was constructed, the whole stone-walled Maze had been built up around it, for reasons that now seemed not only mystical but often totally obscure. For generations the rulers of the city and the island seemed to have taken up the erection of more walls and tunnels as a holy task. The reasons underlying this tradition remained obscure.

I found the Artisan about where I had expected he would be, not far from the center of the relatively small area in which he had chosen to confine his labors.

"Greetings, Daedalus."

"Asterion." He had been sitting cross-legged in a shaded corner, perched on a kind of bench or table that was made of some ancient, incomprehensible material, seemingly neither wood nor rock nor metal, dark and smooth and hard. Once he had told me that such tables were antique workbenches.

As I approached, Daedalus was studying intently a small fragment of twisted, ancient metal, holding it up in both hands close before his eyes. When he heard my voice he looked up at me, startled and yet not really surprised to see me, the vagueness in his eyes showing that most of his thought was still elsewhere, engaged I suppose upon some baffling problem. Yet he was not displeased to be interrupted.

Nothing that I had ever seen in the Artisan suggested to me that he was a violent man; but the story that had come with him, on which I had never sought his own comment, was that he had fled to Corycus after killing his nephew and chief assistant, Perdix, in some quarrel on the mainland.

The master artisan, said to be a widower, was a lean man of about forty, of no more than average height, with a large nose, his brownish, gray-streaked hair tied behind him with utilitarian string. Nothing ornamental about Daedalus. Today, as usual when he was on the job, his only garment was a kind of combination belt and apron of patched leather, equipped with pockets and loops to hold small tools. His arms were all lean, practical strength. All of his fingers were ringless as a slave's, both hands callused and scarred from the use of every kind of tool, and marked by accidents. Even now one knuckle was bleeding slightly, from a fresh scrape.

I had heard that while laboring for his previous patrons on the mainland, Daedalus had usually worked with many assistants. But since Minos had set him the task of making sense of the ancient apparatus of odylic force, he was almost always alone.

When we had exchanged a few commonplace remarks, I asked him, "What do you know of a youth, a man, called Theseus?"

"Who?" It was plain from his blank look that Daedalus knew nothing. "Who is he?" Now he was giving me his full attention, his technical problems for the moment set aside. Even the fact of the Tribute was news to this dedicated worker, who seemed to know even less than I of events outside the Maze.

I shook my head to show it did not matter. "Never mind, I will ask elsewhere. Is your work successful?"

"Successful?" Daedalus's brows knotted. He searched the sky with his fierce gaze, and blasphemed several gods. Savagely he hurled aside the bit of twisted metal he had been examining, so that it bounced on stone pavement and vanished somewhere. "The truth is, I have been here on Corycus for almost four months now and I still don't know what I'm doing. I curse the day I became entangled with these mysteries they call odylic. That's why I currently have no assistant. My ignorance would be hard to conceal from any intelligent person who might spend an entire day with me."

"I don't suppose you've confessed to the new king that you still don't know what you're doing?"

Daedalus snorted.

"Do you wish that you were elsewhere?"

He looked at me sharply. "To you, Asterion, I will admit that I curse the day I ever came to Corycus. But what I wish on that subject does not much matter. King Perses is not going to let me go."

"You have asked him?"

"I don't need to, I know it would be useless."

I tried to let my concern show in my voice; my face does not much lend itself to the expression of emotion. "Well, I'll help you if possible. Is there anything I can do?"

"I doubt it. But I suppose it's conceivable that you might be of help sometime, and I certainly thank you for the offer." The Artisan drew a deep breath and let it out. "You've spent more time in this damned Maze than anyone else, myself certainly included. My question is quite fundamental: What in the Underworld *is* all this stuff?" And Daedalus gestured with one scarred hand toward all the heaped-up business, unidentifiable, strange enough to be unearthly, almost indescribable, upon the nearest bench.

"I don't know," I admitted simply. "You've been here four months; I've been here most of my life, and I have no idea." It did not seem the kind of question that could be answered by pursuing it in dreams.

"Look at it! Table after table of it, room after room. Long glass tubes to make connections in the mass. They stretch from one chamber to another here on ground level, they go down at least two levels lower. But they convey nothing at all that I can see, or imagine."

Here the Artisan paused, and fixed me with a gaze of burning intensity. "Asterion, do you know anything of the art of handling molten glass? No, how could you. But let me tell you, just to duplicate one of those tubes would be a serious challenge to the finest glassblower. And that's only the beginning. Strands of copper, intricately woven, binding other objects. Glass, metal, other materials I can't even tell if they're mineral or vegetable—or maybe some kind of horn, or bone. No two rooms are quite identical, nor are the contents of any two tables, but to a casual inspection most of them are very much alike. If these are tools, then it can be no ordinary matter on which they are designed to operate, no ordinary task that they were meant to do.

"I am not entirely sure that I have even found all of the rooms in this section of the Labyrinth, let alone examined them minutely, or even determined their exact number—though I suppose I will do that. That would at least give me something quite definite to report, which might at least sound like progress." He glanced over his shoulder at the shaded doorway of the modest roofed room in which he and his small son had taken up their residence; at the moment there was no sign of anyone.

Then Daedalus added, as if in afterthought, "And there is supposed to be a god's Face discoverable somewhere in all this."

"What?"

The Artisan nodded. "The king, the new king, is convinced of it, for some reason, and so it must be there." Daedalus took a deep swig from an opaque water bottle that stood by him and set it back on the bench with a thud, like a workman putting down a tool. It occurred to me to wonder if there might be something besides water in the bottle; but I had never seen him appear to be the worse for wine.

"Really?" I asked. "The Face of what god?"

"Actually I didn't ask, because I didn't think it mattered. Because, whoever it might be, I have no idea of how to go about such a task. Asterion? Have you ever seen a god's Face? I suppose the great majority of people never do."

"Not I." As usual, I found Daedalus's calm acceptance of me as a person, despite my grotesque shape, very heartening. "Except in dreams, where I am liable to see almost anything. How should I see a god? Shiva has never summoned me, or visited the Maze—which suits me fine. Have you ever seen one?"

The Artisan nodded slowly. "Once, long ago, I may have done; not a detached Face, but a being who looked almost like a man, though I believe it was one of the gods."

"You said: 'a detached Face'?"

Daedalus patiently explained what everyone more or less knew about the Faces, and how the king was interested in a particular one, unspecified.

"He came to visit me a while back, and without much preamble demanded, 'Where is the Face of Dionysus?' I said to him, 'My lord king, though I am Daedalus, I am only a mortal man, and there are things I do not know, and that is one of them. The missing Faces of the gods may be here, somewhere within reach, or they may all be at the far end of the earth. I can only go on searching.' "

"And what did our new Minos have to say to that?"

"He grumbled, and told me to go on looking, and that was about all. But I tell you, Asterion." Here the Artisan paused to look around, and dropped his voice. "I regret the day I came here, and I devoutly wish my son and I were somewhere else."

"I suppose it is not impossible that a man of your talent should find a way to leave. If you do, I wish you would tell me, and soon. I know others who have the same wish."

"Ah," said the Artisan, sounding slightly and hopefully surprised. He gave me a long, guarded look, then nodded slowly. "These others you mention . . . have they taken any steps toward a practical solution of the problem?"

"I think not. No, I'm sure they haven't. Would it be impertinent to ask if you have done so?"

"Impertinence should be the least of anyone's concerns when

such matters are discussed. No, I have taken no pragmatic action. But now perhaps it is time I did so."

And with that he went back to talking of other things. What Daedalus had said to me on the subject of Faces tallied with much that I had heard before. It was a story so common that I supposed it had to be fundamentally correct: how ordinary mortals could, when given the opportunity, put those Faces on, clothing themselves in divine power.

Then he added, "Now that the subject of gods has come up between us, Asterion, there is a personal question I would like to ask you, if you do not mind."

"I don't mind it from you, Daedalus. I suppose I can even guess what the question is."

"There are folk who say great Zeus himself was your father."

I nodded. "There seems reason to believe that is the case. But I know no more about that than you do."

At that moment Icarus came running up to us, a wiry boy of seven or eight, clad only in a small copy of his father's leather apron. Daedalus had never mentioned the boy's mother, who she might be, or where she was, and I had never asked. Evidently the child had seen that Daedalus was not, at the moment, concentrating upon his work, and thus could be safely interrupted. Icarus had been frightened of me, months ago when we first met, but had soon adopted his father's cosmopolitan attitude.

The Artisan's son was willing enough to help with his father's work, when his parent told him to do so, but I thought Icarus showed no great native skill or interest in such matters.

Absently Daedalus stroked his small son's uncombed head. "If this were some ordinary job, I'd have the boy assisting me. But this . . ." The artisan shook his head. "I must come up with some kind of an answer here. Or the king will be seriously displeased."

Studying Icarus critically, I said to him, "You have grown taller since I saw you last. I think you are old enough to swim, and I could teach you. We wouldn't have to leave the Labyrinth. I know where there is a pool quite long and deep enough, not many miles from here. No one else ever comes to that place, only the birds, from year to year, and sometimes a big fish."

For some reason, what I had just said had caught the father's interest. Slowly he came back from his dreams of work to look at me. "How big? The fish, I mean."

I raised my hands, almost two feet apart.

"What species?"

"A sort of salmon, I think, judging by its resemblance to a fish I have seen people eating."

"I would like to see this pool," said Daedalus, and at the same moment his son said, "I already know how to swim," in a tone that expressed his scorn of anyone who might not.

"Then I won't need to teach you," I agreed. "And I will show you both the pool," I said to Daedalus. "But it will have to wait until another day." Looking up at the sun, I estimated how many hours must pass before it set. I turned away to go, and then turned back. "Remember what I said, about how others share your wish."

"I will remember."

At an hour before sunset, Ariadne was waiting for me at the agreed meeting place. This was a little plaza, wider by a stride than most such in my domain, that my sister and I in our private talks had come to call the Courtyard of the Three Statues. Because indeed there were three marble carvings, of a man, a woman, and a satyr, each on its own pedestal, carved by some unremembered artist in some lost century before our own.

But on that afternoon I paid little attention to the statues as I approached; I was surprised to see that my sister was not alone. The small figure of a single companion stood beside her, anonymous and sexually ambiguous in an elaborate mask and costume.

Ariadne was carrying a mass of fabric in her arms; it might have been another costume, or a small tent. As soon as I appeared, she told me that she had brought something for me to wear when I went exploring in the town. The chosen outfit included loose trousers, and a large, baggy shirt or blouse that I thought rather strange-looking, to say the least. Both garments were of coarse cloth and gaudy colors. On a bench nearby rested a lacquered box that I thought I recognized as her own modest makeup kit. "And who's this?" I demanded, pointing. Ariadne giggled and pulled the mask from the face of the short figure by her side. I was not really surprised to see the face of her regular attendant and frequent companion, Clara, a pert slave girl with dark, straight hair.

Clara had accompanied Ariadne on many of my sister's earlier visits to the Maze, but I had not expected her or anyone else today. It had seemed to me that the fewer people who knew about my planned foray into the outside world, the better.

Ariadne was smiling, as if daring me to guess what these preparations were all about. I took the gaudy shirt from her hands and shook it out. It was enormous, too big even for me. "Where in the world did you get a garment like this?"

"We found it in a storeroom. It was made for the last Festival, and then it didn't quite fit the straw dummy that was going to be burned, and they had to make another. I happened to remember that this one was just left over."

I waved the mass of fabric like a flag. "And wearing this is supposed to make me inconspicuous?"

"Actually, yes. You'll see."

"And Clara. Why is she costumed?" The slave girl smiled at me uncertainly.

"She's going with you," Ariadne informed me, observing my continued puzzlement.

"Oh." My first impulse was to protest, but on second thought I could see advantages. Clara's outfit was a showy one, I suppose on the theory that it would also serve to distract attention from me.

Now I turned my attention to the box of cosmetics. "Do you imagine that with a little paint you can make my head look human?"

My sister shook her head at my obtuseness. "No, silly! But what I *can* do is make your head look like a mask. One of those great, hollow masks that people often wear at Festival."

"I don't know . . ."

"I do. Come over here, where the sun still shines." She patted the stone bench beside her. "Sit down. Sit still."

Over the next few minutes the two women busied themselves making up my horned head with rouge, lipstick, and paint, so that in the end they assured me that it did indeed look like a giant mask. And they helped me, as if I were a child who needed help, to pull on the huge blouse as a costume, and the oversized, awkward gloves. Now I began to appreciate the plan. Had I gone out without a costume, I would necessarily have spent my time lurking and scurrying through shadows, trying to avoid being seen by anyone.

When I had been thus thoroughly disguised, my sister assured me that I could pass, for a while, and at night, as an ordinary human, though indeed a man of impressive size. Clara had brought with her in her kit a small mirror, and I was now encouraged to try to see the alteration for myself. Fortunately or not, the small mirror was of but little help.

Studying the total effect, Ariadne planted her fists on her hips and sighed. "There's no way, short of magic, to disguise your height; and I don't know any magician I'd want to ask to do that job." But the huge blouse covered just those upper parts, those portions of my body that looked least human.

At last the artists were satisfied. "When are you going?" my sister inquired.

"Now. It'll be dark by the time I get out. It will take us half an hour to walk from here to the nearest exit, on the city side."

"Longer than that, surely."

"Not by the route I'll take." I had good reason to be confident that no one else knew the Labyrinth as well as I.

Ariadne sighed, and rubbed my gloved hand in a proprietary way. "Then go, and the gods of fortune with you. I am half tempted to go with you myself—I want a full report tomorrow on your adventures."

"You shall have it." I paused, wanting to change the subject before my sister could convince herself that she should come along. "Have you had any further word of your Theseus?" I had no fear in speaking that name in front of Clara, taking it for granted that the slave girl shared all her mistress's fears and schemes.

Ariadne shook her light brown curls. "Not since I spoke to you a few hours ago. Why?"

"I have had a talk with Daedalus during the interval. I think that you, and he, and this Theseus now all have something very important in common—a wish to be away from Corycus."

Both young women were listening with keen interest. "Then I think I should meet with Daedalus," Ariadne said.

I bowed lightly. "Allow me to arrange it—tomorrow."

needed no one's help in accomplishing my actual emergence into the world. I had managed that feat several times before in my young life, quite without assistance or companionship. There were a number of doorways, spaced around the eight-mile perimeter, and to the best of my knowledge four of them always stood open between the outermost layer of the Labyrinth and the rest of the world. There was nothing physically difficult about getting out, once you could find one of those doors. And of course the doors were infinitely easier to discover from the outside, so it was not at all hard for outsiders to get in. People had done so, of course, at irregular intervals over the years. Every now and then, some fanatic or adventurer, drawn by the urge to explore a mystery, bemused by some foolish rumor of hidden treasure, or simply acting on a dare, would venture into what I considered my domain. Certain evidence obtained in dreams had convinced me that most of these explorers were newcomers to the city and the island.

These occasional wanderers caused me no trouble, and I seldom gave them any thought. Only twice, while roaming the Maze during my childhood, I had stumbled upon human bones that must have belonged to members of this ill-fated fraternity, dead of panic and despair, or possibly of starvation—vast regions of my domain offer little or nothing in the way of food. In each case the remains were lying miles from the nearest entrance to the Labyrinth—which, of course, might not have been the portal by which the unfortunate one had entered. In each case, again, a rusted weapon lay near the skeleton; doubtless the intruders had come armed to protect themselves against the monstrous Minotaur. Or possibly they planned to collect my great horned head and lug it home as a trophy.

How many similar fallen ones might still lie undiscovered,

even by me, in the remoter byways, was hard to estimate. I felt most comfortable with the belief that the majority of such experiments ended with the adventurer making it safely out of the Maze after an hour or two's adventure. No doubt some of them carried balls of string to unwind as they explored, in an attempt to keep from getting lost. But I had no fear of ever being overrun by trespassers. As I had once told Ariadne, I was confident that none would carry a thousand miles of string.

My own previous excursions beyond the walls of the Labyrinth had all been brief, and unaccompanied, impulsive midnight dartings into a world that I had never really known outside of dreams. My last such sortie had been years ago, and my memories of the world that I had seen outside were old and hazy, like troubled dreams.

This time, as on those earlier occasions, I naturally waited until after dark. And as before, I carried no ball of string to help me find my way back through the mysterious city to my home. I planned to go much farther this time than I had ever gone before, but this time I had a guide to help me, and in any case I was willing to rely on my own sense of direction.

Meanwhile, my sister, having bidden her brother and her slave farewell, turned away to make her way home to the palace alone. I had no more fear of Ariadne's ever getting lost in the Maze than I did of losing my own way. From our real father she had her own special inheritance, which fortunately for her was far less conspicuous and troublesome than mine.

Now, walking beside Clara, I made an effort to observe more details of her true appearance, but the effort was thwarted by her mask and the clothes she had put on.

My escort's costume was of colors considerably brighter than my own—but that she should draw attention away from me was, of course, a key part of Ariadne's plan. Clara's mask was of papier-mâché or something of the kind, and it altered the shape of her whole head, though it gave her feline rather than bovine form—of course there was no need for her to match me in that way.

From the sound of my companion's occasional laughter behind her mask, from the feel of her hand when I took it to guide her through certain turns of the passages, I thought that she was still a little afraid of me. She had seen me often enough in the company of her mistress, but this was the first time the two of us had ever been alone.

Now that darkness had fallen, had already become impenetrably thick in some of the roofed areas, the Maze was more confusing than ever. Once, as I led her down a byway that must have looked particularly unpromising, I am sure that my companion started to ask me if I knew where I was going. But then she bit her tongue and did not fairly launch the question.

As we walked, I described to the girl a certain winter night that I remembered very clearly. One night, several winters ago, when snow fell briefly, out of a cold and moonless, starless sky, swirling and drifting in the roofless stretches of the endless passageways. That had been the first and only snow that my waking eyes had ever seen, excepting the occasional white stain along the crest of the distant mountain ridge. Several times, on that long-past night, even I had begun to be confused about directions.

My girl-companion evidently did not know what to say in response to my little story. Eventually she murmured something. I took her small hand in my great gloved one as we walked, and being a slave she made no effort to pull her hand away. She asked, brightly enough, "Where are we going? I mean once we are out in the city?"

"I'm not sure. Perhaps I'll leave the final decision on that up to you. I want a place where I can see many people, face to face. And where it is likely that they will all accept me as a man in costume."

Clara was ready with a suggestion. "I know a place where many of the soldiers, the enlisted men, go when they're off duty. At night during the Festival, there will be many fantastic costumes there."

"What Festival is this?"

"Quite a new one, I think. It's been proclaimed, in connection with the Tribute."

I asked her, "And have you been to this place of celebration with the soldiers? Is one of them perhaps your lover?"

"I am a slave, Lord Asterion." Clara raised a hand to finger her silver collar, beneath the concealing fabric of her costume.

"I know that, but does that mean that you can have no lover?"

"My Lord Asterion's questions are too profound for me to understand. I would be overwhelmed, if my lord was suggesting that he and I—"

"No, nothing like that. I have no lovers, in the way that we are talking about. I want and need none. I thought my sister would have told you that much about me."

"No, Lord Asterion. My lady has told me very little. Only that the stories that you are some kind of a cruel monster are all utter nonsense—not that I would have believed them in any case, when I saw how she regards you."

"That's good." For a moment I thought of asking Clara to tell me exactly what some of those stories said; but quickly I decided I did not really want to know. "Lead on."

The doorway, or gateway, through which we left the Labyrinth that night was one of those that I knew were generally unlocked and unguarded, and so indeed we found it. Somewhat to my surprise, I noticed now that this high-arched portal was no longer furnished with any real door at all. Holes in the masonry showed where bolts must once have secured strong hinges. The only hindrance to intruders was what I took to be a warning, graven over the arched opening, on the outside of the high wall. The message was written in what appeared to be three languages, all so old that I was unable to read any of them. In passing I reminded myself to come back here sometime in a dream; then, more likely than not, I would be able to decipher all the words.

When my companion and I had emerged from the Maze and were standing in an open street, it was dark and at the moment almost unoccupied except for ourselves. Turning to my left, I could see the palace, less than a mile away. The huge, daunting House of the Hammer (as it was sometimes called, for what reason I know not), level after level of it rising up, lights burning on certain corners of the roof, and in many of its windows. Having visited that building in many dreams, I felt I knew it very well.

Indeed, I supposed it very probable that I had been born inside it, but that of course I could not remember. No one has ever told me the detailed story of my birth, nor had I ever sought to learn it. When in dream-life I found my steps tending in that direction, I always shied away.

Looking in the opposite direction from the palace, Clara and I could see out over the harbor, where there were berths for many mighty ships of war, as well as the bottoms of a busy trade. Most of those berths were empty now, but there was moonlight enough for me to see a scattering of ships, skeletal masts and spars, furled sails. Including some moored biremes. Here and there the orange flame of some warning beacon burned. If the whole world did not fear Minos, as they had once feared his predecessors, at least most of the people who knew him did. Of course, as always, a great part of his formidable navy was at sea.

As soon as we were fairly out of the Maze, Clara seemed to lose all her remaining timidity regarding the Minotaur who walked beside her. Now she was eager for a party, and held my hand quite willingly.

"I wonder—" I said aloud.

"Lord Asterion?"

"I was only wondering how many thousand people live here in Kandak. I've heard that it is one of the great cities of the world, but that saying may be only local pride."

"Lord, I have no idea how many there may be."

I still thought it strange that I had lived in the capital of my native land, or more precisely beside it, my whole life, and still had no idea what the number was.

We moved on. Tentatively exploring the darkened streets, steering a course neither directly toward the palace nor away from it, Clara and I were drawn to a scene of music and laughter.

Parties of laughing folk went by us in the street, and on impulse I tugged my partner into following one such group.

There were cameloids in the streets of the city, pacing on their great soft feet, some being ridden swiftly, and others swaying slowly under heavy cargo. Draft cameloids, one-humped droms even taller and heavier than the others, pulled the heavier carriages and carts. I knew that these were common animals, but in waking life my eyes had never seen the like before. From behind the high gates and fences guarding private homes, dogs barked at me as we passed. I hesitated, but Clara murmured reassuringly, "They would bark at anyone."

The group of people on foot we had begun to follow soon turned in through the gateway of a private house—no place for me there, certainly. But my companion knew where she wanted to go, to another building in another street, and in a few more minutes we had reached the place. There was the sound of laughter, and the rich smells of roasting meat and fresh-baked pastry, to me unappetizing. Torchlight came spilling out through all the doors and windows that pierced a certain white adobe wall, while most of the neighborhood around remained in darkness.

A door in the middle of the wall stood wide open. Ducking my head and turning, to get my horns in through the doorway, I entered the hall. I thought that something in the overall shape of the building suggested an earlier history as a temple, but the walls were scarred where symbols must have been chiseled away, and I could not tell which god it had sought to honor. Later, I thought, when we were outside again, I would ask Clara.

Inside the crowded room, the music of drums and strings throbbed loudly, and unclothed bodies whirled in a wild dance. Not professional entertainers, but free folk, mostly of the working classes, dancing for their own amusement. There sounded the lyre, Apollo's instrument. Torches and braziers flared, somehow cleverly made to burn with flames of different colors. Laughter went up in many voices. I was almost entranced. Never, except in dreams, had I even seen so many people in the same place at the same time. I supposed there might have been a hundred in one room. This was not a haunt of the wealthy. I thought a number of the men were soldiers, as Clara had foretold, young enlisted men out of uniform for their night's revelry.

Along the walls of the room and in its corners there were

tables, with people sitting at them, some consuming wine and food. Moving close to the broad table where drinks were being poured and handed out, I heard disturbing comments, and saw startling sights, including a number of people costumed even more spectacularly than I was myself.

Looking closely, I observed that one or two of them were actually versions of the Minotaur, larger and fiercer-looking than I had ever been, with long horns carved of wood or bone. The mouth of one of their great masks sprouted predatory fangs.

And again, something about the shape of the scarred walls nagged at my attention. "I still wonder," I murmured to the girl beside me, "what god they once served here, whose house we are in? Not Apollo. And not Bacchus, surely." I was sure that Bacchus, one of whose other names is Dionysus, was proscribed in every quarter of the island, and had been for the last six months.

Clara said in a low voice, "They might once have served the Twice-Born. I have heard that when the new king came to power, he sent his soldiers here and they tore the place apart; they wouldn't say what they were looking for."

"There are many gods whose interests lie in the same general direction as those of Dionysus. Priapus would do, or any of half a dozen others."

On entering the hall, I had rather foolishly hoped no one would notice me. But even in this gathering, my appearance was more conspicuous, and drew more attention, than I would have wished. This was so even if the other Minotaurs were more monstrous than I.

Fortunately, Ariadne had remembered to give the slave-girl coins, trusting her more than me to understand the details of using money. Presently something to drink, carried in a strange flagon, appeared on the broad table before me. I should mention that I was not entirely unused to wine; Ariadne had brought me some from time to time, and in the old days it had sometimes come, in small glasses, suitable for my youth, with the official meals that were then sent out to me from the palace. That an intoxicating drink would be served in this establishment suggested Bacchus once again. Beside me a loudmouthed man had now ceased haranguing the world long enough to empty a flagon of foaming beer. I had heard that the new god of Corycus frowned on most kinds of merriment; well, people were not going to give up wine, let Shiva threaten as much as he liked.

The noise, the press of the crowd around me, more solid than in any dream, tended to be confusing. I had emptied my first flagon of wine and started on another before it occurred to me that if I drank or ate anything, I risked revealing that my mouth was mobile flesh, not part of a lifeless mask.

But the hesitation was only momentary. To the Underworld with it! I was going to enjoy the wine.

The unaccustomed drink produced a swaying of the room, a roaring in my ears. I had to wait for a long moment, until everything began to settle down again. Then I banged the empty flagon on the table, and made a bull-sound deep in my throat. I wanted to drink still more, and yet I was afraid.

Only now, with the drink beginning to act upon my senses, did I begin to pay attention to a large mirror, hanging on the wall behind the long table where the drinks were poured. The broad, smooth glass was as long as the table itself, and from that position it reflected all the dim lights of the large, low room.

Looking at my image in the mirror, I beheld a figure seven feet tall, weighing, as I knew, a little over three hundred pounds. Two sharp horns on the head, large brown eyes set wide apart, on a long bull-like face, now painted in stripes and dots that struggled to give a look of artificiality. Muffled in the great shirt were massive shoulders and arms, the latter terminating in hands that were trying to hide their almost inhuman size in grotesque and fancy gloves. The face and most of the body (now concealed by my costume) was covered with short cattle-hair.

The removal of a glove, the better to deal with a drinking glass, revealed long fingers, heavy nails.

But my gaze kept coming back to the reflected image of my face. Here it was, at last exposed for everyone to see, and had been ever since I entered the hall. But no one had really seen it yet.

Standing in the middle of such a crowd, it was hard to know what to think, what to do next. In all my life, my waking eyes had never seen more than six or eight people at one time at close range, and fewer still had ever seen me. Men and women were almost as unfamiliar in a mass as cameloids. Now to be surrounded, almost imprisoned by swarming humans, was more unsettling than I had expected it would be.

One of the young women, whose costume, or rather lack of one, suggested that she was a hired entertainer, put a hand upon my arm, only to withdrew it suddenly, a moment later. She must have felt skin that had the touch of fur, of something very much like cattle-hide.

Suddenly brutal voices rose up nearby, and I feared that my disguise had been somehow penetrated—but no, it was only being ridiculed, by drunken celebrants.

"What is it, man or monster?"

"Not very convincing, if it's supposed to be the Minotaur."

I turned toward the voices, but could find no words. Looking back at the situation now, I can see that my lack of ready speech must have only encouraged those who were looking for an opportunity to torment a victim.

"Hey, cow-face!" The speaker was large, though not, of course, as large as I. He was in costume too, some kind of parody of a military officer—not, of course, of the Minoan Palace Guard.

I was being picked on, first from one side, then another. Emboldened by drink, I shouted back at them. My voice, tolerably human when I am calm, sometimes escapes control when I am greatly excited, making a braying noise. What words I might have used have escaped my memory now. Certainly I meant them as insults, but I lacked all skill in such matters, and perhaps I only sounded stupid.

"Your mask is uglier than mine," was perhaps my best attempt, addressed as it was to a lounger who, like myself, wore none.

With that, the space around me grew ominously quiet. Clara had taken me by the arm, and was trying, first gently and then fiercely, to tug me away. But even when she pulled with all her strength, it was hardly possible for her to move me. And some accidental surging of the crowd in our immediate area had made the press so thick that quick movement was hardly possible.

The tugging and shoving grew more violent. My tormentors and I were thrust together. It would have been hard to pinpoint a moment when the fight began. Someone swung into my midriff with a clumsy fist; I scarcely felt the blow. This was not why I had come here. Neither reality nor my world of dreams had prepared me for anything of the kind.

I had, and have, no particular skill in personal combat. I could send bad dreams upon someone I hated—if I hated anyone—but that is all. But the sending of dreams required me first to go to sleep, and at the moment that was not feasible.

Some of the men who joined the brawl were soldiers, off duty and here to spend their pay, and some were not. Several were armed, though weapons were not drawn at first. One struck me with his fist, a much harder blow than the first attempt, and I struck back, and he went down, flat on his back.

My own more serious armament, such as it is, is always ready. When the brawl started, one of my opponents grabbed the bull by the horns, no doubt with the intention of tearing off my mask. What kind of shock he experienced when he discovered that the horns were of one piece with my skull, I do not know. Perhaps he was too far gone in wine to notice. I am no skilled fighter, but I am very strong, and my temper is not always mild. With an awkward heave of my bull's neck and shoulders I cast him loose, so that his body flew across the room, sweeping a table clean, reducing a chair beyond to kindling.

Someone else came at me with a weapon, and I saw the gleam of steel, but a young man whom I took to be a soldier, though now out of uniform, intervened on my side of the fight, helping to protect my companion. Clara, her mask dislodged in the scuffling, was huddling on the floor, trying to protect her head with folded arms. I hurled a chair at the man with the drawn knife, and he was seen no more.

"Call the Watch! Call the Watch!" First one voice, then three or four, were bawling.

The brawl had not become a general riot yet, but neither was it over. I realized that I had no choice but to flee, back to the Labyrinth. Quite possibly some of those in the room realized my true identity, but there was no general awareness, or alarm that the monster had actually come out. Those who screamed that they had seen the Minotaur were laughed to silence by others convinced that the witnesses had mistaken one of the cruder costumes for the real thing.

If this was the real world, I thought, I wanted no more of it. In my innocence I then imagined that I had really begun to understand what the real world was like.

After the figure in the monstrous costume had been driven out into the outer darkness, the young soldier Alex, who was in the room but taking no part in the fighting, recognized the slave-girl who served the princess that he worshipped from afar.

She had run out into the street, following the costumed Minotaur, and Alex ran out after her.

"Clara?"

The sound of her name stopped her in her tracks. She stood looking over her shoulder, waiting fearfully. In the distance sounded the whistles and rattles of the Watch. Alex knew he had a little time in which to act before they could arrive.

"You serve the Princess Ariadne, don't you? I've seen you with her more than once."

"Yes." Now Clara turned fully around.

"How lucky you are!"

"Why do you say that?"

"Why? Because—because you can be near her, every day."

The girl paused for what seemed a long time, as if she were unsure just what to make of that. At last she said: "Your name is Alex, is it not? A soldier of the Palace Guard."

"Yes." Then, as if involuntarily, the secret that had been poisoning him for half a year burst out. Still, his voice was so low that no one but the girl standing directly in front of him could hear. "Tell your mistress I must see her."

"Why?"

"There is something of great importance that she needs to know."

"What?"

"Something about her father, and the way he died."

"You must see her. Very well, I'll tell her that."

"And, slave-girl—repeat to no one else what I am telling you!"

Clara nodded, wide-eyed. The young soldier got the impression that what he had just said had frightened her, perhaps more than the fight itself.

Clara had already screamed, and run away in the direction of the palace. She had seen that I was loose, and knew I could certainly run fast enough to overtake her.

Some man with a loud voice was bellowing, "The Watch is coming. Look out for the Watch!"

I ran, my very manlike feet in sandals pounding the pavement in the direction where I had seen the young girl who was my escort disappear. I can move very quickly, and I had no fear that they would catch me, unless they came on cameloids.

How ironic it would be, I thought, if I became bewildered, lost my way in the city, and had to ask directions back to the Labyrinth. But once I was out in the street, I looked up to see the familiar stars and moon. They had followed me out of the Labyrinth as if they intended to stay with me, and now they were on hand to guide me home.

$\mathcal{O}$n returning to the palace, the slave-girl Clara found, as she had expected, that her mistress was waiting up in their shared bedroom for her report on Asterion's adventure.

As Clara closed the door behind her, the Princess Ariadne pushed aside the small harp on which she had been practicing, and jumped to her feet. "What happened? Come in and tell me everything!" She blew out the single candle, leaving the room to the moonlight that entered by the high window.

With the doors closed, the two young women were as safe from being overheard as it was ever possible to be inside the palace. While discarding her costume and mask, Clara hastened to pass along what the young soldier had said to her in town.

Ariadne was immediately fascinated, but wary. "It couldn't be some kind of trap, could it?"

"I really don't see how, my lady. That would mean someone knew I was going to be there, and arranged for Alex to tell me what he did. But neither the Lord Asterion nor I were sure where we were going, until we were well on our way."

"Did anyone recognize him?"

"I really don't know, my lady. I couldn't tell. Many people looked at him strangely, of course . . ."

"Of course."

Quickly the princess decided to take the risk of arranging a secret meeting between herself and Alex, at a time when the young soldier would be off duty again, and might be expected to be in town enjoying himself.

"First we must find out when he will be off duty again."

"I expect I can easily do that," said Clara. "I know a certain corporal, who keeps track of the rosters."

* * *

A day later, Alex received a summons to a meeting, whispered to him by one of the greasy kitchen scullions, who managed to catch the soldier alone as he was leaving the small mess hall. For the next twenty-four hours his head was awhirl with the news that the princess wanted to see him. At the end of his next shift of guard, on being relieved from duty, instead of walking into town or back to the barracks, he made an excuse of weariness that separated him from his fellows.

Then, still in his workaday uniform though without armor and unarmed—only guards on duty were allowed to carry weapons inside the palace—he walked around the huge building, entering the grounds through a side entrance at a good distance from the barracks.

In the gardenlike expanse just inside the gated wall, he was met by Clara, dressed inconspicuously in ordinary servant's garb, who seemed to be waiting for him.

"Good day," Alex offered timidly.

"Good day to you, corporal."

"I'm only a private." His lack of any insignia of rank was plain enough.

Clara smiled faintly, and Alex supposed she had only been trying to flatter him a little. She said, "The princess is waiting for you. Come this way."

As he followed the slave girl, it occurred to Alex, not for the first time, that there must be many members of the royal household, even as he knew there were in the barracks, who loved the princess, though some of them had not cared for her father all that much. Certainly most of them cared even less for her ambitious uncle and his terrifying god. One thing Alex was sure of was that there could be none who loved the Princess Ariadne more than he.

Somewhat to his surprise, his guide led him not into one of the side doors of the palace itself, but in almost the opposite direction, along a small gravel path that curved across a corner of the parklike grounds. Now he could see that they were headed straight toward one edge of the mysterious Labyrinth, which here immediately adjoined the palace grounds. The Maze's outer wall of stone, tall and slightly curving, loomed up ominously ahead of them. Soldiers were warned frequently against ever entering that realm on their own.

"We are going there?"

His escort tried to be reassuring. "The princess goes into the Labyrinth almost every day. She's done so for a long time, and no one takes notice."

"Why does she go in every day?"

He expected to be told that what her royal highness did was none of his business. But Clara responded readily enough. "Mostly to see her brother."

Alex, like the great majority of the Corycan people, and of visitors to the island, had never set foot inside the Maze. What little he knew about it came almost entirely from the legends and the stories. It was a vast construction, sprawling over some four square miles. It was also the home of the legendary Minotaur, and the almost equally legendary Artisan, Daedalus—and rumor had it that for the last six months the god Shiva had also made the Labyrinth his chief place of residence.

At any given time there were sure to be two or three different rumors, stories, jokes, circulating in the barracks about the horrible monster who dwelt inside the Labyrinth—and two nights ago, in town, he had seen for himself someone, or something, who . . .

But it was going to take more than a Minotaur to frighten him when he had a chance to be of service to the princess.

Now the arched entrance to the great Maze was looming close ahead of them. "They say," said Alex to the slave girl, "that there are monsters here."

"People say many things that are sheer nonsense," Clara told him briskly. Without slowing her pace, she turned her head to give him a penetrating glance. "There is no monster in the Maze—unless perhaps you mean a certain god. The only mortal creature who lives there is the brother of the princess. You saw him the other night, when he was in costume."

"Yes. All right." Alex nodded. If the being he had encountered in town two nights ago was not to be considered monstrous, whether it was costumed or not . . . well, so be it.

He paused briefly, on the very threshold of the arched doorway. Ahead were blank walls, and a quick choice to be made of sudden turnings. "Is this the same part of the Maze where the people of the Tribute are being held?"

"No, they're over there." With a slight movement of her head the girl seemed to be indicating some other section of the Maze.

And even as she made that gesture, she went in. Alex followed, keeping close behind his guide, who led him first beneath a grating that striped the sky with iron bars. They turned right at the first branching of the passageway, then left at the second. In these early stages the passage between tall walls of smooth stone was so narrow that Alex walked with his elbows almost brushing on each side. Then abruptly the overhead grating was gone, but the way was wider, so wide that a man could not hope to climb by bracing himself between two walls.

Three more turns inside the Labyrinth, three choices of branching roofless corridors, brought Alex and his guide to a place where the walls opened out a little more, making a kind of narrow courtyard. The soldier felt his heart leap up inside his chest. The Princess Ariadne, today almost as plainly dressed as her servant, was seated there on a stone bench, waiting for him, while the afternoon sun awakened glories in her light brown hair.

Alex dropped to one knee on the pavement. This was the woman he had come to worship, helplessly, beginning on the first day he saw her. His escort had somehow vanished, and it came upon him with overwhelming force that now he and the Princess Ariadne were utterly alone, surrounded by the grotesque, curving pattern of the tall stone walls, as if this were only some fantastic daydream. Alex assumed that Clara had remained nearby somewhere, probably keeping watch to see that they were undisturbed.

"Your name is Alex?" Her voice was achingly familiar; of course he had heard her speak in public now and then.

"Yes, my princess!" For a moment he was afraid that the words were going to stick in his throat.

Of course she was not going to offer her hand to a mere private soldier. Her marvelous eyes were well-disposed toward him, but they were not patient. "Yes, I think I can remember seeing you on duty now and again, as a member of the Guard." She paused to draw a breath. "Last night you told my servant that you knew something about my father's death."

So, he had made some impression on her memory! The revelation was immensely heartening.

"Yes ma'am." In his own ears, every word he said sounded utterly stupid.

The eyes of the princess were not only kindly, but enormous. They were pools in which a man might lose his way forever. Under their gaze, Alex made two false beginnings to his story, tried a third time and was not doing well. Eventually she had to prompt him. "So you were there, in the great hall, on the night of my father's murder?"

"Princess, I was there. One of the men guarding the main door, when you came in."

"I remember only that there were some soldiers. Never mind, tell what you have to tell."

And Alex, with much sincere worship, finally told his story. It was not, of course, the version of events the general had forced upon all witnesses, but the version his own eyes had seen.

It needed a couple of minutes to stammer through. When Alex was done, and the eyes of the young woman before him were clenched in tears, he added, "Gracious lady, I am so sorry to reopen the wound . . ."

"The wound has never closed." She wiped her tears away, and in a few moments it was almost as if they had never been. She said to the young man before her, "I thank you with all my heart, for telling me the truth, when no one else has dared to do so. You may stand up. Yes, now I seem to remember seeing you in the great hall that night. I would like to give you a present to show my gratitude."

"All I want is the chance to serve you, Princess!"

"The gods know that I may call on you for help. But you should have something finer and more immediate than that." And, rising to her feet, she impulsively pulled a small medallion up on the golden chain by which it hung around her neck. It looked like a thin disk of gold, between two and three inches in diameter, one flat side welded somehow to a disk of silver of the exact same size. Both gold and silver circles bore in low relief an image of the sun, surrounded by intricate fine metalwork suggesting leaves and vines.

"Come closer," she commanded.

And when Alex had nervously edged closer, so close that he hardly dared to breathe, the princess reached out and with her own hands put the chain around his neck. On each side, her fingers touched his skin. "You will probably be safer if you wear it inside your shirt, where no one will notice."

Obviously she was not familiar with living conditions in the barracks; but Alex could not possibly have raised any objection at this point. "Yes, my lady."

Somewhere in the distance, probably in some remote portion of the palace grounds, one of the officers of the guard was shouting something at his men. The voice was a familiar sound, but at the moment it had nothing to do with Alex.

And now, having sealed his loyalty even more tightly than before, the princess insisted on his going over once more the events of that terrible night. This time she craved more details, in particular the identities of the other soldiers and servants who had been there at her father's death, and who had never come forward with the truth.

"You can give me their names, can you not?"

"I could, lady, and of course I will if you command it. But . . ." Alex slowly shook his head.

"Would any of them be willing now to tell me the truth, as you have done?"

"Great princess, I think that's very doubtful. I don't know about the servants, but I think that after what the general said to us, the other soldiers almost certainly will be too much afraid."

Suddenly Ariadne seemed to be really looking at him for the first time. "But you are not. You are willing to disobey orders, coming here and talking to me like this."

"Majesty, lady, for you—I would do anything. I . . ."

"I thank you again for your loyalty," said the princess, her attention sliding away from him again. Then her gaze shifted, sliding over Alex's shoulder to a point not far behind him. He turned to see the Minotaur regarding him, standing on two human legs not ten feet away.

No trace remained of the facial paint the monster had worn two nights ago, so his head and face were even more inhuman than Alex remembered them. The loose garments of carnival costume were gone, the huge body clad in little more than a kilt, leaving the massive chest and shoulders exposed in their coating of short cattle-hair, in black and white. Here was the beast of legend, in the full light of day.

Ever since that night six months ago, when he had witnessed the arrival in the kingdom of two gods, Alex had been ready to accept, to believe in marvels when he saw them. Now his blood seemed to freeze in his veins. He couldn't interpret the expression on the Minotaur's face, if that inhuman countenance could be said to have an expression at all. Alex's first impulse was to reach for the sword he wasn't wearing, following an instinct to defend the princess.

If either the princess or the monster noticed the aborted movement of his arm, they paid it no attention. Instead they exchanged with each other a few words of almost casual conversation.

Then the terrible, frightening figure turned to Alex, and said in its strange voice, towering over him, "I am the Lord Asterion. We recently saw each other in town."

"Yes. Yes, lord."

"You have spoken to others about my presence there?"

"No . . . sir."

"If you would serve the Princess Ariadne, you will say nothing. About last night, or about this meeting here today."

"I will say nothing, Lord Asterion."

"Then you may go."

As soon as the soldier had been escorted away by Clara, Daedalus emerged from the place of concealment from which he had been watching, and bowed deeply before the princess. The slave-girl had kept him waiting until the coast was clear. Icarus had been left in the care of the woman who usually looked after him whenever his father was busy.

Ariadne wasted no time in getting to the point. "Theseus wants to meet you, Artisan—you know who Theseus is?"

Daedalus made a perfunctory bow. "Your brother has told me, my lady. Let me say that I advise against it, unless there is some reason stronger than mere curiosity. The fewer meetings we have, the less chance that anyone will suspect our plot. My suggestion is, let the Lord Asterion go back and forth, and act as go-between."

"That sounds wise," said Ariadne cautiously, and looked to her brother.

The horned head nodded in agreement. Then Asterion asked, "Daedalus, have you devised a means of escape we might all use?"

The Artisan cleared his throat, and spoke with modest satisfaction. "It was your mention of the deep-sea fish, my Lord Asterion, that gave me the essential clue."

"How is that?"

"They are a kind of fish who spend most of their lives in Poseidon's domain of deep salt water, but once or twice in their lives ascend freshwater streams to spawn. Somehow those fish in what you call the Deep Pool must have got there by following an underground conduit, open only at intervals to light and air, all the way from the coast of the island to a place well within the Maze."

Having deduced this much by logic, Daedalus, bringing his son with him, had spent almost a full day following the hidden stream, down to within sight of the sea, and within the sound of its waves.

"It was not a very long walk—say three miles down to the sea, and three back—but over most of the distance it was not possible to move quickly."

Then Daedalus had warned his child fiercely to say nothing to anyone about having recently seen the sea.

"Why did you take the boy with you?" Ariadne asked curiously.

"Because, gracious princess, I thought it quite possible that I would not come back."

"I am not sure that I understand."

"I mean, my lady, that had I been able to pass one final obstacle on that day—and had my son and I been able to find a boat at the water's edge—and had we been willing to brave the sea alone—then I must admit to you, princess, that the two of us might have left this island forever behind."

"I see."

"But to obtain a suitable boat, or passage on a ship, we are almost certainly going to need help."

"That will not be impossible to arrange. But tell me, Daedalus, what is this 'final obstacle' you speak of?"

"My princess, with your permission, it will be easier if I show it to you when we reach it—if it is agreed that we are going." They both looked at Asterion, who nodded silently. "And rest assured that this time I will be prepared to overcome it."

"I see. Yes, I think that we are now agreed to go . . . I will speak for Theseus, since he cannot be here to speak for himself. Then the only remaining question seems to be, how are we to obtain a boat? No, I suppose there is one more: when we put out to sea, can we escape the patrols of my uncle's navy?"

She stood looking at the two men, and they at her. At last Ariadne added, "I must speak to Theseus about this."

In the early evening of that same day, Ariadne and Theseus met secretly once more. Like all their other meetings, this one took place in a corner of a walled-off passageway of the Labyrinth, very close to the palace. When communication by smuggled notes and surreptitious glances had advanced their relationship to the point where a place of rendezvous was certainly required, the princess had closed her eyes and taken thought, in the special way that had come to her as a legacy of her divine father. A familiar scene, recognizable to her as a portion of the Maze, had appeared as if it were a product only of her imagination. And in the scene there appeared two glistening parallel lines; the princess had been following those lines almost all her life, through one kind of imaged background or another, and they had never yet led her astray. As always, they reminded her of imaginary spiderwebs; and on this occasion the lines had run straight from just below her own eyes to the next corner of the Maze, where they took a sharp turn to the left. Ariadne had relaxed. From lifelong experience she knew that she had only to follow the two lines and they would almost infallibly lead her to the thing that she most wanted or needed at the moment—in this case, a place where she might meet in secrecy with her new lover.

It had needed no more than a trifling bribe to a sympathetic guard to enable Theseus to slip from one pocket of the Maze into another, out of sight of guards and of his fellow prisoners as well. So easily was it possible for him to leave behind the section in which the eighteen young people of the renewed Tribute were still confined, waiting to meet their doom in a few days.

On the following day the couple had met in the secret place again. Since then, hardly a day had passed without a rendezvous. Today, as soon as Theseus saw her, he caught her in his arms, with princely boldness, and kissed her feverishly. So far, faced with the constant possibility of being observed, he had not attempted any further demonstration of his love.

How beautiful he was! Taller than any other man that Ariadne knew, her brother of course excepted. Her new lover's body, clad now in the special kilt and cape that all the young men of the Tribute had been given to put on, was fit to be that of a young god. A thick curl of golden beard adorned his square jaw.

In an urgent whisper, she told him, "It's been decided. You are going to escape, and I am coming with you, and so are several others."

He heaved a sigh, as if a large weight had just dropped from his shoulders. Then he asked, in his usual quiet voice, "Others of the Tribute?"

"No! It won't be possible to get them all away. You must say nothing to them."

Immediately Theseus was suspicious. "Who is coming with us, then?"

"One is Daedalus—you've heard of him?"

"I think that everyone in the world has heard of Daedalus. And most people know that he has come to Corycus to work for the new king."

"Yes. And now he has his own reasons for wanting to escape my uncle, and this island. Also, he has discovered a way by which we can reach the seacoast."

Still her lover's suspicions were not entirely allayed. "How?"

"Daedalus doesn't want to say, until the day comes. Probably that's wise, and I believe him."

"Then when are we going? How will it be arranged?"

Ariadne lowered her voice to an even softer whisper. "We are going to depart, from somewhere near the very middle of the Labyrinth, on the very morning, the very hour, when the sacrifice is scheduled to take place."

Obviously Theseus did not understand. "In broad daylight? Why then?"

"Because Asterion—he's my brother, and he's coming with us too, at least I think he is—has learned in a dream that that will be the best time."

Theseus was obviously not impressed by such a revelation. "Are we to be controlled by our dreams, then? Shall I tell you what mine was last night?"

But the princess lifted her chin and defended it. "My brother's dreams are as different from those of most men as his body is from theirs. As I believe Daedalus when he says the thing is possible, so I believe Asterion."

When her lover saw how serious she was, he did not press the argument. But he had more questions. "And how am I to get free? Somehow I must reach the starting point of this secret route that Daedalus has discovered."

Ariadne grabbed up one of his big hands and kissed it. "All these details will be worked out. We will meet in a certain place, inside the Maze. Those who do not already know the way will be guided when the time comes."

"Fine. Reasonable, I suppose. And then—?"

"Daedalus has not revealed the details of his route yet. When the day has come, and we are all together, he will show it to us."

The prince still brooded, not quite satisfied. He took a pace or two, all that the confined space would allow, and then came back to her. "And this is all you can tell me now?"

"It's all I know, my love. Many details must still be worked out, of course. If you don't want to trust Daedalus, can you come up with a better idea? He seems to be a good man, and he wants to escape almost as much as we do."

Theseus had no concrete suggestions of better ways to offer. He kissed her, and said, "I am a stranger on this island. If it were up to me to plan an escape, I'd be at a dead loss. If you trust Daedalus, I will too."

"Good." Then a shade of new concern grew in Ariadne's face. "How is it with you, among the other prisoners? Are the others . . . ?"

"Are they what? Trying to escape? No. Terrified? They really don't seem to be." Theseus shook his head. In a different tone he said, "The truth is that I don't understand them. Even if I had not found you—"

"Don't say that, dear."

"Oh, my darling! . . . But my point is that no matter what, I would still be trying to get away. Making some kind of effort. What I can't understand is that none of my fellow inmates seem to care a fig for their own lives. It's beyond me—having been told that they are doomed, they accept the judgment without a murmur. They've given up and said goodbye to the world. Well, I haven't."

"I should hope not." Ariadne snuggled into the curve of her prince's arm, which seemed to soften to accommodate her. "I sup-pose they think it hopeless to struggle against a god—or even against my uncle. Still, I worry that your absence will be noticed, when you come here to meet me."

"I really don't think we need worry much about that. It's not as if all eighteen of us were being kept in a single room. No one is taking roll call every hour. One of Shiva's priests does that, usu-ally only once a day."

Theseus went on to describe the interior layout of the quarters he shared with the seventeen others of the Tribute. Ariadne had not seen that portion of the Labyrinth since it was partitioned off from the rest. The young people of the Tribute were rarely all in sight of one another at the same time—in fact no one room of their quarters was big enough to hold them all. The section in which they were confined was in itself a maze of narrow passages and small compartments. Here and there draperies had been hung, affording some measure of privacy.

The captives were being well fed, provided with wine and certain pleasant drugs, allowed and even encouraged to spend their time amusing themselves with each other's bodies, or with the entertainers who were brought in from time to time.

The princess was relieved that her lover was not being cru-elly treated. But at the same time she was vaguely perturbed. "What luxury! Of course I hope you have no interest in the oth-ers' bodies."

"Of course I do not! Believe me, dear one, from the moment I laid eyes on you . . ."

When another prolonged kiss had been concluded, Ariadne said: "I am relieved. Somehow, though I should have known better, I was picturing a kind of dimly lighted dungeon. Rats, and dirt . . ."

"Not at all. It seems that nothing is too good for those who are to be blessed by Shiva."

The princess winced, and her voice dropped. "Have you caught a glimpse of my uncle's god yet? I have seen him only a couple of times."

"No, the Lord Shiva has not honored us poor folk of the Tribute with his presence," Theseus observed dryly. He paused, then added, "Nor have I yet been able to speak to your uncle the king."

That made the princess blink. "Why should you expect to be able to do that?"

Theseus drew a deep breath, like a man coming to a decision. "I didn't say anything to you about it, not wanting to cause you extra worry, but—many days ago, I sent a message to King Perses—addressing him as King Minos of course—saying I was willing to act as go-between in arranging an alliance between him and my father. On the condition, naturally, that my life should be spared, and I released."

Ariadne's eyes widened in surprise, and she held her breath. "And what did Uncle say?"

"Nothing at all; at least I have received no answer. I suppose the new Minos—no, I really shouldn't call him that—I suppose your uncle doesn't trust me. I'd be a fool to rely on any promise he might make. Not that he's likely to make any."

Ariadne said impulsively, "I will go to him, and plead for your life."

Theseus was shaking his head slowly. His face was grim. "I don't think so, princess. I believe we ought to rely on some other means, more dependable than your uncle's word—even assuming that you could persuade him to give his word. No, I'd much rather trust the plans of the clever Daedalus. Your pleading should be kept as a last desperate resort."

After that the couple tried to work out some of the details of the effort they were soon to make.

The princess said, "Daedalus swears that he can somehow

lead us all the way to the seashore, with little danger of discovery. But after that of course we'll need a ship."

Her lover was listening intently, squinting with an effort at concentration. "To what point on the shore is he going to lead us? There are hundreds, maybe thousands, of miles of coastline on this island, taking into account all the inlets and promontories."

"I don't know where, but I'll find out."

Ariadne told Theseus she was going to smuggle a message out to certain sailors, men who had remained loyal to the memory of her father. The new king was feared and obeyed, but he was not enormously popular among the people.

But Theseus assured her that it would be much easier for him than for her to summon ships and sailors to their aid, provided her secret allies could get a message out for him. He felt confident of being able to communicate with seamen who would be loyal to him. Vaguely he spoke of elements of his father's navy.

"In fact," he added, "I had better give you the message now. Take this." And he slipped from one of his big fingers a distinctive ring. It was of bronze, thought Ariadne, of little intrinsic worth, but curiously wrought. "So my friend will believe it truly comes from me." He gave her also the name of a man in the city ("he is one of my father's agents") who would pass it on.

The name of the ultimate recipient meant nothing to Ariadne, and she commented on the fact.

Theseus shrugged. "There's no reason why it should. It's only a kind of code word. He is really an officer in my father's navy."

The princess was daring, but seldom careless, and she wanted to make sure that the whole escape effort was as solidly organized as possible. "How many will we be, then, besides you and myself?"

"Is Princess Phaedra coming too?" her lover asked.

"No." Ariadne answered calmly, but without hesitation. "I know my sister, and she will not leave the island. She would see running away as deserting her suffering people. Besides, Phaedra is one of those people who become transparent whenever they try to keep a secret—everyone who looks at her can see at once that something is amiss. No, she mustn't even suspect what we are doing."

"All right. I leave your sister to you. Not that I have any choice about it."

"Fine. Let me see, where were we? You and I, and Asterion, if he will come with us, makes three."

Ariadne's lover raised a golden eyebrow in a perfect curve. "Will your brother be willing to leave the Labyrinth?"

"I don't know, but of course I have offered him the chance, and he hasn't yet said no. And Daedalus, who will be our necessary guide, makes four—and little Icarus, five. I'm sure the father has no intention of leaving the son behind."

Theseus nodded thoughtfully. Then he suggested, "What about this soldier—you say his name is Alex?—the one who confirmed the manner of your father's death. How deeply involved is he in the plan?"

"Quite deeply, now."

"Then I think he should join our party too. Or at least it would be wiser for us not to leave him behind, alive. Now that he knows so much of our plans."

Ariadne tossed back her hair with a decisive motion. "That makes sense. Say half a dozen, then. And we should also add my personal attendant, for the same reason. Clara will make seven. That is a lucky number, is it not?"

"A large number, to keep anything a secret. But it seems we don't have much choice."

The couple's talk moved on, to the things that would have to be managed at the last moment. Ariadne had learned, and now warned her lover, that the maidens and youths were to be given a slow-acting poison, in a ritual cup, just before they were led deeper into the Maze, and to their deaths. "A few hours later they will all be dead. They will disappear from the world forever, and their fate will of course be blamed upon the Monster."

Just at sunrise on the chosen day, the eighteen were to be guided, by priests of Shiva and a detachment of the Palace Guard,

to a spot near the center of the Labyrinth. "It's only a short distance from where Daedalus is working, and he says that a crew of
maintenance workers from the palace are building a kind of holding pen. Some of the walls of the Labyrinth have been knocked
down to make an open space."

"What method is to be used to take our lives?"

The princess had heard rumors about that, but it was not the
kind of thing she wanted to mention to her lover. "It's not going to
happen to you. It's not!"

"Of course not." And Theseus patted her arm. "Now, while
we have the chance, let us try to consider some of the details.
Where things might possibly go wrong."

"Of course."

"But before we get into that—I've wondered, how does your
uncle plan to explain to the world what he is doing with the people
sent to him as tribute?"

"From what I hear, the world had already given them up for
lost. As for my uncle, he sees no reason why a king has to explain
anything. Dear, what will you do when they hand you a poisoned
cup and order you to drink?"

Theseus shrugged impatiently. "I can manage that somehow.
I might just pretend to drink the stuff. Hold it in my mouth and
spit it out, it can't be instant death, if they mean to march us a mile
after we drink. Or, if you can find out what the poison is, it might
be possible to get an antidote—but that's even chancier. I hope we
can get away before that moment comes."

He went on to relate to Ariadne a rumor that had been allowed
to spread among the victims themselves: Minos secretly hoped to
create from these fine specimens of mainland youth the nucleus of
a legion of powerful and fiercely loyal warriors, with the girls of
course destined to be the mothers of warriors. With such a legion
he hoped to be able to conquer the world.

Ariadne's eyes were wide. "Do you believe that?"

Theseus shook his head. "Frankly, no. There are few of the
other intended victims that I would choose as fighters."

Another tale that had gained some currency was that the
youths and maidens were simply to serve for a year as attendants

in a temple, containing the altar of some god whose help Minos considered vital, perhaps Mars, or Hermes; and after that the eighteen would be returned safely to their homes.

"Maybe some of the seventeen others have swallowed that one," Theseus speculated. "That might account for their complacency."

Ariadne was shaking her head slowly. Her voice was more frightened than he had heard it yet. "The truth is, of course, that Shiva wants you, and the others."

"To be his servants?" The question was asked in mockery.

She answered solemnly. "He wants you to walk the road that so many slaves and prisoners have already traveled in the last few months—in the form of sacrifice."

The prospect did not seem to disturb the youth unduly. "But why? I don't doubt what you say, everything points to it—but still it puzzles me."

"Why does any god want sacrifice? And yet almost all of them seem to find it pleasing."

My horns rather limit the number and kind of positions in which it is possible for me to sleep. When I, the Minotaur, awakened, I was exactly where I had lain down, in a certain small plaza of the Labyrinth where I liked to sleep in the warm weather. My big body was suspended in a hammock I had tied up between two trees, within a ring of murmuring fountains. I lay in a curved position, clasped hands under one cheek, supporting my head.

I, Asterion, slept and dreamt deeply, for several nights before the morning on which the great sacrifice was scheduled to take place—I experienced vivid dreams, in which my spirit wandered far abroad, over sea as well as land.

When asleep, I can sometimes gain ready access to the minds of others, through the medium of dreams, my own and theirs. I can sometimes exert considerable influence upon my fellow dreamers, often without the subject suspecting the presence of an intruder. In a lifetime of such nocturnal wandering, out of my misshapen body, I have had many strange encounters, some of them with figures that I gradually began to recognize as gods.

As the day of sacrifice and escape approached, I was not certain yet whether I would be one of the fugitives. But in any case my sister and her party were certainly going to require a ship.

Ships were virtually always in the control of men. Sending my dreaming spirit drifting out from the Labyrinth, out from the island, over the waves, through the breezes of a spring night, I posed the question to the universe, or perhaps it was only to myself: *Where is the man I have to find?*

Tonight the beauty of the sea had no attraction; my thought was too much concentrated upon our needs. But I knew it was on the sea that I must search. At last my search was rewarded, a good contact established with the dreaming captain of a small merchant ship.

The detachment of the Palace Guard who were detailed to watch the youths and maidens of the Tribute took head counts only casually and sporadically, generally leaving that business to the priests of Shiva, who took them about once a day. The portion of the Maze in which the youths and maidens were confined was only casually sealed off from the rest—none of the victims seemed inclined to try to escape. And, after all, where would they possibly go, with the wide ocean between them and their homes? The two doors which had been cut into the old walls to connect their quarters with the outside world were steadily if not very intensely guarded.

From time to time the young soldier called Alex the Half-Nameless, like many of the other men in his barracks, pulled a shift of guard duty at one of those portals.

There Alex was able to observe, to his relief, that most of the guards were deployed on the wrong side of the people they were trying to guard. The escape plan, as it had been stealthily conveyed to Alex, in bits and pieces by the slave-girl Clara, did not require Theseus to break out into the palace grounds. Rather he was to accompany the others of the Tribute on their forced march deeper into the Labyrinth. Ariadne's lover was a superb athlete, and, as he assured her, confident that he could get right over the

wall, at a certain point she had described to him in detail, where
the barrier was no more than about ten feet high. All he would
need was a moment or two to prepare himself, and a little space in
which to run and jump. Alex himself, along with the princess Ariadne and Clara, would be waiting on the other side, ready to lead
Theseus away to join the others who were taking part in the
escape.

Before the time arrived, the plan had been worked out in
some detail. The planners, chiefly Daedalus and the princess, were
proud of their achievement. If all went well, it seemed entirely
likely that seven people were going to vanish as if the earth had
swallowed them up.

In the course of their secret meetings, Theseus several times
expressed to Ariadne his admiration for the famous Daedalus, and
said he looked forward to meeting the Artisan. Theseus was also
intrigued by the participation of the Minotaur, whom he had not
yet seen, and he questioned Ariadne about her brother.

"So, he eats no meat at all? Then it's a pretty good joke to
think that all these people are supposed to be somehow devoured
by him. He eats no meat, can't handle wine, and goes to bed with
no one. And we are all supposed to be terrified of this—cow."

Ariadne's face suddenly looked swollen around the eyes, and
her voice quavered. "Asterion is my brother. He is placing his
own life at risk to help you get away."

Theseus looked at her, and something altered in his face. "I
am sorry." The words had a sound of beautiful sincerity.

When they had kissed again, Ariadne observed, "I don't suppose the Lord Shiva is really going to eat seventeen people either.
Is he?"

"Not exactly." At the moment, Theseus wasn't much interested in Shiva. "But tell me more about Asterion. I'm sorry I
spoke rudely about him, I didn't understand. Is he really a child of
Zeus? And does he really have prophetic dreams? And what is his
contribution to the escape plan going to be? Apart from dreams, I
mean."

Her response was sharp. "He is as much a child of Zeus as I

am. Asterion is my brother, and to me he seems . . . almost ordinary, despite his strange appearance. And don't laugh at his dreams. Over the years he has told me many wonderful things, gathered in his own dreams and those of other people."

The young man smiled faintly. "I think it is your dreams that interest me more than his."

"I would like to hear about what you do in the land of Oneiros, when you sleep," Ariadne breathed.

"And I of your adventures there."

"And I will tell you of them."

Theseus said intensely, "What I would really love, is to lie beside you as you dream."

Fiercely Ariadne squeezed his hand. "I, too, desire that very much, my love," she whispered. "And it will come about, I promise."

"I believe you."

Moving back half a step, she drew a deep breath. "As to how my brother will help you, on the day of the escape, that depends. If I should be delayed for any reason, he will appear when you need a guide. You can trust him with your life."

"I am trusting him with your life, too. And to me that is infinitely more valuable than my own."

"Oh, love!"

---

everal days before the sacrifice of the Tribute was scheduled to take place, the priest Creon had approached the
Princess Ariadne quietly and discreetly, conveying to her official
notice of just where and when the ceremony was to be conducted.
The ceremony would definitely not be open to the public. It would
take place in the presence of a select few witnesses, in the assured
privacy of a certain restricted domain within the Labyrinth, and not
far from its center. At Shiva's orders a new ritual site had already
been created there, by flattening and removing some of the old
walls across a circle about a hundred feet in diameter. A semicircu-
lar viewing stand had been erected in about half of the cleared
space, and an elaborate stage upon the other half.

Creon, obviously enamored of his subject, seemed about to
go into greater detail, when the Princess Ariadne interrupted to
make it plain that whatever the arrangements were, she had no
intention of attending.

The priest had obviously expected that response. "Your uncle
and I assumed that that would be your attitude, your royal highness." And he seemed content to let the matter go at that.

But now that the subject of Tribute and human sacrifice had
been raised, Ariadne was not going to let it pass without further
comment. She said, "You are going to murder people, to please
your damned new god, and it is a foul and vicious business."

At that the high priest managed to look pained and shocked.
"If I may say so, highness, that is not a very constructive attitude
to take. It is even rather dangerous. Our lord Shiva has graciously
consented to accept the offering of our most royal king, your
uncle."

"Since you use the form of asking my permission, no, you
may not say so. What kind of god is it who demands an offering of
human lives? What kind of king, who struggles to provide it?"

Creon's countenance seemed to have become a mask. He bowed slightly, and silently took himself away.

The morning on which the sacrifice of the Tribute was scheduled to take place dawned clear across the island of Corycus, on a day that promised to be very warm for spring.

Ariadne had given everyone to understand that on this morning she would be visiting her brother, as she often did, in some remote portion of the Maze.

She and Clara were just about to depart when the princess Phaedra was announced. Phaedra had come unattended, paying an unusual visit to her younger sister's room. "Have you heard what kind of sacrifice is to be performed?"

Ariadne was eager to get rid of the unexpected visitor, without arousing her suspicions. "Of course. I have even been officially invited to attend it—haven't you?"

"I have." Phaedra shivered. "But of course I am not going."

"Nor am I."

Meanwhile the slave-girl Clara was standing by, trying to conceal her nervousness, watching and listening to the conversation, but taking little part. None of the Princess Phaedra's personal attendants were granted anything like the freedom of speech and action that Clara generally enjoyed in the company of her own mistress.

Now Ariadne was saying, "Today's will not be the first human sacrifice Shiva has claimed here in our homeland."

"I know that. There have been prisoners, slaves—"

"Do you know who the first one was?" the younger sister interrupted. She paused briefly for effect, before adding, "Our father, Minos."

Phaedra was aghast. She had to admit that the suspicion had crossed her mind, but until now she had been inclined to give their uncle the benefit of the doubt.

When she stammered some remark along this line, the younger woman quickly cut her down. "Nonsense. Perses killed his brother." Ariadne spoke with firm conviction.

"Why do you say that?"

"Because I know it to be true."

"But *how* do you know—? No, don't tell me!" Phaedra paced nervously among the feminine furnishings of the room. She glanced several times at her sister, who continued to regard her silently.

At last the elder sister stopped her pacing. "I must think deeply about this."

"I wish you would."

"We must not—not take any hasty action. I must consider all these things, very carefully."

"Yes, I agree. Oh, if you are concerned about Clara here, you need not be. I trust her with my life."

The older princess knew that well enough, and was not worried about Clara. She was thinking again of the ceremony of sacrifice, due to get under way in less than an hour. She said, "I will not attend any such horrible event. What is our uncle thinking of?"

"What he's usually thinking of—his own power. I suppose he will not be satisfied until he rules the world, may the gods forbid that ever happening." Ariadne paused, then added deliberately, "That is why he killed his brother."

Phaedra turned pale, and this time involuntarily glanced toward Clara. Again she said, "We must talk of this later."

"You keep telling me that, Phaedra. Yes, I agree, we must."

For a moment Phaedra seemed on the brink of breaking down, under the weight of confirmed suspicions. "Ariadne, what can we do?"

"At the moment, nothing."

"But who is going into the Labyrinth today, to watch this horror? Ariadne, I have sent our uncle word that I am indisposed and will not be there. Will you stay with me this morning?"

"Today there are reasons why I must be elsewhere," the younger told her tenderly.

"Reasons? What reasons?"

"I have promised Asterion."

"Oh." Phaedra never spoke of her half-brother in the Labyrinth, much less went to see him. And the sisters embraced and kissed each other, a rare occurrence with them.

One of the regular household servants now appeared on schedule, ready to serve the usual morning tea.

But Phaedra protested that she was too upset to think of tea, or any other food or drink. Moments later she had taken herself away.

"Thank all the gods," Ariadne murmured when her sister was gone, and the innocent servant too. "She dawdled until I feared that she would make us late. Clara, see that you have good sturdy sandals on. Beyond that, we dare not make any preparations."

"I have, my lady."

Clara and her mistress had already put on their ordinary clothes.

As the princess looked down from her window, only the leaves of nearby treetops prevented her seeing into the section of the Labyrinth where the young people of the Tribute were being held.

What might have been the entire crew of odylic priests and wizards who attended the new king and his strange god, perhaps a dozen men in all, were busy arranging and decorating a table in one of the larger plazas of the Labyrinth, an open space that served the captive youths and maidens as a kind of common room. Two or three sections of wall had been taken down, enlarging the plaza by converting sections of several passageways into a single open space.

Ariadne could not exactly see just what the servants of Destruction might be doing down there, chanting as they did so. But it was an easy guess that they were drugging the wine which was to be ritually served to the victims just before the young people were led off to their doom, in another recently created plaza perhaps a mile away.

Ariadne looked sharply at Clara, who was now visibly trembling. "Do calm down. You're as nervous as my sister."

"Yes, my lady."

Then she asked Clara, "Did you hear anything in the room last night? See anything?" For about a month now the princess had addressed those same questions to her servant almost every morning—and on the few mornings when she failed to do so,

Clara had asked them of her. The ritual of questioning had been going on ever since one memorable night when the suite of rooms shared by the two young women had been plagued with a mysterious flurry of strange midnight whisperings. The unintelligible voices, coming from no visible sources, had been mixed with other sounds, hard to identify but suggestive of small objects being moved about.

On the following night, similar phenomena had taken place. Each occasion, both occupants of the room had arisen, Ariadne from her huge canopied bed, Clara from her cot nearby, and had consulted in whispers as to whether they should call the guard. But neither young woman put much trust in the guard, since their uncle had taken over. Neither mistress nor servant had been molested in any way, and a careful inspection of the contents of the rooms by daylight showed nothing was missing.

On the second night of the strange visitation, which had turned out to be the last, Ariadne had dreamt, or thought she dreamt, of a shadowy figure bending over her in her bed. But in the morning her jewelry—quite a modest collection for a Corycan princess—lay in its strongbox undisturbed, and the gold and silver medallion, the gift of Daedalus, still hung on its fine chain round her neck, lying just above and between her breasts.

"I heard nothing last night, my lady," Clara said now. "I saw nothing." For almost a month, inhuman intruders had been as totally absent as any of the human kind.

"Do you suppose anything of the kind has been happening to my sister?"

"I doubt it, my lady. Today would have been the Princess Phaedra's chance to tell you all about it. And . . ."

"And she probably would have done so, had there been anything to tell. But she said nothing."

The princess and her slave-girl had both felt confident from the start that at least the trespasser, if there really had been one, had not been Shiva. The thought of an unknown power was somewhat disturbing; but whatever it might be, they feared it less than they did the one which now had the kingdom in its grip.

Now, on the morning of the Tribute, Ariadne put the matter of strange intrusions completely out of her mind, and looked out of the window again. She breathed a prayer to her favorite goddess, Artemis—and then to be on the safe side, she added silent pleas to Athena and Aphrodite.

He was down there; and she was going to save him.

On that morning of mixed omens, good and bad, I, Asterion, awoke somewhat earlier than usual, my sleep having been tortured by strenuous and disturbing dreams. These were only partially concerned with the escape plan, in which my personal part was simple. Because of my own uncertainty as to whether I was really going to escape or not, I had been assigned no duties in the way of helping others.

I opened my eyes about half an hour before dawn, when certain stars, and a single planet, that I could interpret as favorable omens, were still visible. The Morning Star, that humans have sometimes identified in a mystic way with the Goddess of Love, was plain in the slowly brightening sky. But Venus had nothing to say to me.

Much, much closer to where I lay, but still at a considerable distance, I could hear loud chanting from the priests of Shiva, and I muttered useless curses under my breath.

My slumber had been fairly long, and my body should have been rested, though my mind had labored even while I slept, but in fact even my flesh and bones felt tired. Near the middle of the night, in a determined search for allies, helpers, wherever I could find them, I had once more visited the dreams of a certain seafaring man named Petros, the captain of a small trading ship, and had reinforced the message I had conveyed to him on the previous night, and also on the night before that.

Now I knew, in the effortless way one knows such things in dreams, that Petros, still at sea and many miles distant, was the one I needed to accomplish the second stage of the escape. With what seemed to me the willing assistance of Oneiros—though I was aware of no direct contact with the God of Dreams—I had planted in the trader captain's mind the vision of a particular swampy cove, at only a few miles' distance down the coast from the main Corycan harbor.

Then, in the hour before waking, when come some of the clearest visions, I had dreamt, involuntarily and quite naturally as it seemed, about the coming into my world of the eighteen young folk from the mainland. It was an ambiguous perception, which I took to indicate that the impact of the business of the Tribute on my life was going to be so violent that there could be no certainty about my future for a long time afterward.

Uncertainty was rising about me like a sea. I was not to be left simply to manage my own affairs. Once I had pledged to Ariadne that I would do all I could to make sure that Theseus escaped, she had taken me at my word and begun to assign me tasks. When the ceremony began, I was to be in a place from which I could watch the sacrifice itself—just in case the inconceivable should have happened, and at that point Theseus was still penned in with the other prisoners. Then it would be up to me to somehow contrive to set him free.

And in the back of my mind I was somehow satisfied that I would be able to witness the horror, or part of it at least. Not, of course, that I expected to derive any kind of pleasure from the sight; rather, Shiva's worshipers had contrived so egregious an evil that I dared not turn my back on it, and feared to let it out of my sight.

On the morning of the sacrifice, shortly after the sun came up, the youths and maidens of the Tribute were thrust into the great Maze and began to tread the path marked through its windings, I, Asterion, was actually somewhat more than a mile away, the distance measured as a bird might fly, or the sound of a scream might carry. They could be singing at the top of their lungs as they marched, and banging drums, and I would never hear them. There might well be a thousand miles of twisted passageways between us.

I wondered what the young folk might be saying to one another, as they talked among themselves on this last morning of their lives. Probably nothing that made sense, after the massive doses of drugs they had ingested. With Theseus, I marveled at their passivity. And what fears they did have were all of harmless shadows, and would be as useless as their songs. As they walked, or danced, or were dragged unthinkingly to their doom, some of them at least would be looking over their shoulders to see if I was about to pounce on them from behind.

I might easily enough have probed their dreams during the night just past, and discovered their secret thoughts during the last sleep of their lives. But that was something I preferred not to know.

And now it was time for me to close off my mind from the realm of dreams. Today's issues were going to be decided in the less manageable world that men and women call reality. Before setting out I breakfasted, forcing my stomach to accept more than it really wanted, not knowing when my next meal might be. I picked up and weighed in one hand a small pack I had prepared. At that moment, I was still uncertain whether I might today be leaving forever the Labyrinth, my lifelong home. After a few moments' indecision I left the pack behind, telling myself I would have time to come back for it later.

As I had expected, I found Daedalus and Icarus waiting in the spot designated for our rendezvous, close by what the Artisan called the Deep Pool.

As soon as I appeared, the small boy jumped to his feet. His father, almost literally pouncing on me, demanded, "Have you seen the princess this morning? She has not changed her mind?"

"I assume you mean Ariadne. I have not seen her, but she will not change her mind in this. Today is the day when Theseus must either escape or die, and I think my sister will die rather than be separated from her lover."

"And you are coming with us, Asterion? I don't see the pack you spoke of bringing."

"There will be time for me to get it."

Having, as I thought, a little time to spare, I briefly joined father and son in their silent vigil. We all three sat waiting for the princess and her servant and her lover, and for the young soldier who was also supposed to attach himself to our party. Icarus fidgeted, so that periodically his father scowled and muttered at him. Daedalus had packed a very few things, which he carried in a small pouch or wallet secured to his belt.

The place where we were waiting was half a mile from the center of the Maze, and a somewhat greater distance from the small area where the youths and maidens were confined.

Daedalus was unarmed as usual, except for the plain knife, more tool than weapon, that he habitually carried at his belt. He explained to me that he had been up through much of the night preparing a balloon, and getting the feathers ready.

I doubted that I had heard his speech correctly. "Did you say 'a balloon'? What are we to do with a balloon, and feathers?"

"Nothing. Oh, I didn't tell you about that, did I?"

"No."

"It is a matter of misdirection." He went on to describe, in the gray predawn light, how the balloon, stitched together from some kind of treated fabric, would be released by a timing device of his invention, just as the escape was getting under way. How the flying machine once launched, sustaining itself in the air, would automatically drop the false clues of feathers, and so on, even as the wind carried it out to sea. "With any luck, they will think we have escaped in a balloon. That I have fashioned wings."

"Well . . ."

"They will, depend upon it." Now it was the Artisan's turn to look me over. "You are unarmed, Asterion?"

"Not really." And I moved my head slightly, so that the sharp tips of the two horns drew circles in the air.

The father nodded grimly. His whole bearing was tense, and the look around his eyes indicated that he had slept but little. The son, who today was also wearing a small knife on his small belt, was fretting at not being allowed to roam as usual. But Icarus was old enough to understand that today they were going to leave Crete.

"Where are we going, Father?"

The answer was a growl. "Haven't I told you not to talk about it, before we start? We'll see where we're going when we get there. It'll be another island, or maybe the mainland."

I, Asterion, had but little time to visit them this morning.

You must also understand a thing that seemed impossible for anyone else on the island to realize: that although I had spent something like fifteen years inside the Labyrinth, almost my entire life, there were still many passageways—by my best estimate, hundreds of miles of them—within that marvelous creation that I had never seen, at least with waking eyes. I had heard that some foolish folk now ascribed its construction entirely to Daedalus.

I mentioned that idea to him, on the morning when we waited to escape. The Artisan himself smiled at the thought, even in the midst of his fretting about today's desperate adventure. No more than a tiny portion of the Maze could possibly have been his doing, and in fact he had not built any of it at all.

"The work of Hephaestus, then?"

"I think not; I have seen some of the divine Smith's constructions, and they are marvelous. Looking at them, one understands what it means, or ought to mean, to be a god." Daedalus shook his head, and his voice dropped. "But the Labyrinth is not particularly marvelous, except by reason of sheer size."

"Really? There, Artisan, I might disagree with you for once. Consider the strangeness which lies at its center."

"If you include that, yes, of course. I am already dizzy from months of considering it."

I was talking to Daedalus, as we waited for a little time to pass, while Icarus lingered nearby, playing some private game that involved hopping on one foot—I noticed that he, like his father, was now wearing sandals—alternately fretting and trying to come to grips with the sudden changes in his childish world. It seemed we were all of us as ready as we could be to set our rescue/escape plan in motion.

Eventually I had to admit that it was time for me to perform that certain thing I had promised my sister I would do. Ariadne had not been able to rid herself of the idea that Theseus might need help to get away. I was more inclined to credit her forebodings, because dreams had warned me that a great chance of difficulty lay there. On this morning I felt some concern also for the young soldier who was to join in the escape, for in the normal course of events he would have less freedom of movement than any of the rest of us, except perhaps for the prisoner Theseus.

But it was not, of course, the soldier's fate that concerned Ariadne. She had asked me to go to the very scene of the ceremony, because nothing must prevent Theseus from escaping.

$\mathcal{D}$ays ago, Alex the Half-Nameless had told Clara what the duty roster showed his assignment would be on the morning of the escape—interior guard. That meant a comfortable station inside the palace. This considerably simplified the secret arrangements being made for the escape.

The next time Clara saw Alex she informed him of the details of the plan as they concerned him: When, on the fateful morning, the princess Ariadne left her rooms on her way to the rendezvous, with Clara at her side, they would keep an eye out for Alex as they passed the various guard stations. When the princess saw him, she would simply and openly beckon him to come along.

Alex nodded. "Yes, I see. That should work." There was nothing very unusual about a soldier being summoned by a member of the royal family or some high official, to perform some chore, undertake an errand, sometimes to administer punishment to an erring slave or servant. It seemed highly unlikely that anyone who saw Alex walk away in obedience to Ariadne's summons would pay much attention. With the exception of a few key locations in the palace, there was no very rigid requirement that men on interior guard remain precisely at their posts at all times.

And at last that dawn arrived, in the light of which all their fates were to be decided.

Alex had not slept much during the night. He awakened in his bunk a little before dawn, as he did on almost every morning of his life—the sergeant saw to that. Around him his comrades were likewise launched on their regular morning routine, groaning and farting and complaining of tiredness, grabbing for their garments and weapons. Despite efforts at disciplined cleanliness, a vague stink hung in the air, the result of too many men in too little space. Amid the predawn grouching, grumbling and scratching in the dim and crowded barracks, the only men excused from duty today were those few who had manned guard posts through the night.

As usual he had taken off his clothes before rolling into his bunk, but this morning, as on other recent mornings, no one appeared to notice the gold and silver medallion that for the past few days he had been wearing around his neck. Alex had hoped and expected that that might be the case, because at least half the men wore some kind of charm or amulet, and many were of metal that resembled gold or silver.

Around him now, some of the men were muttering prayers to various gods, Mars—whose other name was Ares—and Priapus being the most popular. Several soldiers were conducting a variety of small rituals, some rubbing their amulets or breathing on them. Traffic to and from the latrine was busy as usual.

"You look a little worn this morning, Al." This was Sarpedon, who slept in the next bunk, a tall young soldier with curly dark hair and a world-weary look that belied his village background.

"I'm not a short-termer like you, Sarp." Sarpedon had only six months to go on his enlistment.

The other nodded. "Can't wait to get out."

"What'll you do when you get home?" Everyone in the barracks knew that Sarpedon was looking forward to returning to his home on the northern coast of Corycus.

Rummaging in his duffel bag for a clean shirt, Sarpedon mumbled something.

Though every move Alex made on this morning was routine, for him today everything looked and sounded different. Every commonplace detail stood out with eerie clarity, as things did sometimes when he had a fever. Consumed with worry, more for the princess than for himself, he had been unable to sleep much.

All day yesterday, from dawn until he rolled into his bunk at the usual time, he had forced himself, by concentrating with all his will, to do nothing that would cause any of his fellow soldiers to notice that he was under any unusual stress, or about to undertake anything out of the ordinary. Fortunately the great majority of them were anything but keen observers, being wrapped up in their own plans and problems.

And then Sarpedon, coming back from the latrine, sent a chill through Alex by asking him if anything was wrong.

"No." There was a rote response to that kind of question, and he repeated it now without enthusiasm. "Another day, another copper coin. Two coins for the corporal."

Then, looking over his friend's shoulder, his eye was caught by a group of men standing near the front door of the barracks, clustered around the place where the duty roster was posted on the wall. The voice of someone up there was raised abruptly, uttering crude words describing various bodily functions. Alex felt a sudden premonitory shifting, as if a heavy weight had abruptly intruded somewhere near the pit of his stomach. Shouldering forward, jostled by other men moving in the same direction, he reached a position where he could read the listings. The paper was crisp and new, not the thumb-printed sheet that had been up there yesterday.

Assignments had been changed. There was his name, but no longer in the list of those who were to draw spears from the armory and pull interior guard. Instead, he and a number of others from his barracks were to arm themselves with short swords and join the detail assigned to convey the people of the Tribute to the place where they would honor Shiva.

There was no way out. It would be unheard of, of course, for a mere private soldier to protest any assignment. Unless he reported himself sick; but the only sure result of that would be to draw unwelcome attention to himself.

Fiercely Alex tried to resist showing any of the sudden turmoil welling up in him. What was he going to do now—now that he was going to be right on the scene when Prince Theseus made his break for freedom? In the back of his mind, apparently, he had been unconsciously preparing for some such eventuality as this. Because he knew without thinking about it that he was not going to stand inertly by. For the princess's sake, he, Alex, would do whatever was required at the time to make sure the prince got away. And then he would simply have to do the best he could for himself.

The best tactic might well be to allow Theseus to break away, then give chase, but in such a manner that the quarry was in no real danger of being caught.

That might work, though of course he could hardly expect to be the only one chasing the fugitive.

But almost as soon as Alex began to try to make a plan, he gave it up. It was impossible, without knowing the specific situation he'd be facing. There was only one thing Alex could be sure of now: For the princess Ariadne he would do anything.

Back at his bunk again, cleaning up the area in case there happened to be a barracks inspection, he was aware that Sarpedon was once more looking at him strangely. Sarpedon was now going to be on the same detail. They exchanged a few routine grumbles. "Not a job I wanted. Well . . ."

So far this morning nothing was really out of the ordinary—roster changes, including some that seemed wildly arbitrary, were not that uncommon—and yet nothing was the same at all. Even if Alex somehow managed to join in the great escape as planned, he was about to set out on the longest and most dangerous journey he had ever undertaken. There had been no question of his packing anything, or even stuffing anything into his belt pouch, to take with him on the journey. When he fell out of the barracks this morning, with his squad, to stand in formation for roll call, he would be carrying with him his short sword and his usual clothing, practically nothing else.

Of course, if the escape plan should fail . . . but he wasn't going to let himself think about that possibility.

It had already occurred to Alex that as soon as his defection was discovered, as he had to assume it would be within a couple of hours at the most, everyone in his barracks would be called in, methodically, for questioning, and those among his fellow soldiers whom he considered his best friends—Sarpedon, for example—were going to be in for a hard time, whether the escape succeeded or not. But there was nothing in the world that Alex could do about it.

The sergeant was now calling names of the detail set to guarding the Tribute youths and maidens. Alex and Sarpedon stepped forward in their turns.

Minutes later, they had joined a squad from another barracks. The whole detail, some twenty men in all, were marching in loose formation under the sergeant's command, crossing the parade ground behind the barracks to the place where the youths and maidens of the Tribute were being held.

Muttered exchanges as they trudged along soon established that none of the men of the detail had been told exactly how the sacrifice was to be accomplished.

Looking around him in formation, taking note of who was present and who was not, Alex decided that men of proven reliability had been wanted for this job. Probably this was one reason why he had been chosen, since he had happened to be on duty in the great hall on the night of the usurpation, and there—to his own lasting shame—he had acquitted himself well, in the Butcher's estimation.

Standing at ease in one of the little plazas just inside the Labyrinth, waiting for the people of the Tribute to be brought out of their quarters, the soldiers of the detail continued muttering and speculating among themselves. When the actual ritual got started, were they going to see another skull or two stripped of flesh and dried for Shiva's necklace? Or maybe more were needed, to be mounted in his new temple, which was outside the Labyrinth but in easy walking distance of the palace.

One rumor whispered among the soldiers now said that the priest-experts were intent on creating a god-face for Shiva's consort, Kali, by in essence boiling down parts of human victims. The hearts of ten brave men, and so forth. Each rumor sounded worse than the one before it, and Alex was sure some of the men were making them up on the spot, trying to outdo each other in gallows humor.

The nine girls, according to a murmured rumor passed along from the other side, were scheduled to be used up in an effort to summon the goddess Kali, traditionally Shiva's consort. Another claimed that the real purpose of the whole sacrifice was directed toward finding the Face of Zeus, supposed to be buried somewhere within the Labyrinth.

Alex had been too long in the army to give credence to any rumor that lacked supporting evidence.

Now it was time to supervise the administration of the ritual drinks to those whose lives were now forfeit to Shiva.

When Shiva's priests brought the victims out of their confinement, Alex had no trouble recognizing Theseus, and had to admit to himself that Ariadne's secret lover looked as if he might almost be worthy of the part. But Alex was curious: Of what kingdom was this man a prince? He had never heard anyone name the place; and he wasn't about to suggest his own interest by asking.

Watching the priests begin to serve their victims what was widely supposed to be drugged wine and water, he saw how Theseus took the cup into his hands as readily as any of the others. But no one besides Alex seemed to be watching the actual consumption of the wine all that closely. If the tall prince let some of it run down his chin in the act of drinking, and more dribble from his mouth after he'd handed the cup back, no one else was going to know about it.

Presently all eighteen had been served the ritual draught, and the soldiers began the business of escorting the people of the Tribute to the place where they were to die.

As the march got under way, following the marked route through the Labyrinth, Alex wondered if Shiva would be waiting for them up ahead. It seemed likely.

He wondered also if Theseus would recognize him, and decided that was highly unlikely.

Even if the princess had mentioned Alex to her lover, at one of their secret meetings, there would have been no point in her describing the soldier who was to accompany them on their getaway.

Alex wondered again what had caused the princess and Daedalus to choose this exact time, the very hour of the sacrifice, for the escape. Not that it was up to a mere private soldier to question anything such folk decided; but he had once tentatively raised the question with Clara.

It might have been troubling her too, for she'd had a kind of answer ready. "The Lord Asterion says that the time that seems the worst may sometimes be the best. We go when the Lord Shiva will not interfere."

That was too much for Alex to understand. Why would Shiva

not interfere, when everyone knew he would be present at the ritual? He could only hope that the dreaming bull-man knew what he was doing.

And at the moment when the squad of soldiers, and the eighteen victims they were escorting, reached the cleared site where the sacrifice was to take place, Shiva was very much present, reclining nude in a throne-like chair of silk and leather, on the very stage of the sacrifice.

The scene of the planned sacrifice was the recently constructed small amphitheater, with concentric semicircles of seats, enough to hold forty or fifty people, far more than it seemed were going to be needed today. Facing them, a kind of elaborate altar, built upon a stage.

The very complexity of the arrangement suggested ominously that today's sacrificial harvest would not be gathered by means of a swift roasting with the Third Eye. Alex supposed that might be too quick and bloodless to produce the desired effect on victims and onlookers, and even in the celebrant himself. There were human beings, he knew, who took great pleasure in inflicting pain; and he supposed that the same was true of certain gods.

Shining cages of a peculiar construction had been set up. Also, at the base of the scaffolding, a kind of holding pen, crudely constructed, in which the prisoners were evidently meant to wait until their turns came to mount the stage.

The sun had been barely at the horizon when the younger princess, attended only by her usual companion, Clara, walked out of the princess's suite of rooms in the palace.

In the freshening morning light, the two young women traversed one corridor of the huge palace, went down some stairs, and then followed another long, broad hall. Here and there, as usual, were soldiers of the Palace Guard, on duty. But none of them was the man Clara was watching for. To cover all the guard posts, it was necessary to make a circuit of the ground floor, and this they did. And now they had almost reached the exit.

They had entered the last corridor on the ground floor before she touched the princess on the arm, something she ordinarily did only in private. "Where is Alex?" Clara dared to whisper.

"I don't know," came the soft-voiced answer. "I haven't seen him anywhere. I'm not going to stop and look for him, we haven't time."

"But my lady . . ."

"No. Either he'll find a way to catch up with us, or he won't. There can be no more delays."

"If *he* dies today," the princess added, obviously no longer speaking about Alex the Half-Nameless, "I will die too."

"Don't say that, my lady!" Clara seemed near tears with fear and worry, and her mistress grimly ordered her to smile. With an effort the slave-girl got herself under control.

Past another pair of soldiers at the door—neither of them the man they hoped to see—and the young women were out of the palace altogether, walking in new morning light, over well-tended grass now glistening with dew. And now the familiar entrance to the Labyrinth loomed close ahead, open and unguarded. And then they were in among its windings, out of sight of the rest of the world.

It occurred to Alex, as he quivered in suspense, trying to look calm while waiting for Theseus to make his break, that no one among the group of plotters had really considered the possibility of doing anything to help the other seventeen scheduled victims. It would have been inconceivable to get them all away, even had they not been more than half-stupefied with drugged wine.

Of course, if a man could somehow set them all loose, running in a panic, that might well create a distraction to help a chosen few to get away . . .

Without much hope, Alex tried to come up with good possibilities. Setting them loose, even for a little while, would entail opening certain doors in the Labyrinth which the priests of Shiva wanted to keep closed; leading or driving the sacrificial victims down alternate paths, so that confusion reigned, and time and effort would be required to get them back.

*   *   *

Having left the palace and its grounds behind them, Ariadne and Clara were now traversing the Labyrinth by means of the marked path, about a mile and a half in its frequently curving length. Perses in his crown and formal robes would soon be coming along this way—it was how he was wont to travel to and fro between his palace and the center of the Maze. And then the intended victims, under guard. There were of course many intersections, and sometimes the chosen route went under or over crossing passageways.

Daedalus no doubt had traversed the intricacies of this way several times, when he came to the island and was set to work, and when Perses called him out to give a progress report.

This way was marked through the Maze by painted spikes driven into the pavement.

The princess and her attendant followed this first portion of the route each time they went to visit the Prince Asterion. And today, as on most other days, on reaching a certain point, Ariadne calmly turned aside, as if she were going to one of her regular meetings with her brother.

From this point on, she walked part of the time with her eyes closed, relying on the web-strands of her inner vision. And during the intervals when her lids were shut, her small feet in their sturdy sandals moved as surely as before.

Presently, after a look back to make sure that she and Clara were unobserved, she turned aside again, leaving the route that usually brought them to Asterion. The two women were now on a way that, if all went well, would take them to Theseus.

The king and Creon were also traveling the marked path. They had the two women briefly in sight ahead of them, and naturally assumed that they were going to see Asterion.

King Perses, dressed in rich ceremonial garments, had given few signs as to whether he expected to enjoy the forthcoming spectacle or not. Not that Perses had any real choice; Shiva would certainly insist upon his being there in any case.

"I suppose, lord, that neither of your nieces are going to attend today's ceremony?"

"So they have both informed me."

"I don't know what the Lord Shiva will think."

Perses frowned, but considered this was not the proper time for a real test of wills. "Really, Creon, I don't know why their presence should make any difference to him."

When the king arrived on the scene, well after dawn (no one really expected any elaborately planned event to start sharply at the scheduled time), he found Shiva waiting, surrounded by his priests. The emaciated body of the God of Destruction was perched on an improvised throne that was higher if not more glorious than the one in the great hall of the palace.

Only the cages were higher than the throne, in fact almost directly above it, so that if Shiva, his scrawny frame lounging naked in a silk and leather chair below, wished to luxuriate in the rain of blood from them he had only to move his body slightly.

The god shifted his position, as if he were growing impatient.

The mortal king, who was now arriving with Creon at his side, would have to be content with a place of secondary importance.

The Butcher and perhaps a dozen lesser officers were in eager attendance, occupying portions of two rows of seats. Alex and the rest of the cohort of the Palace Guard had been deployed casually around the space.

I, Asterion, having taken leave of Daedalus and his son, trotted quickly back through the Labyrinth, to a vantage point I had been careful to select beforehand, which would provide me with a good view of the actual site of the sacrifice. I suppose that if I had applied to Perses for permission to attend, it would have been easily and even eagerly granted. But of course I had not thought of doing so, any more than the usurper had thought of volunteering an invitation.

One of the refinements of the Maze, known to comparatively few, is the existence of movable panels, which on casual inspection are indistinguishable from sections of a certain type of solid wall. With strength only a little beyond that of an ordinary man, it is not hard to move the panels, and the judicious shifting of a few of them can, if the shifter knows what he is doing, redesign whole regions of the Labyrinth.

In the current situation my object was not so ambitious. I was using a loose panel, carved into a kind of lattice-shape, to block off a short section of passage. Peering through this latticework, and the screen of greenery which came attached to it, I expected to be able to look on at the ceremony without being seen.

I would not have been surprised to observe, on the newly-constructed stage, blood drained by stone knives in the hands of priests. I feared that if my monstrous shape were suddenly to appear before the doomed ones, even drugged as they were, total panic would be inevitable. Of course, just such an effect could have been calculated as part of our escape plan. My form would not only be monstrous in their eyes, but the very shape of all the nightmares that the Maze engendered. But when it was desirable to create confusion, then total panic was just what we wanted.

I had known in a general way what was going to happen. Still, I was utterly horrified when the details actually began to take place right before my waking eyes.

The first of the eighteen, still glassy-eyed with drugs, was separated from the group, stripped of his ceremonial garments and led up the steps to the stage, from which another skeletal stair to the small, twin cages above. A young woman soon followed.

Now both of the iron-ribbed torture chambers were occupied, almost above Shiva's throne. From every side of the interior of each cage, sharp dagger-blades projected toward the naked victim there confined, the clearance between skin and dagger-point being never more than a few inches. None of the blades were long enough to inflict a single, fatal wound.

Now one of the priests approached on a catwalk outside the cages, carrying a bar of iron whose free end was heated red. The object soon became plain—recoiling involuntarily from the hot iron, the victim's body would inevitably be punctured repeatedly by the sharp blade-points that drained their blood, one small wound at a time. Life would run out slowly, with the trickling blood that ran to bathe the God of Destruction who was taking his ease below.

The eyes of almost everyone were on the hot iron in the torturer's hand. The eyes of Alex were still on Theseus, who had pasted a foolish smile upon his face, and stumbled about restlessly among the other intended victims, singing as they sang.

Then, choosing his moment with superb skill, Theseus abandoned his pretense of being drugged.

The sergeant spoke to him sharply. "Get back in line. Where d'you think you're—?"

Despite Alex's determination to be ready, still Theseus moved so fast that the young soldier was very nearly taken by surprise.

An armed sergeant moved quickly to block Theseus, who did not shy from contact as the soldier must have expected. Instead, the prince, already running at full speed, lowered his shoulder into the sergeant's midriff, knocking him down, and with almost the same fluid motion grabbed up the short sword that had fallen from his hand.

Then Theseus went bounding and climbing over a wall, under his own power. He threw the weapon he had just captured up and over the wall ahead of him. Then, with one more explosion of strength, he was up and over after it.

And Alex was running at full speed after him.

Watching from behind my screen, I saw that the alarm caught Shiva in something of an awkward position in his silk-and-leather chair, just beginning to enjoy the bath of young blood that trickled on him from above. The God of Destruction was immediately convinced that his life was in great danger. I saw him leap into action, calling the bull Nandi seemingly out of nowhere and jumping on the creature's back. It seemed that with decisive action he might have recaptured Theseus in short order; but my dream-omens were proven accurate. Shiva's purpose was only to break away and take flight, and in a moment he and his mount were dwindling together in the distant sky.

Meanwhile, Theseus had escaped, as far as I could tell, without the need for any last-minute heroics on my part. But before I could turn away, I beheld something else that froze me in my tracks. A young woman whose name I did not know, one of the eighteen, inadequately drugged and running desperately, seemed to be appealing to me for help.

No dream, and of course no conscious effort to foresee possibilities had ever warned me that such a thing might happen, and for just a moment I cursed mentally the chain of decisions and impulses that had caused me to become so entangled in the real world.

When seen from its other end, the short spur of passageway at whose end I waited was, to all appearances, a dead blind alley, and so no guard had been posted at its entrance. But the girl by running into it did put herself momentarily out of sight of the watchers in the tiers of seats (who of course were themselves just out of my field of vision). She came running toward me as if she believed, or trusted, that a way to salvation must exist somewhere, as if unaware or unwilling to believe what her eyes reported, that only a few feet ahead a solid barrier walled her in.

In such circumstances, I suppose it was impossible for me to do anything but what I did.

Behind the one who had awakened to reality, the other drugged ones were groaning and moaning now, turning and trying to stumble away as a vague consciousness of what was happening began to get through to them. Others had been made so happy by the drugged wine that they kept on singing.

Many of the guards had run after Theseus (I had noted that Alex was first among them), and everyone had witnessed the shocking fact of Shiva's taking flight. Only a few soldiers were left at the scene of sacrifice, and the rest of the scheduled victims were largely forgotten in the uproar. Not that any of them actually got away, but some were not retaken for many hours.

Bursting from my place of hiding, I charged at full speed, brushing past the petrified girl in the narrow passage. A moment later I had smashed my horned head into the torso of the unready priest, so that the stone knife fell from the man's hand and his gored body, much less massive than my own, went flying.

*   *   *

The priest of Shiva I had so brutally struck down lay flat on his back, blood already puddling under him. Whether he would survive to accuse me I did not know, nor at the moment did I much care. In the open space beyond the stub of passageway, men and women were running to and fro, none of them yet paying me any attention. The noise of mass panic suggested that I still might have a few moments in which to act. It was quite possible that no one but the priest and girl had noticed my rash interference.

The girl I had just saved had slumped to the pavement. Bending swiftly, I scooped the drugged and helpless figure up into my arms, and carried her away.

Having quickly regained my original hiding place, I stopped and turned to restore the screen-barricade that made the stub of passageway look like it was blocked. Then, gently carrying the girl, I turned away and raced on.

Behind me, the sounds of panic and of rage lingered in the morning air, fading only slowly.

Theseus, having vaulted over the wall, came down catlike on his sandaled feet, steadying into a fighting crouch, ready to spring. But he was utterly alone. He found himself now in another passage, practically indistinguishable from the one from which he had just departed so precipitously. There was the sword he had just captured, lying on the pavement where his toss had landed it, and he hastened to grab the weapon up.

A hasty glance to right and left, and away he ran. There was no one here to guide him, but he had not been relying on that anyway. It was ingrained in him never to trust that people were going to do anything they promised.

Ariadne had given a list of directions to memorize and follow—turn right, right again, then left at the next corner, and left again, after a longer run than either of the two preceding.

The whispered words were carved into his memory. *Then you will see a kind of alcove on your right. Turn into it, though it looks like a dead end, and behind the column in the rear you will dis-*

cover a small door. Come through that door, and someone will be waiting for you.

If anyone had noticed him going over the wall, then almost certainly some pursuit would follow. But they would have to spend a little time in scrambling to get over, especially if they carried weapons.

The tumult behind him was increasing in volume, but so far no one was right on his tail. He could hear voices shouting in confusion, and screams that spoke all too eloquently of blood and death.

Theseus sprinted on.

◦ *T e n* ◦

*T*heseus, running as fast as he could through the memorized list of turns, rounded a corner in the Labyrinth to find Ariadne and Clara hastening toward him. Smothering a cry of joy, the princess threw herself into her lover's arms. Moments later, she was leading him and Clara on a sinuous path toward the place where they were to meet Daedalus. Ariadne's eyes were closed at least half the time, as she strode surefootedly ahead.

The prince had not yet noticed this fact. "How can you find anything in this place?" he demanded, after the third or fourth additional branching of the ways. "My head is spinning already."

"I can always find what I need, my love." The princess smiled at him proudly. "Especially in here."

As far back as she could remember, the Princess Ariadne had always been willing to put aside the comforts and privileges of her high birth, for the sake of an adventure—she had endured considerable discomfort for the sake of much less exciting outings than this one promised to be. And this, of course, was vastly more than a mere escapade. For Theseus, she would have sacrificed everything she had, her very life.

In a few minutes, when they had reached the Deep Pool, Daedalus greeted them with relief. Asterion and the young soldier, Alex, were still nowhere to be seen, and the newcomers reported that Alex had not been in the palace. The princess and her lover huddled democratically with Clara and the child of the Artisan. They were all about to put their lives into the hands of Daedalus, relying utterly on his word that he would be able to provide them with an effective means of escape.

Icarus was a study in wide-eyed, silent fear, caught from the tension among the adults around him. He clung close to his father as much as possible.

All of them but Theseus were now sitting, while he paced nervously on the edge of what Asterion called the Deep Pool. The artificially constructed basin, some ten paces long by five wide, looked fresh and was evidently filled and drained by unseen subterranean flows. It was a surprisingly large body of water compared to the few other ponds Ariadne had seen in the Labyrinth—though after years of roaming in that immense complexity, often by herself, nothing she discovered there really surprised her anymore.

Right now, her instinct urged her to trust to Daedalus; but when she gazed into the unplumbed depth of water before her, she knew that she could find her own way to the sea if that ever became necessary. Closing her eyes, willing her thoughts into the proper channel, she could see the beginnings of the thin, ghostly filaments that would lead her to the correct path. Though it wasn't possible just yet to see which way they led . . .

The agreed-upon time to begin the next stage of their journey had now arrived, the sun was several handsbreadths above the eastern wall of the little courtyard. But still, two of the group's original seven had not appeared at the meeting place.

Theseus told the others he had no idea whether Alex might have been among the detail of soldiers from whom he had just escaped.

"I thought that one of them kept watching me, and then the same one took a cut at me when I ran. But the fates were with me, and he missed."

"About middle-sized, with a straggly brown beard?" Daedalus inquired.

The prince stared thoughtfully at the older man. "He might have been. I wasn't paying much attention to the details of anyone's appearance."

Ariadne and Clara were worried about what might have happened to Asterion. But the princess comforted herself with the thought that her brother had never seemed firmly committed to joining in the escape, and had probably simply decided at the last minute not to go. Knowing him as she did, she would not have been much surprised if it were so.

Clara, despite her mistress's earlier command to do no packing, had managed to tuck under her dress a small belt pack with what she considered a few essentials. There were now some dried dates in a kind of purse that ordinarily held for the princess a mirror, a hairbrush, and a few cosmetics, all trinkets that had been left behind.

Theseus suddenly halted in his pacing, and announced commandingly, "We can't wait any longer. Whoever is not here by now is probably not coming."

The princess quickly agreed. "You're right, we mustn't wait."

If Ariadne was not determined to wait for her brother, no one else was either. And certainly no one was going to suggest a delay in hopes that the young soldier, Alex, might, after all, be able to catch up with them. Nor was there any real discussion of his possible fate. He might have lost his way, might have been killed or captured, or perhaps had simply lost his nerve at the last moment. As Theseus observed, "Anyway, he didn't know the place of rendezvous, or the escape route. He won't be able to tell them much."

For Ariadne, the fact of overwhelming importance was that her lover Theseus had managed to get this far, and for the moment he was out of danger. It seemed to the princess that her whole life was now invested in her concern for his welfare. As long as *he* was safe, nothing and no one else, herself included, counted for very much.

It would have been almost impossible for anyone to accidentally stumble on Daedalus's secret way, even had there been daily visitors to the site of rendezvous, which there certainly were not. People might have camped here for years and caught no inkling that it existed. Now, speaking quickly, in a low voice, the Artisan explained how he, trying to determine for himself how large saltwater fish could have come this far inland, had spent some time investigating. Once he had located the underground stream, he had fashioned a secret entrance, at the edge, just below the waterline in the deep pool that Asterion had once described as being long and deep enough for swimming.

Immediately agreeing that they should wait no longer, Daedalus quickly explained to the others what they were about to do. Then he, with his son clinging to him, drew a deep breath and slid down into the dark waters of the pool and disappeared, with scarcely a ripple, under the water-lily pads that covered a portion of its calm surface.

Without hesitation Theseus, still clothed in the cloak and kilt of sacrificial garments, and with his captured sword in hand, drew a deep breath and went after the man and boy. One after another, the other members of the party followed, each keeping the one ahead in sight. Each ducked underwater, groped along the side of the pool beneath an overhang, slid through a hole, and popped up again on the other side of the wall, where the pavement was higher than that immediately surrounding the Deep Pool. There they all found breathing space, though there was no room to stand up properly. They were in a dark and clammy cavern, where the noise of running water was somewhat louder than it had been on the surface, while the occasional shouts of soldiers in the distance had faded almost to inaudibility. Only enough of the brilliant morning sunlight filtered in through chinks and crannies in the upper rounds of masonry to turn the cavern into a half-lit grotto.

When it came Ariadne's turn to immerse herself in the pool, a stray thought momentarily crossed her mind: what a thorough way to ruin one's fine clothes. There was a curious satisfaction in the image.

When all five had crowded into the dank little cavern, Daedalus murmured a few words of encouragement and led the way again, his son still clinging tightly to his back. This time the Artisan plunged boldly into the descending course of the underground stream, managing to keep his head above water. Theseus, as if jealous of the leadership position, kept close behind him. Here the current was swifter. Water gurgled and rushed around them, sometimes as high as the adults' armpits.

Now and then, in muttered comments, the Artisan tried to explain how water from mountain springs flowed in diverse channels through the Maze, across its almost-level tableland, while other streams had been diverted to the streets of the city. Various aqueducts and channels had been added over the centuries.

From time to time Theseus raised a hand, calling a halt so he could listen carefully for sounds of pursuit. His cloak, now water-soaked, was weighty but he did not discard it. Each time, after only a slight pause, he shook his head and motioned them on again. There was no sign that anyone was coming after them.

Now and then the slave-girl, Clara, took a turn at helping the child through some of the more difficult places, and Daedalus looked at her gratefully. Ariadne noted the fact in passing; in these circumstances, she herself certainly did not need the constant attendance of her slave.

After perhaps an hour underground, sometimes wading, sometimes crawling over wet rock, the party had reached a half-lit cavern a little bigger than most of the similar rooms they had passed through. Here, as they paused for a rest on a dry ledge, the Artisan told the others about the hot-air balloon he had put together, the fire that kept it inflated, and the timing mechanism, involving a slow-burning rope, he had devised for its launching. If all had gone well, the balloon should have risen in morning sunlight from near the middle of the Maze, and should even now be riding the prevailing winds out to sea. The idea was to deceive the army of searchers, who by now were sure to be hunting the escapees, into believing they had made an aerial escape.

"Look!" It was an urgent whisper from Icarus, who stood peering up through a crevice in the masonry, at the world outside. "Look!"

Looking up through other gaps, where tree roots met the pavement overhead, Ariadne and one or two others were able to catch a glimpse of the Artisan's balloon. The princess saw a crude sphere bound in some kind of ropes, with a basket hanging beneath it, soaring overhead. There were dots, that at such a distance could be mistaken for human heads, showing just above the basket's rim.

The slave-girl, having seen the balloon, turned openmouthed to stare at its creator. She obviously found Daedalus interesting.

Theseus, a new respect in his tone, said to him, "It seems that going through the air might be a better, faster way than this."

Now they were getting under way again. The Artisan replied, "Watch out for the bottom here, all slippery mud. No, my balloon was not even large enough, you understand, to carry one man, let alone a party of five or more. And it will come down, as soon as the air inside cools off. A balloon, or any flying device, big enough to bear us all away would be a vast project—though a truly interesting one." For a moment Daedalus could not keep himself from being distracted by the challenge of such a task.

Once more the party moved on. Ariadne kept close behind Theseus, and close behind her came the slave-girl, tugging the child along by the hand.

There were places where the stream, in its long rush seaward, went through ancient culverts, one of which it almost filled. Fortunately a sufficient breathing space remained open along the top.

Now and then their guide muttered and mused that parts of this escape route seemed to have been designed, by some ancient engineer, to serve the function of a tunnel, and other parts were only the natural course of the stream bed.

Who knew, thought Ariadne, how many hundreds of years the little creek might have been flowing here—or any stream anywhere, for that matter? This one had been at it long enough, certainly, to carve its way deeply into the ground, forming a channel that enabled a few big fish to swim all the way up into a portion of the Maze. Any fish ascending as far as the Deep Pool were evidently required to leap up one or more waterfalls in the process.

When they had stopped once more to catch their breath, Daedalus explained that in the course of his earlier reconnaissance down this stream, only a few days ago, he had briefly toyed with, then quickly discarded, the idea of improvising some kind of boat. For most of its length the channel was simply too shallow and narrow for that to be practical. A true underground stream of more than minimal length would have made breathing apparatus necessary, but fortunately that was not the case.

After about a mile of progress, carried out in a generally southwesterly direction, Ariadne was sure that they had left the Labyrinth behind them. Looking up through the occasional aperture, past natural rocks, exposed roots, and spiderwebs, it was no

longer possible to catch a glimpse of its distinctive walls or pavement. Neither were they beneath the grounds of the palace, or the
city, both of which lay in a different direction. The route now
seemed to lie beneath a rocky wasteland, and the spaces that let in
light and air were mere crevices between outcroppings, or piled
boulders. Here and there, at the bottom of an otherwise almost
impenetrable ravine, the little stream came fully out into the open
for a few yards, before it once more plunged under the earth.

Ariadne, more familiar than anyone else in the party with the
island's overall geography, announced that she knew approxi-
mately where they must be. "Little or nothing grows here. The
land above us is good only for grazing goats."

By dint of walking, crawling, clambering, occasionally swimming, once or twice going underwater again, the fugitives continued their descent, almost all the way to the small stream's inevitable
junction with the sea. Eventually it would become a creek, which
must find its way down to the marshy wetlands, and then the sea.

Daedalus gave his estimate that the whole journey would be
about three miles long. At the best rate of progress the little band
of fugitives could manage in the circumstances it took them more
than two hours.

Once the slave-girl asked her mistress timidly, "What do we
do when we reach the sea?"

Ariadne was silent for a time, hoping someone else might
come up with a better answer than she had ready. But no one did,
and at last the princess said, "If there's no useful ship or boat
immediately available—and of course we can't count on there
being one—we must find a hiding place, and wait."

For a moment Clara seemed on the point of asking: *Wait for
what?* but then she let it go in silence.

Two days before the morning of the escape, Theseus, with
some help from Ariadne's sympathizers, had dispatched by secret
means a message, to a man he said was an officer in his father's
navy. It would of course take time for that message to reach his
pirate cohorts, and more time for them to respond. But Theseus
hoped that they would come looking for him on a series of nights,
beginning only a few days from now, on a certain practically

uninhabited stretch of the island's rugged coast, long familiar to pirates and smugglers.

The trouble was that that stretch of coast was halfway around the island from the area in which Daedalus's discovered tunnel seemed to be about to bring them out. But Ariadne had been given some encouragement by her brother as well; her lover had not been the only one trying to arrange transportation.

Theseus was aware of the difficulties, but remained grimly optimistic. "We'll get to a place where we can be picked up. Or we'll find a way to take a boat from someone."

After struggling down the narrow waterway for several hours, more often than not wading in its bed, picking their way with difficulty down slippery rocks beside the falls where the salmonlike fish came leaping up, the fugitives reached what was undeniably the end of the tunnel, blocked by a coarse grillwork of thick, rusty metal bars. Just beyond that the stream emerged into full sunlight, then went wandering on, beyond a fringe of small trees, to lose itself in a marsh, under an open sky. A gull cried in the distance, and they could hear the encouraging sound of surf on hard rocks. Theseus, gripping the bars of the terminal barrier, announced hopefully that if he craned his neck he could just see a blue sliver of watery horizon beyond the reeds and bushes of the marsh.

From inside the tunnel it was possible to see occasional furry movement in the middle distance. Daedalus called attention to the fact that there were mutant beavers living and working in the waters that drained the Labyrinth. The stream the fugitives had been following emptied here into a kind of wetlands. From the nature of more distant vegetation, it appeared likely that the area soon became a salt marsh, and would be a good place for pirates or other surreptitious folk to land.

Evidently some authority had once at least suspected that the stream offered a pathway directly into the heart of the Labyrinth, and had attempted to seal it off. Rusted iron bars as thick as a man's arm, some underwater and some above, ran both horizontally and vertically across the opening where the small stream debouched at last into the open air. There was plenty of space between the bars for fish to go in and out, but not nearly enough for people.

The others all looked at Daedalus. "This is the 'final barrier' you mentioned?" asked Theseus.

"It is." The Artisan proceeded calmly. He had carefully studied the details of this problem on his earlier scouting trip, and it was soon obvious that he had been thinking the matter over ever since.

"We need a tool," he said. "And on my first visit I marked one that I believe we can use."

Taking from a pouch attached to his belt a small coil of thin, strong-looking cord, he handed it to Icarus. Now, moving at his father's orders, the boy squeezed his small body through the largest of the irregular openings in the grill, and went splashing off downstream toward the fringe of trees. When he got there he followed directions called to him by Daedalus. Soon he had knotted one end of the cord to a green log or pole, as thick as a man's arm, that lay where it was visible from the end of the tunnel. Ariadne, watching, supposed it was probably a small trunk chewed down by beavers.

Icarus had to draw his little knife, and work industriously at the log for several minutes, trimming off twigs that got in the way of his knot-tying. Meanwhile his father, watching from behind the iron bars, continued to call out instructions and encouragement, while the others managed to keep quiet.

As soon as the boy had a firm knot in the right place, he ran splashing back to the end of the tunnel, swimming through a couple of deep spots in the stream, carrying with him the free coil of the cord, unwinding it as he came.

Moments later the Artisan had the loose end in his hands. Drawing it taut, he raised it to one of the higher openings in the coarse grill, then engaged in some skillful and energetic tugging. In response, the distant pole leaped up, and began to progress in fits and starts toward the grating.

Icarus, who had run back again to stand beside the pole, now kept pace with it as it moved, and when necessary cleared its pathway of minor obstacles. Now and then he helped with a tug or push on the weight that would have been too great for him to lift or drag unaided.

Ariadne, not fully understanding the plan as yet, still let out a whispered cheer as the slim log came loose from the last entanglement of brush. A minute later it came sliding right up to the bars. Working together, with hands extended through the grating, Theseus and Daedalus turned the log endwise and pulled it through, a process delayed by the necessity of hacking off one more branch.

Once the two men had the long lever in their hands, inside the tunnel, they needed only moments to force one end of it into the gap between one side of rock and the nearest bar, only a few inches distant. Then, using a conveniently located bulge on the side of the tunnel for their fulcrum, they leaned their weight against the free end of the lever formed by the log.

The green wood of the fresh timber bent, but stubbornly refused to break. The metal barrier was very old, and the rock around it had started crumbling years ago. Presently there came a rasping sound of tortured metal. Now the men were able to force their lever farther into the aperture. They heaved again. First Clara, then Ariadne, came to try to help, but space near the end of the lever was limited, and the women soon stood back out of the way again.

Once more the two men strained their muscles. This time they made some progress. Ancient bolts and rivets formed of bronze, much thinner than the bars, were giving way, one at a time, in small, sharp explosions.

Daedalus stood back, wiping sweat from his brow with a bare forearm. "Prince Theseus, if you would help me, please. There are some hard rocks here of a handy size to make good hammers." There was no use, at this point, in trying to be quiet.

Theseus picked up from the stream bed a stone the size of his two fists, and with it delivered powerful, clanging blows to a bolt that now stood with almost its whole length bendably exposed. Then he dropped the hammerstone and went back to stand beside the Artisan, once more laying hold of the lever.

"It's tougher than I thought," Daedalus grunted.

"We'll get it, old man. This is a brilliant idea of yours. Now heave!"

After a few more minutes of grunting, straining effort, the massive, rusted iron tore loose from rock with an explosive noise. One whole side of the grating sagged.

An exit two feet wide stood open to the world.

○ *E l e v e n* ○

---

*W*hen Theseus went over the wall and vanished from sight, Alex was already running in hot pursuit. There was no need for him to hold back or deliberately stumble. Compared to most men Alex was fast and agile; matched against Theseus, he was clumsy and slow, and on his best day he would not have been able to overtake the prince.

Nor would he ever be able to match the leap that enabled Princess Ariadne's lover to catch the top of the wall, or the strength of arm that pulled him over and out of sight in just the blinking of an eye. But Alex remained grimly determined not to let the fugitive permanently out of sight. Whatever route Theseus might be following to reach the point of rendezvous with the princess and the others, it would presumably work for Alex also.

All this ran swiftly through the young soldier's mind as he darted round the first corner in pursuit. There was no trace of Theseus to be seen, and with a shock Alex observed that the passageway he had now entered seemed to curve in the wrong direction, and was going to carry him farther from the spot where Theseus must have come down.

But at this point Alex had no choice. Hoping that the next turn would bring his quarry in sight once more, he dashed on, committing himself entirely to chance.

Behind him, the uproar attendant on the shattered ceremony faded quickly, the noise baffled in the endless turnings of the Labyrinth. Before his racing feet there appeared always another branching of the way, and then another. The occasional stair going up or plunging down beneath ground level. Each time he had to choose, Alex followed his instincts; but his instincts were evidently wrong, for there was never a sign of the fleeing prince, or indeed of any living being.

In this way Alex ran until he was exhausted. When at last he stopped, chest heaving for breath, he turned and looked about. There were the twisting walls on every side, and the sky above. The realization came to him, with a blending of horror and relief, that he was now hopelessly lost.

Resting, he thought he heard someone approaching, the steps of a single pair of feet, coming along the way that he himself had come.

He could see no place to hide. On he went, desperately crawling through one odd low passage that was really only a small tunnel, breaking his fingernails on the rough stones that paved its floor. Now it seemed to him that he could hear the sounds, padding feet and clinking metal, of armed men running in pursuit, behind him and around him. On his hands and knees, peering round a corner, Alex's worst fears were confirmed when he caught a glimpse of one such figure. These were men who until minutes ago had been his comrades, but who now might well have been ordered to cut him down on sight.

For the moment he was still safe, but he might be discovered at any instant. If he simply waited where he was, they were certain to find him sooner or later. But if he ran on, turning corners at random as before, he might very well run right into the men who were looking for him.

Near despair, he almost called aloud to the Lord Asterion, and to Prince Theseus, for help; but with an effort he kept himself from doing that. Even when the enemies of the princess caught and tortured him, as now it seemed almost certain that they would do, he must do his best to keep from naming names.

Fighting to shake off the grip of panic, Alex told himself firmly that it was possible, even likely, that he was not yet being hunted, or even under suspicion. Of course people must have seen him running after Theseus, but that could be easily explained as his attempt to catch the fugitive. Other soldiers must have gone pounding in pursuit as well. He might, he probably could, rejoin his comrades now, assuming he and they could find their way out of the toils of the Labyrinth, and perhaps remain free of suspicion.

But meanwhile, every passing minute and hour would see the

princess getting farther and farther away, by means of whatever cleverness Daedalus had chosen to employ. And he, Alex, would be able to do nothing at all for her, never see her again or have a chance to serve her. Never again would she look at him with approval; nor would her fingers ever touch his skin, as they had when she gave him the medallion—though she was unlikely ever to touch him again in any case. Ah, if only he could be sure that she was safe!

Restlessly he moved on, and soon began to run again, driven by a sense of urgency to find the princess. But in a little while he stopped, aware that he had not the least idea where she was, or where he was headed. Flattening himself against the wall, he thought his own gasping breath was so loud that the sound of it must betray his presence to any searchers who came near. If only he could keep from breathing! But he was likely to reach that state of perfect silence soon enough.

Now it seemed to Alex that not only soldiers, but also the priests of Shiva, carrying their instruments of torture, must already be searching for him, and that the men who sought his life must hear the pulses pounding in his head. At any moment they were bound to come upon him; and a few minutes after that, if he was lucky, he would be dead.

His mouth was dry, with normal thirst as well as with fear. Too bad that a canteen had been no part of this morning's prescribed uniform.

He moved on, still nursing a fading hope to join the princess and her party. But gradually it was borne in on him that it probably made no difference whether he tried to desert or rejoin his squad; he was now hopelessly lost. Maybe if he climbed one of these walls, he could at least see where he was, in relation to the palace and the city . . . but when he looked up he saw that here the high walls, difficult enough in themselves, had been topped with a stiff growth of some mutant thorn. It would be impossible to walk on that.

The sun as it progressed across the sky could give him some clue as to the points of the compass. But since he did not know in which direction he wanted to move, knowing them would be no help.

Once, encountering a cheerful fountain, Alex paused gratefully, long enough to plunge his head into the pool at its base, and drink deeply. There was no telling when he might have another chance.

After resting a few minutes, he felt unable to sit still, and moved on at a steady walk. Now he had to fight against a helpless feeling much akin to that of drowning. For a long time now, he had not had the slightest idea whether or not the path he was following was bringing him any closer to the princess and her party. For all he knew, his every move was carrying him farther and farther away from her.

Turn right.

Alex stopped in his tracks, body swaying with the impetus of suddenly arrested motion. The voice that had uttered those two words had been so plain, though soft, that he did not doubt for a moment that he had really heard it. But it had issued from no visible body; his eyes assured him that he was still utterly alone.

Only once before had Alex ever heard a similar voice. Half a year ago, on a certain never-to-be-forgotten night, a night of wintry wind and bloody horror; and the voices he had heard then had been those of the auxiliaries of Dionysus.

Now, even as he stood waiting, listening, beginning to fear that imagination was after all playing tricks, the breathless little voice came back again, as clearly as before: *Turn right, then up the little stair, and right again.*

In his disoriented state of mind, the next thought Alex had was that the beings who spoke to him had somehow joined in his persecution, and he cried out, "Why are you doing this to me?"

But at the moment he could get no answer to that question. The only sounds that came, very faintly, were those of music and merriment.

Then at last, a few words: *Not to you, for you. We want to help.*

And then, as if his interlocutors grew impatient, Alex saw a mysterious, insubstantial figure, beckoning to him from around a corner. At once he recalled a glimpse of a similar presence, on that night of death and horror in the great hall, six months ago.

Above the loins, the body was that of a naked human male, while all the lower parts, including the two hoofed legs, were thickly covered by the rough fur of a beast. Whatever it might be, it at least was not a soldier, or a priest of Shiva, and Alex instinctively obeyed the wordless summons.

And now, off in the distance somewhere, he could hear soldiers shouting excitedly, fired with the excitement of the hunt.

And in the same instant, the rapid voice in his own ear: *They chase after phantoms.*

The inhuman presence was frightening, and he tried to run. Gasping, sobbing for breath, he plunged back into the windings of the Labyrinth.

Once more the sounds of pursuit, or of a search at least, grew less and faded away. Still, in spite of everything, he had not been caught. Luck seemed with him, and luck might count for as much as an army.

Then, there it was again, in front of him, the ghostly figure waving a beckoning arm. Again, having no hope of any better chance, Alex followed.

Apotheosis will be a good treatment for any wound—therefore see the apothecary. A voice that certainly sounded like a woman's giggled those words into his ear. Alex only wished that he could have known what the two big words in the statement meant.

Rest here.

And gratefully he sank down.

If only he'd been able to find Asterion, who would have told him where to go and what to do . . . but Asterion was probably long gone now, with his sister, and Daedalus, and the others. If only the Lady Ariadne had managed to escape! That, after all, was far more important than what might happen to a half-nameless soldier.

At last Alex heard the horn, the usual signal for a recall of the troops. Now the officers would be reorganizing, planning a methodical search, and in a little while they would be back in earnest. The Maze might shelter him from that. But by the same token, he was still lost in the Maze, utterly and hopelessly lost . . .

Sitting against a wall, Alex dozed, to snap awake again with a nervous start. The sun was gone now, light fading from what he could see of the sky, darkness beginning to enfold the Labyrinth. He had been on the move since dawn, and had accomplished nothing, except to keep himself alive. Which he might have managed just as easily by sitting still. Would there be searchers through the night, groping about in the Maze with torches? He couldn't guess.

Trying to burrow his way into the deepest, darkest hole he could, in which to hide, he tumbled into the closest thing to a hideaway that he could find. Not underground, but the cramped dead end of a coiled passage that just wound in on itself, going nowhere.

He lay there breathing deeply, feeling utterly worn out. Now he was bottled up for sure. Never in his life had he felt so weary and alone. If only he could find some reason to hope that what he had done today had been in some slight way a service to the princess . . .

Totally exhausted, Alex knew despair. He had missed his appointed meeting with the princess and the others, he had no idea where they were going or how, and he would certainly be unable to follow them. The only bright side of his situation seemed to be that if he were captured he would be unable to betray them. Even the Butcher, even Shiva himself, would not be able to extract information a man did not have.

But if only the princess could get away! He kept coming back to that, which was the all-important thing. But the truth was that he would probably go to his own death without ever knowing what had happened to her—or to her lover.

Alex had to admit that he would have been unlikely to find a better hiding place than the one to which he had been led. If the powers that had brought him here were as friendly as they claimed to be, then it might offer real refuge for a time. Alex had slept very little on his last night in the barracks; and his weariness soon overcame him now.

He was not even aware that he was close to falling asleep again, until a jolt of nervous tension jarred him abruptly awake. For a moment he lay there afraid to breathe. Then there came a rustling in the darkness, and a faint glow, and once more the help-ful powers were on hand.

Someone—or something; he barely felt a touch upon his hand—handed him a smooth stone cup, brimming with cool liq-uid. A taste informed him that it was wine, fine wine, and water mixed. Not only did the draught quench his thirst, but it sent him right back to sleep.

He was awakened again, with another jarring start, this time from dreamless oblivion, and with the conviction that someone, or something, had just said to him in a clear voice, *Now it is time.*

Had he been dreaming after all? No, because he suddenly realized that he was not alone in his small stone refuge. For a moment he could remember that the vast Labyrinth enfolded him, and wonder whether he was waking in a prison, or a tomb.

"Time for what?" he whispered back. "Who are you?"

In answer there came a giggle, then a whisper of what sounded like nonsense words. With a deep inner chill, Alex sud-denly remembered that madness was the real signature of Diony-sus. But the being confronting him now was only some satyr, sprite, or other minor power.

Gradually he became aware that there were two or three of them—he could not be certain of the number—with him in the confined space. They glowed in the dark, with a gentle light to which only the corners of his human eyes seemed sensitive. Each of them interchangeably took on and put off again the appearance of man and woman, child and goat, sitting or standing or lying at full length. Somehow his new companions seemed to occupy little or no room, but it was hard to be certain of anything about them. Whenever Alex tried to look closely at one of the figures, it dis-solved into grayish back-of-the-eyeball blurs, exotic shifting shapes that made no sense and had no permanence.

"Tell me who you are." He breathed the words as much in weariness as fear. If something horrible was going to happen, then let it happen and be done.

Only a faint whisper came back, and at first Alex couldn't be sure that he was hearing anything but the wind. Still he could see them moving, and he knew that they were with him.

Once the Lord Dionysus was like you.

"Ah," said Alex. On any ordinary day, the fact that any non-human being had chosen to speak directly to him would have stricken him with awe. Today, however, he seemed to have no capacity left for such emotions.

After a pause he continued, "Yes. Yes, I remember he told me that himself." Alex paused again, waiting for an answer.

Faint, very faint and far away, the music of a single flute. Of course they were the creatures of Dionysus; what else could they be? But even the mad must sometimes tell the truth.

Alex swallowed, then got out a whisper through a tight throat. "Lord Dionysus? Where are you?"

Our god is dead.

"Oh." He swallowed. "Then what do you want of me?"

Come. A little patch of blurred fog. The ghost of a pale hand, beckoning.

Shakily Alex rose to his feet. He wondered if he was weakening, though at the moment he felt no particular hunger. Led by the sprite, for no great distance, but by a convoluted path, to a cranny, a buried recess, that he would not have found unaided in a hundred years of searching, Alex came upon the body of the previous avatar of Dionysus. At first, all he could recognize was the cape.

A swirling of half-visible forms was followed by what sounded like a whispered consultation, and then one who had been delegated to do so came back to the young man again, an image becoming minimally plainer, the mere outline of an old man, bearded like a goat. *When no one wears the Face of Dionysus, we grow weaker and weaker. If our god stays dead much longer, most of us will fade and die.*

Alex looked about him on the dusty pavement, starting at the spot beneath the mummified head of the late god. Nothing. "Where is the Face? Does one of you have it?"

The vague form gestured, with what might have been its hands. *None of us can ever wear it, for we are not human. We are allowed to touch it only briefly.*

A spotted panther, looking like a creature from somewhere deep in the mainland jungles, south of the Great Sea, came into view, silent as a ghost, regarding him gravely. It was a very strange sight indeed, though not the strangest that Alex had seen today. And now there were two panthers, enough like each other to be twins. And, just behind the great cats, an image as of a small chariot, hardly more than toy-sized. In a moment the animals withdrew, or disappeared. The great cats had looked neither more nor less unreal than all the other visitants; and as soon as they moved away, the chariot too was gone, if it had ever been there.

For a moment Alex recoiled in fear. But then he moved forward again to look. At last he knelt down, cautiously, beside the inert figure.

As a soldier he was no stranger to death in all its phases. Obviously the god had been dead for a long time. Judging from everything he knew about the case, Alex concluded that six months would be about the right interval. Dionysus—this avatar of Dionysus—had probably hidden here half a year ago, on the night when he fled from Shiva.

"Who are you?"

This time he was asking about the individual who spoke to him, not the whole collection of them, and so his question was understood. *My name is Silenus. But that does not matter. What matters is that spring has come again, and yet our god is dead.*

A second voice now joined in the ghostly whispering. *Our god is dead, yet spring has come to the world regardless. Is that not strange and unbelievable?* It was a weird, affecting lamentation, all the more intense because it was so inhuman.

This was one turning of the year when the previous avatar was not going to revive. The body was little more than a skeleton by this time, but the rich cape that Alex remembered was here, now only a weathered rag. The golden winecup Dionysus had drunk from in the great hall now lay near the skeletal right hand. Dionysus, at least in this most recent avatar, had not bothered to bear weapons, at least none of any ordinary sort. If a divinity became so weak that he needed a commonplace sword or spear, they weren't likely to do him any good.

The fleeing god had left his *thyrsus*-staff in the great hall, where it had been incinerated by Shiva. Alex wondered whether the staff might have reconstituted itself somehow, as sometimes the tools of the gods did in legend. If so, it was not here.

And there was no sign of the Face.

Overcoming first his awe, then a growing distaste at this disturbance of the dead, Alex began to search, first carefully, then more vigorously. But what he was looking for was not to be found.

The countenance of the corpse, eyeless and noseless now, was still utterly and routinely human. No more and no less horrible than that of any man long dead, a kind of placid and routine horror. Nothing that ought to frighten an experienced soldier, or raise his hopes. Yet a wild hope, that had in it a strong component of new fear, had been born in Alex now. He repeated his question, this time as a demand. "Where is the Face?"

We took it away. We wanted to make sure that it remained out of our enemies' reach.

"You mean someone else has put it on?"

It would be a mistake to bring about our god's rebirth just now here on Corycus. When the Twice-Born lives again, he must be given time to grow, develop, become familiar with his powers before he needs to use them. Here and now, Shiva would allow him no such time.

"Then where is the Face?" Alex persisted. "You've hidden it somewhere?"

When you have arrived at a certain temple of Apollo, we will tell you more. In that place you may discover our god's Face, and put it on.

There was a silence that seemed long. Those last three words kept echoing in the young soldier's mind, while their meaning seemed to stay just out of reach.

"I?" Alex cried at last. Abruptly he was very conscious of the strangeness of the Labyrinth around him. The passageway in which he crouched seemed to be constricting around him. "*I* am to put it on?"

On the night when our god last breathed, he spoke favorably of you.

Suddenly Alex could remember again the fallen avatar in the great hall, looking directly at him and saying, with something like envy, *Once I was like you.* It seemed to the young man now that he could hear in the echo of that booming voice all the false heartiness and bravado that had concealed a great fear.

Aloud he asked, "And this—my discovering the Face—is to happen in some temple of Apollo? Not one of Dionysus?"

No response.

His mind was whirling. Sudden dreams of unbelievable glory alternated with sharp pangs of terror. "Anyway, I think there are no longer any temples of Apollo on this island. Shiva has ordered them all destroyed, or converted to base use."

The only answer was faint music, and fainter laughter. The man could hear nothing of joy, but only a kind of madness in it.

"All right, so I must reach a certain temple of Apollo. Where does it stand, if not here on Corycus? And how am I to get there?"

We are weak. Without our god to give us strength, the long trip over the water may be too much for us.

The voices babbled all together suddenly, sounding confused, not to say mad. But what else to expect from the entourage of Dionysus, God of Frenzy? Alex resisted the urge to repeat his search of the immediate area, to make sure that despite their babble, the Face was not simply lying here unclaimed.

Struck by a sudden thought, Alex raised his head and whispered into the air, "Does Shiva know that your god is dead?"

The God of Destruction does not care. He has not taken the trouble to search for Dionysus. Shiva is very much afraid of certain other deities. But not of our lord. Not yet.

There came an eerie sound, a kind of high-pitched rumbling, rolling down one of the twisting corridors—Alex could not at first be sure which one. Soon the chariot, pulled by the two ghostly panthers, pulled up in front of him and stood there, waiting, its car unoccupied. The whole equipage seemed much bigger now, too

wide to have negotiated the narrow pathways of the Maze—yet
here it was.

Get in.

Drawing a deep breath, Alex put a hand on the low side rail of
the vehicle, just in front of one of the two tall wheels. The sensation of solidity beneath his palm and fingers wavered once, then
firmed. It had the feel of ivory, or horn.

Drawing another deep breath, and holding it this time, he
vaulted up onto the wheeled platform. Before he could locate the
reins, or even confirm that any existed, he heard a warbling of
flutes and a clash of ghostly cymbals, the panthers sprang forward,
and the chariot shot up, lurching into the air.

At that moment the rattle of wheels on pavement ceased
abruptly. Gripping the railing with all his strength, Alex groaned
and involuntarily closed his eyes. The last thing he saw was the
moonlit vast complexity of the Labyrinth falling away beneath
him, many of its thousand miles of twisted passageways now visible all at once.

When he opened his eyes again, moments later, most of the
island of Corycus was spread out below, with faint points of light
outlining the sprawling city, and marking the other settled places.
Here and there a lone spark from lamp or hearth marked, he supposed, an isolated dwelling.

Everything was quiet, except for the rush of air. The soft feet
of the leopards, running over a soft carpet of mere air and cloud,
made no sound that human ears could hear.

At last his ears were able to pick out a fainter murmur in the
air around him. He understood that the tattered remnants of the
minor powers were accompanying him upon this journey. Somehow the little chariot was able to contain them all, or drag them
with it through the sky.

he last thing that Edith, the girl from Dia, could remember was . . . a monstrous, animal-like figure looming in front of her . . . her own voice, shouting in terror, pleading with Apollo, *Alexikakos*, averter of evil, to save her from the bloody horror that threatened.

Standing in line with the others of the Tribute, she had been shocked by an outcry, and had looked up in utter amazement to see Prince Theseus escape. She had watched, as with startling fury he struck down a guard, with what speed and strength he hauled himself over a wall and out of sight.

Such feats were not possible for her. But suddenly it was no longer possible to simply, meekly, wait for pain and death. In a moment, she too was running as fast as she could . . .

Now, regaining consciousness with the sense that hours of drugged sleep must have passed, she remembered few details of the peril from which she had been rescued. Her head ached, and thirst was parching her mouth and throat.

Then, with a shock, something like full memory returned, and she sat up.

Even on the last morning of their lives, many of the eighteen had not believed that they were doomed to die. The upcoming ceremony meant only that they would be initiated somehow into Shiva's cult.

For days she and her doomed companions, an assortment of young folk who seemed to come from every quarter of the Great Sea, had been aware that this was the morning when they were to meet the god. Shiva, the Compassionate, as his priests described him, who took an interest in their welfare . . . then the first victims were marched up to the cages, and shut in. There followed the glowing iron and sharp, cruel knives, the dripping blood. What Edith now remembered most clearly of all was her own body's reaction, the burst of panic breaking through the fog of drugged wine, to send her running madly for her life . . .

Now everything around her was silence, tranquility giving at least the appearance of safety. Bright sunlight, coming at an angle not far from that of midday, touched part of one high wall above her. *Apollo, lord of light, you have not yet entirely forsaken me.*

She had awakened lying on a kind of curved stone bench, built into one wall of the Maze at a place where several passages came together, forming a clear space roughly circular, about three yards in diameter. The miniature courtyard thus created had five entrances or exits, five doorless apertures, each leading to a different corridor. Three of the connecting ways were roofless, and all of them curved out of sight after only a few yards. She was still dressed in the clothing of the ritual. There was more cloth beneath her body, a kind of blanket that she had never seen before, padding her away from the sun-warmed stone, and a folded robe to serve as pillow under her head.

There was no need to ask herself: where am I? For the tall, laterally curving stone walls that shut her in told her with certainty where she was—still inside the Labyrinth. Some of those walls seemed waves of stone, frozen in time, about to topple in and crush her. For all she knew, she could still be near the very place where the sacrifice was to have been carried out. But she sat up with a sudden movement, provoking a wave of dizziness. And now she began to wonder what could have happened.

Her belt had been loosened, and a cup of water and some fruit placed at her side. Indeed, she was very thirsty, and drank the water in a few quick swallows. She had had nothing to eat or drink since that early morning draught of delightful wine and water, administered by Shiva's helpers. They had poured hers carelessly, filling the goblet less than halfway. Something in *that* cup must have been potent enough to begin to dissolve even the fear of death.

Now she had drained the last drops from the simple cup of water before it occurred to her to wonder whether it too might be drugged. But the taste of this drink was clean and cold, not like that poisoned wine at all.

Every part of her body ached as she forced herself to get to her feet. Repeated waves of dizziness made her sway as she stood listening. Somewhere in the distance she could hear what sounded like soldiers' voices, shouting back and forth, though it was impossible to make out what they were saying, and even hard to tell how far away they were.

Had she been retaken, then? Carried to this spot by soldiers, who might reappear at any moment, to carry her back to the place where Shiva's victims bled and died?

But no soldiers appeared. Instead, there came a slight sound behind her, and she turned quickly. She of course recognized the shape before her as the Monster of the Maze, dreaded by everyone. It was the last sight she had seen at the place of horror and blood. Whimpering, she shrank back against the wall. She might have run, but was engulfed by another wave of dizziness, motes swimming before her eyes.

The monstrous figure paused, spreading huge manlike hands as if to show they were empty of any threat. In an unlikely, low-pitched voice it said, "You needn't be afraid. I'll keep my distance, if that will ease your mind."

Desperately Edith pressed her body back into the curved corner, feeling rough stone against her back. "What do you want?"

The beast, the monster, answered as calmly as before. "My name is Asterion; at moments of formality, the Lord, or Prince, Asterion, though we needn't be bothered about titles. And you are—?"

The possibility that the creature might have a name, might be *someone*, had somehow never occurred to her before. Automatically she told him her own name.

"Edith. Yes, I like that. I am the one who brought you here, you know, after snatching you away from the killing." Here he paused, as if to give her time for some response. But Edith could only shake her head, and Asterion went on. "Or perhaps you don't remember. But I am not one of those you must fear." There was a longer pause. The creature sat down on the opposite bench, and as it ceased to tower over her it became a touch less threatening. "As for what I want—well, to start with, you might oblige me by answering a question or two."

"Yes?" She managed to get out the one word clearly.

"To begin with: Just what is it that you're afraid I'm going to do to you? Eat you? I don't even eat lamb chops."

It took her almost half a minute of confused effort to come up with a kind of answer. "I remember the blood . . ."

"None of it was of my spilling. Well, only a little bit, perhaps."

Still the young woman had very little to say, but I could see that her fear of me grew less as I sat at ease and conversed with her.

It was all very well to congratulate myself for having rescued one of the eighteen, and I had no second thoughts about having done so. But now, I was growing more perturbed as she grew calmer. Minute by minute, a certain question was becoming more urgent: what was I going to do with her?

I had no means of inducing the girl to fall asleep again; all I could do was listen to her hopeless weeping until it ceased. Later on, when she slept again, I ought to be able to prolong her slumber by a little bit, and also to see to it that her dreams were pleasant, and reassuring. Maybe, if we were very lucky, I could do more than that.

But such plans failed to come to grips with the basic question: what *was* I going to do with her? Certainly by now it was too late for me, let alone my new companion, to join my sister and her desperate band of escapees. Daedalus and the others would not still be waiting for me, and I could only hope that they had all gotten away. In dreams lay my best hope of getting an accurate report on what had happened to them; but that would have to wait. Dreaming required sleep, and it was pretty plain that I was not going to sleep again for many hours.

Within an hour or so I began to realize that Edith might have to live with me in the Labyrinth indefinitely. While she was still unconscious, I had carried her to a remote area, where it seemed practically impossible that the inevitable searchers would ever find their way. Here, a human presence of any kind was exceedingly rare; the grass grew thick in many places between the paving stones. Probably none of Shiva's priests, or the Butcher's soldiers, had yet come closer than a mile—which meant that they were effectively hundreds of miles distant, by any route that they were at all likely to discover.

And now, as the young girl lost her immediate fears, the larger difficulties of her situation became plainer in her eyes. "I want to go home!" she moaned, again and again.

I did my best to remain calm and soothing. "No doubt you do. But I don't know when that will be possible." I thought, but did not add: *probably never*. I could understand, being so attached to my own terrific home that I was ready to die rather than leave it.

"Where is home, Edith?" I asked, after a little silence. I was thinking that gentle talk was probably the best thing for her just now.

"The island of Dia."

"Is that so? I've heard of it, of course, but never been there. Tell me about it."

And soon she was able to take food, and enjoy an almost-peaceful sleep. But soon I felt I had to awaken her from that. Time was passing, and there were things I had to do. I explained to my guest and new companion that I had to leave her for a little while. "There has been much excitement, as you can imagine—as we have both heard." Indeed, certain phases of the great search had been quite noisy, some of the military trumpet calls audible a mile away. "I expect there may be messages waiting for me, and I had better see them."

The shade of alarm that crossed her face was flattering. "Asterion, you won't—?"

"Abandon you? Certainly not." But I emphasized, and repeated, that she should stay where she was. "I can almost guarantee that no one will find you here." That guarantee would be void if Shiva ever nerved himself to take an active part in the proceedings; but I saw no reason to mention that. "And where would you go? Believe me, you won't be able to find your way out of the Maze. On top of that, you wouldn't *want* to find your way out, because everywhere outside are the soldiers of King Perses, and the priests of Shiva, and I have no doubt that they are all still looking for you.

"Besides, if you go wandering about inside the Labyrinth, you may lose yourself so thoroughly that even I won't be able to locate you when I return. There is fruit growing here in this courtyard"—I pointed to a patch of exposed soil, where two trees grew, as well as the mutant vine—"and running water. And I promise you, I will return, as soon as I can. With some more food for you, and with good news, I hope. Though naturally I do not promise that."

By the morning after the escape, Uncle Perses had become exceedingly eager to interrogate me. During the previous afternoon, the usurper king had taken time out from his other efforts to send messengers into the Maze, who claimed to know where I could usually be found. One of these messengers, actually an old woman who had once been my nurse, had succeeded in leaving a written message for the Minotaur.

Dutifully I checked in certain odd locations, nooks and crannies of the Labyrinth which my sister and I had used, in our early years, as places to exchange communications. Today there was no such good luck as a note from Ariadne. But I did find a brief note, as sort of memorandum, from the usurper.

To judge by the contents of the note, Perses had already questioned Princess Phaedra extensively, and I silently congratulated myself on our wisdom in keeping all knowledge of the plot from her. Nor had Phaedra any idea of where I might usually be found inside the Labyrinth; Ariadne had almost never discussed such things with her. My elder sister had met me only a few times, generally in dreams. I could not remember whether we had ever laid eyes on each other in waking life; if that had happened, it must have been when I was very small. I knew that Phaedra wished me well, but couldn't help being profoundly upset by the mere sight of her half-brother.

But the main point of the king's written message was a proposal, almost a supplication, for a meeting with me. It did not mention Ariadne, and the wording of it raised my hopes that the attempted flight had succeeded.

The usurper and I had had very little contact with each other at any time, and none at all in the six months since Perses came to power.

Somehow it did not concern me greatly that I had irrevocably missed my chance of escaping with the others. It seemed to me almost as if someone else had made the decision for me, knowing I would approve. Maybe I had known somehow, even when I so impulsively rescued the girl, that her presence would prevent my flight.

Nor did I greatly dread my coming interview with the usurper. Even if Perses was aware that his monstrous nephew had aided the princess and others to get away, he was not going to kill a son of Zeus. And now, looking back, I see that there was another possible reason for my remaining where I was: I might simply have been too much afraid to leave the only home that I had ever known.

Our meeting took place in a portion of the Labyrinth that lay quite near the place where most of the youths and maidens of the Tribute had been done to death, and from which Theseus must have made his escape.

My uncle was wearing full battle dress, as if he thought an invasion was impending, and was attended by a bodyguard of half a dozen soldiers, all picked men from the Palace Guard. Also present was a priest of Shiva, who with his necklace of small imitation skulls was obviously trying to cultivate a similarity of appearance with his dread master.

The monarch's rage grew as the evidence mounted that Daedalus and his son were among the missing. That made six people in all who were unaccounted for.

"Vanished as if the earth had swallowed them." The priest decked out in imitation skulls seemed to think he had just invented a particularly apt comparison.

"All the inducements I showered upon the man," Perses grumbled again. "I made him wealthy."

The Artisan's simple quarters near the center of the Maze had of course been found deserted. A small room containing two small beds, and nothing special in the way of furnishings. A few of their scant belongings were lying about, but there was nothing to indicate whether the man and boy might be coming back. I saw that a satchel containing a set of fine, small tools had been opened and its contents scattered.

"Surely he would have wanted to take his special tools with him?" I suggested helpfully.

"Maybe they were too heavy for the balloon," muttered one of the searching officers nearby. I gave no sign that I had heard.

The woman who sometimes cared for the child, a duty she had shared with other members of the regular Cretan palace household staff, had been going about her routine business of cleaning and preparing food. No, she could tell nothing about where the Artisan and his son might have gone. Both man and boy tended to be irregular in their habits.

And, though he remained reluctant to admit the fact to me, Perses was forced to acknowledge that his niece Ariadne was also among those who had disappeared. No one had a clue as to where they might be now.

My heart leaped up in joy. For me it is always easy to keep my emotions from showing in my face.

The concern in the usurper's voice was very real when he informed me, "Princess Phaedra is greatly worried about her sister's welfare."

For once I could easily believe that the murderer spoke the truth. "Naturally," I responded. "As I am."

In the course of this conversation I refused to show any sign of respect to the priest, whose name was Creon. Looking him up and down, I observed, "Somehow I was expecting to see the god himself."

"Be glad that you do not," snarled the priest.

"Why?" the king demanded of me. "What do you want with the Lord Shiva? Some favor to ask?"

I returned the usurper's gaze curiously. "I want nothing from him. Certainly no favor."

The new Minos was obviously trying to repress his loathing when he looked at me; and yet, I could tell that he was impressed, almost intimidated, despite himself.

"Asterion, you are my nephew, and I wish you well."

"Half-nephew, at least, half-uncle."

He was not going to try to respond to that. "They tell me you have all the understanding of a normal man. Despite the shape of your head."

I was already angry at this man. Very angry, because of the killing of our father, the pain he had caused Ariadne, and for the lies he spread and encouraged about the Minotaur. "They tell me the same thing about you," I returned sweetly.

At that the king's anger flamed, so that his bodyguard looked at him expectantly, and tightened their grips upon their spears, as if they anticipated an order to attack the warped creature before them, and put it out of its misery. But, as I had expected, Perses gave no such command. He had business to transact with me. Obviously there was some kind of help he wanted from the impertinent monster, and he managed to control his temper.

Motioning Creon the priest to withdraw to a little distance, the usurper said to me, placatingly, "Your father and I were never bosom friends. But neither were we enemies."

"Does your majesty mean my father King Minos, or my Father Zeus, the ruler of the universe?" That last was perhaps an exaggeration; though not, as I thought, by much.

"I am speaking of my brother."

On rare occasions in my childhood and youth I had tried to explore in dreams the question of what my foster father, or adoptive father, Minos, had really thought of me. But in truth I was afraid to learn the whole truth on that subject. Minos had not slain me in my monstrous infancy, even though my horns, already present at my birth, had cost him the life of his unfaithful queen. Of course, for a wife, especially a royal wife, to betray her husband with a mere man is one thing, and for her to bear the children of the Great Lecher Zeus is quite another. Also I found it not always easy, and sometimes quite impossible, to cause the visions of the night to develop in the exact way I wanted them to go.

I said, "I never considered King Minos my enemy, and indeed I hardly knew him. When I heard that he was dead, the news at first had little impact. But having had half a year to think about it, I find I'm truly sorry." I paused for a moment. "Of course my sisters are still grieving deeply."

"So are we all, my boy. So are we all." A stranger would have believed his sorrow, his willingness to be reconciled, perfectly genuine. "Now, speaking of your sisters: tell me, where is Ariadne?"

"I do not know," I said quite honestly. Once more I could be glad of my inhuman face and voice, which make it vastly easier to conceal my emotions.

"If you did know, Asterion, would you tell me?"

I tried to give the impression that I was thinking the question over very seriously. "Any answer I might give you now, majesty, would be only speculation."

The usurper, his face totally expressionless, stared at me in silence for a full ten seconds. Then he tried once more. "Also among the missing is a certain slave-girl, Clara, who is the regular attendant of the missing princess. You know the girl I mean?"

"I may know the girl you mean, Uncle. But I don't know where she is now. Probably with Ariadne."

I thought our noble uncle winced slightly at the familiar form of address. But he remained outwardly calm.

"Another is a young Dian woman named Edith, one of those who were to have been honored by the Lord Shiva."

"I have no information to give you about her either. So, am I to understand that only one of the eighteen is missing? What exactly happened? How many are still alive?"

"Actually two of the Tribute are among the six people unaccounted for. The second is a youth named Theseus. We have learned from a servant that he held a private meeting with your younger sister, several days ago."

"A private meeting?"

"Yes."

I shook my head, expressing ignorance.

With an effort at patience, Perses went on with his list of questions. "Have you seen anything at all, since the day of the ceremony, of Daedalus, or of his child? Or of a lost soldier, who may be wandering in the Maze?"

So, I thought, *Alex also may have got away.* My horned head continued to shake slowly from side to side. "Don't tell me they are missing too? But if I do encounter any of these people, my uncle, I will inform them of your concern."

"Make sure you do." Our noble uncle paused to draw a deep breath. "But I see you are still here."

I inclined my head in a slight bow; let him make of that answer what he would.

"Where were you, Asterion, when the sun came up yesterday morning?"

I considered pretending to have difficulty remembering. But that would have been childish. "Uncle, I was busy trying to explore the world."

The usurper leaned forward, frowning. "Trying to explore—what do you mean?"

"In the only way possible for one whose movements are so restricted. I explore the world by means of dreams."

It seemed to me that our uncle did not have much belief in his nephew's dreams—but likely he could easily be convinced.

Now he said, "You and I, Prince Asterion, have not always gotten on very well together." He said it with the air of a man who had recently made a discovery that gently pained him.

"I fear that is true, Uncle."

"Will you believe me when I say that I would like to be your friend?"

"How could I doubt my true king?"

Impulsively, or so it seemed, he reached out to grasp my hand in friendship. At that moment I might have seized the opportunity to jerk him toward me and wring his neck. But moments after doing that, I too would lie dead, and Edith would be left completely unprotected. And the death of Perses would have achieved nothing, really, to my sisters' benefit. There would still be Shiva, ready to put some other human puppet on the throne.

And still I wondered why Shiva was not present at this meeting. It seemed to me that the king, and even the chief priest Creon, might be uneasy over the same question.

Naturally Shiva had been enraged at the disruption of the sacrifice, and the loss of some of the youths and maidens whose painful deaths would have fed his cravings. But the question kept looming larger and larger—where had the God of Destruction gone when he departed so suddenly? And, where was he now?

Even gods—some of them might say, *especially* gods—had enemies. Envy and jealousy raged among them as violently as in any merely human group.

"I see that bravery is not the Destroyer's most conspicuous quality." The people around me blanched when they heard me say those words.

The usurper said he did not find it surprising that Shiva was not available just now for consultation, or to inspire his followers and allies. The hunt for the escapees would have to be conducted without divine assistance. The God of Destruction, before vanishing, had told Minos that he had more important things to worry about. "You must see to these details yourself. Other powers of some kind are near, I tell you!"

But Uncle Perses and the Butcher had wasted no time before organizing a mass search of the Labyrinth for the escapees. The king also dispatched riders on cameloids, commanding that all the coasts should be watched. But it was a long, long, winding coastline, that with its many bays and promontories extended for hundreds of miles. The king's word would need at least a day to reach the farthest points of the island; and how comprehensively it would be honored was a question. Any fugitive who once got clear of the palace and the city was in a fair way for getting away entirely.

And the king suspected that, if Daedalus was seriously

involved in their escape plot, the fugitives might well enjoy some extraordinary means of transportation. "If you know the man's reputation as I do, you will worry."

The Butcher agreed.

And Shiva agreed, but had little thought to spare for Daedalus, or any of the other humans involved. Rather he was consumed by his suspicion that the escape was only a diversion, planned by certain other gods who were jealously trying to destroy him.

The attempted search of the Labyrinth, by a hundred men of the Palace Guard, had achieved little but to get half a dozen of the Butcher's soldiers fairly seriously lost. In spite of some measure of planning, military discipline, and stern precautions, several of those men became separated from their comrades, and did not find their way back for several hours. By sunset on the day following the escape, almost all had been recovered, but the new Minos was left with the uncomfortable feeling that if he ever chose to deploy his soldiers in those endless passageways, an entire army could easily be swallowed up, like water flowing into sand.

At last only one man remained unaccounted for, a certain private soldier known as Alex the Half-Nameless, last seen running after the escaping Prince Theseus. None of other members of his squad seemed to have any idea where Private Alex might have got to. Of course it was possible that he had caught up with some of the plotters, they had killed him, and his body lay undiscovered in some winding of the Maze.

Before our conversation was quite over, an urgent report was brought to the king, concerning the finding of some parts of a balloon, and feathers, in an outlying portion of the Maze.

"A scattering of feathers?" Creon's voice went up in an unseemly squawk.

Several people had reported seeing a kind of balloon-shape, heading out to sea. The thing was visible only at a distance, and it was impossible to gauge its size.

To those who knew Daedalus by reputation, it was entirely possible that he had contrived a miraculous escape.

*O*n emerging from the mouth of the secret tunnel, the princess and her companions immediately scanned their surroundings, looking for the best hiding place nearby. The land nearby was mostly waste, with a small marsh where the stream they had been following trickled into the sea. There were no houses in sight, and no sign of human presence, apart from a couple of narrow paths, so the danger of accidental discovery appeared to be no worse than moderate.

A cluster of small caves offered the most convenient hiding place, and virtually the only one in the immediate vicinity. The caves were clustered forty or fifty feet above the marsh, near the top of a sandstone cliff, the highest point of land within half a mile. Within a minute or two the fugitives had scrambled up to the high ground and were established in the caves. The stream was still near enough to provide a source of water. Obviously the lack of food would soon become a problem, if they were forced to stay here for any length of time.

Looking inland from the top of the cliff, it was easily possible to see the towers and walls of Kandak, less than four miles away. In the circumstances this was not a reassuring sight.

The openings of the high caves also afforded a good view of the sea. Theseus, sounding confident, assured the others that it would be easy for him to spot the sail, or the hull, of the ship he was expecting to come looking for them.

Of course the five people spent most of their time doing their best to stay out of sight, keeping their heads down in one cave or another. At any moment a patrol of soldiers might come along to take them alive and drag them back to Shiva and King Perses, or perhaps to kill some of them on the spot. Or some vessel of the Corycan navy might sail by, and spot them on the shore. Or the God of Destruction himself might finally decide to come looking for them, mounted airborne on his bull. Everyone suffered with the heat and the confinement, but the threat of a much worse fate, if they should be overtaken by Shiva or his followers, stifled protest.

All day, at intervals of half an hour or less, Daedalus or Theseus, or sometimes both together, would emerge restlessly from a cave and crawl to the top of the small cliff. There, crouching or lying flat to avoid presenting a conspicuous silhouette against the sky, an observer had a view of the sea that was both broad and deep. Now the men searched the horizon anxiously. Once or twice during the day a distant sail came into view, but none headed for the island.

Meanwhile the slave-girl Clara moved about restlessly, going back and forth between the two most habitable caves, until her mistress ordered her sharply to settle down somewhere and be still. At that, Clara seemed to pull herself together and concentrated on inventing quiet games to play with the child.

Theseus spent most of his time, between visits to the cliff top, waiting in a cave, looking moodily out to sea, or tossing pebbles, one at a time, at sparrows that came near. He never managed to hit any of them. Ariadne spent most of her time looking soulfully at the man she loved, and trying to think of ways to cheer him up.

Icarus whined, sometimes, when Clara's games grew boring, until his father threatened to cuff him. Daedalus fretted, and drew in the sand before the entrance of the largest cave odd diagrams that none of the others could understand.

When darkness fell, and it was no longer possible to keep a useful watch on the sea, Theseus took the princess by the hand and pulled her into the smaller of the two most easily habitable caves. At the moment the two of them had its modest space entirely to themselves. Willingly enough she allowed herself to be drawn to him, and there they lay together through the night, while no one else came near them.

Shortly after the two lovers came together, the slave-girl Clara appeared at the entrance of the largest cave, only a few yards away, into which there now began to drift soft, eager moaning sounds made by the princess.

"If you do not object to my presence, sir," Clara said to Daedalus.

"I do not mind at all." The Artisan spoke in a low voice; he glanced toward his son, who, worn out by the day's adventures, was already asleep, huddled on a patch of sand where the warmth of the day's sun still lingered. Daedalus had partially covered the small boy's body with the warm sand. "I suppose your mistress is not likely to need you for anything?"

"Not tonight, sir." The girl answered quickly and with certainty. She tilted her head, listening to the soft sounds from the other cave, and wrapped herself more tightly in what had been a fine linen dress twenty-four hours ago. The garment had sustained serious damage in the travail of the escape, and patches of Clara's smooth skin showed through holes. "She and Prince Theseus are busy keeping warm together."

"I understand. And do you have a plan for keeping yourself warm tonight?"

"Not really, sir." Her long eyelashes flickered. "But I am open to suggestions."

In the other cave, there came an interval of sleepy rest, and relaxed murmuring. "I am glad, Prince Theseus," whispered the Princess Ariadne, "that your plans for the future include me."

"Absolutely—certainly they do." His voice sounded vague and tired, as well it might, after all he had been through.

"Isn't it strange?" the young woman mused. "A year ago—six months ago—I had no idea that anything like this was going to happen."

"How could you have had?"

"Did you?"

"Did I expect to meet the woman who would become dearer to me than my own life? No."

The princess moved a little, snuggling herself more comfortably against her lover. "Where were you a year ago? I suppose you were safe at home, in your father's palace."

That brought a chuckle from Theseus. "My father doesn't have a palace."

"You said he was a king."

"Well, yes, but . . ." The prince seemed to be groping for words. "He has a nice big house. Even if he had a palace, neither he nor I would spend much time in it. We are both men with many affairs—affairs of state, I mean—to keep us busy."

Ariadne raised herself on one elbow. "I want to know all about your family. So far you've told me practically nothing. What is your mother's name? What's she like?"

"She's been dead for many years."

"Ah. Like my own mother. I'm so sorry for you. How about your brothers, sisters? Tell me everything. I can't believe I don't even know the name of your country, or how far away it is."

"All that can wait. Right now isn't it enough that we are both alive? And that we have each other?"

Theseus and the princess who loved him lay together in the soft, clean sand of the cave floor, keeping warm through the night. Ariadne kept exchanging whispers with her lover in periods of sleepy talk, between the bouts of feverish activity.

"If you don't want to talk about your family, then we can at least plan what kind of wedding we are going to have. I mean when we have finally reached your mysterious homeland."

"All in good time. You know what I would much prefer to think about right now."

"Tell me."

"This."

"Ahh."

And still later, the princess returned yet again to the subject of her lover's family and home. But the more Ariadne tried to press him for the relevant details that she so craved to hear, the more he put her off.

When she pressed harder, Theseus curtly broke off the discussion. "I don't want to talk about all that just now."

"Really? Then when?"

"When I feel we are truly safe, my princess. Then I'll be able to relax."

The best way to break off the discussion was to change the sub-ject. Fervently Theseus protested his love for Ariadne, doing all he could to insure that she remained devoted to him. He never ceased to marvel at her beauty—for a few seconds at a time.

Privately he also marveled at the fact that she seemed really to have been a virgin—until this night. But then he supposed that was not really surprising in a princess.

Theseus slept fitfully, between bouts of passion and sleepy intervals of talk. Whenever his attention was not totally engaged with the body of the princess, he nursed his dreams and plans, which in general had little to do with her. Meanwhile he never entirely gave up watching and listening for the patrol of Minoan soldiers, who wouldn't be making much noise when they came, but would be carrying plenty of power of their own, in the form of weapons. It was important not to sleep too soundly.

Under a brilliant moon and piercing stars, Theseus stood con-fronting Asterion, deep inside the Maze. A night breeze whis-pered, and there was as always the faint sound of running water.

But he wasn't even thinking about Asterion at first. Instead his thoughts were confused, as if he were on the point of falling asleep. Theseus's next plan, now that his own survival seemed assured for the time being, was to get Ariadne away somewhere. It would have been great if he could have brought her sister away too. Then he might even have held both of the girls for ransom—though in his heart he would have been better satisfied if it had been Phaedra who had fallen in love with him at first sight, and who lay with him tonight. He thought she would have been more interesting, perhaps only because Phaedra had never paid him any attention. But he had done all in his power to seduce Ariadne, because she *was* clearly interested. And after all, he had no intention of ending his life as a mere sacrifice, one of a row of sacrificial dummies.

On second thought, he rather doubted that their Uncle Minos would really want either of his nieces back on Corycus, as a potential rallying point for the disaffected, once someone had been so obliging as to kidnap them. Trying to collect ransom would have been useless.

And, besides saving his own skin for the moment, Theseus wanted to find out whatever this girl knew—if she knew anything at all—about the god-Face supposedly hidden in the Labyrinth. That rumor had been passed around even among the youths and maidens of the Tribute.

Already he had tentatively questioned Clara on that subject. She had heard the same rumors as everyone else, but had been able to tell Prince Theseus nothing concrete that he did not already know.

Prince Asterion (as far as Theseus could determine, that seemed to be a genuine title, his real name) was half a head taller even than Theseus. His massive, hairy upper body was exposed above the beltline of his kilt, making Theseus, for all his muscular development, seem no larger than an ordinary man. The strange voice from the bull-throat said: "I am sorry to see that you have come carrying a sword on your visit to me, Prince Theseus."

"As a prince and a warrior, it is my business to carry a sword. Whether strange creatures approve of the practice or not."

"I only said that I am sorry. *Are* you a prince indeed? I know you've told my sister that you are."

Theseus made a little jerky motion with the bright blade, stirring sparks of starlight. "I am whatever I say I am. Whatever *this* says. Are *you* a prince indeed? Are you even a human being?"

"I am the brother of the woman you say you love. Does that mean nothing to you? If not, consider this: I am determined that she will take no harm through you."

Theseus made no answer to that. He was pondering whether he ought to kill the monster right away. The act would doubtless boost his reputation mightily in some quarters—but of course he would be damaged irreparably in the eyes of Ariadne, and right now that was much more important. Also, it would be much better if he were somehow able to put Asterion's powers to work for his own benefit.

Taking the bull-man hostage, holding him for ransom, seemed yet another possibility. But the objections that applied to kidnapping the sisters were valid here as well. No one, except possibly Ariadne herself, was going to pay ransom to get a monster back.

In a bright glow that impressed the dreaming eyes of Theseus as intense and silvery moonlight, the two of them still faced each other, somewhere deep inside the Maze.

The odd voice from the bull's head said to him, "What you and my sister need now, prince, if you are in fact a prince, is not a sword but a ship. I am doing my best to provide one, and if all goes well it should soon be there."

But Theseus refused to be distracted. "I don't fear your powers, monster."

"Why should you? Powers? What powers?" The creature spread his vast and leathery hands, as if to show their emptiness. "The only powers that I have exist only in dreams."

Theseus was not at all sure that he ought to believe that, of the supposed son of Zeus. The prince cast a hasty, nervous glance over his right shoulder, then very quickly another over his left. He was reluctant to take his eyes off the monster before him, even for a fraction of a second, but he could not escape the uneasy feeling that the Maze was closing in ominously around him.

"Set me free," he demanded, brandishing the blade again, "or I will kill you!"

The monstrous hands were still spread out and empty. "I do not hold you prisoner. If you would depart from me, all you need do is turn and walk away."

This time Theseus turned fully around, but saw only the endless Labyrinth, hedging him in. The walled space in which he was standing seemed to have a million doorways, but he knew, with the certainty of dream-knowledge, that they all led nowhere. With a great cry, he spun around again to face the Minotaur, leaped forward and thrust with his sword, aiming for the middle of the barrel chest, where he supposed the heart must be. The sword plunged home; the monster went down quite easily, and lay in a great heap, leaking blood.

For a long moment the prince stood frozen, in the position in which he had finished his thrust, staring at the weapon with which he'd struck the Minotaur down. Dark blood was on the blade, running down toward the hilt when he tilted up the point. How and where had he obtained so fine a tool? He could not remember. Somewhere, somehow, he'd laid his hands on a sword of fine steel—although in the moonlight he was suddenly reminded of a weapon of his father's he'd once envied, the blade of magically hardened and toughened bronze.

Certainly what he held now was not the common sword that he had taken from a common soldier, in the midst of his desperate scramble to escape the Labyrinth. Dark blood, almost black in the moonlight, oozed onto his hand, and he shifted his grip on the sword and tried to wipe his fingers clean against his thigh, realizing as he did that he was naked. How had he come here without clothing?

The monster was dead, a mound of fallen meat, but the monster's Maze still held him prisoner.

Above him now, what had been a clear night sky was darkening, immense thunderheads rolling into position, emitting a cosmic grumbling. Beneath such power, the Labyrinth itself seemed meaningless, shorn of terror. Theseus cowered down, suddenly terrified of the wrath of Zeus—what had possessed him to actually kill a son of the Thunderer? Then he wondered, with a more immediate pang, how he was going to justify to Ariadne what he had done.

He was going to have to give her some kind of explanation, because she was already watching him—how could she be here—?

—But in fact she was, and her face came looming over him, faintly visible in starlight, as were her bare breasts. Anxiously watching her lover Theseus, calling him repeatedly by name, even as he at last broke some chain of sleep, and woke up in their hiding place in the little sandstone cave.

The night was far advanced. His hands were empty, and the only available weapon was the cheap sword that he had taken from the soldier, and even it was lying now on the other side of the narrow cave. He, Theseus, had killed nothing and no one tonight. Only in a dream, under the spell of divine Oneiros, had he been anywhere near Asterion or his Labyrinth during the past few hours.

Groggily, Theseus said, "I thought I was . . ."

"What is it, darling?"

"Dreaming," he got out. Rolled over, wiped sweat from his face, looked at her intently. But her eyes were innocent, as usual. Her body as naked and innocent as a baby's. She knew nothing of what her brother, the invader and changer of dreams, was trying to do to him.

The sky outside the cave was starting to brighten. Soon it would be time to go up on the clifftop again and look for ships.

Early on the next morning, beginning the second day of their escape, great excitement spread among the fugitives when a small ship, moving under a single sail, came to stand by just offshore.

Theseus and Daedalus crouched together atop the little cliff, squinting into the morning sunlight, holding consultation.

The Artisan said at last, "It's only a trader. Not Corycan, as far as I can tell, so I can't see that they're likely to pose us any danger."

Theseus nodded. "Come, let's go down. Make sure they see the women and the child, they'll be less suspicious of us then."

The men called to the women to bring the child and follow them. Theseus put on the cloak that he had shed during the night, Daedalus slipped on his workman's belt and apron, and both men went down to the shore to make contact with this alien captain and his crew.

Theseus, striding forward across the little strip of beach, greeted them boldly and heartily. "Good day to you, captain—and to all of you. We are five, altogether, and we require passage across the sea."

The sailors soon relaxed—these five seemed a harmless enough bunch. The captain, who introduced himself as Petros, was a short, bearded, pot-bellied man wearing a single earring, his hair and beard of curls so dark as to resist the slightest bleaching by the sun. He had a red cloth tied around his head, and was wearing a pair of shorts and a worn vest of some leather that had once been fine. He stood with arms folded, watching the approach of the three refugees with no particular surprise. Meanwhile the half-dozen men of the trader's crew stood by their captain. They were a motley group, varying in age from a white-bearded elder to a beardless boy. About half of them were armed, like their leader, with long knives or short swords.

Captain Petros looked over his prospective passengers, while the crew of the small trader regarded them with what seemed wary speculation. Then almost at once, to the fugitives' surprise, Petros promptly agreed to take them to any reasonable destination within range of his craft. And the faces of the crew showed no objection to this decision, only a kind of watchful waiting.

Theseus accepted the offer as if he had expected nothing less. But the Artisan was more circumspect. "Captain, are you accustomed to taking on odd lots of passengers?"

Under cautious questioning by Daedalus, Captain Petros offered an explanation: for the past two nights in a row, he had been promised by a strange figure in a vivid dream that his fortune would be made if he put in at this particular beach, and accepted an offer that would be made to him when he had done so. No one, especially a seafaring man, could ignore such a message.

Now Theseus was interested again. "This strange figure in the dream—did it seem entirely human?"

"Now that you mention it, no. There were great horns on its head. Why?"

"That's fine, I was just curious."

Petros explained that he had discussed the series of dreams with his crew, and by a unanimous vote they had decided to stake their fortunes that the promise he had received was true—the business of carrying cargo had not been prosperous of late.

Captain and crew were still worried, however, about the patrols of the Minoan navy, whose prowess was almost legendary. So far they had been lucky in that regard.

So it was best not to waste any time. Yes, he was willing to take them where they wished to go. "Where will that be?"

"Away from this coast, to begin with," said Theseus. "As soon as Corycus is out of sight I will consult your compass-pyx."

Nor did Petros press his new passengers as to when he might expect to receive his reward, and exactly what it was to be. All his life the captain had believed earnestly in dreams, and he expected much from this one, which had promised him great things.

*A*s the chariot drawn by two swiftly pacing leopards bore Alex westward into the sky, even the practical fear of falling could not distract him from his steady anxiety about the princess.

Vertiginously he clung to the thought that the creatures of the god would not have whirled him to this giddy height simply so that they could watch him plunge to his death. Alternately, his thoughts soared with dreams of glory, in which he triumphed over some nameless, faceless enemy of the Princess Ariadne. Gradually his opponent took on the form of the king, her uncle—but in almost a year of pulling guard duty in and around the palace, Alex had seen too much of royalty to be overawed by the mere thought. Even if he had to fight against the Butcher himself, Alex could still face him.

Now he had a god as an ally, even if it was a dead god. A deity known for, among other things, his many names: among others, Dionysus, Bacchus, the Twice-Born, for which last name there was a legendary explanation. A god renowned also for the yearly cycle of growth and decline to which he and his powers seemed to be subject—and also for a tendency to fits of madness, sometimes bloody, in which his followers were constrained to join him.

Hastily Alex tried to think of something else. That last attribute was not one he wanted to contemplate in an ally.

The leopards paced on, their paws spurning the air, running as firmly as if they were on solid ground.

Gradually Alex came to understand that his terrifying distance from the earth was easier to bear when he did not look down. Therefore he spent much time studying the sky. He could tell by the moon and stars that the chariot was still carrying him to the west.

Several minutes passed, while his terror and confusion slowly diminished. When at last he changed position, his hand fell by accident upon something that felt like fine leather. He had discovered the reins, which had been tied around one of the carved spindles which served as support for the rail that encircled the car at about the level of the occupant's waist. But the knot of leather strips would not yield easily when Alex tugged at it, and after a minute he let the reins stay as they were, and went back to gripping the rail.

Even had he been able to establish control over his exotic team, he would have been afraid to use it. His experience at driving any kind of animals was minimal, and it seemed that the powers who had launched him on this flight were much better equipped than he was to see it to a safe conclusion.

His hand went more than once to the medallion the princess had given him.

He had been able to bring his soldier's short sword with him, and it was still vaguely comforting to be armed, though at the moment keen edges and hard metal were of no help at all.

Hours passed as he stood clinging to the rail, swaying on his feet with the motion of the speeding chariot. At last, exhausted by the tension in his muscles, he let himself slump into a sitting position, with the wooden spindles of the railing at his back. Maintaining a grip on one spindle with his hand, he let his eyes close, though he could not sleep. As long as he had no control over the direction of his flight, there was no use in even trying to see where he was going.

The time, as indicated by the rotation of the stars, had been a little past midnight when the inhuman auxiliaries of Dionysus had scooped him up into the air, and the flight lasted long enough to afford Alex the privilege of seeing the dawn in all its glory, the world and the morning coming to life over the flat immensity of the sea, the boundless domain of Lord Poseidon. By the time that daybreak was starting to wipe the stars away, he was shivering violently in the endless rush of air. The fugitive thought, but could not be sure, that some of the sprites managed to warm him a little as he flew, or at least to break the force of the wind with some invisible shielding.

There were certain minutes when he slept, in spite of his precarious position. Each time he awakened with a start of terror, sure that Shiva had somehow overtaken him.

Shortly after one of the awakenings, his invisible escort furnished him, somehow, with a fragile crystal goblet almost filled with wine. The drink went straight to Alex's head, with in its way a sharper impact than any cheap, throat-burning soldiers' booze he'd ever swallowed. Yet this was totally different from the last drink these Dionysians had given him, which had put him utterly to sleep. He was not sleepy now, but energized, keyed up to the brink of some extraordinary effort. When he had drained the goblet he set it down on the chariot's wooden floor. When he looked for it again a moment later, it had disappeared.

On departing from Corycus, Alex had had the idea that the whole diminished host of Dionysian powers, or at least all those strong enough to make the journey, were accompanying the chariot. By daybreak he had a definite impression that their numbers were diminished, though he still had no clear idea of what the count should be. Perhaps, he thought, the wind of the chariot's passage could not support them all, and those who had been left out had trouble keeping up. Even as that idea occurred to Alex it seemed to him that one of the unseen beings cried out faintly, as if it were swiftly dropping behind.

Only a few moments later he became aware of an odd-looking flight of birds, visible in the growing morning light, bearing in from the dim, gray north as if to head the chariot off.

Perhaps five minutes after first sighting the flying things, Alex realized that they were not birds at all, at least in any ordinary sense. His blood chilled as he realized that they seemed little more than large, inhuman heads with great wings attached. Of course the true scale of size was difficult to determine, but surely such shapes lay outside the ordinary forms of nature.

The creatures were closing upon the chariot with remarkable speed, and before Alex had time to be fully alarmed, there came a midair clash between his own half-visible escort and a dozen of the winged heads, all streaming long, tangled hair. Flying near, the attackers opened beaked mouths that shrieked and honked with laughter, then swerved away as the leopards unsheathed their claws and snarled, causing the chariot to rock wildly in its flight. A moment later, the pair of great cats had somehow increased their pace.

Alex, on his feet again, drew whatever weapon he had, and tried to shout defiance, but the wind of flight whipped his words away so that he himself could scarcely hear them. Some of the heads and faces were more birdlike, and others more batlike, than human in design, and he thought they were built on a scale somewhat larger than humanity. Still it was hard to be sure of size, with nothing near them to judge by.

He could feel his own hair trying to rise upon his scalp, when his eyes told him that the visitors' scalps were each thickly overgrown with a crop of hissing, writhing snakes.

Moments later the largest of the things, wings laboring frantically, drew close enough for him to see its bloodshot eyes, squawked words at him. The language was one that Alex had never heard before, but the content of menace, the intention to inspire terror, were unmistakable. And now from the chariot's other side, another creature suddenly swooped close, near enough to strike at him, it seemed, although he could not see what weapon it might have.

Suddenly it displayed a thin, bonelike arm, wielding a kind of twisted javelin. Evidently the damned thing had six limbs in all, counting its wings. And Alex could also see the claws in which its thin legs terminated. Another of the beings gripped in one hand what appeared to be a living snake, thick as a man's arm, and raised it like a weapon, ready to strike with the reptile's fanged and gaping mouth. Two long snake-fangs came thudding down with a hard impact, to remain embedded in the wood.

A moment later he saw, almost too late, that the flying horror, whatever it might be, also used its beak for a weapon. A savage thrust of head and neck just missed Alex as the chariot swerved, and tore splinters from the wooden railing.

There was no way to retreat, and no place to run. Instinctively Alex thrust back with his blade, feeling the steel go into solid flesh. Then he dealt a hacking blow, decapitating the snake, whose head stayed where it was, while the thick body writhed and fell away.

One of the flying creatures he had struck dropped like a stone. Another, wounded, screamed and fell away, laboring to stay airborne with a damaged wing.

Meanwhile the chariot was rocking and bouncing in midair, as if it had encountered some kind of obstacle, so Alex was terrified of being thrown out; then once more the motion of the vehicle straightened out, and it bored ahead at increased speed.

The leopards were bounding straight for a cloud. Moments later they plunged into the insubstantial barrier and through it at high speed, so that it passed in a mere flickering of disorienting whiteness.

A second cloud was skewered in the same way, and then, after some broad intervening spans of empty sky, a third and then a fourth. Gradually the monstrous enemy was left behind.

Now the passenger noticed that two thin streams of smoke emerged from the wood around the two embedded fangs of the snake's detached head, to be quickly blown into nothingness by the wind of passage. Using the tip of his weapon he pried the thing loose and let the wind of passage whirl it away.

Alex kept looking back. After the last band of clouds had been passed, he thought that the flying heads retreated, falling back farther and farther as the Eye of Apollo rose fully clear of the horizon, launching itself on its long daily passage across the sky. At last, with a reaction of relief that left him feeling weak, he allowed himself to be convinced that they had abandoned the chase and turned away. Soon they had shrunk to mere elongated dots against the far clouds on the horizon, and not long after that disappeared altogether.

A few minutes later Alex, looking ahead and to the right, past the spotted backs of the rhythmically coursing leopards, thought that he could see some kind of island, though at the distance he could not be sure that it was any more than a low-lying cloud. Details were impossible to make out.

Abruptly the chariot altered course, so that now the cloud, or island, lay straight ahead.

"Is that our goal?" the passenger demanded loudly of the rushing air. "The island where I am to find the Face?"

Nothing and no one answered him.

"What's wrong now? What's going on? Why don't you speak?"

He had to shout his questions again and again before at last there came a few words in response: *We grow weak.*

"But is that the island we want?" He was sure that they were now gradually descending.

We must land somewhere soon, or the chariot will fall and you will perish.

The island—now he could see that it was certainly more than a cloud—may have been farther away than Alex had first estimated, or else the great panthers' pace had slowed considerably.

Another hour of the day wore on, and then another. With nothing below him but the trackless sea, it was hard for the weary passenger to even guess at his altitude, but he felt sure that they were considerably lower. And now at last he could see clearly some of the details of their goal. It was a mass of land with the shape of a thick, rough horseshoe, curving a strip of beach around a narrow-mouthed harbor, which at the moment held no ships.

At this range he could still distinguish nothing that might be a Temple of Apollo. Indeed he began to get the impression that there were no buildings at all.

Without warning, the chariot wavered again, not only in its course but, as the passenger thought, in its substantiality, the very reality of its existence. There was a long, horrible moment when Alex thought that he could see right through the rims of the spinning wheels, and even the floor beneath his feet. Then solidity came back, but the vehicle was rapidly losing both speed and altitude. Now abruptly the leopards and their burden plunged down at a sickening angle, the water coming closer with frightening speed. Alex gritted his teeth, then screamed unashamedly in fright.

Keeping his eyes open, he waited until what he judged was the last possible second, then leapt clear of the plunging chariot.

Inevitably he had misjudged the height, and endured a longer free fall and a harder splash into the sea than he had expected. Warm salt water closed over his head, and he struck out blindly. Heavy metal was dragging him down unmercifully, and he unfastened belt and harness, let go all his weapons. A moment later he had slid out of what remained of his clothing, realizing he was going to need all the buoyancy that he could get.

Holding his mouth closed, he framed a silent prayer to Poseidon, a promise of rich sacrifice if his life should be spared. After a frighteningly long struggle he popped out on the surface, gasping. When the motion of the sea lifted him to the top of a gentle swell, he could see the island clearly, with its shoreline still a quarter of a mile away.

Alex had never been better than an average swimmer, but fortunately the sea was calm, the surface water warm. By now the sun was well along in its climb toward the zenith. It remained high in the sky, but it seemed that a long time had passed, before Alex finally waded and crawled ashore, to lie shivering on a sand beach, his naked flesh shriveled with immersion, feeling more like a drowned rat than any kind of conquering hero, or even a useful servant on which the princess might be able to depend. When the last small wave slapped at him from behind, he felt immensely grateful for the last little push of Poseidon's helping hand, though he doubted that any conscious effort by the sea god was involved.

All he could be reasonably certain of was that at least one powerful god, Shiva, would probably be very angry to see Dionysus returning.

The one thing Alex had not even considered abandoning to the sea was the medallion given him by the princess, and the thin double disk of gold and silver still hung on its chain around his neck. He now raised it to his lips and kissed it fervently.

As soon as the castaway felt a little stronger, and had distributed a few heartfelt prayers of thanksgiving among various deities, he got to his feet. Shading his eyes, he turned to scan the sea from which he had emerged. The chariot seemed to have sunk immediately, or perhaps simply disappeared on contact with the water. The two panthers had also vanished without a trace, along with the rest of his inhuman escort. He could only hope that they were not all entirely dead.

Facing inland, he studied the thin scrubby woods beyond the beach. There were a few palm trees, and the ubiquitous laurel on the modest heights inland. There seemed to be no coconuts. Along the first edge of solid land, a few feet above the pale sand of the beach, there straggled a row of dying olive trees.

As soon as he had recovered his breath a little, he started to explore inland.

Alex felt a little better as the sun began to toast his back and shoulders, already heavily tanned, and his activity warmed him too. More than a day had passed since he had eaten his last meal, a poorly digested breakfast in the mess hall, in a place and among people that, if he was lucky, he would never see again.

Here and there he found a few berries he couldn't recognize, but which looked and tasted edible. He wondered if the island held any permanent inhabitants.

Over the next few hours, while the sun slowly declined toward the west, his wandering investigation confirmed the impressions he had gained on his approach. The island was roughly horseshoe-shaped, its outer shoreline perhaps a mile in diameter. The neat natural harbor that Alex had observed while still airborne was indeed currently unoccupied by any ships. He also discovered, to his relief, a small stream flowing right into the harbor, and he immediately bent to drink. The water was brackish close to the beach, but when he had followed it upstream for a quarter of a mile, to near the springs where it had its source, it became good and fresh.

For the first hour or so he found himself looking frequently over his shoulder. But gradually he became convinced that he had the entire island to himself.

He soon came to the conclusion that there were indeed no buildings anywhere, but in several places he found traces of recent human occupation, an occasional footprint and discarded bits of trash. Any place with fresh water conveniently available was likely to be visited frequently by ships.

Thirst was evidently not going to be a problem while he was marooned here, but hunger could certainly become one. There were no cultivated plants, and what grew wild was not reassuring. Scarcity might be due, of course, to the land having been picked over by frequent visitors. There were a few mushrooms that he could recognize as edible, and some berries growing in the patch of woods that covered the island's central elevation. On the next hill he could see what looked like wild grapes, and he walked that way to investigate.

If only he could know that the princess was somehow safe— but he could not know that. He was no closer now to being able to help her than he had been when he was lost in the Labyrinth. Assuming she had been able to escape at all, she was probably getting farther and farther away from him all the time.

On reaching the hilltop, he discovered that the fruit of the wild vines growing there was still much too green to eat. But rummaging around among them soon led to an intriguing discovery. Almost completely hidden by the vines and the surrounding bushes of tall laurel, a few whitish bones of marble came poking out. Digging into the mass of vegetation, the castaway discovered the shattered and age-worn remnants of a building.

There was not much of the structure left, only the skeleton of a single room, a paved floor covering a somewhat larger area, enough for two or three more rooms perhaps, and a low rim of surviving stone wall. If only this could be the temple of Apollo that the sprites had spoken of—but that possibility seemed remote in the extreme. On this island the best that Alex thought he could hope for was survival.

At sunset, some hours after Alex's arrival on the island, one sprite came back to talk to him, much to his relief.

He greeted his almost invisible companion joyfully. "Thank all the gods! I feared that all of you were dead."

Not all the gods are worthy of your thanks.

"Well then, I confine my thanks to those who are. Tell me, tell me, what of the Princess Ariadne? Did she get away from Corycus? And what of the others who were with her?"

There was only a whispering, as of a faint wind, before the contact broke, the visitor vanished. Alex got the impression that the auxiliaries of Dionysus were grown too weak even to talk to him at all. He could only hope that now they might somehow be able to rest and regain some strength.

"Tell me, tell me I beg you, is the princess safe?"

But that question received no answer.

Captain Petros and his crew were eager to put out to sea again as rapidly as possible, and energetically assisted the five fugitives as they scrambled aboard. There wasn't much room on the small vessel, and comfortable spots to sit or even crouch were at a premium, but no one was complaining. Petros and his crew kept casting worried looks about, and their comments indicated that they were chronically worried about running into some ship of the Corycan navy, who were likely to demand tribute. But so far their luck was holding.

Ariadne repeated her earlier question. "Where are we going?"

"I have an idea or two about that," her lover said, frowning into the distance. "But Petros is right, the first thing is to get away from this coast as fast as possible."

At first the wind was unfavorable, and a great deal of maneuvering with the sail was necessary. Theseus was not shy about giving the captain advice on the details of how to do this, while Daedalus grumbled that the whole design of the ship was inefficient. Petros mainly ignored the arguments of both.

It would also be possible to man about ten oars, now that the fugitives were available to pull. Theseus and Daedalus as potential crew members added two strong men, and Ariadne volunteered herself and her slave-girl to row if necessary.

The offer was received in bewildered silence. When the princess proudly announced that she had often rowed for sport at home, the crew looked at her without comprehension.

In any event, the men took care of the oars, while the women contributed by keeping out of the way as much as possible. An hour of rowing was necessary before the wind came around to the right direction, and gained enough strength to be useful. The shoreline receded only slowly.

At last the peaks of the island's small mountains disappeared under the horizon.

The breeze kept on after sunset, and the stars provided guidance. The Princess Ariadne, clinging to her lover's arm, was in a mood to contemplate romantic tales, and she began to relate some of them, that Theseus said he had never heard. There were legends told about some of the constellations, and the role that Father Zeus was supposed to have had in creating them. One was called the Bull, and another, small and comparatively obscure, the Princess. Theseus listened, saying little, now and then nodding indulgently with approval.

One of the crew, perhaps inspired by listening to the stories, began to twang an untuned lyre. In a surprisingly true voice he began to intone an ancient song, in which the singer bragged that he knew more than Apollo—

"—for oft when he lies sleeping,
I see the stars at bloody wars
In the wounded welkin weeping—"

Ariadne had never heard that song before. "What is the 'welkin'?" she asked, perpetually curious, hoping that at least one of her shipmates could provide the information.

But no one knew; or at least no one was interested enough to want to answer.

"What had you planned as your next stop, captain?" Theseus's tone conveyed the idea that the question was not entirely an idle one.

Petros sounded relieved, now that Corycus was out of sight. "Refuge Island. Not too far, and it's a good place to take on water."

It was really necessary to replenish the store of water on board before undertaking a voyage of the length required to satisfy the hopes of either Theseus or Daedalus. For the time being the Artisan pronounced himself content to be leaving Corycus behind.

Refuge Island, as the captain had said, lay at no great distance and offered a dependable supply. Theseus nodded, and said that he had some acquaintance with the place. Ariadne grudged the delay, but when she looked at the depleted water casks she had to admit that it was probably necessary.

The first night the fugitives passed on board the trader was almost uneventful. Ariadne had to fight off seasickness, and got little sleep. Icarus, who had slept longer ashore, now kept people awake reveling in the adventure of it all, and several times came near falling overboard. Petros from time to time questioned his passengers, trying to get a clue as to what his reward was going to be, but they could tell him nothing helpful.

The princess was determined to be gracious. "I repeat, captain, that we are grateful for your help."

"Thank you, ma'am, thank you."

Captain Petros continued to be accommodating. He explained that all his life he had depended heavily on dreams, and had picked up the fugitives after being promised, in a remarkable dream, that his fortune would be made if he did.

When Ariadne questioned him, she was comforted to hear that in his dreams he had spoken with a figure that looked like the Minotaur.

But he hadn't wanted to delay on the shore of Corycus long enough to get water—not a moment longer on that coastline than was absolutely necessary, not even long enough to fill some jugs. Besides, the water there at the marsh had a bad reputation among seafaring folk, it just didn't look or taste right.

Use of the compass-pyx was well-nigh universal. Navigation across the open sea, out of sight of land, was difficult enough even with the help of such devices, and would have been all but impossible without it. The basic device was proven, but Petros, like many sailors and fisherfolk, relied upon some special private magical addition to the instrument that he was keen on keeping secret.

What Petros's secret addition might be was hard to say. The compass-pyx that Ariadne was inspecting now looked much like the instruments that she had been required to practice with in the course of a royal education.

The pointer, or cusp of the device, balanced on a needle-sharp pivot, consisted of a narrow crescent of horn and ivory. A sliver of each of the disparate materials, identically curved and not quite as long as a man's hand, were bound together in a particular way. Some swore that silk was the only proper material to use for the binding, but Ariadne saw now that Petros, like a number of others, preferred the web-stuff of certain mutant spiders.

That gave her pause. She closed her eyes, but no vision came immediately.

Once a pilot or steersman had attuned his mind to the device, it indicated with great accuracy the bearing that the ship should take to bring him to his goal. Few people placed any reliance on the compass-pyx on land; its effectiveness on the Great Sea was credited to Poseidon's having long ago given the device his blessing.

There were of course refinements in the construction and operation of the compass-pyx. Some extremely simple versions were good only for indicating true north; others, if the cap/cover was shifted to the first end, pointed to the nearest dry land.

Many swore that the compass-pyx worked best, indeed that it was only reliable at all, if hooked up with a strip of pure copper that ran deep into the central timbers of the ship.

Daedalus looked at the device mounted in a binnacle near the steering oar of Petros's craft, and pronounced it of tolerably good workmanship. Coming from him, this was a high compliment.

Early the next morning, despite patchy fog, the merchant raised the small island he was seeking, and maneuvered in through the narrow mouth of the harbor.

Petros's crew dropped a small anchor in the still harbor, and then, wading ashore from the shallow-draft vessel, broke out water jugs and wooden kegs from below the single deck, and began to carry them inland. About half a mile upstream, the captain informed his passengers, they could fill them from where a spring flowed pure, into a little rivulet that soon became the brackish stream.

Hardly had they begun this operation, when a larger craft of ominous appearance materialized out of a drift of fog at the mouth of the harbor, and soon dropped anchor there, blocking the narrow entrance.

Everyone froze and stared at it. Giant eyes, suitable for some legendary sea monster, had been painted in bold colors on the bow, and glared threateningly at the pirate's potential victims.

The newcomer appeared to be manned by an energetic crew of twenty, who, even at a distance, gave the impression of being all too eager to drop their oars and pick up weapons. Blades of steel or bronze glinted in the distance.

About half of the merchant crew, loaded with every empty container aboard, had been just about to hike inland and get some fresh water. But the stranger's appearance stopped them in their tracks. The merchant crew knew at a glance that they had no chance to get away from the newcomer, bottled up in the harbor as they were, nor any hope of outfighting her if matters came to that.

Ariadne, bewildered for a few moments, took her cue from the trader captain, who quickly identified the newcomer.

She cried, "*Theseus, they're pirates!*"

Everyone but Theseus seemed perturbed to hear this rather obvious discovery so flatly stated, although no one but Ariadne herself appeared surprised.

Her lover only raised one perfect eyebrow, then nodded, smiling ruefully. "I'm afraid they are," he acknowledged.

"What are we going to do?"

"Well, I wouldn't worry about it if I were you." And then, instead of leading Ariadne inland as she expected, running into hiding on the heels of Petros and his crew, he strolled casually in the opposite direction, out across the sand, waving across the narrowing gap of water at the new arrivals.

A minute later the pirate put a small boat overside, and two men got into it, one of whom rowed energetically for the beach, while the other sat with massive bare arms folded. Theseus walked down toward the water line, to stand, fists on hips, with the wavelets washing over his sandals.

When the little rowboat was close enough for handy communication, he waved an arm, and called in a loud voice, "Hello, Samson. I see you got my message. It took you long enough to get here."

The other acknowledged the greeting with a friendly word of surprised recognition. "Theseus." It was a familiar mode of address, and for a moment Ariadne wondered if this fierce-looking man could be her prince's brother, or some other close relation. "What message? I've had no message from you, or anyone."

What she saw of the passenger as he drew closer was not reassuring. He was an evil-looking man dressed in a loincloth and a vest, his whole body massively muscled. The hilts of blade weapons protruded from three separate sheaths at his belt. Hair grew on his scarred and tattooed shoulders as thickly as on his chest. He wore two rings in each ear, and what appeared to be a small, straight piece of bone in his nose.

"Was expecting to meet you, mate, but not here."

"Don't worry about it. Matters worked out all right."

Looking around her in bewilderment, the princess observed that the trader captain and his crew had now entirely vanished from her sight, having disappeared in the general direction of the center of the island. Only a couple of empty water containers, dropped in haste, and the stirring of some bushes about a hundred yards inland, indicated which way they had gone.

Ariadne moved a step closer to Theseus, and rested one hand on his arm. Her love, and her lover, provided all the protection she would ever need.

The two men who had rowed the little boat ashore were appraising the beached merchantman. One of them climbed aboard, took a quick look into the tiny space belowdecks, and reappeared nodding his head.

"Small, Cap'n Sam, but sound. We can find a use for her. Or get a price."

"Cargo?"

"Not much."

Captain Samson squinted inland. "Too bad the crew's run off. I'll be short-handed for two ships. Think any of your people might be ready to take shares in our enterprise?"

"They won't have gone entirely out of sight just yet," Theseus put in. "Let me see what I can do." Giving Ariadne's hand a reassuring squeeze, he dropped it and strode inland. After a moment's hesitation, the princess followed.

Her lover walked steadily toward a screen of bushes about a hundred paces from the beach, where the princess herself had already noticed movement.

Stopping before he got close enough to alarm anyone who might be there, he called out in a clear, calm voice, "How about it, lads? Samson here's ready to take you on as shipmates. I can vouch for him, he's not a bad sort as a captain. What say you to a different kind of cruise, that has a little profit at the end of it? Otherwise you'll be left here. Not the worst place in the world to be marooned, but . . ."

Slowly, cautiously, part of a head appeared from behind a bush. The trader's captain and at least some of his crew were in there listening.

Daedalus and Icarus, who had already started upstream along the brook when the pirate ship appeared, continued to hurry inland, determined to hide out. Clara had been walking near them, and with a look of mingled fear and determination, had attached herself to them, and the Artisan with a brisk movement of his head unhesitatingly signaled her to come along.

Theseus, who seemed to be blithely assuming that he had full power to represent the pirate captain in negotiations, was now heavily engaged in bargaining with the people who remained hidden in the bushes. At issue now were some details, regarding matters such as the food available on the buccaneers' craft, and the plan according to which future booty would be divided. Meanwhile Samson kept aloof, with folded arms, waiting for the result.

When several questions had been answered, Theseus stood back and folded his arms too, awaiting the decision of Petros and his people. He seemed perfectly at ease, though his manner was absent when he returned Ariadne's anxious smile. There were dozens of questions she wanted to have answered, declarations she wanted to make, but this did not seem the right moment to bring any of them up.

Presently there was a rustling in the bushes. After less than a minute of discussion, the trader captain and his small crew, having evidently discussed and voted on the matter among themselves, emerged as a unit, announcing that they had vowed to stick together.

When Theseus had shepherded them all back to the beach, the pirate captain took his time looking his new recruits over, with the attitude of a man considering the purchase of slaves. At last Samson nodded as if reasonably satisfied.

While these negotiations were being concluded, Ariadne, giving her hair its familiar toss, stood waiting proudly beside her prince, trusting in the calm assurance he had already given her that everything was going to be all right.

Belatedly remembering Clara, she looked around and observed that the girl was missing, as were Daedalus and his child. Briefly the princess was annoyed by her slave's defection. But when she thought about it, she could hardly blame the girl for running off, given the way that any female of low rank was likely to be treated by pirates.

Theseus was back at her side, smiling at her. Only now was it really sinking in. She repeated, "These men are *pirates*!"

He frowned slightly. "There are nicer terms, my love, like 'gentleman adventurer,' or 'soldier of fortune.' I'm one of them, you know. Let me be plain about that, just in case you were still harboring any doubts."

"But your father! The kingdom . . ."

He was quite ready to debate the point. "Well, everything I told you is quite true—in a sense. My father is a pirate too, only much wealthier than I. But of course he's been at the business much longer. He lives in a big house when he's ashore."

"You told me he was a king!"

"And so he is. King of the Pirates—a lot of people call him

that. Ariadne, I suppose I should warn you that often Dad and I don't get along. That has a lot to do with how I found myself shanghaied into being one of the Tribute people sent to your damned uncle." Theseus sighed, with the sound of a man finishing a disagreeable chore. Then he brightened. "Anyway, since we are home now, I thought it was time I filled you in on the family situation."

"Home?" The princess looked around her blankly.

Her lover's gesture took in the sea before them, and the two ships, on the smaller of which Captain Samson was now affixing a striped banner that was evidently his own flag, from the pride he took in fastening it to the mast.

"Home." Theseus pronounced the word with an air of finality, and a certain pride. "I don't have a big house, let alone a palace, anywhere. Not yet."

Ariadne took a step away from him. "Then you lied to me," she got out at last. Her voice was low, almost choking.

"Maybe I did stretch things a little." Theseus paused and grinned at her. "Can't really blame me, can you? After all, I didn't want to take any chances. Not with what Shiva was planning to do to me."

*S*uch cargo as the pirates had been able to discover in the small hold of the trading vessel—water casks, oil jars, dried fish, and extra coils of rope—was nothing to cause wild jubilation in their ranks. But, as Theseus explained to the princess, such modest hauls added up, and formed a large part of the business of pillaging. What they could not use, they could probably sell in some congenial port, and make a small profit thereby. The ship itself, of course, would fetch a nice price—if it were not quickly used up, consumed in the general wear and tear of pirating, which tended to be stressful on men and equipment alike.

Samson manned the captured ship with a prize crew composed mainly of his own people, and including only two or three of the trader's original crew, the captain not among them. Petros accepted the decision philosophically. Despite the fact that the best deal Samson felt able to offer him was service as a simple seaman on the original pirate vessel. "But once a man decides to trust his dreams, he might as well go all the way. I've been a soldier of fortune before. No reason I can't be again."

Petros expressed his philosophy forcefully. But still he continued to appear just a little worried.

Theseus assured him heartily that he had nothing to worry about. Then he turned, and, looking thoughtfully inland, said he was considering whether it might be worthwhile to try to find Daedalus and bring him along. "There are a lot of places where a man like that would bring a very good price."

The princess at first could not believe that she had heard him properly. "You mean—you'd sell him? *Daedalus?* After he helped you to escape?"

Theseus looked at her blankly for a moment, then shrugged. "I thought the idea had some merit; I won't insist on it."

In turn, Ariadne was staring at her lover as if she had never seen him before. She thought that the prince—she had still been thinking of him as a prince though it seemed he really had no legitimate claim to that title—was demonstrating a poor attitude.

"If it weren't for Daedalus," she said to him, "you wouldn't be here now. You'd probably be dead."

Theseus shrugged. "He helped us, we helped him. If he had power over me, and I stood in the way of his solving some problem, how long do you think I'd last?"

Samson overheard some of the talk about trying to chase down Daedalus, but decided quickly that it would involve a lot of effort for a doubtful return. The same went for the slave-girl—it was annoying to have a valuable and entertaining girl get away, but there were plenty of others in the world, and in general they were not too hard to find.

Presently both ships put out to sea.

Ariadne had not been aboard ship long before she became aware that the crew were eyeing her with several varieties and degrees of speculation. Much of this attention was not at all of the kind a princess had been brought up to expect.

"They stare at me," Ariadne said to Theseus, the next time he stood beside her.

"I'll bet they do, you're well worth gaping at. But none of them are going to forget that you are mine—I'll see to that."

"How long are we going to be on this ship?"

"Depends on where we go. As I said before, I've got a couple of ideas about that. I haven't quite decided. It's just great to have a ship again." And he filled his lungs contentedly with ocean air, and let his gaze roam the horizon.

Ariadne continued to be troubled. "You say you 'have a ship.' "

"Mm-hmm."

"But this one is not yours, is it? It's still going to be Samson who decides which way we sail? That's the impression I got from listening to him."

As if regretfully, Theseus ceased his enjoyment of the view. Looking at the princess again, he smiled thinly. "That reminds me. I suppose Samson himself probably still clings to that opinion. I'd better go have a talk with him." And Theseus gave her a wink and presently moved aft, to engage the captain in serious conversation.

Which soon began to grow heated. Ariadne could not hear much of what Theseus and Samson, at the other end of the ship, were saying to each other. But it was plain enough from their faces, and certain gestures that they made, that they had begun to disagree.

The dispute had nothing directly to do with her; she felt reasonably confident of that. From the few words drifting her way, she gathered that it was about what the next object of their pillaging should be. Most of the men were listening too; enough of a breeze had come up to make the oars temporarily unnecessary.

The princess still couldn't hear much of what was said, but the key point of contention was not hard to discover. Theseus was claiming authority, simply as his father's son, and Samson had no intention of turning over his ships and crews to an upstart, on that basis or any other.

Now Samson at last raised his voice. "Once and for all, *Prince*, I understand that's what you like to be called, you'd better get it through your head that both of these vessels are mine now. Both their crews follow my orders, no one else's. I plan to build up a fleet the way your father did."

"My understanding is not the same as yours, Samson."

"Well, I s'pose your father will understand, if I have to feed you to the fishes."

The two men were now standing tall, staring each other levelly in the eye. There was still no murmuring among the crew, but rather a watchful stillness. Ariadne had the impression that some of the men, at least, knew Theseus, though they hadn't seen him for some years. Earlier she had heard one remark that when the prince was last seen he had been only about two-thirds his present size. It seemed obvious to Ariadne that few or none would be ready to side with him in a mutiny. A number of the crew, like the newcomer Petros, obviously didn't know what to think, except that any threat of serious trouble aboard ship made them nervous.

What the usual code of ethics among pirates might be, Ariadne had no idea, but to her it seemed a bad idea for her lover, or anyone, to try to steal another man's ship right out from under his feet. The princess had already edged away from the developing conflict, as far as it was possible to go on a small ship, which was only a few feet—and in her own mind was trying to construct excuses for her lover's unacceptable behavior. Now that they had fallen among pirates, he must of course try to look and sound as much as possible like one of them.

Suddenly turning her back on the argument, she scanned the seas ahead, then closed her eyes. Useless. Now was one of those times when it seemed almost impossible to generate any kind of inner vision—

Ariadne was aroused from fruitless inward contemplation by a shout behind her, and then the sound of some kind of impact, like that of one chunk of solid flesh and bone against another.

If there had been a blow, it seemed to have left no physical mark.

Samson, blaspheming the names of several deities in the process, was telling the young upstart that it made no difference on *his* ship whose son anyone else might be.

Theseus's face was turning red with anger, but his voice stayed steady. "And if I have a remark or two to make on your own parentage?"

The crew had long since given up any pretense of going on with any of their shipboard duties.

The newly acquired ship, Petros's former trader, had been sailing close enough for those aboard to see and hear something of what was going on, and now she was maneuvering closer alongside. This was a matter in which all members of both crews were deeply interested.

There was evidently a protocol for how these things were done. A formal challenge had evidently been issued, Ariadne was not sure exactly how, and a space for the fight was swiftly being cleared on deck. The sun was going down in a welter of bloodred light, and a couple of men were lighting torches against the coming dark.

One of the older crew members had taken charge of managing the formalities.

Ariadne could hear him spelling out the rules, reciting mechanically and grimly what sounded like a well-known formula. A loser who was forced into the sea, or jumped in to escape, would not be picked up again. If both contestants went into the water, neither would be helped out, until the fight had been concluded.

One point remaining to be decided was the choice of weapons. Theseus seemed gloriously indifferent. "Knives if you like. Or hands and feet are good enough for me."

Samson smiled at that. He had respect for the youth's quickness and ruthlessness with a blade, but retained as usual supreme confidence in his own strength and rough-and-tumble skills. "Hands and feet it is." And he shot a meaningful glance in the direction of the princess, which she had no trouble interpreting.

Each man was allowed to wear only a loincloth, doubled and knotted in such a way as to provide some protection against disabling blows to the crotch.

Empty-handed, the two men faced each other. A signal was given and the fight began. The men struck at each other with clenched fists, in boxers' blows, and tried to use their knees and elbows to good effect.

Gripping a railing, Ariadne watched. Just looking at them, she was sure that Samson must have an edge in brute strength and ruthlessness. The only advantage she could see for Theseus was that he looked quicker, and more agile.

If Theseus loses, she thought to herself coldly, *I will throw myself into the sea.*

Again the combatants exchanged blows—Samson missed twice in rapid succession—and then they grappled, wrestling. It was hard for either to obtain a grip. The princess could hear the animal sounds of their lungs working. And now, somehow, Samson's nose was bleeding heavily.

The crew, silent at first, soon erupted in cheers and grunts of sympathy. Ariadne could not tell who they were for, or if they really cared who won, as long as they had the spectacle of the fight to entertain them.

Then somehow Theseus was taken by surprise, tripped, shoved or knocked off his feet. However it had happened, he was down. Ariadne's heart leaped up like a wounded bird inside her, and she uttered a small cry as Samson leaped on his fallen victim. But the leaner body of the man below twisted and writhed away. Several men jumped to their feet, but none attempted to interfere, as the grappling bodies on the deck rolled back and forth.

First Ariadne could not see what was happening, and then she dared not look. Her eyes were turned away when she heard first a horrible choked cry, surely that of a dying man, and then a great mindless roar from the men who had been watching.

Slowly she turned her head back, compelled to know her fate. Theseus was standing erect, his golden curls visible above the ring of watchers' heads surrounding him. Now he seemed to be pushing hard, with one foot, at something on the deck, something that Ariadne could not see for all the men's legs in between. And now that something had gone into the water with a weighty splash, provoking another cheer from the assembled crew.

Scarcely had the waves closed over Samson's body, when Theseus proclaimed himself the new commander.

Looking around him at the crowd of men, he asked, "Anyone else in need of a workout?"

No one else was minded to challenge the victor, who took a plunge in the sea to rinse off the blood and grime of combat, and then was showered with congratulations. Ariadne thought a number of the men were genuinely pleased to be rid of Samson, who had been blustering and unpredictable. Unexpectedly she was reminded of the situation at home, when Minos was overthrown, and Perses hailed and acclaimed.

Theseus was looking back toward the spot where the body of Samson had vanished tracelessly among light waves. "One owner, two ships," he mused. "Yes, I like that idea." He smiled at Ariadne. "We're making progress."

Unable to think of anything to say, she smiled back.

Now in command of two vessels, he had a new look about him, that of a man who felt much more at home in the world than the harried prisoner Ariadne had helped to escape. Now Theseus began to plan what work of piracy he wanted to accomplish next. Ariadne heard only bits and pieces of these plans, as he commented on the jewels and furs she would soon be able to enjoy.

"I had jewels and furs at home," she remarked.

"Why, I suppose you did." Her lover's glance turned speculative, as an idea occurred to him. "Didn't smuggle any gems along with you, by any chance? No? Too bad."

Her reply broke off in the middle of a sentence, for it was obvious that Theseus was no longer listening to her at all. His gaze was fixed somewhere high over her left shoulder, and the look on his face made the princess spin around quickly, eyes searching the sky.

There was a figure there, approaching swiftly, traversing the air like a bird, without any visible means of support, though its shape was all wrong for any bird that she had ever seen, in dreams or waking life.

Shiva had flown within a hundred yards of the ship before the princess recognized him. Ariadne had seen the God of Destruction only once before, and had paid him little enough attention on that howling autumn night, as he stood in the background while she crouched over her father's corpse.

Now the whole crew, eyes wide and jaws dropped in consternation, were watching the god approach.

Some of them still did not understand. "What in the Underworld is that?"

"There's only one thing it can be."

The crew were absolutely in awe, and Ariadne shrank back in terror of this being who had played a role in her father's murder.

When Nandi made his first pass over the ship, most of the crew went down on their faces, prostrate on the deck. One or two got no farther than kneeling. One actually hurled himself overboard, convinced that he personally was the target of divine vengeance. But Shiva ignored the man, and a couple of his shipmates fished him out.

Shiva had never taken a close look at any of the youths and maidens of the Tribute—except for the two or three who had actually been used up. But now, making a rapid survey of the assembly on the deck, he had no doubt from the first moment which of the men was Theseus. Only one still stood erect, and had actually drawn a short sword.

And there beside her lover stood the Princess Ariadne. True to her heritage of royal blood, the princess was standing as straight as she could on the pitching deck.

Shiva flew low, hovering for a moment only a few yards from the ship, studying the man he had come to see.

The young man holding the drawn sword called out in a clear, loud voice, "Dark God, if you mean to claim me as your sacrifice after all, I don't suppose I can stop you. But I mean to try."

There was a long moment of silence. The bull-figure, posing in the air, was steadier than the wooden ship riding the light waves below. Then the god said in his harsh voice, "I have chosen you for greater things than that, son of Aegeus. Perhaps I want for you exactly what you want for yourself. You have not been easy to locate, but as you see, I have taken the time and trouble to do so." And Shiva on his wonderful steed swooped low, and, disregarding the drawn sword, seized the prince of pirates by one arm, and snatched him up into the sky full of low-scudding clouds.

Ariadne and the others watched them go, and she expected her lover to vanish at any moment from her sight—and as soon as that happened, she would hurl herself into the sea.

But that was not to be. Shiva was circling the ship at no very great distance, holding before him on the bull's back the larger body of the mortal man, as he might have held a child. Theseus seemed to have sheathed his sword again.

Several minutes passed before the wingless bull, hooves gracefully and powerfully treading the air, swooped low again, slowly passing directly above the ship, and Theseus was deposited casually on deck, so smoothly that he needed only one brief running step to keep his feet. Then the bull with its divine rider once more shot high into the air, and this time soon disappeared into the distance, in the direction of Corycus.

Theseus waved after it, the gesture of a man speeding some departing friend on his way. But the rider did not look back.

"What happened?" Ariadne breathlessly demanded of her companion. "What did he say to you? What did he want?" Around the couple, most of the crewmen were daring to raise their eyes.

Theseus was standing with his fists on his hips, still gazing after their departed visitor. He had a look on his face the like of which the princess had never seen there before, and had never imagined he would wear. As if he had been stunned, then treated to a vision of glory before he had quite regained his senses.

Time passed, but still her question hung in the air unanswered.

$\mathcal{S}$hiva, having concluded his meeting with Theseus, was coming back to Corycus, wind howling in his ears as he traversed the sky astride the galloping bull-creature, Nandi.

He had delayed his return and prolonged his journey in order to search out alliances and information in certain other portions of the world. Unfortunately for himself, the Destroyer had not succeeded very well in either effort. It seemed to Shiva that other gods had secretly arrayed themselves against him, and he was stubbornly determined to discover who they were who so stubbornly plotted his destruction. That such a conspiracy existed, he did not doubt for a moment.

He had some very good candidates in mind, but he wanted to be absolutely sure.

The more he brooded on the matter, the broader and deeper grew his mental image of the plot against him. It was becoming more and more obvious to Shiva that his divine enemies had engineered the whole course of events over the last few months. The escape of the youths and maidens of the Tribute, the defection of the Princess Ariadne—all these events and others took on sinister meaning as part of an elaborate scheme to attack him.

He brought his mount down on the flat roof of the king's palace, an acre of stone and timber and hardened plaster, presenting to the sky a variation in levels in accordance with the layout of the various rooms below. Welcomed home by Creon the high priest, Shiva informed his human servants that he wanted to determine the full roster of his active enemies.

Creon looked groggy, and was shivering with cold. Rain had wet him while he was waiting for the god's return, though he was accompanied by a pair of acolytes who were trying to hold a silken cover over him.

The Destroyer's Bull of course needed no stabling, in the sense that any ordinary animal would require it. In obedience to his master's will, Nandi had already disappeared.

Shiva looked forward to the time when he would be able to identify his foes with certainty. Then he would rapidly proceed to build an alliance against them—and then, no matter how great they might be, how high in the hierarchy of divinity, he meant to pull them down. And he thought he saw the means of forming a coalition that could accomplish that.

Descending from the roof of the palace, with Creon walking beside him, and the two acolytes following at a respectful distance, Shiva said, "One very important thing that must be remembered about the Faces of the Gods is that they cannot be destroyed. Nor, as history and legends testify, can they ever be buried deeply enough or hidden well enough to keep them out of human hands indefinitely."

"Very true, lord," Creon said. He had no idea why Shiva was suddenly talking about the Faces of the Gods, but he presumed that the reason would be made clear in time.

The god went on, "Since it is very likely that some human will again wear the Face of Dionysus in the near future, I would much prefer it to be a human of my own choosing—so I intend, if I can, to put that Face into the chosen human's hands before some unreliable person, or even one of my enemies, can pick it up."

Creon asked deferentially, "Is it permitted to ask whom you have chosen to be the Twice-Born, great lord?"

It was only natural, Shiva thought, that at least one of his own worshipers would like to claim that privilege for himself. But the god considered that that man would be too ambitious, as a divinity.

He looked sideways at the wet and worried man walking beside him. "My dear Creon, you make a much better high priest than you would a god."

The other's face fell. Bitter disappointment, obviously. But such was the fate of human dreams in general.

Shiva continued thoughtfully, "But you wanted to know my choice. A fair question. Easy enough to say, that it should be someone easily led. Who would continue to take my orders, even when he felt the divine power flowing in his own veins. But strange things happen to mortal men, aye and to women too, when they undergo that transformation."

Creon had regained an appearance of calm. He said, "Your Lordship's own power is certainly greater than any that some mere mortal might gain by putting on the Face of Dionysus."

"Yes, of course. Greater where it counts most, or so I should like to think. More direct, at least. The abilities of the God of Many Names are . . . subtler than my own. Nevertheless, they are considerable. Whoever gains those talents, those attributes, will want careful watching.

"Therefore, my chosen candidate is—Theseus, Prince of Pirates. And I have just come from telling him so."

"Theseus?" Creon was shocked and uncomprehending. The infant skulls of his necklace displayed their almost toothless grins, as if mocking the dismay of the one who wore them.

Maybe, thought the God of Destruction, this man was not even worthy of his present office. But who was better qualified?

Shiva said to him, "I know the objection you are about to make—he is far too ambitious, and as a god he could become a mighty rival. However, I think you are mistaken. The prince of pirates is aggressive and unpredictable as a mortal, true. But with his talent for self-defense, I think Theseus will last a long time in a position of divinity—as did his predecessor. Why bother to give a Face to a weakling? Likely he would soon manage to lose his life, and the business would have to be done over again."

Creon bowed low. He had managed to recover fully, and was once more projecting his usual appearance of happy subservience. "Your will be done, lord. The ways of your wisdom are unfathomable to mere humans like myself."

"And, unlike yourself, the pirate prince displays an almost unlimited capacity for wine, women, and song. When he finds all the opportunities of godhood lying open to him in those directions, I think he will have little energy left over for serious matters."

* * *

Having now reached an interior courtyard of the palace, Shiva dismissed his high priest and the other attendants who had begun to follow him. Now he entered a covered passage through which he could pass privately to a certain nearby temple, which had now become his own. On the way the walking god encountered only a few humans, all of them bowing deeply, or crouching in attitudes of terror, faces averted. All this was as it should be.

As soon as Shiva had passed inside his private citadel, a place where he felt relatively safe, a divine weariness came over him. With a gesture he banished the temple prostitutes who had been waiting; all his energies must be conserved, channeled into the purposes for which they were needed most. Dismissing also the few remaining servants, he entered a hidden room where he lay down to sleep. In this inner sanctuary, a private retreat within a fortress, he knew he would be fiercely guarded by the humans and the things of magic that he commanded. Still it was not without misgivings that he barred the room's only door and went to his couch.

Even a god, it seemed, was not exempt from the requirement of having to sleep sometime. And even here, in his stronghold, strange dreams continued to annoy him.

Slumber claimed him quickly, and Shiva was plunged promptly into a bewildering dream. There was a bull, with baleful eyes, whom he could not recognize. It was certainly not Nandi.

This vision included, among its other strange events, a troubling vision of Apollo. Turning restlessly on what should have been a comfortable couch, the God of Destruction saw the beardless youth, wrapped in his white robe, gripping his Silver Bow, and engaged in what seemed a friendly conversation with the Minotaur.

Even while he remained asleep, the man who was an avatar of Shiva suspected that it was Asterion who was sending him this vision. Someday he intended to meet the bull-man, face to face in waking life. But dreaming or waking, Shiva was in no hurry. He had many enemies, and one could never be too careful.

Next in his dream he saw the seared and wasted ghosts of

those he had destroyed. The nearer ones, the more recently slain, were plainest in his sight. These included the caged and naked youths and maidens of the Tribute. But Shiva was able to see many of the others clearly too. There was a long, long line of them, and the previous Minos stood among them. Their shades would still be active in the Underworld, and it would be reckless to assume that even from there none of them could ever act against him in revenge.

Memory, accumulated by a long series of previous avatars, held substantial evidence that Shiva had sometimes played a constructive role in the world—but he who wore the Face at present was not interested in such matters.

Rolling over on his couch he muttered, half-asleep, "Perhaps my predecessors did not understand what power is for."

He could gladly endure some troubling dreams, if only they would provide him with the information that he needed.

In a few hours he awakened fully. Though he felt far from rested, there were things he must do. Unbarring the door of the small secret room, he quickly called in his attendants to report to him on all that had happened while he slept.

Shiva listened to a series of reports, all rather useless, from his Corycan priests.

Left alone again, Shiva returned obsessively to his chief concern, determining exactly the identity of certain other divinities who were conspiring to destroy him, and what their next move against him was going to be.

Of the names of one or two he could feel absolutely certain. He had no doubt that Apollo must be his enemy, and gods and men alike might well tremble to have such a foe.

The latest avatar of Hephaestus, said to be new in his position and recently allied with Apollo, had given no signs of friendship for Shiva either.

On the other side of the ledger, Shiva's most reliable supporter would probably be Hades, Lord of the Underworld, and it would be hard to find a mightier ally than that.

Some help could be expected from a host of less eminent

denizens of the Underworld. Thanatos came especially to mind. Not that any of them were particularly trustworthy; but most, and Hades in particular, could be counted on to try to help any enemy of Apollo.

Later in the day, Creon was back, once more talking matters over with his god. The chief priest toyed with his necklace of imitation skulls, perhaps with the stuffed cobra he also wore, and said, "And . . . the Thunderer?"

The skulls in Shiva's own necklace were all genuine bones, and of course all human. As adult human crania would have been awkwardly large, the god found it more convenient to use only those of infants and small children. Sometimes he wondered how his predecessors had managed. The available memories on the subject were fragmentary; the current avatar took this as a sign that the question had not much interested the god, whatever his mortal predecessors in the character had thought.

To his priest he said, "I think that for a long time, no one has had certain knowledge of the whereabouts of mighty Zeus." A lowering of the voice. "It might even be that his Face lies unclaimed, somewhere."

"My lord, I believe King Perses has had this idea for some time. I assumed that he had communicated it to you."

Shiva nodded calmly, trying to remember whether Perses had ever said anything of the kind to him. Sometimes his memory was not all that he could wish it to be.

"Somewhere in the Labyrinth," added the god at last, making it half a question.

"That is the indication, lord."

Creon always swore that his sources were reliable, even though for magical reasons he was forbidden to reveal them. Of course it was impossible to check on them directly now.

"The most priceless object in the universe could be here, waiting to be picked up!"

Once the idea had begun to grow in Shiva's mind, it was impossible to forget it, or to keep from speculating on the subject. But neither god nor man could be sure. A hush followed that declaration.

Shiva considered ordering his priest-magician to try to arrange a face-to-face meeting with Hades. But, in truth, even he, the God of Destruction, was somewhat afraid of that dark power. In the accepted scheme of classical theology, Zeus, Poseidon, and Hades divided the rule of the whole universe among them, being respectively the lords of sky, sea, and the Underworld. But in this late age of the world it seemed that gods seldom or never did anything except through the medium of their Faces, and then only when those were worn by humans. However the system might have been established, great confusion and uncertainty resulted.

Pondering all these matters intensely, the God of Destruction decided that he would first try to call Asterion to account. "I am going into the Labyrinth. We must talk to this great beast and see what we can learn."

But even Shiva, like everyone else, would think twice before doing grievous harm to any child of Zeus.

It occurred to him to wonder whether Asterion might know where the Face of Zeus was hidden. And what might happen if the Minotaur himself tried to put it on and become a god?

Looking for Asterion, determined to try to settle the matter of the dreams, he once more called up Nandi, and on his wingless, galloping mount went flying back and forth over the four square miles of the Labyrinth, looking down into the thousand miles and more of tedious windings.

Whether he skimmed low or soared to an eagle's height apparently made little difference. There were literally thousands of places where man or monster could be hiding, in the scattered clumps of vegetation or in any of the many roofed segments of passageway. The God of Destruction could not escape the uneasy feeling that Asterion, mortal or not, was not likely to be found, even by a divine power, unless he wanted to be found.

But at last he spotted the Bull-man, standing still on his two human legs and looking up.

Shiva commanded his mount to land.

Even before dismounting, he said, "This time, monster, we are both of us fully awake. That should put you at something of a disadvantage."

I, Asterion, had been looking over the mysterious central portion of the Labyrinth when the God of Destruction came upon me. Most of these windings I had visited a hundred or a thousand times before in waking life, and so I was not sure what I expected or hoped to find. If Daedalus had not been able to fathom the secrets of this ruin, how could I expect to do so?

For some time I had observed the God of Destruction in his cruising search over my domain, and when he descended I was as ready for him as I could be. Meanwhile the girl, Edith, who had begun to grow accustomed to my Minotaurish presence, still cowered down when Shiva appeared. At the last moment, his close approach proved too much for her. Reminded inescapably of the horror of the day of sacrifice, she panicked, screamed that the devil had come for her again, and ran away.

I did not even attempt to call her back, but hoped that she might safely lose herself for the time being in the endless convolutions of the Labyrinth.

The god, perhaps annoyed at having to cruise for so long above the Maze before he could locate me, dismounted promptly. While Nandi stood snorting and pawing the pavement in the background (perhaps wondering who this being might be with a head so like his own) his master exchanged chilly greetings with me. Then Shiva demanded, "Where is the Face of Dionysus?"

The question startled me at first. "Still buried in the head of the human who was wearing it last fall, for all I know." But as soon as I began to think about the question, I was no longer surprised. The avatar of the Twice-Born who had visited the palace in the autumn had certainly seemed unhealthy.

The lid of my visitor's Third Eye cracked open just a trifle, offering me a hairline glimpse into a pit of molten silver. "You will show me some respect, Bull-man. Or suffer for your impudence."

At last I was beginning to be frightened, but I reminded myself that it is always a great mistake to show fear when confronted by a dangerous wild beast. I folded my huge human arms and looked straight back at the Third Eye. "The world holds greater gods than you, Destroyer. I give respect where it is due."

And then I winced and moved involuntarily when a lance of fire darted from the Third Eye, passed close over my right shoulder, and with a sizzling sound incinerated a small section of one of the Maze's walls behind me, stone and wood vanishing together, as I saw when I slowly turned my head to assess the damage. Of course my movement would have been much too slow to save me, had the beam been directed at me.

Wisps of smoke had been left hanging in the air. But so far Shiva had been careful not to harm a hair on the heads of the children of Zeus.

Now Shiva's hoarse, strained voice dripped words on me like liquid acid. "You persistently intrude upon my dreams, Minotaur."

Still I stood with folded arms, not retreating an inch, though I could feel a fine trembling in my limbs. I hoped that I could conceal the effort that it was costing me to be brave; my antagonist seemed excited beyond the point where he could pay any attention to subtleties. "I might say the same about you, slayer of infants." My voice remained reassuringly steady. "Understand that I do not particularly enjoy your company, either waking or asleep."

"Listen, monster! You ought not rely too much for protection upon legends concerning your illustrious parentage."

I could think of no quick answer to that, and I could see in the three-eyed face that Shiva believed he had made an impression upon me. After a moment he added, to press the point, "There are the princesses, your sisters, to be considered."

"Harming either one of them will not endear you to the people of Corycus."

Shiva's expression showed what he thought of the great mass of ordinary humans.

"Or to the Thunderer, either," I added.

"I have warned you not to rely on that. No one wants to claim you as a son—certainly Minos never did. It seems to me he spent almost twenty years plotting ways to be rid of his monstrous burden—you are a rather ghastly creature, after all."

The idea was hardly a new one to me, and I was able to confront it calmly enough. I shook my horned head. "Whatever Minos may have thought of me, he never contemplated my destruction. It would have been perfectly easy for him, as for any king, to quietly dispose of any infant born in his household and under his control."

"Still," said Shiva, "he did choose to hide you from the world."

"Did he?"

"Of course." My enemy's gaze moved about, taking in the Maze. "What do you mean?"

"What do I mean? Just think about it." And I gestured at the surrounding walls. "What a flawed and futile way to try to conceal someone's existence! To house him in the center of one of the world's most famous mysteries, making it impossible for people ever to see him—or forget him. Creating a legend, demanding international tribute in his name.

"No, it seems to me much more likely that my royal father—or stepfather if you will—had some goal in mind for his wife's offspring, Zeus's bastard. And my uncle is planning something now, you may be sure."

Shiva's lip curled, a sign of contempt for any plans that Perses might be making. "What other gods have approached you lately, monster?"

Again he had surprised me. "Other gods? None. What do you mean?"

But a silent sneer was all the answer I received. My visitor called Nandi to him, and in a moment had sprung into the air again.

When Shiva was gone, I looked around for Edith. At first I assumed that she had not gone far, but soon I became worried and began to search for her. At last I called her name repeatedly, aloud.

All in vain.

For days now I had been trying to think of some way to arrange for Edith to get home—as well as to get the Princess Phaedra out of house arrest—but even if that could be managed, I feared it was even possible that Edith's father, when he saw her return home, would assume she had escaped unlawfully, and, fearful of the wrath of Minos, send her back to Corycus.

But, as I discovered later, only minutes after Edith fled in panic from Shiva's presence, she had fallen into the hands of some of the Butcher's soldiers, who were using the marked pathway to maintain a presence near the center of the Labyrinth. She was soon put aboard Aegeus's ship and dispatched toward Dia.

The next time I fell asleep, I had a dream of darkness, in which I heard the voice of someone (I could not see who) observing, "What do you suppose would happen if—but no, that's too grotesque."

"What?" responded another invisible being.

"*Suppose the Minotaur tried to put on a god's face?*" The unknown speaker sounded shocked.

There was a murmuring, as of an audience. It seemed that no one felt confident of what might happen in that case. But several were frightened by the thought.

Including me. I stirred in my sleep, and must have groaned aloud. Suppose I were to come upon the Face, the power, of Dionysus—or of Zeus himself? What would I do with it? Would I be too frightened to put it on, or too frightened not to do so?

Shiva was holding audience, for a group of flying heads, creatures similar to Furies, the product of ancient odylic engineering. They came before him, groveling extravagantly, nightmare things, some of them with snakes for hair, others with the heads of dogs. They entered his chamber hovering in a swarm; those that entirely lacked legs or bodies were more or less compelled to remain air-borne at all times.

In some jockeying among them for position, one of these last had been forced down to the ground, and now for the time being it could only lie there, like a winged egg, the ugly face tilted far to one side.

These creatures reported, to Shiva or his priest, that one morning, very recently, they had seen the usual entourage of Bacchus in full retreat, leopard-drawn chariot and all, westward bound from Corycus, high above the sea. The Dionysian powers had been carrying a mere mortal with them in their retreat, and they were obviously weakening.

Shiva demanded, "They were carrying only one?"

That was confirmed, in a chorus of ugly voices and jerky gestures.

"This is very important. Can you be sure that the figure in the chariot was a mere mortal?"

The heads—some mutant version of Harpies, it would seem—pirouetted on their wings in midair, and tried to find the breath to laugh. They could be absolutely sure.

Speaking of the Dionysian powers they said, "They know where the Face of their dead master lies; and they are carrying someone there to put it on."

"Do they indeed?" the God of Destruction questioned. "If they were originally headed for Dia, perhaps so. But my candidate ought to get there first." That too was very likely. But the leopard chariot had changed course abruptly when the heads attacked, and made for a scrap of land known as the Isle of Refuge, a place where human sailors of all kinds often took refuge in storms and other emergencies, and stopped to replenish their stores of fresh water.

Doubtless the satyrs' and sprites' original destination had been some other island, more directly to the west, and more distant from Corycus. Dia was a good possibility. Or maybe they had even been heading for the mainland in that direction, beyond the rim of the Great Sea.

"No doubt the Face of your enemy can be discovered there, Lord Shiva."

"Very likely. Who was the man the leopards were transporting?"

The heads, the Furies, did not know. They had never seen him before.

$\mathcal{A}$lex, after spending a few hours in exploration of the small island, mastered his impatience as best he could, and settled down to wait. For his vigil he chose a spot on one of the higher hills, very near the ruined temple, from which he could conveniently keep an eye on the harbor. Everything he had observed about the island so far suggested that ships put in here fairly frequently, to get fresh water, or to take refuge from bad weather. But it would be important to be able to look each visiting vessel over, from a safe distance, before applying to be taken aboard.

Since coming ashore he had been mentally rehearsing a short speech, in which he intended to present himself to the populace as a shipwrecked mariner, and appeal for their help. But within a couple of hours of his arrival, he had been forced to the conclusion that there was no permanent population at all. He was going to have to make his speech to another crew of sailors.

The ruined temple—on second look he thought it had probably been no more than a shrine—occupied a position where, except for the overgrowth of greenery, it would have been fairly conspicuous, on one of the highest points of the island. Its location was further disguised by the fact that most of the walls and roof had fallen in. What was left of the building was almost completely overgrown by wild grapes and laurel, the latter in the form of evergreen shrubs and small trees.

He had never tried the taste of laurel berries before; he sampled one now, making a face at the bitterness and spitting out the single seed. One was enough to convince him, despite his hunger, that they must be poisonous.

The building, temple, shrine, or whatever it was, could never have been large, even when it was intact; that much was shown by the limited size of the foundation, and the relative thinness of the remaining walls. The higher portion of one of those walls bore inscriptions, carved with an air of permanence, doubtless as old as the building itself. They appeared to be in several different languages, none of which Alex could begin to read. The only section of roof remaining, a kind of miniature dome, was small and covered a chamber that must once have been a kind of anteroom. Now birds had adopted what was left of the dome, as a good site for nest-building. Well, it would offer some shelter from the rain that was sure to come.

Alex spent what seemed an interminable series of hours impatiently watching for a ship, meanwhile trying to stave off hunger by nibbling such fruit and mushrooms as he could find, and were not too bitter to be eaten. Once, when the tide seemed at its low, he went down to the beach, to search for shellfish in the shallows. The effort proved futile, shellfish being absent while other small creatures darted away over the sandbanks before he could try to grab them; had he been able to retain his knife, he would have tried to whittle a fishing spear.

In this manner he passed the remainder of the day. Most of his hours were spent in the shade, out of the broiling sun, brooding on the possible meanings of the various things the Dionysian spirits had said to him, and on the problem of what he was to do if he should never hear from them again.

The moon was getting on toward full, appearing vague and blue in the eastern sky before sunset; and when, after sunset, Alex watched it from his high place, it made a vast shimmering on the sea, like silver burning. When he slept, choosing for his bed the anteroom of the shrine or temple, he tried to keep watch in his dreams for the Lord Asterion. But such visions as came held nothing that he could recognize as helpful, and when he awoke even their trivial content had slipped from his memory like water from a clenched fist.

As Alex had expected, he did not have very long to wait for the next ship. On the second morning after his own arrival, two of them appeared in rapid succession. First a small trader, rather nondescript, entered the harbor. Then within the hour a larger vessel, of perhaps twenty oars, hove into sight, blocking the entrance.

Watching as closely as he could from his vantage point in a tree well up on temple hill, perhaps two hundred yards above the harbor, Alex didn't like the look of the bigger vessel, with the ominous painting on its bow. He had no personal experience of pirates, but like everyone else had heard some hair-raising stories.

Anxiously he shifted from one observation post to another, working his way closer to the beach, trying to get a better look at what was happening. A few people were milling about down there, but he couldn't see any of them very well. He had about decided that he must work his way closer still, when he observed three people, energetically making their way inland together. In the lead came a nearly naked man whose brown hair was turning gray, closely a young woman and a child, neither of them much better clothed. Already the three had put a substantial screen of vegetation between themselves and the people on the beach. They were all looking back frequently over their shoulders as if in fear of pursuit—there was none—and were coming toward Alex at a good pace, though they had not seen him yet.

Quickly he decided that he must question these folk, and dropped down from his tree.

The trio had not come much closer before he realized that there was something familiar in the woman's appearance.

Alex had never actually seen the Artisan, who had spent almost all his time on Corycus in the middle of the Maze; but this man certainly fit the descriptions he had heard of Daedalus.

The man and boy stopped in their tracks, staring at the naked man who seemed to have popped out of nowhere, perhaps thinking they had come upon some savage native of the island. But the slave-girl hardly paused, having recognized Alex at once.

And Alex was now close enough to be certain that she was Clara. Eagerly he looked downhill past the girl, nursing a faint hope that the princess might be following her slave in flight. But it was not to be.

As soon as Clara had finished the necessary introductions, she said to Alex, "We had given you up for lost. What happened to your clothes?"

"They're gone. I couldn't help losing them, I had a long swim getting here. I very nearly drowned—and I didn't know whether any of the group managed to get away or not. Tell me, where is the princess?" It came out as an urgent plea.

"Down on the beach." The slave, sounding not terribly concerned about the fate of her mistress, turned her head slightly in that direction.

"Really? Is she—is she—?"

"She was quite all right a few minutes ago, hanging on her lover's arm. But I had no such protector there."

Meanwhile, Daedalus was squinting at the gold and silver medallion, which still hung on Alex's naked chest. "I made that ornament for the princess, soldier. May I ask how you come to have it?"

Alex straightened his shoulders. "The Princess Ariadne gave it to me, sir. It's the one thing I was determined not to lose, even if I drowned."

"She simply made you a present of my handiwork?" Daedalus seemed to find this difficult to understand.

"It was a reward, sir. I was able to tell her something she considered very important."

"But how did you get here?" the Artisan demanded of him. "Don't tell me you swam all the way from Corycus."

"No sir, hardly that far. But you may find the true story not much easier to believe. I was helped by the powers of Dionysus, though the god himself is dead. How about yourself?"

The three new arrivals on the island took turns in relating the essentials of their own journey. Among them the newcomers had nothing in the way of a spare garment to lend Alex, being themselves down to the minimum in that regard. The fine linen shift in which Clara had begun her journey out of the Labyrinth had been shredded in a number of places, and was in danger of disintegrating entirely. The man and boy were still wearing the leather aprons in which they had begun their flight, and Icarus had lost his sandals somewhere. Nor had they any food to offer the other cast-

away, and hope dimmed in their faces when he related the difficulties of foraging.

While Alex led them on to higher ground, the three offered
more details of their escape. There was some discussion of the
recent arrival of a pirate ship, and the different reactions of Theseus and the Princess Ariadne.

On being reminded of the princess, Alex once more scrambled up a tree, and strained his eyes studying the people on the
beach in the sun-bathed harbor. He was a little farther from them
now, much too far away for ready identification, but all the people
he could see down there now looked like men.

Daedalus, grunting, clambered up beside him, squinted into
the sun, shook his head, and said, "The ship we arrived on is lost,
I fear. The pirates have surely taken her over. And I believe the
crew of our ship has joined them."

"But what will happen to the princess?"

The older man remained calm. "That the fates must decide.
The last I saw of her, she was still clinging quite willingly to her
handsome prince, who is quite nonchalant about his real profession as a pirate. She may well be regretting her attachment by
now."

"Why do you say that?"

"Well . . ."

Both men dropped down from the tree. Alex was mightily
upset, having to face the fact that the princess would be taken
aboard a pirate ship, by her lover Theseus, who had turned out to
be no better than a buccaneer himself. Alex feared for Ariadne's
safety—nor did it ease his concerns to hear that in spite of everything she still clung closely to her lover's arm.

In his helplessness he reacted by becoming unreasonably
angry with Clara. "Could you not have stayed with her?"

The girl gestured awkwardly. "I don't know, sir, what good
that would have done."

"No. No, you are right, of course." Alex raised both hands
and tugged at his hair. "Oh, gods! If only I could *do* something!"

It crossed his mind that he might, of course, run down to the
beach even now; if the pirates did not kill him at once, and if they

were willing to take him aboard their ship, he might at least be near the princess for a while. But how could he be of any possible use to her under those conditions?

It seemed that, short of being able to summon some kind of human army or navy, only the powers of a god had a chance of helping Ariadne now. Therefore, before he, Alex the Half-Nameless, could be of any use, he must gain the strength that the helpers of Dionysus had promised him—but to do that he must somehow reach the proper island, and the proper temple!

Another look in the direction of the beach, and the two ships, confirmed that all the people there seemed to be getting along peacefully, at least for the moment. Daedalus, counting heads at a distance, confirmed that the entire crew of the merchant had decided to join the more irregular enterprise.

"Which is not really surprising," the Artisan observed. "The distinction between trade and piracy is often somewhat unclear, and many seafaring men change back and forth several times during their professional lives."

"I suppose so. But . . ." Alex was not comforted.

In a little while, everyone on the beach had gone peacefully aboard one or another of the two vessels. Soon both hoisted sails, and tacked their way out of the harbor, carrying with them Alex's last chance to attend the princess as a mere human. It now seemed to him that on the deck of the larger ship, he could make out a bright speck that might well have been sunlight on Ariadne's light brown hair.

After watching the two ships out of sight, the refugees agreed that there was little they could do now but wait for yet another ship to put in. When one that looked like a decent trader arrived, one that was not Corycan, they would emerge from hiding and ask to be taken aboard.

"If only we don't all die of hunger first," Icarus complained.

Alex led his three new companions back to the heights, near the place where he had been waiting alone, where they established a kind of camp.

Restless Icarus soon returned from a mushroom-hunting

foray into the brush, with the announcement that he had discovered someone's broken house—it was of course the same building that Alex had already started to examine.

Daedalus, perpetually and professionally curious, went to see, pulling some vines away from the crumbling masonry that he might have a better look.

"Practically useless as a shelter," he observed.

The building was mostly ruined, but the Artisan thought that the paintings on the wall-remnants depicted some worship of a sun-god. No one else could tell what the dim and doubtful figures were supposed to be doing.

Daedalus soon produced flint and steel from a waterproof oilskin wallet that he carried attached to his apron's belt, and quickly had a small fire going in a slight hollow of sandy ground. There was a notable lack of things to cook, but at least a symbol of civilization had been established.

The Artisan told Alex that his ultimate goal was to reach a certain mainland kingdom, Megara, whose ruler had once offered the Artisan a place of honor at his court. There he could hope to bring up his son in reasonable safety and stability.

The slave-girl asked, "And will there be room in that household for me, as well, my lord?"

Alex was somewhat surprised to see how familiarly the Artisan reached out a callused hand to stroke her hair. It was the gesture of a man who knows a woman well.

"There had better be," Daedalus said. "I grow fond of you indeed." When his fingers touched her slave's collar he added musingly, "We must soon find a way to get this off."

In his continued desperation regarding the Princess Ariadne and her fate, Alex soon found himself confiding in the others more details of his search for the Face of Dionysus.

After their evening meal of roots and berries, augmented by some eggs Icarus had pillaged from a nest in a tall tree, Alex asked Daedalus, whom he considered a wise and trustworthy older man, for his advice.

The question now having been raised, of what a man ought to

do if offered the chance to put on a Face, Daedalus said without hesitation that he would definitely refuse.

"Would you really?"

The Artisan nodded slowly. "I find that merely being a man presents me with quite enough problems; I have no wish to assume those that must come with being a god." With a finely splintered twig he picked out a bit of eggshell from between his teeth.

Alex found this attitude hard to understand. "But think of the powers one would gain!"

"And what have the gods ever done with all the powers they have accumulated? Do they experience great happiness? Contentment? Such glimpses as we catch of their lives do not encourage that idea." Daedalus picked up a handful of sand, letting it sift through his fingers. "There are other ways for a man to increase his capabilities. To find a plan for dealing with the universe."

The slave-girl, on the other hand, proved to have a head full of glorious daydreams that she yearned to put into effect, if she were ever given the chance.

"If I could only be Artemis—" At that point Clara broke off, evidently deciding that some of her dreams were still best kept private. To cover the sudden pause, she turned to the youngest member of the group. "What god would you like to be, Master Icarus, if you had the choice?"

The boy looked up with shining eyes. "I want to be Ares!"

"Bad choice," his father growled. "Who've you been listening to? Ares means war, and war destruction. Any fool can kill, and break, and burn."

Icarus was subdued, but did not appear entirely convinced that his selection was a bad one.

Clara had returned to her own dreams, and was fingering her simple metal collar. "But what would a goddess do, if she found herself wearing one of these?"

"I have no doubt that it would be gone, in the next instant." The Artisan nodded briskly. "Yes, I must find a way to get that collar off your neck."

Alex offered no comment. In most lands ruled by law, or by

the authority of a monarch, the removal of the badge of slavery, by any mere mortal human, would of course be seriously illegal; but on this island, he supposed, the only lawmakers were the pirates and the gods. Certainly the Princess Ariadne would not begrudge her favorite companion a chance at happiness.

Daedalus was looking at him shrewdly. "What of your future, soldier? We would all of us like to help the Princess Ariadne, who has done her best to help us. But we don't even know where she's going now, or where we may be tomorrow. It's quite likely that none of us will ever see her again. Under the circumstances, you may find it hard to continue your devotion."

Alex explained that the sprites and other Dionysian powers had revealed to him that the Face of Dionysus was hidden in some Temple of Apollo, on some island. "But I don't know which temple, or where to look for it. They were gone again, off into thin air, before I could find that out."

"That is unfortunate," the Artisan observed. "There are a thousand islands in the Great Sea, as a conservative estimate, and shrines to the Sun-god can probably be found on most of them. Not to mention the countless numbers on the mainland."

Alex nodded wearily, and glanced at the broken wall nearby. "I doubt this ruined structure was the temple they had in mind. Or that this island was their original goal, because when I was riding in the chariot we had to alter course to get here; and here I am, and I see no Face. And I very much doubt that the temple the powers were talking about is on Corycus, or they wouldn't have carried me so far away. Besides, I don't think the island where the usurper rules contains any temples to Apollo."

Daedalus shook his head. "Not any longer. Shiva, may all three of his eyes go blind, has seen to that."

When night fell, the fire was allowed to die down; the air remained reasonably warm, and the Artisan felt confident of being able to kindle another when required.

Alex soon found himself alone, Daedalus having indicated in certain polite but definite ways that he and his woman would appreciate a bit of privacy, to make sure of which they retreated out of sight, a little distance down the hill. Well, that was natural enough. Clara was well-shaped and young, and her torn dress was definitely provocative. Had Alex not been obsessed with thoughts of his princess, he would very likely have been trying to persuade the slave-girl to spend some time alone with him.

Sleep would not come at once, and the young soldier soon found himself sitting upright in what had once been the main entrance of the ruined temple—or perhaps shrine—staring out at a sea exotically silvered by moonlight. He was hoping without much hope for some return of the Dionysian sprites, when a slight noise nearby made him turn his head, to see small Icarus emerging from the bushes.

"Hello," said Alex.

"Hello." The boy was naked as an egg, having evidently shed his leather apron in preparation for sleep. "They are keeping each other warm over there, and they wanted me to go somewhere else."

"I see. Well, you are welcome to stay here, if you like. It seems I am to have no other visitors."

Icarus sat down close beside Alex, and immediately reached out to finger the medallion hanging on the man's chest. "My father made this," he said. "I watched him do it."

"Yes, I know. We were talking about that, but I suppose you weren't listening. He gave it to the Princess Ariadne, and she gave it to me."

"Why?" the child demanded.

"To reward me. As I explained to your father, I was able to tell the princess something that she . . . considered to be very important."

"What do you keep in it?" the boy asked curiously.

"Keep in it?"

"Yes. Don't you know? It opens up. Like this." Shifting position, the son of the Artisan worked on the medallion momentarily with two small, nimble hands, and suddenly it sprang open, the thin disk of silver that formed its back separating from the equally attenuated circle of gold that made the front. Only a single hinge of ingenious construction, practically invisible, still joined the two halves together.

And something, a certain object that had been folded with eerie skill, compressed with supernatural cleverness, into the thin secret compartment between the gold and silver—that something now fell out, to land on Alex's right thigh.

It was a transparent thing, roughly the breadth and thickness of a man's hand, and it felt warm and tingled when it touched his skin. Alex made an odd sound in his throat, and a moment later he had jumped to his feet, clutching in both hands what he knew must be the Face of some god—doubtless Dionysus.

Never before had he seen or touched anything of the kind, and yet he had not the least doubt of what it was. It was shaped like a mask, or rather a fragment of a mask, large enough to cover about half a human face. From near the middle of the fragment, a single transparent eye stared back at the man who clutched it in his hands.

Again Alex uttered a strange noise, born of joy, astonishment, and fear. Young Icarus, alarmed by Alex's behavior, jumped to his feet also, and backed away.

For a short and yet unmeasurable time the young man stood there, holding the object that he could not doubt contained the powers of a god. For the moment it seemed impossible to breathe.

The moonlight seemed to show that some substance, or some kind of energy, inside the Face of Dionysus was engaged in rapid movement—a ceaseless, rapid flow of something that might have been ice-clear water, or even light itself.

Inside the semi-transparent object, the waves of—of something—kept reflecting from the edges, top to bottom, side to side, and they went on and on, crossing and recrossing one another in the middle without any sign of weakening.

The most prominent feature of the Face was the single eye—the left—carved or molded from the same piece of strange, warm, flexible stuff . . . around the whole irregular perimeter of translucent shard, edges were somewhat jagged . . . small projections bent easily, springing back to original shape as soon as pressure released.

Alex became aware that the mere touch of the fragment was producing a pleasant sensation, an eerie tingling, in his hands, and the spot on his leg where it had landed still felt warm.

And, just as he knew the identity of the object that he was holding, he was aware, without the least doubt, of what he was required to do next.

The decision to put on the Face was really no decision at all, because it was obviously what the princess must have wanted him to do—otherwise she would not have given it to him.

But Alex had some idea of what to expect from a Face. So at the last moment, even as he raised the tingling thing toward his own eyes and nose and forehead, and despite the joy and determination with which he did so, he had an intimation of something of what a suicide must feel.

But that pang endured only for a moment. He ignored the Artisan's son, who in his childish voice was babbling something that might have been intended as a warning. Alex breathed a certain name, and pressed the transparent thing against his countenance, so that his own left eye looked out through the corresponding transparent lens of the Face of Dionysus.

And instantly something began to happen to him. He was undergoing a transformation that was simultaneously tremendous, marvelous, and horrible.

or the remainder of the day I, Asterion, continued my search for Edith. But she was gone, beyond my power to locate in a few hours, and as the time passed I had to admit to myself that she had very likely been recaptured.

Of course it was still possible that the girl had only fled deeper into the Labyrinth, beyond the range of my comparatively brief search. I hoped that when I had the chance to sleep again, a dream would reveal her fate. But for the moment I was helpless to do anything.

Her loss affected me strongly. Despite the short time that we had been together, I had a strong impression that she had been learning to trust me, perhaps even to feel some regard for me—

Looking at what I have just written, I see a hopelessly inadequate attempt to express profound complications. But if I were to write that Edith had begun to develop an attachment to me, beyond simple gratitude, how idiotic that would sound.

Let me stick to the facts. She had begun to tell me something of her ordinary life, before the dreadful conscription of the Tribute had taken her away from home, and I got the impression that as a girl she had been happy. She'd been destined from childhood to serve some god or goddess, and eventually had somehow become attached to the service of Apollo.

At one point in our talk I asked her, "Have you ever seen him, girl?"

"Who?" It took her a moment to understand. "The *god*? Apollo himself?" Just the thought was enough to make her wide-eyed. "Never. Have *you* . . . ?"

"No. Not I."

The bull with its divine rider had disappeared into the sky above the distant sea-horizon, in the direction of Corycus. Around Ariadne and Theseus, on the deck of the pirate ship, most of the crew were daring to raise their eyes again.

"What happened?" Ariadne breathlessly demanded of her companion. "What did he say to you? What did he want?"

For the time of several breaths after Ariadne had asked her question there was no sound but the whine of wind and the whisper of water past the hull.

The princess was not in a mood to cultivate patience. "What happened?" she demanded again. "What did Shiva have to say to you?" From the edges of her vision she could see that all the faces of the crew were turned toward her.

Theseus, still wearing only the loincloth in which he had won the fight, was standing braced on the deck, his bare feet planted wide apart. For a long moment he said nothing, only shaking his head slightly, staring after the departing form. Then, turning aside, he barked orders at his crew, commanding them to man the oars, establish a change of course. "We are going to Dia!"

As the helmsman bent over the compass-pyx, Theseus turned his face back to Ariadne, looking at her with a strange, unreadable expression. But still he had not replied to her questions.

The princess was not accustomed to such rudeness. "Are you going to tell me or not? It seemed a long time that he held you in the air. What in the Underworld did he want?"

When her companion's answer came at last, his voice was so low that she could barely hear it. "He told me that I am to become a god."

Again a silence fell aboard the ship.

Almost within arm's reach—it seemed to Ariadne that everything on the small ship was almost within arm's reach—some of the crew were pulling at their oars, aiming the ship into what little wind there was. Meanwhile others tugged at lines to get the lowered sail properly out of the way. They had gone back to work at the captain's orders, and were obeying his instructions, being too much afraid of him to do anything else. Meanwhile there was no doubt that they were also listening avidly to the conversation, knowing that their own lives and fortunes were surely at stake in any dealings that their master had with gods.

"Are you joking?" was the next question that burst from Ariadne's lips. She was painfully aware that sun and salt were cracking her lips and spoiling her skin. Her fine linen dress was gone, dissolved into threads and rags, her present clothing a haphazard collection of rags extorted by her companion from several members of the crew. At the moment she was fully conscious of how little she resembled the beautiful princess who had awakened in her palace bedroom only a few mornings ago. If she were to appear at the gate of the palace in her present condition, no one would recognize her.

"Not at all," said Theseus. Now she could see just how elated he was, and how grimly serious in his delight. For the first time the princess realized that, though her lover could smile and laugh as readily as any man, she could not remember him ever making a joke.

She was still angry at him, and felt a growing disgust with her whole situation. "And how and when is this great transformation supposed to take place?"

"As to how, simply enough. I have been told where the Face of a god can almost certainly be found, and Shiva wants me to go there and get it and put it on. As to when this will take place, within the next few days."

"Which god are you to be?" was Ariadne's next question. It came out in a small voice.

"Does it *matter*?" Now his triumph was beginning to show more plainly. She had to face the fact that the look he gave her was actually scornful. "Actually it's Dionysus. Gods and demons, but you're starting to look strange with your nose peeling like that."

"So, Shiva himself promised you this?"

"Shiva himself." And Theseus, shaking his noble head, drew what sounded like a deep breath of pride.

"So Shiva told you this." Somehow she couldn't believe it.

"Are you deaf? That's what I said."

The more Ariadne thought about the strange claims her companion was making, the less she liked them. "Of course it matters! You're not going to be—you can't be—allied with something like Shiva! Not with the demon who killed my father!"

"Shiva didn't kill him." This man had a way of saying things that made them supremely convincing. Sometimes, she had observed, he applied this talent to things she knew were false.

Ariadne was not going to be meekly convinced, and her attitude showed in her look. "I suppose the Destroyer himself told you that as well."

This irritated Theseus. "We had other things to talk about."

"Such as what?"

The Prince of Pirates ignored the question. "As for your father, were you there that night in the palace?" he demanded. "Did you see what happened?"

"I saw my father's body!" As Ariadne spoke, the ship fell smoothly away from under her feet, starting down a swell, her hungry stomach lurched, and for a moment of distant horror she wondered if she was going to be seasick. "My sister and I both saw that."

Theseus, still clinging with one hand to one of the lines that thinly webbed the single mast, seemed oblivious to the plunging of the ship, as he was to so much else. "But you didn't see how he died."

"That was plain enough. He died of . . . horrible injuries." Her outrage had grown so great that she could hardly speak. "Injuries that looked like sword wounds."

"There you are. Shiva strikes down his enemies with a beam of fire. He never carries a sword."

"Not only his enemies does he strike, but a lot of innocent bystanders as well. He would have cheerfully devoured you, had we not escaped."

Theseus was not moved by her arguments, but he had paused. Now she could perceive in his face a shade of something uglier than sheer indifference. He said, "He didn't devour me, as you put it, just now when he had the chance. Instead, he has chosen me as his ally. And what makes you so sure that Shiva is really *your* enemy? He hasn't hurt your sister, has he?"

"Phaedra may be dead by now, for all I know. Burned to a crisp, or tortured in a cage. He's allied with my uncle, isn't he?"

"So's the whole army back there, and you still have friends

among them. I don't say that your uncle is totally innocent, maybe he's not, but why do you accuse Shiva? You admit you didn't see what happened to your father. They say your father also called up a god on that night."

"No, I didn't see him killed with my own eyes. But I had a . . . reliable report."

That made him frown. "A report from who?"

Ariadne didn't care to answer that.

"So, you won't tell me?" But Theseus, hanging with one hand on a rope that ran up to the mast, his eyes probing the horizon, spoke only out of habit, trying to force everyone else to do his will. He really was not interested sufficiently to try to force an answer. Now Ariadne could see that his thoughts had already turned sharply away from her and all her questions. Doubtless he was imagining the glorious adventures that would come within his grasp when he became a god.

But she wasn't going to let him get away that easily. "So, you think you are going to be Dionysus. Why would Shiva grant you such a favor?"

"That's easy enough. No Face can lie around indefinitely unworn, everyone knows that. Some divine power, some kind of law, keeps them all from getting really lost. Sooner or later someone's bound to find it and put it on. And the Lord Shiva would rather see the Face of Dionysus worn by someone he can depend on as a useful ally."

After a pause, Theseus advised her offhandedly, "If the report that worries you came from your brother, I wouldn't put too much reliance on it. He wasn't there either. He dreams things, and then imagines they are real."

Ariadne said coldly, "Sometimes they are. Very real indeed." But despite her anger, a seed of uncertainty had been planted. Theseus's point about the army was well taken—officers and men who called themselves her friends were still willing to serve the usurper and his new god. And she really knew almost nothing about the young soldier—Alex something—who had claimed to have seen what had happened.

Her quest for love and adventure had landed her in a sea of

uncertainty. But it came to her with a rush of emotion that there was one man she must never doubt. Her lover, the only man she had ever allowed to know her body. Theseus was so handsome, and at this very moment he was looking at her, so intently that her knees felt weak.

The Island of Dia had a much smoother coastline than the Island of Refuge, besides being enormously larger, with perhaps a hundred times the area, and several thousand permanent inhabitants. There was nothing that could really be called a city. The last time there had been a strong central government was so long ago that memories were vague. The most prominent topographical feature was a range of tall, rugged hills, locally called mountains, never rising more than about three thousand feet above sea level. These ran down the center of the island from north to south. This range was rugged and barren along its crest, but there was plenty of moisture in the smooth slopes of the lower elevations.

Dia was roughly rectangular, about sixteen miles by ten. Vaguely Ariadne could remember from her history lessons the name of a certain tyrant, Lygdamis, who had ruled here several centuries in the past. The present government was a loose and ineffectual confederation of townships. Exports included beautiful white marble, white wine, and some fruits. The capital and chief port lay on the west coast, the opposite side of the island from that where Theseus's two ships were approaching.

Naturally the mountains were the first landmark to become visible to an approaching ship.

As the pair of raiders drew near, their crews could see a few small sailboats near the coast, craft that seemed to be taking care to steer clear of the attacking force; and they grumbled that now the natives had probably spotted them as well. The locals, given warning, might be able to arrange some kind of a defense, or at least to hide their women and their valuables. "Of course they don't know where we're going to land."

The Dians were among the peoples who had been forced to

send tribute to Minos; in recent years they had not been well organized among themselves.

Theseus took note of the fact that there was as yet no sign of his
father's ship. "Shiva said he might be here, and that I could expect
some other help as well. I expect the old bastard will show up, but
who knows when."

Ariadne asked Theseus, "Are you and your father still on
speaking terms? I thought it was somehow because of him that
you were shanghaied into being one of the youths of the Tribute."

Theseus looked into the distance, smiling faintly. "We have
our disagreements, Dad and I. So far, neither of us has tried to
conceal any of them from the other."

What kind of greeting he intended to give the old bastard
when he came was hard to tell from his manner.

Back on the island of Corycus, Shiva had ordered Perses to see to
it that such forces as were available and could be spared, were dispatched to aid the cause of Theseus.

Fortunately several suitable ships were in the harbor or
nearby, among them that of Aegeus, also known as King of the
Pirates. Theseus had agreed with Shiva, in the course of their brief
airborne discussion, that his father would be a good man to have
along when matters came to fighting. Provided, of course, that it
did not take months to locate him. But as fate would have it,
Aegeus had already put in at Corycus; months ago, King Perses
had let it be known that certain gentlemen of fortune would be
welcomed at his court, and that profitable alliances could be
arranged. Before putting out to sea again, Aegeus had taken
aboard his ship the girl Edith, who had been recaptured in the
Labyrinth. It was thought she quite likely would be useful on her
native isle of Dia, both as a guide and as a hostage.

Now the God of Destruction was engaged in directing the furnishing of his new temple. King Perses had come to the temple, to
make sure, as he said, that the work of furnishing and decoration
was going to the god's liking. Laborers and craftsmen, ordered to

keep the work going despite the immediate presence of divinity and royalty, were pounding and sawing on the upper levels of a high interior wall, now and then ripping out oaths and dropping fragments of wood or stone, so that the god and king who stood below had taken shelter beneath a platform of scaffolding. A faint cloud of dust, pierced here and there by sunbeams entering at windows, filled most of the large interior of the structure.

Perses, paying careful attention, listened to the news that Theseus was very likely to soon put on the Face of Dionysus. The king knew very little about the amazingly fortunate young man, except of course that he had just escaped being part of the recent Tribute, and had by some amazing feat established a romantic connection with Ariadne.

Now it suddenly occurred to Perses, with a sharp inward chill, that Shiva might be planning to depose him as king, and invite Phaedra to take the throne instead.

He said nothing of his suspicion to Shiva, but asked cautiously, "This Theseus bears me no ill will?"

As usual, most of the god's attention seemed to be elsewhere. He was squinting upward past the scaffolding, trying to make important decisions. Should the rows of human skulls on the interior wall run vertically or horizontally? It was a high wall, and broad, and its surface held room for many rows of skulls. Maybe a random scattering would be more effective. "No more than he feels for humankind in general, I suppose."

The king said that if he could be assured of that, then he had no objection. Not that it would have made any difference, he supposed, if he did object.

"How do we know, oh great lord, that the Face of Dionysus is likely to be found on the island of Dia?"

"Because that is what your man Creon assures me, on what he claims is very good magical authority."

"May I ask, lord, what this good reason is?"

Shiva made a gesture of impatience. "Something he has heard from one of his familiars." Actually Shiva had been unable to follow Creon's involved explanation, but he had no intention of confessing any such failure to a mortal. "Of course he may be wrong, but we cannot afford to let the opportunity pass by."

Perses meanwhile was thinking that some of Creon's other predictions, notably those about the Face of Zeus, had not been fulfilled. But the king, dreading his god's reaction, did not want to voice that comment aloud. Investigations, both physical and magical, were continuing. But legend and experience alike assured him that in the Labyrinth, answers of any kind, to any question, tended to be difficult.

The god had fallen silent. Perhaps, thought Perses, Shiva's thoughts were running along the same lines.

Presently they were joined by Creon himself, who brought word that Hades was ready for a meeting.

Shiva drew himself up to his full height. "That is satisfactory," he allowed.

"Will the Lord Shiva be going to Dia personally?" the high priest asked. Then he looked up apprehensively, as another fragment of something fell from the ongoing work above.

"Not now." Shiva's original plan had been to allow Theseus time to get to Dia with his ship, and then to appear to take a personal hand in the proceedings. But the meeting with Hades must come first. By his very nature, the Ruler of the Underworld was vastly more powerful and important than Dionysus was ever likely to become.

He did not wish to try again to explain to this mere mortal how he, Shiva, could be so certain that his many enemies were trying to entrap him. Besides, there were other matters, like trying to arrange his alliance with Hades, that were really of overriding importance. Seeing to it that the right human got to wear the Face of Dionysus was certainly a task worth doing, but Shiva did not think that his own fate depended utterly on the result.

To Perses he said, "The Lord Hades has expressed a wish of forming an alliance with me."

"Great are the ways of the gods," the king murmured placatingly. Now the man was being so ostentatiously awe-stricken that Shiva found his attitude irritating. "How soon does my lord plan to conclude this alliance?" No doubt the humble tone of the question was intended to make it sound less impertinent, but the effort did not succeed.

"Very soon," Shiva responded shortly. Later there would be time to deal properly with impertinence.

The current human avatars of Hades and Shiva had never met, and, as far as Shiva could remember, none of the contacts between their respective earlier embodiments had been more than brief and incidental; so Shiva knew he must approach their impending conference warily.

In a little while the humans who were working as liaison between himself and Hades came to Shiva and told him where Hades wanted to meet him, and when. The rendezvous was scheduled to take place on a new volcanic island, many miles from Corycus, and still almost glowing with heat. Shiva had already scouted the place, airborne, from a distance; he supposed that Hades and his creatures of the Underworld could stand on it unscathed, but Shiva and everyone else would find it excruciatingly hot. Shiva expected that he could stand there and shield himself from damage, by an exertion of will, but he could not be comfortable.

The attitude of these human servants of Hades toward him was not at all like Creon's. Shiva burned with inward rage at being treated with arrogance by these mere mortals; yet he dared not strike them down, or even rebuke them strongly. And they were so confident in their impudence that they did not even flinch when he allowed the lid of his Third Eye to open slightly. Perhaps they did become just a shade more respectful.

These humans were relatively new to their job; their predecessors had been discharged—if that was the right word to describe their fate—in a general shakeup of Hades's staff following last year's encounter with Apollo.

The meeting got under way at last.

Lightning flared, rain fell toward rocks still not cooled very far below their melting point. The falling water, caught up in the rising heat, was turned to steam before it even touched the rocks, and so sprang up again at once, hissing and boiling away in white clouds that spread across the cooler ground, knee deep on mortals and deities alike.

There were no formal introductions made, and most of those present seemed to be taking steps to cloak their identities. For a moment Shiva wondered whether all these who were gathered here were part of the great conspiracy against him. Well, even if they were, it was too late now to simply turn around and leave.

Hades had to remove his Cap of Invisibility before he could be seen, even by his fellow gods. But even before the cap came off, Shiva was certain that he could *feel* that mighty presence near.

And then he saw it, standing where the shadows of the thunderclouds above seemed to be deepest. Not so much a shape, as a gathering of darkness, only vaguely human. It was difficult to be sure of Hades's size, though he received a definite impression of a shaggy head and massive, rounded shoulders, with a dark chain of some kind hung around the neck.

The voice when he heard it was dark and deep, and sounded full of echoes, as if it were issuing from some deep cave.

As was true of all the gods, Shiva's human body had once walked the earth with no name or identity beyond those of mere humanity. But the Destroyer, unlike many other deities, had long labored to force himself to forget that epoch of his existence. He would have given a great deal to possess that Cap. He was impressed despite himself by the power and majesty of Hades, but also vaguely sickened in a way. *An utter blackness, an infernal gloom, that defied the Sun itself to brighten it. It would have swallowed up the lancing beam from the Third Eye, as the ocean swallowed sparks.*

Exchanging whispers with those around him, Shiva began to comprehend the situation. Some of the gods that the Lord of the Underworld had hoped to recruit had declined to join him, while his aides had been unable to locate certain others. Some might be absent because no one was wearing their Faces at the moment. Others simply disliked Hades, or feared him too much to consider entering a partnership.

An alternate explanation could well be that they were might-ily afraid of Apollo. Even those who had never been the Far-Worker's enemies, who considered themselves ready to be his friends, tended to be uneasy in his presence. Of course, very much depended on the nature and behavior of the particular avatars involved. In general, it seemed that the worldwide community of gods—if such a loose assortment of beings could be called a com-munity—was not taking sides in this conflict. Most of the mem-bers, as far as could be determined, were simply waiting to see what happened next.

One god commented, "Too bad that Thanatos is missing. I have not seen his Face on anyone for some time."

"Have never seen him, that I can remember—and won't be too sad if I never do." That got a chuckle.

And another observed, "Yet I have noticed no difficulty in terminating mortal lives, even in the absence of Death himself."

Hades had his own ideas concerning any god-Faces that might be available, and who should put them on. He wanted to make sure that this new upstart avatar of Dionysus was slain without delay, though he was not at all sure which human should receive the prize. Ideally, the Lord of the Underworld would have preferred to carry that Face down to such a subterranean depth that none of his potential enemies would ever be able to get at it.

Shiva protested that he had in mind a certain human who, he thought, was very well qualified to wear the Face of Dionysus.

Well, said Hades, who as yet had no particular human in mind, maybe the candidate of Shiva would be acceptable—this Theseus. "But I must meet him first."

While the gods conversed, they observed a new version of Cer-berus in operation. Cerberus was not a god, of course, and cer-tainly had never been a human. But a formidable weapon and tool in the arsenal of Hades, the creature had just broken open the new gateway to the Underworld.

First a quivering of the ground, then a savage eruption, flying rocks and mud. Powerful limbs moving in a blur of speed, claws harder and sharper than any bone, any tooth or claw, rending the earth, pulverizing even rock.

And now Cerberus, unbothered by the infernal heat, was working to pave the smooth, round wall of a tunnel, circular in cross-section.

"I seem to remember a different creature of that name. Much more doglike."

"That was the old version—Apollo killed it, more than a year ago."

The introduction of Apollo's name cast something of a chill on the proceedings.

Looking at the thing, Shiva decided that it was not, and had never been, alive, even though it certainly had hair—even red hair, calling to mind something he had heard of Apollo's new avatar—and its surface showed some of the complex irregularity of life. Even its eyes looked dead, and there was no sign that it was breathing.

Some kind of artifact, no doubt, of the mysterious odylic process of the ancients.

"Where does Hades get them?" an anonymous voice wondered.

"No one knows."

The thunderheads of the ongoing storm were massing ever more tightly above the island. The suggestion was inescapable that Zeus might be taking an interest in their meeting.

Hades professed indifference, but many of the others who gathered here would have preferred to meet at night, out of sight of the great Eye of Apollo.

The subject of the Sun-God having arisen, Hades assured his prospective colleague that he was quite ready to go another round with Apollo.

"That Bloodless One will not escape me, next time."

Shiva had been impressed by the presence of Hades when the meeting began. As it went on, the Destroyer moved from being wary to being frightened. The dark presence before him was one, with Poseidon and Zeus himself, of the triumvirate who ruled the universe. It had become a habit with Shiva to toy with the lid of his Third Eye, no matter whose company he was in, deriving pleasure from the nervous reactions of whoever he was with. But now the Third Eye stayed tightly closed.

And he remained frightened of Hades even after the conference was over. Even if Hades had promised that his, Shiva's, rule on Corycus would be confirmed and strengthened.

The high priest Creon, making his own calculations, had decided that the unknown power that had advised him about treasure was probably very reliable.

The thought that it might be untrustworthy was very frightening indeed, and he quickly put it from him.

In the moment before Alex slipped the Face of Dionysus on over his own, he had only a vague and general idea of what shape his impending transformation was going to take—but that his metamorphosis would be awesome in some way he had not the slightest doubt. The young man clapped the strange thing over his left eye and ear, and cheek and forehead, in the full expectation of being seized and shaken by all the powers of Dionysus, mentally as well as physically, like a rat in the jaws of a dog.

What actually happened seemed less violent than he had expected, but every bit as thorough.

Through his left eye he now saw the world quite differently than he ever had before. Potentialities of life, perceptible as shimmering, transparent reds and greens, were visible in almost everything he looked at. Not quite everything; the empty sky was least affected, along with certain dark rocks, whose shapes and colors told him they had been unchanged for almost as long as there had been an earth. The vision of his other, un-Faced eye, like the hearing in his right ear, remained unaffected. The dual perception thus created in his senses was disorienting at first, but he soon began to get used to it.

In his left ear there now came sounds that were not quite sounds, only hints of whispers that might have been or were yet to be. And, if he listened for them, the throb of pulse and sigh of breath of every human who was near him.

Outside of the sudden alteration in his senses, the young man was at first aware of very little physical change in his own body. Unthinkingly he had somehow expected to be ten feet tall, but of course that was not to be. It seemed to him that there had been a broadening of his chest, a slight rounding of his limbs. When he wished silently for a mirror, one of the newly revitalized sprites brought it to him, materializing what felt like solid silver and glass out of the air.

Presently Alex realized that he was now able to see the sprites, and the other creatures of his entourage, clearly, whenever he wanted to see them, in somewhat the same way as a human could always monitor his own breathing when he cared to think about it. He could have named them now, or most of them, individually, had he wanted to take the trouble. At the moment about a dozen sprites, also called maenads or bacchantes, were visible, about half their number naked, the remainder wreathed in wispy veils. All were beautiful in both of the young soldier's eyes. Most of them appeared to be no more than half-grown girls, in a great variety of sizes and shapes. Their smooth, bare skins bore all the ordinary colors of humanity, along with several hues that neither Alex nor Dionysus had ever seen on mortal flesh.

Then there were the hairy-legged satyrs, all emphatically male, ranging in apparent age from elderly to hardly more than children. Their leader, as Alex could now remember, was a paunchy and debauched elder specimen named Silenus. As soon as Alex willed their forms into clarity, there they were, satyrs and maenads alike, making obeisance to him as soon as they observed that he was taking notice. The moment he wished them away, they promptly disappeared.

Let them stay vanished for the moment. He needed at least the illusion of privacy, to try to come to grips with a new world, his new self.

Now memory, vastly augmented over what that of mere mortal Alex had ever been, assured him that only the chariot and the two panthers were still missing from his usual entourage. The stored experience of a god's lifetime, a depository of marvels bewilderingly enormous, warned him that the restoration of those items might still take many days.

But it was not only the potentialities of life outside his own which were now open to his observation. New memory also assured him of the possibilities of frenzy, that he would experience and that he would bring to others, embodied so clearly in his inhuman escort. And there were depths now visible within himself, from which he recoiled after his first look.

The moment Alex wondered about the *thyrsus* staff, it suddenly appeared. It had come from nowhere, and now it was in his hand. He knew that his marvelous new memory, if he consulted it, would tell him what miraculous feats might be accomplished with the staff, and how to go about doing them. He would be able to work marvels, he was sure. But first. . . .

The first really disturbing change to manifest itself was a raging thirst for wine, easily enough satisfied. He had only to extend a hand, and a filled goblet appeared in it. Then came a vivid daydream of naked women, sinuous bodies twisting in a lustful dance. But in the very first moments of the experience Alex realized that it was not a dream at all. The sprites were back, as he must have wanted them to be, at least a dozen of them now, as convincingly real and alive as any people he had ever seen.

Satyrs in their several varieties came trooping and cavorting with the females, bearing torches whose flames spurted up wildly in different colors. Romping lustfully, stamping and prancing to the beat of the music, the goat-men, led as usual by Silenus, grappled the girls and women to them in a wild dance that had hardly got under way before it was transformed into an orgy.

His human mind and body had a limited capacity to sustain such passion. Soon there came an ebbing of the tide that had drawn and whirled his blood into such frenzy, The storm ebbed, and was soon followed by an exhausted calm.

How many minutes had passed, Alex could not have said. He came to himself, gasping and with the blood pounding in his head, keenly aware that he had just finished satisfying his own lust on the body of Clara. Now she moved again beneath him, but this time the movement was only a simple, awkward, sexless shifting of her weight, as if trying to ease some painful pressure. With a kind of groan the new god—still Alex, but no longer only Alex—

raised his body, enough to let her get up and withdraw to a little distance. Then he collapsed on his side and lay there panting.

His mind was filled, overwhelmed, with the memory of naked bodies surrounding him, the rhythms of joining and rejoining. When he closed his eyes they were still there. But gradually the excitement and its visions faded.

Evidently Clara had been caught up in the madness of Dionysus almost as fully as he had himself. Nor had Daedalus been immune—but there was another matter that Alex now found puzzling. When the tide of mania ebbed, he retained a confused memory of having been observed, even while the frenzy was at its peak, by the figure of a woman. A beautiful, dark-haired woman, clad in a cloud of fine fabric that shimmered with the ghosts of many colors, she had watched with evident amusement while declining to take part.

Who was this woman, who could resist so successfully not only the grappling efforts of the satyrs, but all the charisma of Dionysus? His vast new vaults of memory held the answer, readily available—Circe, no goddess but a mortal woman, though still in appearance as young and beautiful as she had been two hundred years ago. Beyond that distance in the past, even the memory of the Twice-Born started to grow cloudy, on this subject at least. Dionysus thought it would have been good to speak with Circe, but now she was gone again.

Alex found a kind of ease in the exhaustion of his own, still very human, body. Not sleep, not yet. Sleep would come, as it came to gods and men alike, but it would have to wait.

The *thyrsus* was lying on the ground, and he bent and picked it up. He looked around, but there was still no sign of chariot and leopards.

Thinking about all that had happened to him during the last few hours, pulling up memories of a vast number of similar events in the god's past, Alex gradually came to understand that a great part of what he had experienced during the orgy—but not all of it, by any means—had taken place only in his own mind.

Well, he had never anticipated that the Face of Dionysus, the arrogant intruder he had so eagerly invited into his brain, was going to bring him peace. Tranquility of any kind, physical or mental, was exactly the wrong thing to expect from the god whose nature Alex had come to share. But the change had been more overwhelming than he had expected it to be. The presence of the deity was racking him with madness.

He had just experienced a prolonged wave of divine craziness, that like an enormous ocean surge had drawn him under, and held him beneath the waves until he knew that he was quite thoroughly drowned. The god was used to such experience, surely, and would survive. But Alex was far from certain that his human nature could stand it.

For a few moments he dozed, sprawled on the broken floor of the ruined temple in divine exhaustion. From that slumber Alex awoke with a shock of guilt, for having entirely forgotten the princess for what must have been many hours. On waking he was himself again—as much, he supposed, as he in his new life was ever going to be entirely himself. The god seemed to have partially withdrawn from him, leaving only the confused human, with enhanced senses and capabilities.

In the aftermath of madness he felt, for the time being, thoroughly human, and very weak.

Again his human heart experienced a sudden lash of guilt at the thought of how, at the very moment, the Princess Ariadne might be in desperate need of the help that he had now been empowered to provide. And he, instead of spending the precious minutes and hours trying to reach her, he had been . . . but the god had possessed him, he reminded himself hastily. He had been given no real choice.

That was a good excuse, but he wasn't sure he could believe it.

Through his own, old, human memory, a vision of his sodden, drunken predecessor, sprawled on the floor of the great hall of the Corycan king, came to Alex like a nightmare. It spurred him to move, to get back on his feet.

"Hello." The voice was quietly thrilling, unmistakable. The mortal enchantress Circe, arrayed in fine garments of her own weaving, was once more standing near, this time certainly no vision, but a solid presence. The coloring of her hair, her skin, seemed as inconstant as that of her clothing.

"So, you are the new Dionysus. I see you are enjoying your new body, great lord." He thought the enchantress pronounced the title with just a hint of mockery. "Let me offer my congratulations on your escape from the Destroyer."

"Thank you, my dear." Dionysus spoke as a prince might, to a favorite artisan or entertainer. To Alex the Half-Nameless, the words seemed to come automatically, in the same language that his visitor had used. It was a tongue that he had never heard before—but of course Dionysus had not the least trouble understanding it. "Perhaps next time—?"

"I am invited to join you?" Circe gently mimed surprise. She was standing at her ease, small hands clasped, graceful head tilted to one side. "All things are possible—but I think not. You never seem to lack for willing partners in your madness."

Alex nodded silently. Then the god with whom he shared his body bowed lightly to the visitor, a gesture containing a hint of mockery. Then Dionysus saluted her with his staff. "But none as experienced as you, Circe—and very few as lovely."

"Oh Twice-Born Lord, I very much appreciate the compliment. But in truth, your romps are far too energetic for a poor mortal woman of my years." To Alex's right eye, still purely human, the female figure before him appeared no more than twenty years of age. Even his augmented left eye could discover no trace of the decay that time must leave on mortal flesh, though to vision of divine acuity, subtle hints were visible in plenty. But that, the human realized, was not the sort of detail that Dionysus ever wished to see.

"Where is Apollo?" the god asked.

"I think you need not bother to search for him. The Far-Worker will be seeking you, and he will find you soon enough." Circe paused. "I do believe you two will get along splendidly in your present avatars, different as you are."

"I rejoice to hear it. Where is the Face of Zeus?"

"Ah, Lord Dee, if I knew that . . . would I be standing here, consuming time in idle chat?"

"I see. No doubt you have other affairs of pressing importance."

"You mock a poor woman, lord; but in fact I do. Besides, it is not good for mere mortals like myself to spend much time in such exalted company."

"Do you mock me, woman?" Alex alone would have been hopelessly enthralled by the shimmering beauty before him, not only of form but of voice and gesture; but Dionysus was beginning to be annoyed.

Silver laughter trilled, and before the god could decide whether to pursue his protest, the woman who had been standing before him was gone. No deity could have vanished more smoothly and magically.

Shortly after awakening from the restful sleep that followed, Alex became aware that he was no longer naked, but that his body was draped in a rich purple cloak. He became intimately and vitally aware of everything that grew and lived on the island, and even the nightbirds flying over it.

At dawn, the growing light revealed trampled bushes and discarded garments, discarded sprite-wear—those glorious shreds spontaneously disappeared even while Alex looked at them. This litter was mingled with the stubs of burnt-out torches, whose persistent reality indicated that most of the light must have come from some kind of real fire.

Ready to attend to business once again, Alex found plenty of practical matters awaiting his attention. He knew, even without any warning from Circe, that Shiva, a damned efficient killer, would be hunting him with murderous intent, and that, despite his own new godhood, he was in mortal peril.

So was the entire world, perhaps. If the Face of Zeus was really lying about somewhere, waiting for someone to pick it up . . . Alex alone could never have fully appreciated what that might mean. But Dionysus could, and Alex could feel the god's fear.

* * *

His determination to help the princess had not been in the least diminished by his apotheosis. He felt immensely reassured by the knowledge that he was still fully human, still as much the individual Alex as he had ever been, despite the unarguable fact that he was now also someone else—and something rather more than human. Before putting on the Face, he had been afraid at some deep level that his own identity would vanish when he became Dionysus; but now the very memory of the god himself, recording the fate of more of his avatars than Alex cared to think about, assured him that was not going to happen.

Not unless he was driven mad by repeated bouts of ecstasy and frenzy. Memories that were new to Alex, but ancient in the god now bound to him, assured him that too was distinctly possible. More than one avatar had led only a short life after putting on the Face of Dionysus.

The worn stones paving the floor of the grass-grown shrine were stained following the orgy—but not with blood. The only redness was of wine. There were worse gods by far, and bloodier, than Dionysus. Alex was afraid to probe his new memory for information about them, but he knew that soon it would be necessary to do so.

The great majority of the participants in last night's revelry, never having been burdened with real human flesh, had vanished into the air, or perhaps into the earth—neither Alex nor Dionysus knew. Only four solid, living bodies, including his own, remained in sight. One of the solid bodies was that of the child Icarus, who had slept peacefully through the night, and now, still deep in the absolute sleep of childhood, lay curled in the lingering warmth of the ashes of last night's fire. And none of the four, as far as Alex could tell, had been seriously harmed, though both the Artisan and Clara looked a little worn this morning.

Clara's metal collar was gone, and whether it had been removed by the power of the god, or through the cleverness of Daedalus, Alex did not try to remember. A pale ring around the girl's neck showed where the vanished band of metal had shielded a narrow circle of her skin from the sun. She had reclaimed the torn remnants of her once-fine linen gown, discarded early on in the bout of shared madness, and was clutching them around her, as if in shame. Clara's movements were tentative and slow, suggesting that many parts of her body were sore this morning.

She gave Alex a slave's unreadable glance, but said nothing, and quickly looked away again, as if she were afraid. Memory assured him that as a god he could expect many people, mere mortal humans, to look at him like that.

The Artisan, who had evidently come fully awake even before Alex, had put his apron on again. His face looked pained, and there was a tremor in his fingers as he endeavored by purely natural means to rebuild the ordinary fire. Meanwhile young Icarus was still asleep.

Alex got up and moved a little apart from his three fellow humans, realizing that they would feel easier if he did so. Moodily he began tracing with one finger the ancient inscriptions on the walls of the ruined temple, while he waited for his companions to recover fully. Suddenly he realized that he had gained the ability to read in a great number of languages. In the litter on the ruined floor he located a sharp-pointed fragment of rock, and on a blank section of remaining wall he proved to himself that he could write many of them also, tracing his own name and that of the Princess Ariadne. His new memory assured him that a great many gods shared such linguistic abilities.

Soon he became aware that the Artisan was approaching him, slowly and tentatively.

"What is it, Daedalus? Don't be afraid." Vaguely Alex realized how different his transformed self must now appear to the other humans, even though the changes in him were comparatively subtle on the surface.

Daedalus, as usual, was making an effort to understand the world around him as well as possible. "Lord, was there—was there someone else here, a few minutes ago? Another woman?"

"There was. Circe. But no cause for you to worry." Feeling a sudden, restless urge to explore more of his grafted memories, Alex reached out with the tip of his staff and pointed to one series of weathered markings. "Daedalus, what is this language called?"

The Artisan rubbed his head, as if it were still throbbing with last night's wine, exertions and emotions. Squinting at the words, he could name the tongue in which they were written, and read a little of it. He could also identify a second kind of writing, but was unable to read it at all. And the third script was something he could not remember ever having seen before.

Alex/Dionysus could not only name all three, but could read them with perfect ease; and he could, if he thought about it, tell in what parts of the world each was in use. All conveyed pretty much the same ideas, being litanies of praise directed to the Sun-God.

Now the new avatar of Dionysus could not only see, and read, but feel, with a mysterious new inward sense, that the temple in which he'd found the Face had indeed been dedicated to Apollo.

"Then it truly happened as my powers foretold," he murmured to himself. "Silenus? Where are you?"

Under questioning by Dionysus, the paunchy one readily admitted that of course the sprites and satyrs had known that the Face was hidden in the locket—they had put it there, trying to hide it from Shiva and the new King Perses. "I doubt we could have done better, lord," the satyr concluded.

"Perhaps not," admitted the Twice-Born, and spread his hands—Alex's hands, of course—and looked at them, as if trying to assess the quality of this new body in which he found himself.

Meanwhile Icarus had begun to stir and yawn. When the child sat up, rubbing his eyes, Daedalus, excusing himself from the god's presence with a few murmured words, went to his son and led him away. The faint sound of their footsteps descending the pathless hill went on for a long time, and Alex realized that the Artisan was taking his boy to some other part of the island.

When Clara looked inquiringly at Alex, he nodded slightly, granting permission, and without saying anything she turned and followed the father and son.

Alex sighed, in sudden loneliness. As a result of sharing an orgy, the three of them now seemed more remote from one another than before. But Dionysian memory assured him that some separation now was for the best. The Twice-Born knew that other humans would generally be more comfortable away from him.

But the god also realized that the three mortals would soon be seeking out his company again. Because the divine keenness of his hearing could pick out a new sound in the distance, that of the ocean's surface being crisply parted by the sharp bow of a ship. The sound was steadily approaching; the harbor would soon entertain another visitor.

By the time the sun had risen a good hand's breadth above the sea, Alex and the god were watching it alone, sharing the same pair of eyes. Right now he was content to be alone, but he knew that it would not always be so.

And now the ship that Dionysus had detected at a distance was at hand, coming right into the harbor.

Several hours passed before Alex saw his fellow refugees again. As he had expected, the arrival of the ship had brought the man and woman and child all back to him, seeking protection against the unknown.

But Alex did not yet realize, and the god did not care, what the effect of his new self on them would be. When the three mortals drew near, Icarus and Clara fell down before him, hiding their faces, and even Daedalus assumed a position indicating a certain humility. Alex spoke to them absently, giving reassurance; but his main thought was already far away, considering what he must do next.

The new arrival proved to be another trader, to all appearances reasonably honest, or at least showing none of the outward signs of piracy, putting in to the harbor to take on water.

Unhurriedly Alex walked down to the beach, where he was presently joined by Daedalus and Clara and Icarus. Calmly he hailed the sailors as they came ashore.

Slowly the timidity of the newcomers was relieved. The captain, who gave his name as Ottho, bowed deeply when he stood before Alex. He was astonished to find himself in the presence of a god, but not paralyzed.

This captain knew the Artisan by reputation, and was impressed to meet him. Also his eyes, and those of his crew, lit up at mention of the reward that the God of Joy now promised them for taking on these passengers, and conveying them to where they wished to go.

The crew of this new ship were, like their captain, ready to acknowledge the young man, whose dazzling presence stood before them, as an avatar of Dionysus. At first they took him for some lord, or prince, who had been marooned here by chance; then, one by one, they began to realize the truth.

"Lord Dionysus!" one said clearly. And a murmuring of prayer and incantation began among them.

"Stand at ease, men!" Alex held out his hands as if in blessing. "If you would please me, take my friends here on a voyage to where they want to go." And he gestured with his staff.

Crew and captain eagerly agreed. And they were pleased and enchanted by the presentation that the god now gave them, large bunches of purple grapes, fully ripe and almost bursting with their juice. "If you will save the seeds and plant them, I think you will be pleased with the results."

"We thank you, lord! We thank you heartily!" Once more the demonstration of gratitude was impressive.

The ship's new destination would be a seaport of Megara, the kingdom where Daedalus hoped to find that the ruler's generous job offer was still open to him.

"And you . . . my lord?" Ever since Alex had put on the Face, the proud Artisan gave the impression every now and then that he was about to fall to his knees—and Clara had already done so.

Alex put out a hand to tug at the arm of Daedalus, holding him upright. "Call me your friend rather than your lord. But let me be alone for now. You should take ship away from here, with your woman and your child, while you have the chance. I want to go where Ariadne is—can you tell me where?"

"Not I, my lord."

"And so I must stay here, and gather my strength, until I can find the right place and time to use it."

"My lord, I—"

"No. Leave me now." Alex—though it really came more from his new, internal partner—made a dismissive wave, a regal gesture. "I will miss your company, all three of you. But the battle I must now fight is one that you had better avoid. In any case, none of you are the kind of people who can spend a great deal of time in the presence of Dionysus and escape unharmed."

Daedalus straightened to his full height. Alex thought he was probably curious about what kind of people that might be, who were able to live on easy terms with the God of Frenzy. But the Artisan's question was: "What will you do now—my friend?"

"My full powers will be restored to me—soon, I think." The god's memory of many previous transitions gave him that hope. "And when they are, I must rely on them to tell me that. But they are not yet . . . fully gathered. For now I can only wait."

In quick succession he shook the callused hand of Daedalus, playfully ruffled the child's short hair, and briefly and tenderly stroked Clara's tender cheek. Then he sent his three mortal companions on their way.

In another hour the ship had sailed free out of the harbor, Alex himself was once more the only human being on the island. But this time he was not alone. It aroused in him mixed feelings to reflect that he, whose name had been Half-Nameless, would never be unknown or alone again.

"Princess Ariadne, be calm, be brave, wherever you are. As soon as I can locate you, I am coming to your aid."

Not that he really expected she could hear him. His only answer was the almost mindless singing of his sprites, and a bass chuckle, very distant, from Silenus.

---

*F*or some hours after his transformation, Alex never doubted that the Princess Ariadne had meant to bestow on him the powers of a god. Miraculous as it seemed, this daughter of the royal house of Corycus had chosen *him*, out of all the men who must have been—who *had to* have been—eager to devote their lives to her service. He, Alex the Half-Nameless, the humble private soldier, was the one Ariadne wanted to be her champion, her defender. In effect she had surrendered her fate into his hands. The princess must have had, after all, some idea of the depth of his devotion, because she had picked him to be the one who, when the time was ripe, would descend with divine power to intervene in her affairs, and save her from . . .

From what, exactly? From the man she had chosen as her lover, who now, if Daedalus and Clara were telling the truth about him, had turned out to be a pirate? No, Alex couldn't believe that it was Theseus from whom the princess wanted to be rescued. Although, to judge from the evidence Alex had heard from his fellow fugitives, she'd be much better off without him. The man Ariadne feared most was of course her uncle.

And above all, and with the best of reasons, she must be terrified of Shiva.

Vividly Alex could remember that dark autumnal night in the great hall of the palace, and how his own predecessor in the role of Dionysus had fled in abject terror from the God of Destruction. By all the gods, even had he lived out his human life as nothing more than human, he would never have forgotten that.

Already, he had enough experience of his own new powers to know that they were tremendous. But the memory he had from Dionysus assured him that they were also terribly disorganized just now; a certain period of confusion in the life of any god was only to be expected when one avatar died and another one took over. On top of that, Alex still had no idea just where the pirates' ship might have carried his princess by this time, or how to go about locating her.

From time to time Alex's new memory presented him with an item of disquieting information. For example: the sprites and satyrs could be expected to become distinctly unreliable, every now and then. Not that they had ever engaged in serious, deliberate treachery, or anything like it. But when those auxiliaries became involved in anything more important than an orgy, it would be a foolish avatar indeed who neglected to keep an eye on them. One or two of the members of his entourage in particular required watching.

Distracting the new god somewhat from such concerns was another question, now beginning to nag at both components of the dual mind of Alex/Dionysus. Why had the princess never told him about the treasure hidden in the medallion?

The first explanation to suggest itself was that Ariadne hadn't wanted to worried a callow young soldier prematurely. It would have frightened him, to know what treasure he was carrying, and ultimately the knowledge must have made his mission harder to accomplish. Of course, the princess must have intended at some point to reveal the truth to her chosen champion. She also ought to have let him know just what she expected from him when he became a god. But Fate had intervened to separate her from her servant before she'd had the chance to break these matters to him gently.

It took a little longer for Alex to become aware of a less flattering possibility. Princess Ariadne had trusted him to carry the Face, but only as she might have relied upon a faithful dog or a cameloid, to bear a burden without any idea of what it meant. At some point she would have asked for her medallion back, and her dazzled worshiper would hand it over. Never had the princess intended that such tremendous treasure should be buried inside the skull of Alex the Nameless, for the rest of that young man's life.

He had to face the fact that the glorious Ariadne must have

intended that the Face of Dionysus should be worn by someone else.

It must be that she had intended it for Prince—if he really was a prince of any kind, which was looking very doubtful—Theseus.

Alex the Half-Nameless might well have been overawed by Prince Theseus, but Lord Dionysus certainly was not. And as far as Alex could tell, the Twice-Born seemed to have no innate preference for having his existence inside the brain of one avatar rather than another.

If Theseus had indeed been Ariadne's choice, she might well be displeased when she saw how Alex had taken personal advantage of the priceless object she had given into his care. Well, there was nothing he could do about it now—nothing but prove to the princess that he was worthy. Once a human had put on a Face, only death could separate it from him.

Alex's efforts to deduce the princess's motives inevitably led him to consider a second question, which he thought might well have a bearing on the first: how had Ariadne herself come into possession of the Face? Most likely, Alex thought, some of the invisible, comparatively minor powers who formed the Dionysian entourage had brought it to her, at some time during the interval of six months or so when the Twice-Born lay dead, his Face unworn by anyone.

Of course, once the princess had the Face of Dionysus in her hands, there would have been nothing to prevent her putting it on herself. The legends and stories all agreed, and the god's own memory confirmed, that humans of either sex could wear the Faces of either male or female deities. So it would seem that the only thing standing in the way of Ariadne's apotheosis must have been some innate reluctance on her part to undergo such an irrevocable transformation.

Dionysus now seemed to have nothing to say about that attitude. But Alex thought that his own mortal mind needed no divine help to understand it. Any princess, and particularly this one, was very like a goddess already; why should anyone as beautiful, as perfect, as Ariadne, ever want to change her identity, even to become a deity?

After sunset, a full twenty-four hours after Alex had put on the Face, he thought he had made a good start, but no more than that, on getting accustomed to the fact of his apotheosis. That word now lay handily within his vocabulary, part of the seemingly inexhaustible memory of his new partner. Some of the treasures waiting to be discovered within that memory were ideas which had never occurred to Alex before, even in the form of questions.

The experimental possibilities now open to him were endlessly fascinating. By a mere act of will, which he demonstrated to himself again and again, he could cause vines to grow, bursting from barren ground into the air. And, by the same token, induce even dead or dying plants to burst into bloom, or sag suddenly with fruit that developed and grew at a fantastic pace, and provided welcome food for the human component of the one who had brought it into being. The olive trees in the hills of the small island, and even those that had been dying along the shore, now burst out with a great new crop, the cycle of growth and ripening requiring only minutes instead of months. The god's power of promoting fertility and growth did not seem to fade or grow tired with repeated use, and in a day the whole island was notably greener than it had been. No doubt when autumn came, his new powers would at least decline somewhat—if only he could stay alive till then!

It worried Alex that he was still temporarily without his chariot—but the god's memory, extending back through a seemingly endless chain of avatars, assured the new possessor of the Face that the vehicle and its team of leopards would be restored to him in time. The process might take no more than a few days but it could require as long as months. Therefore he would have to find some other means to cross the sea, and that meant waiting for a ship.

Had he known that his wait to regain the chariot was going to be this long, he would have boarded the merchant ship with

Daedalus and Clara, and started his journey to Dia by that means. But there was no use fretting about it now. Calling up Silenus, Alex asked if anything could be done to hurry the thing along. Silenus was not hopeful, but swore he would try.

And again and again, Alex's new memory brought him back to that scene in the great hall of the palace of King Minos, on what must have been the last night of the previous avatar's life. Now, through the god's vivid memory, Alex could see himself, his earlier, purely human self, as a clearly seen but generally inconspicuous figure in the background of that brief drama. Indeed, he had been, even then, a better-looking young man than he had imagined himself to be. And even, perhaps, a little taller.

Once I was like you.

Sleep and dreams were evidently going to be at least as large a part of his new life as they had been of the years when he was merely human. On the first night following his possession by the god he had not slept, in any sense of the word implying repose, but tonight he was alone and needed rest.

Even the tiredness of a god was somehow of a different quality than the same feeling in a mere mortal human. But Alex soon discovered that he could now see more sharply than ever before the faces and objects in his dreams, and also remember them more clearly when he awakened. This clarity of vision came from Dionysus, he was sure, but he thought much of the content of the dreams was sent him by Asterion.

In this one, his first real dream since his apotheosis, he remained throughout strangely but comfortably aware that he was dreaming. He was wandering a rocky shoreline, not that of the Island of Refuge, nor any place that either he or Dionysus could remember ever having been before. The waves as they broke before his feet were the color of dark wine, and each time the withdrawing water left a fizzing, a whispering, of small bubbles on the rock. Like the sparkling white wine that once—how many centuries ago?—he and his colleagues in divinity had drunk in the crystal halls of a vast palace that he now thought might have been Olympus. But that scene lay beyond such a gulf of time that even the memory of divinity began to be uncertain.

"It *is* you," the odd voice of Asterion said, sounding behind him in his present dream. Dionysus identified the speaker even before he turned. The bull-man gave the appearance of wandering comfortably through this world created by the new man-god's sleeping imagination. He stood relaxed, wearing his usual kilt and sandals, looking around him at the odd scenery, as if he had come to visit an old acquaintance in a strange new house. In one of his very human hands Asterion was gathering what looked like spiderwebs, and somehow Alex knew that this was material used by Ariadne in some private and very mysterious weaving.

In his other hand the bull-man held a long, pointed stick, and with its tip had been sketching in the sand a diagram that Alex knew at once must be the map of the Labyrinth itself. Though each corridor in the map was only an inch or two wide, the whole plan was enormous, stretching over sandhill after sandhill, so that its far end was lost in darkness and distance.

Asterion threw the stick down, as if the diagram was now complete. Then he proceeded to ignore what he had sketched. His gaze remained fixed on Alex. "And yet," he continued, "it is not you any longer."

"Wrong. It is me, but it is someone else as well."

"Of course. You are a god now, and I think that is good." The Minotaur appeared to be pleased, but far from overwhelmed, by the discovery.

"Circe seems to think so too."

"So you know the enchantress now? I've never met her. I am enormously surprised, of course, at what has happened to you. Tell me as many details as you can."

Looking into his own mind as best he could, Alex could discover no Dionysian objections, and he related an outline of his recent adventures. In turn, Asterion told him of Shiva's plan to make Theseus a god.

The Twice-Born asked, "I suppose you have gained this knowledge in a dream?"

"It is the world in which I am most at home. And now in another dream I pass it on to you." Asterion's next question was: "Are you strong enough to oppose Shiva?"

Looking into his new memory for clues, Alex could find little to give him confidence on that point. "I don't know. I will do what I can, when the time comes. Where has the princess gone?"

The horned head turned slowly sideways, back and forth. "The dreams of both my sisters are always hard for me to find, difficult to enter. But I know, I feel, that Ariadne is beginning to consider herself lost. And once she understands that she is lost, she will probably be able to find her own way home."

"*I* don't understand." And now it seemed to Alex that the god inside him was speaking with him, sharing his concern. "If you can't tell me where Ariadne is, how am I to locate her?"

It seemed that the Minotaur could find no answer. From that point on, the dream gave promise of dissolving into the visions of the mad, with parts of the landscape that should not have been alive behaving as if they were. This was not the green and healthy growth normally inspired by the Twice-Born, but something cancerous and gray and ugly. Alex/Dionysus with an effort of will pulled himself free of it, awakening to the second morning of his new life.

He had not been awake for very long on that bright morning before there blew into sight, far out to sea, yet another ship with bellying sail, that appeared to be steering a course directly for the mouth of the harbor. Before it had come within a mile, Dionysus had descended from the hill to sit on the inner shoreline as before. He watched its approach from a seat so close to the water that the waves now and then lapped his sandaled feet, in the luxuriant shade of newly blooming olives.

He was not in the least dismayed to observe that, even at first glance, there was no possibility that this could be anything other than a pirate ship. It was a slightly larger vessel than the peaceful trader on which the princess and her new, crude entourage had departed only a few days ago. Two days ago, the sight of the dark flag, the swarm of armed men, would have sent Alex jumping to his feet and sprinting away for cover. But it would never have occurred to Dionysus to do anything of the kind, and Alex, bonded to his new partner inside the skull they now shared, felt quite secure enough to wait without fear.

It appeared there were a great many pirates in the sea. Well, the waters around the Isle of Refuge were probably one of their favorite hunting grounds. This vessel of freebooters, like its predecessor, anchored in the mouth of the harbor, blocking it while avoiding the possibility of being itself blocked in. Next the visitor, like its sister ship before it, launched a little boat; the difference was that instead of only two armed men, this dinghy contained five, one standing, in an attitude of command, while four others rowed.

Alex felt no apprehension, and little excitement, except that the way was now opening for him to go to Ariadne. With a sense of being intimately connected with the reassuring presence of Dionysus, he sat waiting, watching the men approach. He had no plan regarding them—except that they had brought him a ship.

When the small boat had come halfway across the harbor's inlet, he was suddenly struck by the pirate captain's strong resemblance to Theseus. The closer the man came, the greater the likeness seemed, and Alex was soon firmly convinced that this was Theseus's father, the Pirate King.

Splashing ashore through the shallows, and tugging their boat up after them, the pirates behaved cautiously, lodging only the very prow of their rowboat on shore, as if they feared an ambush, and wanted to be ready to put out again at a second's notice. But very soon they began to relax. The nearest cover that might possibly hide ambushers was more than a hundred paces from where Alex waited.

Alex studied the pirate captain, whose face was burned and wrinkled by the sun, his body richly scarred and tattooed in the course of an obviously eventful life, and hung with the sheaths of what seemed an inordinate number of weapons. With this model in view, it was easy to imagine what the son would look like in twenty or thirty years.

"Captain Aegeus?"

"Aye?"

"I have seen your son, Theseus," Alex told him.

If he had thought to surprise the buccaneer, he was mistaken. "Have you, now?" Aegeus did not seem startled by the news, or much impressed.

On impulse Alex asked the pirate chief, "Wouldn't you like your son to be a god?"

The King of Pirates did not seem startled by the question, or even much impressed; maybe he simply did not take the announcement seriously. "I don't know that it would make much difference. My lifelong tendency has been to ignore the gods, and so far they've done the same for me. Anyway, my son has considered himself to be endowed with divine powers, as far back as I can remember."

"You don't seem surprised to learn that Theseus is still alive; I understand you arranged to have him sent to Minos as part of the new Tribute."

"Did I? Must have slipped my mind." He gave vent to a burst of laughter. "That's one thing that I'll never be surprised to hear of my son. That he's still alive."

The captain and his four men surrounded him, their carefree voices booming now. "Someone's marooned you, hey, matey? How unkind!" And all five demonstrated that they thought it extremely funny.

Alex said no more. To argue with these men now, to try to persuade or threaten, would only delay his getting aboard the ship, if it had any effect at all. When they were at sea again, the Lord Dionysus would make his wishes known.

The most talkative of the sailors had some more to say. "Bad luck for you, good for us. Your family will pay a mighty ransom to have you back—I'll bet your life they will! Haw, haw, haw!"

Now two of the buccaneers menaced him with their weapons, while two others seized him. Dionysus tolerated their roughness, indeed scarcely felt it, nor did Alex—but only because his thoughts were elsewhere, on matters of great moment.

They hauled him to his feet and started to drag him away. In less than a minute they had taken the utterly unrecognized Dionysus into their rowboat, where they pushed him down in the bottom of the boat, so that the glorious youth in his purple robe seemed to be practically cowering at the pirate captain's feet. But the god's mind, melded with the mind of Alex, was focused far ahead, on plans for dealing with serious enemies, and finding the princess. Scarcely did either of them notice the indignity. Now the quest for Ariadne would soon be under way in earnest, and their thoughts were concentrated on that.

The small boat had been pushed off and was halfway across the harbor, the four oarsmen pulling with a good will, when the captain called out something to one Acetes, who was evidently the helmsman among the crew still waiting on the pirate ship.

Roughly the captain cried out that they would be hoisting anchor immediately. A stroke of good fortune had changed his plans, and they would not delay even for the short time necessary to take on water.

Acetes, a lean fellow with a red cloth tied around his head, and a curved sword at his belt, shouted back some acknowledgement of the order. Then he added, with a shade of concern in his voice, "Who've ye got there, mates?"

One man pounded in triumph on the captive's shoulder. "A prince's ransom, that's who! A bag of gold in a purple cape!"

---

*M*inutes later, the little boat was right under the ship's bow, with its painted, staring, devil-face. There was a story in that painting for Alex's new right eye to read, but he would not allow himself to be distracted by it now. Rough hands were pulling and pushing him aboard the ship. Again the minor mistreatment was easy to ignore, with other things to think about. Flies droned, trying to extract nourishment from old bloodstains on the deck. Garbage lay about. Whatever the captain's serious interests might be, they did not include cleanliness.

A faint moan, issuing from some cabin or locker, reached his ears. There were tones in it of great interest to the god. Suddenly concentrating once more on his immediate environment, Dionysus thought in a certain way about the sailors, who were still endeavoring to terrorize him. And the brush of his thought against their minds caused them to forget about him for the moment. As soon as they went slack-jawed and stood back, he reached out a hand to touch the latch that secured the door of the locker or cabin, and the fastening fell open.

Alex tugged open the door and looked inside, wrinkling his nose against the smell of heat and human confinement. A young woman lay slumped in one corner of the small space, barely conscious and obviously in great distress.

Edith had changed in the few days since Alex had briefly seen her in the Labyrinth, so that he did not recognize her at first glance. Even the ceremonial garments she was still wearing were stained and torn and faded out of recognition. Alex, in those distant-seeming days when he had been no more than a young soldier, had seen all of the youths and maidens of the Tribute more than once; and presently he understood that this young woman had been one of them. Somehow she had survived the murderous terror of Shiva, to become a harassed prisoner.

And now, as if dimly aware that the door was open, she stirred at last, muttering what sounded like some desperate prayer to Apollo.

Moving forward into the dim space, Alex bent down and put out a hand to raise her up. He was gratefully aware that the Twice-Born must be helping, for he could lift her as easily as a doll.

He said, "Your name is Edith—isn't it? Of course. You were on Corycus when I was there. How did you come here? Did any of the others in the Tribute manage to survive?"

Gradually, in halting phrases, a story came out. Captivity, as one of the Tribute people. Then freedom for a short time, in the Labyrinth. And finally, a worse captivity by far, a hell of repeated rape and other torments.

"Why have they done such things to you? Because they are bad men, and you are pretty, and young, and helpless, yes—but was there some other, special reason? Take your time in answering. Soon you will sleep, and there will be no more pain."

"I was a servant of Apollo, once," she whispered back. Her lips were cracked and dry.

The right hand of the god accepted a crystal goblet from the air. Carefully he gave the girl a drink. "And will be again, if that is what you want. Is that the reason why these men have so abused and tortured you?"

"They wanted me to tell them the secrets." Her voice was a little stronger now. "They said there must be secrets in Apollo's temples, and I must tell them what they were."

"Secrets? What could they be?" Dionysus wondered aloud. "Of all the gods I know, the Far-Worker seems least inclined to have mysteries."

"They wanted to know about places in the temples in which something could be hidden. I told them all I knew," said the girl in her small, hurt tones. "Which was little enough. I knew of nothing hidden."

"Of course you told them." Alex patted her hand. "Don't worry about that. But why have they carried you here, all the way from Corycus?"

Again, Edith needed a little time to gather the strength to speak. "Lord, they kept saying to me that they would bring me back to my home on Dia, and there I would serve them as a hostage. They also think that I will serve them as a guide, to some particular temple there in my native land."

With human concern Alex examined the young woman. The traces of the terror and abuse she had been through were very plain. Was there nothing he could do to heal her? The skills and attributes of Dionysus offered very little. It would be easy enough to cause her to forget her troubles utterly, for a long time if not forever; and possibly in a little while Alex would use the powers of the Twice-Born to accomplish that. But right now more urgent matters must claim almost all of his attention.

Anger was mounting swiftly in him. But Dionysus was no Shiva, to deal out death in the winking of an eye; and Alex was no Butcher, either.

Slowly Dionysus shook his head. A purpose was growing in him, though he had not yet formed it in clear words, even in the mind he shared with Alex. Backing their shared body out of the cabin, he allowed the crew once more to remember the fact of his presence. Now they stood squinting at the young man they had carried aboard, evidently trying to make up their minds what to do with him next. Alex wanted to demand of the pirates: *What have you done here?* With the memory and experience of Dionysus to draw on, he had already realized that he was unlikely to get anywhere trying to work with and through these men.

Still, he could feel enough human sympathy for them to make the attempt. Also it would be useful to have a full crew, or something like one, to man his ship.

He stood up straight and raised his voice. "Will you not listen to me?"

Sadly, it seemed that they would not. They had given themselves to some darker power, and accepted a kind of blindness. Except for one member of the crew, the man named Acetes, who seemed on the verge of saying something sympathetic—but then the steersman fell silent, when he realized what strange things had begun to happen before his eyes.

*   *   *

Alex had left open the door of the little cabin, or locker, and now Dionysus reached in, with their shared right hand, to stroke the head of the captive girl. Soon he would bring her out into the open air, but not just yet. He feared that she might be frightened by certain things that were soon going to happen on the deck. Her freedom was now assured, and could wait just a little longer.

"All will be well," Alex tried to comfort her. "But tell me again what has happened to bring you here. I'm not sure that I understand. Somehow, you got away from Shiva?"

Slowly her gaze focused on him. Whatever she saw evidently gave her strength to talk, to speak clearly. "I was with Asterion, and he protected me."

"In the Labyrinth?"

"Yes. But then—Shiva came again."

"I see. All right, it doesn't matter now. No doubt you would like to go home, to Dia? In freedom, I mean, of course."

"Lord, if only I could go home!"

Dionysus nodded. "As soon as we can hail another ship," said Alex, "I'll send you home by that one, or by this, whichever is the slower. The faster one I must keep, and use. I would be inclined to escort you to your home myself, but there are other things that I must do. Matters so urgent that they must not wait."

Now a handful of crewmen, suddenly struck by the fact that their lordly prisoner still remained unbound, approached Alex, and were actually making an attempt to bind the youth whom they still imagined to be their prisoner.

As soon as the ropes had been knotted round the god's wrists and ankles, Dionysus, irritated and distracted from the plans he was trying to make, caused them to loosen and slide off.

When he did this, the men who had tied the ropes on simply tried to tie them on again—the madness that had now taken possession of the crew was none of his doing, but rather sprang from their own cruelty and greed. They were too far gone in their own quiet, hopeless insanity to comprehend the meaning of what they were trying to do.

But Edith, looking out through the open door of the cabin where she still lay huddled, had the beginning of understanding. And so did the helmsman, Acetes, whose eyes widened when he saw what was happening, and who began to plead with his shipmates to stop. But they could not or would not hear him—it was as if some kind of curse had seized them.

From scraps of conversation Alex overheard, he soon understood that, in a kind of circular chain of circumstance, the pirate king intended to sell him to King Perses, having heard that the Tribute levied this year was going to be repeated, next year, or even sooner.

In the god's memory Alex could find the image of what he himself ought to look like now. His hair should be fuller and darker than it was, and it doubtless would take on that aspect soon—provided Shiva let him live long enough. Even now, with his purple cloak covering his broad shoulders, he looked enough like the popular image of royalty to account for the sailors' optimism in the matter of being able to collect a great ransom.

Now some of them had picked up scraps of rope and cord with which to fetter him, but to their amazement their efforts along that line met with no success. The ropes would not hold together; the fibers separated, the knots came undone as soon as they touched Alex's hands or feet. And he sat looking at them with a smile in his dark eyes.

"Stop!" This was the helmsman crying out.

"What's wrong with you?" Aegeus demanded, what little patience he possessed now badly frayed.

Acetes said, "You are trying to abuse a god." But his voice had suddenly fallen so low that the others in their impatience, and with their own ongoing clamor, failed to hear him.

"What's that? Speak up?"

Once more the steersman screamed in anguish at his shipmates.

The captain shouted abuse and mockery at him, and with a volley of oaths ordered the crew to get the sail up.

The wind at once filled the sheet of cotton canvas, and the mast creaked and strained, but the ship did not move.

"Are we aground? We can't be!"

"What's going on?"

If they had thought about that question instead of merely shouting it, they might still have saved their lives. The power of a god was taking their ship away from them. Men were splashing in wine up to their ankles, wading in sparkling red that poured from nowhere to run across the deck and into the sea. But for once they found no joy in wine. The lines on which they tugged and heaved turned into green vines in their hands.

Jarred at last into his senses, the captain gave up trying to begin a voyage, and ordered the helmsman to put in to land.

He was too late. Ghostly images of two leopards appeared, and at that sight some of the men began leaping overboard.

Dionysus said to them, "If you will behave like wild beasts, then you ought not to wear the shapes of men." And in midair the bodies of those who jumped took on the smooth and limbless shape of dolphins.

Turning to face the one he had tried to kidnap, Aegeus drew one of his weapons from his belt, brandished it for a moment, and then saw it fall clattering to the deck when his own hands and arms betrayed him, flailing the air in madness.

Now Aegeus was no longer able to grip a weapon, or anything else. The King of Pirates, the father of Theseus, could see and feel his own arms contracting, the bones in them changing, his hands losing their fingers, warping into the digitless shape of fins.

Driven into a frenzy by their fear, the remainder of the sailors, all but the captain himself, leapt for the rail and over it, and even as they jumped, their arcing bodies were transformed in midair, grimaces of fear transformed to mindless dolphin smiles, taking on in midleap sleek streamlined shapes.

All of them losing, among the million other things they lost, any chance of ever becoming gods.

One cried out, just before his mouth took on the mindless dolphin smile, "Lord, mercy!"

The Twice-Born was calm, regretful. "Another god might have done much worse to you than I have done. Be glad that it was not the Far-Worker whom you brought on board. Now leave my ship!"

Now, of all those the god had condemned, only Aegeus himself remained standing on the deck. The pirate captain's hands had disappeared, his feet were now barely large enough to let him stand on them. His clothes were gone, his skin no longer that of a man, but his head and the sound of his voice were human still. It was as if he still maintained them in that form, by a supreme effort of his own will.

"A prophecy once said that I would never hang—by all the gods, it was right!"

Dionysus had nothing to say at the moment. Neither did Alex.

But the King of the Pirates was not quite finished. On the edge of doom he bragged and blustered to the new avatar of Dionysus that his son, Theseus, was going to be a god—he had the word of Shiva for that.

"And you have faith in the Destroyer's word, do you?"

The pirate's voice was failing now, but he could still form words. "My son is going to be a god. Seek out Theseus. Will you do that for me? Seek out my son!"

"Why should I do that?"

"So he may kill you."

"Has he the Princess Ariadne with him?"

Triumph flamed in the pirate's ruined face. "He has her with him. My lad has her, and he'll keep her, too. Go search for them on the island of Dia. You'll find your princess there, and Theseus and Shiva too. Shiva will burn you to a cinder, puny god! And my son will have your Face!"

"That may be. But you will not be there to see it happen. Go!"

And at last the King of the Pirates screamed in despair, a scream that mutated into a croaking and inhuman noise. The change had overcome his head and face before he went overboard.

Now, in helpless obedience, they were all gone.

Dionysus turned away from the suddenly unpopulated deck, and went to stand beside Acetes, who had not moved from his post, though he had let go of the steering oar. Alex put out a hand and laid it on the trembling helmsman's arm, restraining him, when he too would have tried to escape by plunging into the sea, and at the same time giving him the courage that he needed to stand fast.

Now the young man spoke in a different tone, perfectly human and friendly. "Take back the steering oar, Acetes, and don't be afraid."

Obediently the man clamped both hands upon the worn and weathered wood. But both his eyes were tight shut, as if he was afraid to open them. "My lord. Lord Dionysus, God of the Many Names, have mercy on me!"

Gently the god squeezed his arm. "Be at peace, steersman, I say. Open your eyes; now there is nothing terrible to see. The wind will change, and I will need a good sailor to advise me. We are going on to Dia."

Edith had fallen into a faint, and lay where the men had pushed her. Abstractedly, with half a thought, Alex/Dionysus sent a sprite to comfort the young woman softly, and ease her slumber, so that she might rest and heal. The door of the cabin was standing open, and when the girl felt ready to come out on deck she could.

He hastened to tell her the good news: she would see her home even sooner than she had expected, and in far better circumstances.

Then he faced around. "Acetes, I suppose you know the right course for the Island of Dia?"

"I believe I do, great lord. But the wind is wrong."

"I do not have the ordering of winds, so you must do the best you can. I can raise or lower the sail, if you will let me know which way you want it."

An act of will, and the ship was free to move again, once more subject to the mundane forces of wind and wave.

Alex/Dionysus soon discovered that he needed no crew to sail this or any other ship, or at least none beyond his sprites and satyrs. He soon discovered that, with a little help from them, he could drive the vessel anywhere by the sheer power of his will, even against the normal wind. But to have the mundane forces on his side was a great help. He caused the compass-pyx to glow so that the helmsman could read it when the sun had dipped below the sea.

Alex was beginning to find the handholds that he needed, not on ropes and oars, but on the very fabric of reality. There were limits on what Dionysus might accomplish, but they were very far beyond the limits that constrained a mortal.

What was going to happen when he faced Shiva, Alex did not know; his new Dionysian memory seemed to hold no clue, no plan, that would help him survive the Third Eye's dazzling, incinerating lance of light. But now, apart from his lack of any tactical plan, he thought he was as ready for the contest as he was ever going to be.

When they were driving swiftly through the sea, more or less in the right direction, he glanced toward Edith again, and saw that her eyes were open and fixed on him. Reluctant to leave the helmsman's side just now, Alex beckoned her to him, and she crept out of the open cabin, trembling, and came across the deck so Dionysus could hold her in the curve of his arm and gently comfort her.

Then Alex raised his head, and called into the wind, "Princess, be of good cheer. I'm coming to you."

he great escape had indeed turned out to be a tremendous adventure, just as the Princess Ariadne had expected from the beginning. But for her it was also a great deal more. For many days her only real goal in life had been to help Theseus, first to save him from destruction, eventually to claim him as her true lover. Someday, somehow, they would be betrothed, and then, by some means and ceremony, she would become his beloved wife. Eventually she would sit somewhere on a throne beside him—but that was vague in a distant future, and at the moment not at all important. She still refused to doubt that her lover was, or could be, in some sense a real prince—she was all the more determined to believe it, now that she could no longer deny that he was a pirate.

Once more blessed by favorable winds, the ship under direct command of the pirate prince bore on through the sea at a rapid pace, her compass-pyx tuned to the mind of Theseus. The captured trader, once the property of Captain Petros, was sailing more or less with it, sometimes within bowshot, sometimes forced by the vagaries of wind and wave a mile or more away. Near Dia they were going to join forces with whatever additional ships Shiva and Perses might have managed to dispatch, and which could reach the point of rendezvous in time.

As the days passed, Ariadne was increasingly beset by seasickness and fear, but was grimly determined not to meekly let such feelings master her.

"And what are we going to do when we get there?" she demanded. No one had seriously discussed the matter with her yet. Her companion might not be minded to answer questions, but now on the small ship he couldn't very well avoid her.

"*You're* not going to do much of anything. Certainly not

going on shore with the raiding party." Theseus made no pretense of asking, or trying to persuade her. He was simply telling her how things were going to be. "You'll stay aboard ship, locked up, so I'll know where to find you when I get back."

"Locked up!" The idea left her speechless for a moment, so protest would have to wait. But she had no doubt he meant it.

"As for what I'm going to do—the first thing will be to meet with the other captains, the leaders on these other ships, and work out a coordinated plan. Make sure they all realize that I am in command."

"Uncle Perses may have appointed his own commander, if he's sending a squadron."

"I hope he is, we can use the ships and men. But what a mere king says won't matter. Shiva has appointed *me*."

Ariadne's anger at the man who had deceived her had grown great, but even worse than the anger was the hollow feeling that lay beneath it. Sometime, somehow, the anger must recede, and when it did, how much of their love would still be left?

Once or twice she had looked into the ship's single tiny cabin, really only a storage space, and once, shortly after they came aboard, Theseus had taken her there, as the only place on board where the two of them might be together out of sight of the crew. No one would spend any more time than necessary in that uncomfortable space; it was only a little smaller than the second clothes closet in her bedroom back in the palace on Corycus, but crowded with stores and intolerably hot and close, under the baking sun, so that it seemed much smaller still. Even when she had lain there in her lover's arms, she could hardly wait to get out again, into the fresh air. To be shut up in that smelly hole alone—

Finally Ariadne found her voice for protest. "And suppose I don't choose to stay in that oven?"

"You'll stay." His calm assumption of control was totally infuriating. "When we go ashore, I'm leaving a skeleton crew on board each ship. Pegleg, for one." That was the nickname of a sailor who had lost part of a lower limb, and hobbled on a foot carved out of ivory. "Along with our graybeards, anyone who can't move fast on land. But I don't want 'em distracted—and you can be very distracting, in several ways, when you're running around loose."

"I won't be shut up in that miserable hole." The refusal came in a royal tone, one that in the experience of a princess had always produced results.

But the only response it provoked from Theseus was a faint smile. "You'll stay," he repeated. "There's a good strong latch on the outside of the door."

Since she had been a child, no one, not her father or Phaedra, not even her oppressive uncle, had ever told her so flatly what she must do, and she found the treatment intolerable.

She turned her back on him, taking her turn at staring out to sea. He must not see any hint that tears of rage and humiliation were threatening to break out.

Several days passed. The wind held, and the compass-pyx seemed to be working well—though the only sure proof of that was arrival at one's destination. Theseus spoke to her less often than before, and made no attempt to take her into the cabin out of the crew's sight. Theseus had not approached her as a lover since that single hurried and uncomfortable encounter shortly after they came aboard. She slept alone, when she slept at all, in a small space on deck half-sheltered against the outer wall of the cabin in which she would be locked away. Ariadne thought that he seemed to have forgotten first her needs, and then her very existence.

No, he had not quite put her entirely out of his thoughts. Once Theseus demanded to know whether she had visited the Island of Dia before. Ariadne still yearned to be of help, but had to plead ignorance. He was trying to learn all he could about the island and its people, from those of his men who had been there. He wanted the most recent information possible.

About the time that the Island of Dia came into sight, so did a couple of other ships, soon identifiable as two of those dispatched from Corycus by Uncle Perses.

"Is that all the help I'm going to get?" Theseus complained, squinting into sunlight. But it was hard to tell from his tone whether the fact pleased him or alarmed him.

Before sunset, the four small vessels came together behind a tiny islet, little more than a sandbar, that screened them from the Dian shore, and a hasty conference was called.

Any additional ships dispatched by Perses or Shiva would need several days to get to Dia from Corycus. Shiva had not promised any direct, personal help, no doubt having what he considered more important business elsewhere.

It would have been too much to hope that Perses, the new Minos, would somehow have been able to assemble and dispatch a large invasion force on such short notice. A regular fleet or squadron might be on its way, next week or next month, if he used his regular navy; but the two captains who had just arrived had no knowledge that any such effort was being planned.

As matters stood, there were still only four ships. And, as Theseus soon discovered, one of the newcomers was seriously undermanned. Counting noses on crews, he arrived at a total of sixty-four men. As it would be necessary to leave minimal crews aboard each vessel, he would be able to lead only about forty ashore, as an effective raiding party.

Perses had told his sailors that Theseus was to be in undisputed command, so that theoretically there should be no doubt as to who was going to put on the Face of Dionysus when it was found.

Yet Theseus couldn't imagine that even the weakest man among his crew, if that wretch should have the tremendous good fortune of being able to put on a god's Face, would worry much about whether Theseus or any other mortal might be angry at him. Even the wrath of a merely human king, like Perses, could be safely disregarded. The anger of Shiva, now—*that* would be worthy of some consideration.

Theseus remained too impatient to wait for any more ships to show up—whether there would eventually be more or not was an open question. And he was ready, in fact eager, to trust to luck, and his own strength and skill.

The subject of prayers and sacrifices came up in the captain's meeting, and it was decided to let each crew satisfy themselves in that regard.

Theseus said to the other men, "Let Samson be my blood sacrifice, if I am required to make one. It seems to me he leaked enough to please any god who is interested in that kind of thing." He paused and thought before adding, "And at the moment there is no one else who can readily be spared."

Theseus had no personal experience of previous forays against Dia, but most of what he had heard about that island from others in his profession, including his father, tended to raise his confidence. He was ready to assure his shipmates that on the Island of Dia a foray to collect a treasure might, if everything went smoothly, amount to little more than simply sailing in, taking a little stroll on shore, filling one's pockets and sailing out again.

One of the other leaders of the raid, Mochlos, the captain of one of the two ships that had been waiting at the rendezvous, was not convinced. "If everything goes smoothly. Yes. If one knows exactly where the treasure is, and is lucky enough to lay his hands on it at once."

Mochlos was almost as tall as Theseus, of angular build and indeterminate age, dark hair hanging in two braids beside jutting cheekbones.

Theseus gave him a steady stare. "Others have raided Dia before, with little difficulty. My own father many times."

Mochlos returned the stare. Suddenly Theseus wondered if the other might be taking that side of the argument in a deliberate effort to provoke an accusation of cowardice. What kind of madman would do that?

Mildly enough Mochlos went on, in a cultured voice that belied his general appearance, "True, the Dians have never had an army, nor do they continually patrol their coasts—unless they have just recently begun such an objectionable practice. But there are, after all, about a thousand men dwelling on the island, and like everyone else they are doubtless rather touchy about certain things. Such as uninvited visitors coming ashore and carrying off their wives and children, or their cattle, or their works of art. Or their food, or their casks of white wine—I hear they press some fairly decent grapes, in certain valleys inland. They're probably also sensitive about their temples being desecrated. Most people are."

The Prince of Pirates was contemptuous. "A thousand scattered farmers, vinedressers, goatherds and quarry workers."

The other could be stubborn too. "That means two thousand arms with muscles in them, two thousand hands clutching weapons—even if it's only reaping hooks and pitchforks. And you say the object of our visit is to hoist something out of a temple of Apollo . . ."

"It's not only my whim that we do that. Shiva says the same thing."

"Of course. But doesn't the thought of arrows worry you a little bit?" When the others looked at Mochlos, he amplified, "Silver arrows, I mean?" He shook his head, dark braids swinging. "If I had to select a deity of whom to make a mortal enemy, the Sun-God wouldn't be my first choice."

"Any gentleman of fortune who feels much concern about making enemies—well, that gentleman is probably in the wrong business." Theseus drew a dagger and began to play with it, thunking it solidly into the wood and pulling it out again. "And if *I* were inclined to fret about what any of the gods are thinking— mind you, I'm not, but if I were—my absolute last choice as an enemy would definitely be Shiva." *Thunk.*

The others looked at Theseus soberly as he sheathed his dagger and went on. "I have seen and talked to Shiva, very recently, at his invitation. I have looked into that Third Eye when it was partly open. And I'm due to talk to him again, ere very many days are past.

"As for Apollo, I have never seen him, I don't know where he is—and I doubt he's ever paid me much attention either."

The others looked at Theseus with respect. One of them laughed appreciatively.

One suddenly, rapping out a string of oaths, came around to his side. "Spoken like a true prince of pirates! That's the talk for me."

"All right, then," said Mochlos, and paused. "From all that your description tells me, the temple we want may very well be the one that's miles inland. For the kind of raid you contemplate, we had better take several ships."

One of the sailors, who had spent time on Dia and knew the lay of the land fairly well, had sketched with charcoal on the deck an outline of the place that they were going to attack. They talked about the island's dimensions, in miles, and the location of towns and villages, hills and streams and harbors.

"There's only one fort, one real strong point, that I know of. It's on the far side, the north side, and we don't need to go anywhere near it."

Theseus could tell from the attitude of the men who had just joined him, the look on their faces and the questions they asked, that they had not yet been told the real object of the raid. Not even the captains knew.

The second of the newly arrived captains, who had had little to say so far, now asked, "Is this a treasure that will need a crew of many men to carry?"

"Not at all," said Theseus. "One man will carry it easily. Myself."

But he realized that now they were all going to have to know what they were looking for. "There is a god-Face there, that I am to have. Shiva wants me to have it."

That was so impressive a statement that it produced silence instead of murmuring. At last the man who had first mentioned the treasure spoke again. "Oh. Which god?"

"Not that it makes any difference, for our purposes, but the god is Dionysus."

"Ah, well. Wouldn't mind putting that one on my own head." And soon the tension had relaxed sufficiently to allow a round of bawdy laughter.

Mochlos inquired, "I suppose there'll be no objection if the rest of us make some profit from this trip too?"

"No objection—as long as we see to it that the main objective is accomplished first."

The temple of Apollo, in which Theseus first intended to seek the treasure, was right on the coast, so the raiders would not have to fight their way inland. Maybe this temple had been chosen as their first target because of its location.

The leaders in their conference went over their reasons for thinking the Face of Dionysus was to be found in one of these two temples. There were various theories according to which it might be so. But the only real reason to believe it was that Shiva had told him so.

He distinctly remembered Shiva mentioning, as if in passing, that there was a possibility that the information about the Face was wrong. But Theseus wasn't going to tell the captains that.

Ariadne was soon aware that Theseus had explained his mission to the men, for she could overhear some of them arguing about it among themselves.

"How does Shiva know where the Face of some other god is to be found?"

"How does a god know anything? What's the point of mortals wondering about that?"

"If the Destroyer's so interested, why didn't he carry it himself to the man he wants to have it?"

"Maybe he was too busy. How in the Underworld should I know?"

"If the local people know that the Face is there, why has no one put it on?"

"Probably because they're not aware. I'd bet that no one on Dia now realizes that it's there."

The whole business made little sense to Ariadne. But she was beginning to realize that that might often be the case when gods were involved.

She had never seen Dionysus in any avatar; but when she tried to picture Theseus in that role, she did not at all like what her imagination showed her.

The raiders were encouraged, and considered their prospects for success much enhanced, when none of their number who had local knowledge could recall there being any large settlement very near their goal. The nearest village, of about a hundred people, was two miles away. If things went smoothly, they could be in and out, and at sea again before most of the people on the island even knew they had arrived.

The captains were gathered on the deck again. "Now as I recall, there's one sizable house, a kind of country estate I think, on the coast within a quarter of a mile of the creek where we're going to put in." The stick used as pointer made a dot on the sketched map.

"Still, that looks like the best place. Anywhere we go ashore, there's bound to be someone near."

The planner stared at the crudely sketched map. "If we don't find what we seek there—well, getting to the next temple will be tougher. That's miles inland."

"The next one will be impossible, if we give the whole island time to mobilize."

"Time for them to run into the hills and hide, more likely."

"It wouldn't be wise to count on that."

"I thought we had this settled. No one ever took any treasure by being timid."

"It's settled that we're going for it, but no one's even mentioned tactics yet. High time we did."

One of the buccaneers had some fairly recent news to pass along about their potential opposition: the leaders of the Dianite villages, tired of being despoiled, had banded together and sought the help of a man to organize, unite, and command all of their defense forces.

"Hired a professional, did they? Too bad. What's he look like? Maybe I've met him somewhere."

"Wiry fellow called Nestor, maybe about thirty years old. Sandy hair, his nose looks like it was once broken. Not a native Dianite, but a real professional."

"Did this Nestor bring any people with him to the island?"

"Could be one or two. Maybe a small handful. I think no more than that."

During the hours of daylight, one or another member of each ship's crew was always scanning the sea, hoping to sight the sail of the ship captained by Aegeus, Theseus's father. The bow of that ship, Theseus said, was adorned with a distinctive painting, showing a pair of monster eyes.

"I hope he arrives soon," said Ariadne. "I want to meet him."

"I hope he brings some fighting men."

But when morning came again, no other ships had yet arrived. Now and then Theseus sent a small and agile man up the mast, which was little more than a stick of slippery wood, in an effort to see farther.

When the first light of morning showed no helpful sails in sight, he said, "We're not going to wait. We've enough men now. More than we need, in fact." He sounded as if he believed that, but the men only looked at one another.

"So we go in now, as soon as we can get ready."

Before the morning sun had fully cleared the horizon, all four of the pirate ships made their final approach to the island, with crews under strict orders to minimize the noise of oars.

They lowered anchors cautiously in a small sheltered bay, at the mouth of a muddy creek, all prows pointing back toward the open sea, and the raiding parties quickly prepared to go ashore. This was one time when no one wanted to run a ship aground; it might be necessary to put out quickly, and with only a skeleton crew to pull the oars or hoist sail, if the wind happened to be right to make that profitable.

"Time to put you in the coop, my little chick."

When Theseus beckoned imperiously, Ariadne meekly bowed her head and went into the cabin—her fists were clenched so that her fingernails, raggedly uncared-for since the adventure started, bit into her palms, but every instinct assured her that this was not the time to resist. When she did fight for her rights, she would do so with all her strength; but in these circumstances all the strength that she could muster would have done her no good at all.

In the doorway she hesitated. "Water. At least give me some water to take in there with me."

One of the crewmen put a jug into her hands. It felt half-empty, but she took it and went in, making no further protest. The wooden overhead of the cabin was not quite high enough to allow her to stand upright. The place was just as hot and foul, and crowded with miscellaneous seafaring baggage, as she remembered it to be. A folded sail, coiled ropes and cords, dried fish piled on the deck like dark slats of wood. She heard the small splash of an anchor going overboard on the end of a line, and then the voice of Theseus, urgent and energetic.

She sat down on a spare folded sail, and folded her arms. If she had to find some way to get out of here without help, absolutely had to, she was confident that she could.

As long as most of the men still remained on the ship, Ariadne could hear them talking in excited voices, but as soon as Theseus gave the order to go ashore, a sudden near-silence fell, broken only by the sounds of splashing and an occasional oath.

Through the chinks in the walls of the low deckhouse, Ariadne watched them climb away.

The men were all professionals who knew what they were doing, and soon the bulk of them were gone ashore, except for the skeleton crew. For a few moments she could hear Pegleg's oak foot thumping on the deck. Then that noise stopped. In the distance, a gull screamed, and then another.

Time passed. Ariadne sipped at the warm water in her jug. The morning sun warmed rapidly, its heat beat down upon the decks and walls, and the cabin became even less endurable. Of course there would be some way out, and if she absolutely had to have it she would close her eyes and find it. There would be a loose plank somewhere. Or—

She sat imagining her web. When the thing was difficult to get started, as it was today, it helped to visualize a giant spider, weaving a web-pattern with concentric circles of fine strands. And then the imaginary creature growing, moving away, leaving one glistening filament to mark the path of its departure—

The eyes of the princess suddenly came open at the sound of an alarm, if not a panic, among the skeleton crew. Their voices were not raised, but the princess could hear a rapid muttering that was all the more alarming because it was trying to be quiet.

All the cabin walls had chinks in them, as did the overhead, and these defects had the accidental benefit of allowing a certain amount of air to circulate. Presently Ariadne, peering out through the small gaps between boards in the shoreward wall, caught her breath. A gang of men she had never seen before were approaching at a run, carrying among them a random, amateurish assortment of weapons. Each man had a white scarf tied around his upper arm, evidently as a kind of emblem or insignia; otherwise they were casually dressed as field-workers or artisans. One loosed an arrow toward the ship. She heard the impact smart against the planking.

Looking out through a chink in the cabin wall, Ariadne could catch a glimpse of the man they were calling for, standing with folded arms on the very edge of the shore, and looking about him alertly. He was perhaps thirty years old, sandy-haired and wiry, simply clad, with nothing amateurish or showy about the sheathed sword at his side.

A couple of the men on shore were waving torches, their flames only marginally visible in the bright sunshine. Suddenly terrified by the thought of fire, Ariadne screamed to let whoever was out there know that she was in the cabin, and pounded on the thick door with ineffective hands.

Pegleg and the other limpers and graybeards of the skeleton crew had begun, too late, a futile effort to put out to sea. Oars clattered and clashed and fell; as far as Ariadne could tell, there was no attempt to hoist sail. Cowering unarmed in the cabin, she heard the struggle, the swearing and the screams.

Every minute or so some excited Dian man or boy, running at full speed, would come pounding up on shore, calling for someone named Nestor and then shouting to the leader some kind of a report as to where the main body of the raiders now were, what they were doing, and how many they were. Each report, it seemed to Ariadne, was more likely than not to be contradictory of the one just preceding it. The consensus on the number of pirates who had come ashore seemed to be around two hundred.

Applying a rule of thumb learned from experience, Nestor

decided in the privacy of his own mind that if he cut that number in half he would probably be somewhere near the truth.

"They're headed for the Temple of Apollo?" The leader was keeping deliberately calm, but he sounded mystified. "What do they expect to find there in the way of loot?"

Ariadne could not hear the response clearly.

"Well, maybe more are landing elsewhere, and they're using the temple as a rendezvous point. Or else they're just confused—that happens a lot. Or possibly they know something that we don't." He raised his voice in the tone of one giving a decisive order. "Let's see how well she burns!"

The scream seemed to come bursting out of her throat without any conscious intention on her part, and it threatened to tear the top of her head off.

She had really been locked in the cabin—a firm try on the door proved that—but moments after the scuffling was over Nestor opened the door, in response to her screams. She could see blood spattered on the deck when she came out.

The ship was already actually on fire; at least the sail was burning spectacularly.

She shrank back momentarily when the grinning man confronted her, not at all certain what treatment she was going to be given. But then she gritted her teeth and burst out of the cabin, regardless of whether missiles might still be flying. Ariadne had determined that if she was to die, it would not be in that miserable hole.

The lean man called Nestor caught her effortlessly with his left hand, as she would have gone running past him, and at the same time lowered the sword that he was holding in his right. Briefly he looked past her, satisfying himself that no one else was in the cabin.

He was not nearly as big as Theseus, she thought, but possessed of all the wiry strength he seemed to need, and moved and spoke with the same air of confidence.

When the man who had caught her spoke to her it was in the common language that everyone who traveled much on the Great

Sea, or dealt with travelers, learned to use. "You're free now, lass. Where're you from?"

He thinks I was a prisoner, Ariadne suddenly realized. And in the next moment she realized that he was right.

One of Nestor's men barked at her to answer.

But Nestor only shook his head. "That's all right. After all she's been through, it's only natural that she's mightily upset."

Then he faced back to Ariadne. "Who's the leader here, girl? Of the people who locked you up?"

"A man called Theseus." The name came simply and automatically, and called up no emotion.

Nor did it seem to mean anything to her questioner. "Don't know him. The two ships that got away looked Corycan."

She nodded.

"And what do they think they're after here?"

Some remnant of loyalty, or maybe it was only innate stubbornness, kept her from blurting out the truth, or giving any reasonable answer. She could hear herself repeating, idiotically, "I don't know, I don't know."

Nestor did not press her but turned away again, conferring with his men. Presently he once more turned back. "You don't talk like a slave or servant. What's your name, girl?" His voice softened. "Don't be afraid, no one will hurt you now."

"Ariadne," said the princess softly, without thinking. And a moment later she felt a faint pang of fear for having revealed her identity, because it was more than possible that these folk would be unfriendly to the lords of Corycus. But Nestor heard the name without blinking, and it was borne in on her again how far she was from looking the part of a princess now.

For many days, until now, Ariadne had continued to assume, without really thinking about it, that if she remained loyally with the romantic prince she had come to love so terribly (not that she could really imagine herself doing anything else), then her life, barring a few exciting and odd adventures, would continue to be that of a princess.

But the time had now come when she could no longer make

excuses for her lover, not even to herself—there was no getting around the fact that Theseus had been downright cruel to her.

Not that Theseus had ever physically mistreated her—unless you counted his locking her in the cabin. But she could almost wish he had been moved to slap her—that would at least have shown strong personal interest.

"I see now," she murmured to herself, "that to be a princess is really nothing in the great world. To be loved is perhaps everything—but now I doubt that Theseus loves me. If only I were a goddess—but I am not. There is no Face of Ariadne that anyone can put on—the only one who can wear the Face of Ariadne is myself."

She, Ariadne, had her pride. She was the daughter of King Minos of Corycus—the real king, who had been unlawfully deposed and murdered—and of his true queen, Pasiphae. And she was the younger sister of Princess Phaedra; and the older sister of Prince Asterion, known to the vulgar as the Minotaur.

In her imagination she could hear her own voice now, trying to explain all this to the man called Nestor. Meanwhile she knew quite well that it was really herself to whom she was trying to explain, how in the name of all the gods she, a princess of Corycus, had come to be here in this situation. And in any case, Nestor seemed to have given up listening to her, once he decided that she was babbling.

mmediately on coming ashore, Theseus had picked out half a dozen of his men, choosing the youngest and most agile, and sent them straight for the seaside villa that practically overlooked their landing from its nearby cliff. It seemed to him that the first thing he had better do was to prevent any local people who might have seen the landing from getting away and spreading the alarm.

The small band of fast-moving pirates went scrambling up the rocks in the gray light of dawn, soon broke into the stable behind the large house, where, shouting their reports downhill, they said they had found no one at home, but were able to report the capture of two cameloids. Shouting up the hill, Theseus quickly ordered a couple of his agile six to mount these animals in swift scouting probes. He thought it an ominous sign that the house was unoccupied. Whether any of the inhabitants might already be busy spreading the alarm he couldn't tell.

He had come ashore with forty men, and now the thirty-odd who made up the main body of the raiding party were quickly moving inland. Theseus was already able to make out, in the distance, the classical white rectangular shape that had to be of one of the temples they were looking for.

The band kept advancing rapidly on foot, following the course of a ravine. The bottom of this natural ditch was mostly dry, with only a puddle or two here and there along its twisted length, and the head-high cliffs of crumbling earth on either side would offer them concealment part of the way to the seaside temple. Halfway there, the ravine went twisting off inland, climbing gradually into higher country, and the attackers had to climb out of it and go running across an open pasture.

"Let's go, lads!"

Moving at a quick trot, some with weapons drawn, they began to cover the uneven space of land between them and their goal.

One of the men who had gone on an impromptu scouting mission on a cameloid came back in a few minutes, driving his mount in a quick pacing run, with a report for Theseus.

"No signs of opposition, cap'n. Saw only three, four people, all running the other way."

"Good. Which way did Hector go?"

"Couldn't say, chief."

"All right. Get off that damned animal and come with us." If he'd had twenty or thirty mounted men, that would have given him a considerable advantage, but one just drew attention to the raiders' presence.

Theseus was not making any plans beyond the moment when he was going to find himself inside the temple. Somehow he had been visualizing the treasure as lying out in the open, on an altar or table of some sort, waiting for him to come along and pick it up. He had to keep reminding himself that there was no reason to believe that getting his hands on a Face would really be that easy.

Scanning the landscape for signs of potential opposition, he could see three or four buildings, all on hilltops, that had the look of temples of one kind or another. All were more than a mile away, and Theseus gave them no thought except to suppose they were dedicated to other gods, deities who might be expected to be neutral in this present conflict.

Now the raiders, moving on foot, were rapidly drawing near the temple on the shore. Nearby, just a few yards inland from the formal erection of marble walls and columns, there clustered some shabby wooden outbuildings, not nearly as fine to look at. Even the most austere temple, dedicated to the most exalted god, needed a latrine nearby, if humans were going to spend much time there. Suddenly it occurred to Theseus to wonder, for the first time in his life, whether men when they became gods still required such a facility. Soon he ought to know.

With Theseus still in the vanguard, and men bunched closely at his heels, the raiding force covered the last few yards. They went bounding across a grassy terrace, up the broad steps of Apollo's temple, and in between the massive columns. There were no doors here to be locked or broken down.

The walls and columns, the decorated entablatures and cornices, were all of the fine local marble. The structure was only partially enclosed, standing broadly open to the sun and air, oriented less with regard to the cardinal directions than to the shape of its natural rocky base.

On the very verge of crossing the threshold, some of the raiders hesitated before intruding upon the shaded solemnity before them. Trying to squelch this reluctance before it could get a foothold, their leader strode right in, and bellowed, "Are there any gods in here? If there are, damn you, come out and fight!"

When Theseus shouted that, his companions looked at him, and the terror and awe they felt were briefly visible in their faces. But he roared his laughter at them, and they got on about their work.

The handful of people already in the temple froze in place after a single look at the grinning men who were advancing toward them so rapidly with drawn swords. A moment later most of the worshipers of Apollo were running away at top speed.

By chance the raiders had interrupted a ceremony in progress. A short procession, consisting of five or six men and boys, all but the chief priest ritually naked, had been approaching the altar. A bearded man who was evidently the priest in charge was bearing in both hands a slab of wood, and piled on the slab like food on a platter were the offal and bones of some newly slaughtered animal, the portion traditionally due the gods. Two boys in the procession were carrying strips of the edible meat, already cut up and wound onto wooden spits, ready to be cooked.

Two of the worshipers, one of the boys and the bearded chief priest, did not get out of the way fast enough and were cut down. Terror sent the others flying out onto the seaside rocks behind the temple, past the place where the animal had just been slaughtered, and from which the smoke of the cooking fire went up. It was not the best choice of directions in which to flee, because from there their only escape from pursuers would be to hurl themselves into the sea. But today was a lucky day for those who scrambled to the rocks; this pack of raiders was not interested in hunting them down.

Whether the tubby, bearded priest was foolhardy enough to try to stop the raiders, or whether he was simply slow, was a question that remained unanswered. When the priest lay on his back on the stone floor, with a dead acolyte beside him, Theseus tried to interrogate him on the subject of hidden treasure in the temple, but his mouth was bubbling blood, and there would be no useful answers.

Theseus took a deep breath, stood back, and looked around.

Temples of Apollo were common enough everywhere, but Theseus had rarely been inside one before. This one was big enough to hold perhaps a hundred worshipers, if they didn't object to a little crowding. Or weren't bothered by getting wet when it rained—most of the roof seemed to have been deliberately left off. The structure had been positioned on a rocky promontory, so three sides of it were only a few yards from sunlit water. From inside it was quite possible to hear the waves, of only ordinary size, eternally patient at their work, casually smashing at gray rock, not many yards below the portico.

Most of the interior of the temple was one open, central space, and at one end of this, behind a wide-spaced row of marble columns, were arrayed the hearths and altars used in offering sacrifice. There were no old bloodstains here, nothing that crude in this austere environment. The actual killing of sacrificial animals would take place somewhere outside. Within the temple, everything was clean, well kept.

The intruders stood looking around them, wasting precious moments, stalled by the lack of any evidence of treasure.

"Where is it, chief?"

"We'll find out."

Other men were rummaging through a kind of cabinet on the other side of the broad interior open space, pulling out rich cloths, ritual vestments, knives for slaughtering animals, tossing them on the marble floor. One called over his shoulder, "Not here either."

On the floor, the lungs of the dying man kept bubbling, like a kettle on a fire. Theseus's men were beginning to stand around, as if they had run out of interesting things to do. "Keep looking!" he shouted at them.

Meanwhile the statue of Apollo, his bow in one hand, lyre in the other, looked down on the scene from a pillar behind the altar. The marble Apollo in this case was a little more than life-sized, and executed with some skill, showing a beardless but well-muscled youth gazing into the distance. It had been crowned with a circle of real laurel, the stiff oval leaves clinging close to the marble head.

At one side of the temple, behind the first row of towering white pillars, were a few wooden storage chests, all quickly up-ended and their contents turned inside out. One was empty, the others filled with common-looking cloth and various instruments of ritual. Nothing of mundane value but a few delicate tools of silver, and not enough of that for any of the men to argue when Theseus commanded them to let it be.

The structure of bare stone, scoured by the sea wind, standing open to light and air, did not appear to offer much in the way of possible hiding places.

He strode back into the open center of the temple, looked about him, and then pointed with his sword. "Maybe it's under the altar. Heave on this chunk of rock, you bastards, tip it over."

So heavy was the stone, so low its center of gravity, that they wanted to drive a lever under it to make any progress; but unfortunately there was no suitable tool on hand.

At last, with six strong men tugging and pushing, the tall stone went over with a breaking crash. And there was nothing under it, not so much as a spider or an ant, nothing at all but the blank solid stone of the floor, not even the suggestion of a hiding place, let alone treasure.

Men swore, and blasphemed the gods. But none of their curses mentioned Shiva by name. Or Apollo, or Dionysus. It was as if an unspoken agreement existed among the men, that to speak such names just now would be pushing one's luck just a bit too far.

"It must be in the other temple, then," Theseus muttered to

himself. "The one inland." Or the possibility that Shiva had hinted at was real, and the Face was not here on the Island of Dia at all.

And he turned, trying to catch a glimpse of that distant structure through the spaces between the nearby columns, to see just how far away it might be, as if he did not already know.

He was starting to have serious doubts. *It appeared that Shiva might have been wrong. Or deliberately lied to him? But why should a god do that? Simply as a joke?* No, Shiva might be many things, but not a joker. When Theseus thought about it, he was aware of no reason why a god could not be misinformed, or simply wrong, just like any human.

Maybe someone, or something, had lied to Shiva, trying to provoke a wild goose chase. If so, they had succeeded.

At that moment came the unmistakable sound of an arrow, launched at some distance but passing nearby at deadly speed. The veterans around Theseus did not even look round for the bowman. They came close to ignoring the missile's faint whir, as they might have a droning hornet. Something of the kind had to be expected when you went around tearing up people's houses and temples, and one arrow though certainly unwelcome, was not in itself cause for genuine alarm. Still, it had to be taken as a definite portent, like the first snowflake of a northern winter.

The raiders, after withdrawing in good order from the first temple, advanced to the second temple, dedicated to Dionysus, some three miles from where they'd left their ships. This time there were no worshipers on hand—evidently word of the raiders' coming had spread ahead of them.

Time was passing.

Having actually got into the temple of Dionysus, Theseus thought maybe the Face he wanted might be hidden in the larger-than-life-size mask, mounted on a sturdy column, which to the devotees represented their god if it did not actually embody him. That would at least be a good place to start looking, as long as they were here. He strode to the column and seized the effigy.

The lower half of the mask's face was covered by a heavy black beard, probably formed of cameloid hair, from some of the dromedaries of the northern mainland, or from the rarer shaggy pelt of horses.

Not quite the Face I wanted. Right now it was only a puzzle, an obstacle. And only lightly fastened in place. Theseus ripped it from its mounting and shattered it on the floor. Fragments flew, and cameloid hair and marble dust went drifting in a beam of sunlight. But the smashing revealed no secrets that he could see.

"Nothing here."

Occasional arrows and slung stones began to come at them out of nowhere, whizzing into the temple between stone columns. One or two of the stones, hurled at invisible speed, chipping the solid marble when they struck.

It was in that sacred space that the first of the raiders fell, struck down by stone and arrow, both hitting him at the same time.

"Lucky man," one of the others standing near Theseus remarked, when the body was turned over. "Never knew what hit him."

One of the pirates yelled at the marksmen outside, "Hey! Quit shooting that stuff in here! Don't you know this is holy ground?" For a minute there were no more missiles; then the slow shower resumed, tentatively at first.

"Let's go, men. Back to the ships."

But when another quarter of an hour had gone by, it was ominously apparent that resistance was developing from somewhere among the people of the island. Arrows and slung stones were now beginning to come in occasional flurries, and the possibility of a real storm had to be recognized. Along the flanks of the raiders' small, irregular column, armed locals could occasionally be seen, running in groups of two or three, from one spot of shelter to the next.

So far the raiding party had lost only one man. But Theseus was now virtually certain that enviable record would not last until they got back to their ships.

As he moved, he kept hoping to catch sight of the second scout, one of the two men who had ridden out on stolen animals to reconnoiter. One had come back, but one had vanished. That was not a good sign.

Meanwhile the main body of the raiders kept moving of necessity on foot. The locals on the other hand had the benefit of mounted speed, at least for a few important messengers. Within an hour or two of the landing, a formidable number of defenders could be mobilized.

Gradually it became easier and easier to believe that the defenders had received some warning of the impending raid, an hour or two at least, and had started to rally their forces and make a plan.

"Gave 'em time to hide their treasure, too."

Very quickly a second raider fell. The stone that had knocked him down had struck him in the back, high up near his neck; but the man was not hit squarely, or killed instantly. A couple of his comrades got him up, wobbly on his feet. Theseus yelled at them to keep moving; if they wanted to slow themselves down trying to help him keep up, he was not going to make an issue of it.

Maybe, thought Theseus, the Dians had learned somehow that he was coming for the thing he wanted, and had hidden it away; but on the other hand, maybe Shiva had been misinformed, and it had never been here at all. Surely if any of these Dians knew where a Face was to be found, one of them would have picked it up and put it on; and in that case Dionysus would be here to defend his house in person. And that would be that—unless, after all, Shiva came to help his men.

But Shiva had never promised to do anything of the kind. No, Theseus kept coming back to the idea that the Face he wanted had never been here at all.

Fiercely he put down his suspicions. It was not that gods were above lying, most of them at least, far from it. But why would Shiva lie to him, about a thing like this? What would be the point? Theseus could not conceive that the god would have had any motive, any possible reason to do so.

Now Theseus, talking with Mochlos, observing certain maneuvers in the distant landscape, began to wonder whether the enemy was less intent on driving them away, than on cutting them off from their ships and destroying them.

A third man went down, felled by a slung stone to the head. One look was enough to know that there would be no helping this one to his feet again.

There was no point in trying to count up losses. But it was becoming obvious that a great many Dianite men had not reacted to the raid by heading for the hills in panic.

"Guess maybe you were right about this fellow Nestor. I wonder if he's really any good?"

As if in answer, a stone came buzzing by within inches of Theseus's nose.

Theseus was an intelligent commander, as well as a bold one, and his troops were experienced men. But now he was becoming convinced that the thing he was trying to find was really somewhere else, probably right back on Corycus.

Theseus could see no reason to believe that the Face of Dionysus, or that of any other god, had ever been in any of these temples. If it had ever been in the temple they had already ransacked, certainly he couldn't find it.

It was a bitter disappointment, but life was full of disappointments, and the only way to deal with them was to plow ahead.

So far they had ransacked two temples, killed about a dozen people, and suffered almost that many casualties themselves. They had found no sign of the marvel they'd come looking for. Theseus supposed there could possibly be a third temple of the kind Shiva had been trying to describe, somewhere on the island. But if such an establishment existed, he obviously wasn't going to get to it today.

His men grumbled when Theseus began to lead them in a forced retreat. Some were laboring to carry a couple of wounded comrades with them, and these were ready to withdraw, while others argued that they should turn in the direction of the nearest village, and try there to take something that would compensate them for their time and trouble.

Overruling this latter group, Theseus kept his people together, pressing on toward the landing site.

Suddenly his eye was caught by a faint column of smoke in the air, rising from very near the place where the raiders had left their ships. His anger flared, and he felt something like the beginning of real apprehension. It was, as usual, a sharply enjoyable sensation.

As soon as he could see that his ship, or one that he now counted as his, was being burned, he cursed at the loss.

Neither Theseus nor his lieutenants had really expected such an effective counterattack, but still had planned for the contingency. The men who had been left aboard the ships were to put out to sea, and keep watch over a long stretch of shore, waiting for their comrades to reappear.

"There they are, I see 'em. Two ships."

Suddenly he remembered Ariadne. Now he was going to have to make a quick choice on what to do about her—assuming she had survived the burning of the ship. It was an irritating decision to be forced to make, but certainly not a hard one.

For a few minutes, at least, he had totally forgotten about his woman. Well, he had certainly enjoyed her, but her real usefulness had ended as soon as they were away from Corycus. Anyway, she did not match his idea of a pleasant companion for a long cruise.

Someone aboard one of the ships had the idea of lowering a single small boat into the water, but that wasn't going to do the thirty or so survivors of the landing party a whole lot of good.

Theseus and a few others plunged immediately into the surf and swam out to the waiting ship. As soon as a few more men had got aboard the ship, they managed to work the vessel a little nearer shore. Moments after the leaders took the plunge, the whole band was in the water, some abandoning their weapons and helmets.

Strong swimmers did their best to drag the wounded along. One man had found a handy log to push into the water to provide additional support. A few missiles, launched from far away, came pattering ineffectually down.

Theseus, ever mindful of his personal reputation as a leader, and himself a very strong swimmer, went back to the beach, this time in a small boat, into which he loaded a man who wasn't going to survive even an assisted swim. Determined to make sure that all his men who were still breathing had gotten offshore, he contemptuously ignored the missiles that sailed from inland to patter around him in the water and on the sand.

In moments when he had nothing else to think about, Theseus found himself wondering briefly what might have happened to Ariadne. The pair of ships that had got away did not include the one on which he'd locked her up. Then he caught a glimpse of her on shore, a distant figure readily identifiable by her hair, and her odd grab-bag selection of clothing. She was waving both arms, doubtless trying to attract his attention, for her face seemed to be turned directly toward him.

It appeared that no one else was near her. The spot on shore where she was standing would be difficult, but not impossible, to reach with a small boat. It would only take a couple of minutes to row over there and pick her up, and the risk of doing so not much different from the risk he was already taking.

"There's the lady, cap'n. Do we get 'er?"

"No. Pull on for the ship." The answer was given without hesitation. The memory of the body now hidden beneath her ragbag clothes caused him to sigh faintly with regret. Very nice, yes—but on the whole, his best move right now was simply to leave her here. Her presence aboard ship was always threatening to cause problems among the men, and sooner or later those problems would erupt. Everything in his earlier plans had given way to the chance of becoming a god, and Ariadne was only going to get in the way of that.

His life that he was risking was no longer merely a human life. The prospect of immortality, or something very like it, made a difference. No woman compared in importance with the possibility of obtaining godhood.

Besides, there was a good chance that she would do all right where she was; any good-looking woman could usually talk some man into being her protector.

Theseus wished the Princess Ariadne well.

he moment after the young woman came popping out of the ovenlike little box of a cabin, Nestor had started impatiently barking questions at her. She was a strange-looking wench, too young-looking and healthy to have long been a pirates' girl, though she was dressed like one. To his great disappointment, she had nothing meaningful to say to her rescuer, only mumbled a few words and looked at him dully, as if she was in shock, while around them Nestor's men were doing the best they could to encourage the fires they had set aboard the vessel.

His urgent need for knowledge kept him trying for a while. "Who are they, girl? How many ships are coming in? Did any of them talk about that?" The raiding force as reported so far seemed ridiculously small, and Nestor kept wondering if this might be only a diversionary attack. If so, where was the main body going to strike? Somewhere near the fort? He had done all he could to put his people on that side of the island on alert.

Naturally he was also wondering about the identity of this bedraggled prisoner, and where she might have come from. But her personal story could be put off until later. Anyway it seemed not to matter which line of questioning he followed, because the answers she kept giving him were practically incoherent anyway.

Well, there was nothing strange about a pirates' prisoner being shocked and terrorized into a state approaching idiocy. Or possibly she'd been an idiot to begin with. Still Nestor kept hoping from minute to minute that if he allowed the girl just a little more time to pull herself together, she might be able to tell him something useful.

So far only four raiders' ships had been spotted, and two of them had managed to escape his counterattack by putting out to sea. A third vessel, drifting away and abandoned by her crew, was now satisfactorily on fire, sending up a good column of smoke that was sure to alert the raiders who had gone ashore. The fourth, on whose deck Nestor and the strange girl were standing now, was soon going to be ablaze, if only his half-trained home guard troops could show a little competence.

It seemed to Nestor, shading his eyes with one hand and squinting out over the sun-shimmer on the water, that neither of the two escaped ships were able to put more than four oars in the water—not enough men aboard. Therefore it should be possible to overtake them, if any Dian ships, most of which were ordinarily harbored on the other side of the island, could be gotten around here in time.

Long hours would have to pass before that happened, though of course he had sent messengers riding inland. Anyway, Nestor had more immediate things to worry about. His men, local militia lads who'd come aboard the pirate with him, kept giving the impression of intense activity, but they weren't the most skilled arsonists he'd ever seen. Even now one energetic youth came running up to Nestor, breathlessly complaining that they hadn't any fire with them at the moment.

"What happened to your torches?" Nestor inquired, reasonably enough as he thought. In an effort to calm down his amateur troops, he was now sitting on one of the rowers' seats, affecting a pose of tranquility he didn't feel. His hands were clasped in front of him, and he was thinking of twiddling his thumbs.

"We threw them in the sea when the other ship caught fire. We forgot we'd need 'em for this one."

Nestor nodded thoughtfully, and looked about, silently calling upon various spiritual powers for assistance. He forcibly reminded himself that people weren't always as stupid as they sounded at their worst. There were times when it paid to lose your temper, but he didn't think this was one of them.

The youth had dashed off again, without waiting for an answer. Nothing like tight discipline—there was nothing like it around here, anyway. Where to obtain fire in a hurry? There was, of course, a whole burning ship in sight, but that source of ignition had now drifted well out of reach.

One of the local men, a sturdy farmer and council member

who had turned out to be a brave fighter, and was willing to go to great lengths to protect his property, protested, "These are solid vessels. We should be saving them for our own use, not burning them!"

The professional commander raised an eyebrow. "Want to grab one for yourself?"

"That's not the point!"

Nestor shook his head. "I've no crew of sailors to put aboard, and if I did I wouldn't want to tie up that many of our people. Our fight ashore's just getting started. Most of the crews from four ships must be in the landing party, I'd guess between fifty and a hundred men, and they're not just going to drops their blades and say the joke's on them. Besides, it would just fit the pattern of pirate raids if there were twenty more pirate ships coming right after these."

"Twenty ships!" The young farmer had dark skin to begin with, and was deeply tanned, but still he seemed to pale. Nervously he scanned the horizon once again. "That could be—what? A thousand men?"

"I don't say it'll happen, but it's possible. If they see one or two of their comrades' ships on fire, they may be discouraged enough to stay offshore. No flint and steel?" This last was addressed to the eager youth who had earlier reported difficulty with torches. Now the lad was back again, panting, seemingly waiting for orders.

"I don't know, Nestor—I mean captain. I'll ask the others." In a flash the boy was gone again. At least one volunteer was hugely enjoying his first experience of war.

Nestor blasphemed the names of several obscure deities, and shouted after him, "If you can't get a fire going, chop a hole in her bottom."

Now he did start twiddling his thumbs. Ariadne, watching from only a few feet away, thought that if this man was only trying to give an impression of being perfectly at ease, he was doing a good job.

She had cast herself down on another rower's bench, where she sat huddled and silent, not really frightened at the moment, vaguely aware of the strangeness of her own mental state. Now that she was freed of the immediate terror of being burned alive, she felt only a remote curiosity about what was going on around her, as if it were some kind of staged show, not particularly interesting. She had no doubt that this fellow called Nestor and his men were going to kill Theseus if they could, and she could scarcely blame them for that. Right now she felt profoundly numb, and anyone or everyone in sight could have been killed without exciting her very much.

Now a sound strongly suggesting the solid blows of an ax falling on heavy wood began to come from somewhere behind the low cabin. Now it sounded like two axes working.

Meanwhile, a couple of members of the Dianite ruling council, pudgy men in merchants' gowns, had come aboard to confer with Nestor. These were his employers, and he sat up straight and began to explore options with them. With the situation as it now stood, he thought it would be best to lure the raiders farther inland, and destroy them, rather than merely drive them away.

Nestor was strongly in favor of this plan. But the ranking civilian, president of the ruling council, let it be known that he would actually be better satisfied with a less drastic result.

The other man from the council was wringing his fat, white, merchant's hands. "Captain Nestor, if the attackers are now *trying* to withdraw, then does it make sense for us to be standing in their way?"

"Seems to me the whole idea is to keep these bastards from doing whatever they want."

"What *we* want to do is get rid of them!"

"Of course, chief. But you don't want them coming back next month, do you?" Nestor paused, staring at his two visitors. Then he added, "By all the gods, I think you're scared you're going to make them angry."

The civilian drew himself up. "I'm afraid of what may happen to our people."

"Right now, I'd say your people are winning. Sure, war is a scary business. But as the proverb says, there are four or five things in the world even worse than war, and most of them happen to you when you're defeated."

Nestor was telling the truth; he viewed the current situation as a considerable victory in the making. There was a good chance that most of the enemy who had come ashore could be trapped and slaughtered.

In fact the council president, listening to the list of his own dead and wounded, was beginning to view the situation as a disaster. Someone had just brought him a paper bearing what appeared to be a list of names, and he shook the paper almost in Nestor's face. "Have you seen this? Have you heard the reports of the slain? Fifteen massacred in the Temple of Apollo. Is this what you call victory?"

Conflicting reports kept coming in from scouts who had been ranging inland, as was usual when a protracted fight was on, even a small one like this. Nestor was sure that many of the details of slaughter and destruction would prove unfounded, while others would be unhappily confirmed.

One of the merchants suggested that it might be a good idea to deliberately allow a few of the marauders to escape. "Let them spread the word among their pirate brotherhood, all across the Great Sea, that Dia is now well armed and capable of resistance."

"That's not a bad idea," Nestor admitted. "But you see, two of their ships did pull out before we could board them. Looks to me that some of these mother-humpers are likely to get away whether we want 'em to or not."

Presently the excitable young man reappeared again, panting, to report that there was now a hole in the planking of the hull, and some water coming in.

"That's what I kind of expected, once you made a hole." Nestor got to his feet, dusting off his hands as if the thumb-twiddling might have dirtied them. "Let's go ashore." After a last glance around at the still-smoldering fires, Nestor took the rescued prisoner gently by the arm. "We're going ashore, lady."

Ariadne came with him meekly, saying nothing.

While guiding her splashing through the water toward the shore, he tried the young woman again with more questions, thinking maybe a moderate dunk in the sea would prove refreshing enough to wake her up. But she came out of the water as glassy-eyed as she went in. She still couldn't or wouldn't give him any helpful answers. Vaguely he wondered if whatever the pirates had done to her might have driven her completely mad. That would be too bad, but meanwhile other folk were dying, including men under his leadership, and he didn't have time to worry much about one girl.

Nestor made sure that Ariadne got safely ashore, a process which required swimming a few strokes, as well as some heavy wading. The brackish water near the creek mouth felt good, cool and clean after her confinement in the cabin. But she let out a gasp of relief at the feel of solid ground under her feet once more.

Nestor urged her along a path that ran inland.

"Take her back to headquarters," he told a small group of armed youth, who were standing around with the air of being temporarily unemployed. "Go easy, she's had a rough time."

"She's a prisoner, Nestor?"

"Not our prisoner, by Hades. Not anyone's anymore. Just take care of her."

The princess hadn't gone far with her new escort, when he was summoned away to attend to some other emergency. Before leaving, he assigned a gray old man to carry on as Ariadne's guide. In the background men were cheering. Now it appeared to her that the ship she'd just left, the one with the hole chopped in her bottom, might be going to catch fire after all.

The way along which she was now being conducted led past the intermingled bodies of slaughtered attackers and defenders. Ariadne had rarely seen such gruesome sights before, and never on such a comparatively large scale. It crossed her mind that one or more of these inanimate things might have been her living shipmates for the past several days, but she could recognize no one. And in any case she would have felt no sense of loss had Theseus's entire crew been wiped out.

What she could see of the landscape stretching inland from the rocky coast looked peaceful and pastoral. In one place she could see the red, tiled roof of a distant farm. Most of the grass in the rolling fields seemed to have been cropped short, though at the moment she could see no grazing animals. She wondered if these efficient defenders had somehow rounded up their herds and driven them to safety.

The silent old man who now had Ariadne in charge, ushering her along courteously if not very helpfully, was following a path that ran along the bank of a small creek or stream.

Part of the time they were walking knee-deep in the stream, so the banks on either side reached over their heads, and kept Ariadne from seeing much of what might be happening in the nearby countryside. Here she wished earnestly for shoes or sandals; the stones in the stream bed and along the path were too much for her tender feet. When she limped and stumbled, her elderly escort showed not the least concern, and it appeared fantastically unlikely that he was going to offer to carry her. Had he done so, she would have been afraid to accept.

When the path brought them up out of the creek again she was able to see, beyond two or three miles of rolling countryside, a building of white marble on a rocky promontory, bathed in brilliant sunlight. Without thinking about it, she knew that building must be the temple of Apollo where the raiders had launched, or were going to launch, their main attack.

To distinguish individual people at such a distance would be impossible. Some figures were visible at a range of two or three hundred yards, but Ariadne could not tell if they were soldiers or shepherds, or even if they were men or women. Certainly they were not in uniform, but then none of today's combatants were regular troops.

So far, since she'd come ashore, everyone had been treating Ariadne kindly, as a rescued prisoner. But the terrible numbness that had settled over her mind and spirit still had her in its grip. Now and then someone asked her a question. All the princess could think of in the way of answer was to keep murmuring that she did not know. Since they were assuming she had been a prisoner on the ship, they seemed to find this acceptable—until another man in his excitement began to question her all over again. But no one pressed her very hard.

Exactly where Nestor's senior auxiliary was taking her, she did not know, but as things turned out, it didn't matter what goal they had in mind. Before she and her escort could reach their destination, some other men wearing white armbands appeared in the middle distance, shouting something to the old man. Ariadne couldn't catch the words, but they must have indicated some military emergency, for her escort immediately turned his back on her and scrambled away at surprising speed to join the others. Whether they were trying to get into the fight or away from it she couldn't tell, and didn't care.

Ariadne ran away.

Their weapons were urgently needed somewhere, and they all ran away from her. Barefoot, she could not have kept up with them had she tried—and she felt no wish to try.

Now she was left to her own devices.

Glancing back to the ships she had just left, she saw how a second one was burning now, smoke black with the tar and pitch of caulked seams, the resin of pine and fir, going up and up into the clear sky.

Looking inland, she saw the pirates, twenty or thirty men in a band, running along a distant trail. They appeared to be hell-bent on getting back to their ships, at the moment dreaming no dreams of pillaging or conquest. Ariadne's heart was briefly in her mouth. But they were out of sight again before she could distinguish Theseus among them, and for one more moment that was her chief concern.

For the space of a couple of breaths she came to a full stop on the path. Then she left the path and moved off at a fast walk, sore feet notwithstanding, instinctively heading away from the sounds of fighting. Somehow the worst fate she could imagine for herself at the moment was being retaken by Theseus and his corps of raiders.

The princess slowed her pace as soon as she felt herself out of immediate danger. But she kept moving, away from the screams and the sound of clashing metal, away from the column of smoke that still went up from the burning ship. Still her feet refused to take her far inland. To a Corycan princess the sea was much less strange, after all, than the rocks and vegetation of this alien island.

Eventually the last sounds died away. When she thought she must have come at least half a mile, she paused to catch her breath and rest.

Wondering if the man called Nestor had already forgotten about her, or if he had set some of his men to searching, she sat down wearily and closed her eyes, only a pebble's toss from the shoreline. Now she had got clear away from all the men of both factions, and all their fighting. Here on this desolate portion of the coast, all she could hear was the sound of seabirds, and unhurried waves as they came in splashing and gurgling between huge rocks. Here it might almost be possible to believe that she had the entire island to herself.

But now the numbness that had gripped her all through the fight, ever since Theseus had ordered her shut up in the cabin, was failing, like a broken dam. She could no longer avoid coming to grips with the truth: the man who had played the role of her lover had locked her away as a kind of afterthought, a toy he might someday want to play with again. And then he had abandoned her. Maybe he was dead by now. But the truth was, she no longer cared whether he was or not.

A storm of rage and weeping swept the princess now, followed by helplessness and hopelessness.

Ariadne fell asleep, in a total exhaustion of mind and body, nestled in the sand between a pair of wave-worn boulders.

She woke again after only a short doze, feeling hungry and thirsty and cold, just in time to see, at a distance of less than a hundred yards, her lover and one of his men in a small rowboat. The face of Theseus was turned in her direction, and Ariadne was sure he saw her, but he made no response to her calls and waves.

She stood up, waving with both hands, and he would have to be stone blind not to see her now. A strong arm might have thrown a stone across the gap of open water in between.

"Theseus!" One last time Ariadne stretched out her arms to him.

He saw her clearly, there could be no doubt. He must have heard her calling. But when he spoke to the man with him, the man only rowed the boat away, intent on making sure there were no more pirates in need of rescue.

*M*uch later the bards would sing it, and most of those who heard them would believe: how the hero Theseus abandoned the Princess Ariadne, shortly after he had carried her to the Island of Dia. In the songs the reasons for his behavior were left obscure. There was no reason to doubt that the princess was still a very young and attractive woman when he left her there—but heroes were generally considered to have their pick of attractive women, and those who listened to the bards were generally more interested in hearing about heroic deeds.

Above all, the Prince of Pirates intended soon to become a god, and to a god, no woman ought to be worth the effort to woo and keep her. It was a law of nature that to a prince, let alone a god, all women should be readily available.

She watched Theseus climb aboard the ship, the size and beauty of his body conspicuous amid a tangle of other men. Soon he had them getting up sail, and when everyone who could make it to the ship seemed to have been gathered aboard, the vessel headed out to sea. It remained in sight for what seemed a very long time, and Ariadne had sat down on the rock again long before it disappeared.

Once she had possessed a home, and family, and friends, and it seemed an evil dream that all of that could have been swept away so rapidly. Half a year ago her vicious uncle and his cruel god had deprived her of her father, and now, over the past few unhappy days, fate had robbed her of all the rest. Everything had been sacrificed for Theseus, who had pledged her his eternal love—and now he, too, was gone, and his promises had meant no more than the whisper of a stableboy to a kitchen maid.

In a profound sense he, the man she loved, had never existed. Now she supposed the best fate she could reasonably hope for was to be taken captive by the Dianites and held for ransom. Not that

Uncle Perses, who if he thought about her at all must consider her a threat to his power, was likely to reward anyone for bringing her back—more likely her uncle would judge himself well rid of her. Quite possibly he would even pay someone to make sure she never did come home.

The only ray of hope the princess could discern, and that not very bright, lay in the fact that her brother Asterion would almost certainly be doing all he could, working in the world of dreams, to try to help her—but in her current situation, she needed much more than dreams. Not even visions as powerful as those her brother could invoke were likely to bring her any benefit.

But she couldn't even be certain that her brother was still alive. He had stayed behind on Corycus, perhaps by his own choice, and Shiva and Perses might well have taken their anger out on him. That thought in itself was enough to bring on tears.

The questions kept forcing themselves upon her tortured mind. *Why* had Theseus abandoned her? How was it possible for the man she had loved so desperately to do a thing like that? Maybe there was some other woman in his life. Maybe . . . but a storm of weeping came, wiping away all thought in pure emotion.

He wouldn't have had to fight his way to me, or anything like that. Only a short row across an open stretch of water. *He saw me, but he turned away.*

He might have come to get me, as he went back to the beach to pick up his pirates.

Ariadne roused from an exhausted sleep in her lonely hiding place. For a moment she was utterly confused, then she remembered she was on Dia. She had just awakened from a strange and twisted dream in which her supposed lover, Theseus, had returned and come ashore to watch her sleeping, and then had faithlessly stolen away again. In the dream he had come and gone without even leaving her any message, and the only explanation she could think of was that he had never learned to read or write. Somehow that seemed unlikely.

Her body ached, as if she had been through some great physical exertion. Slowly, cautiously, she moved to a slightly higher spot where she could see more of the sea. All the ships of the raiding party were completely out of sight by now, the hulk of the one that had been burned evidently sunk beneath the waves, and she could just see in the distance, along the shore, the mast of the one that had been sunk, protruding above the water.

A wave crashed on the rocks, almost at her feet, wetting her borrowed pirates' clothes with spray. The tide had changed, she realized, and now was coming in.

Now, once more left to her own resources, Ariadne remained in hiding. Theseus had sailed away, but she imagined there must still be pirates on the land. And the defense forces, the irregulars captained by the man called Nestor, might be searching for her. She preferred that they not find her either, though perhaps that attitude did not make sense, because sooner or later she would have to come out, if only to beg someone for food in this alien and probably unfriendly land.

Hunger was fast becoming a problem, and the princess could foresee that it was quickly going to get worse. In her last day on the ship she had eaten only some hard biscuit, and a couple of raw carrots, gone rubbery with dehydration. It seemed to her that she had not had a hearty, solid meal since the evening before the great escape effort had begun. If she now had one of those boardlike dried fish from the cabin floor in hand, she would have tried to chew on it.

As the tide came in and the wind shifted, the spray from incoming waves kept wetting her, so she moved. Then she moved again, cowering first behind one rock and then behind another, but reluctant to go anywhere out of sight of the sea—it was as if with part of her mind she still expected her lover to come splashing up boldly out of the waves and rescue her. But that was not going to happen. The truth was that she had no lover, no such being existed. Men had paid court to her from time to time, and one of them, to save his own skin, had managed to seduce her. (There were names for men who behaved like that, though a Corycan princess was not supposed to speak such names.) But there was no man who loved her, and probably there had never been.

And another truth was that she was hiding now because she hated and despised them all, all the men with swords in their hands, like the one who had killed her father.

Now she must find her own way; and since her earliest childhood, she had never been entirely helpless. Settling herself in the driest corner she could find between tall rocks, in a position that minimized her various discomforts as much as possible, she closed her eyes and tried to visualize a web.

When the familiar, gossamer strands began to glisten in her inner vision, they formed a pattern that Ariadne had never seen before. They came together to form a great, complex network, with herself at the center, nexus, of many radiating filaments.

In the circumstances the vision was frightening, and she quickly opened her eyes again. Never had she seen the threads do that before. They seemed to be telling her to stay right where she was—advice that did not seem to make any sense at all. Unless it meant that her condition was now utterly hopeless.

For most of her life, she had relied upon her own almost unerring ability to find, to locate, whatever she was looking for. But today, after what had happened, she no longer quite knew what that was. Certainly she was not making an effort to locate Theseus.

"Father Zeus, why have you deserted me?" It was the first time in Ariadne's life that she had ever uttered such a prayer aloud. There was no answer. Of course she had not really expected one.

Homeless and friendless and lost, the princess considered hurling herself into the sea and dying. Maybe Poseidon would welcome her, grant her the peace that had escaped her on the earth.

She needed no extraordinary perception to be aware that something very strange, but something very real, that was not an inner vision, was approaching the island from well out at sea.

The president of the ruling council saw the strange-looking ship approaching before Nestor did, and called his attention to it.

"Another pirate?" the merchant demanded anxiously.

Nestor looked for a long time, shading his eyes with one hand. At last he said, "I don't think so. If it is, it's the weirdest-looking pirate I ever laid eyes on."

On second thought, when he had looked a little longer, he decided it might well be the weirdest-looking ship of any kind he'd ever seen. The vessel's mast and lines were festooned with greenery, its sides growing grass and vines that trailed in the sea as if they could be nourished by salt water.

As the princess watched the same ship from a different distance and angle, the thought momentarily crossed her mind that the craft might belong to Theseus, that he was engaged in some trick or magic, coming back to get her after all. But she could not convince herself of that, and did not try.

Now Ariadne could be sure that the strange vessel was coming in to land. But of course it was not going to land within a quarter of a mile of her, where the coast was all jagged and forbidding rocks.

Dionysus, immediately on landing, escorted Edith ashore, and tenderly sent her on her way homeward.

A smooth plank, magically supported, ran ashore and steadily supported those who walked on it.

Alex had done what he could, but had not been able to work any miracles of healing on the girl. But freedom and the prospect of being reunited with her family, along with a couple of days of proper nourishment, had had a strong beneficial effect. Edith now seemed quite capable of making her own way home through a friendly countryside.

Alex also dispatched a couple of sprites to dance attendance on the girl, to see that she came safely to her destination.

She was wearing soft, clean garments now, there were flowers in her hair, and she had passed a full day without weeping. "Thank you, thank you, my lord!"

"You are welcome. I envy you the joy of your homecoming. And I envy your family when they see you. There will be much rejoicing when you arrive."

Before walking away from the vessel that had brought him to Dia, Alex gave her to her faithful steersman, who was still with him. "This ship is yours now, good Acetes. Make what profit from her you can."

"Thank you, great lord!"

Ariadne's presence on Dia had been strongly suggested by Aegeus, before he was turned into a dolphin.

Some of Alex's sprites and powers, sent ahead to look around the island, now brought him a report.

But at first Alex could not believe what he was hearing. "Theseus has done *what*?"

The whisperer told him. Alternate waves of outrage and joy engulfed the latest avatar of Dionysus. She had been badly treated, mortally offended—but she was physically unhurt, and she was here.

Despite his recent access of divinity, Alex still felt very shy at imagining himself in the presence of the princess—he thought that with the Twice-Born to support him, he could face another god now, calmly enough, if required. But somehow this was different.

"She is only a mortal woman, why am I so nervous?"

His entourage had no answer to that question, but to chide him. *It does not behoove a god to take the presence or absence of mortal flesh so seriously.* These were the words of the disreputable Silenus.

His reply was stiff. "Thank you for your advice. But I am the god, not you." And it occurred to Alex to wonder, not for the first time, how and why Silenus, who had no real body, should show in his image all the ravages of dissipation.

You see me as I am, lord; your true servant, incapable of guile or deception.

Even Dionysus seemed to be taken aback by such a fabulous claim, and unable to find words for an immediate reply. Eventually Alex got out, "Oh, compelled to be absolutely truthful, are you?"

My devotion to the truth, Your Divinity, requires me to qualify

*that description. In pursuit of the highest truth it is sometimes nec-
essary to deviate from strict accuracy in less important matters. In
such a case—for example, in my service to yourself—the greater
good to be accomplished must work to purify the means that are
necessary to achieve it.*

"I see. Of course. This is your roundabout way of admitting
that you are an incorrigible liar. I ought to have remembered that
fact before now."

I am most honored that Your Divinity remembers me at all.

Wondering how best to approach the woman he so desperately
loved, Alex could this time find nothing very helpful in the long
memory of Dionysus. Probably the god's usual approach to such
matters was simply too different from his own. Left on his own,
and feeling strangely awkward, the young man pondered how to
introduce himself. To say "I am a god" would be no more than the
simple truth, but an unaccountable shyness held him back from
that approach. He was a god, but like the avatars of other deities,
he was also something less—or something more. To say "I am
Alex the Half-Nameless" would also be the truth, or at least a
half-truth, but now seriously misleading.

In the end, Alex decided that he would neither announce his
name to the princess at once, nor make any effort at disguise. Let
Ariadne recognize him if she could—though, as he reminded himself, she had never been very familiar with the face of the young
soldier whose only name was Alex. Nor had she ever seen him
dressed in any other garments than the uniform of the Palace
Guard.

He was still wearing around his neck the medallion of silver
and gold that she had given him long days ago, but all of it except
the chain was hidden under his purple cloak, where that garment
was clasped around his neck.

When Alex saw her crouching in among the rocks, and the image
of her as it appeared in the eye of Dionysus assured him that she
had taken no great harm, his relief was so great that for a moment
he could not speak.

When Ariadne suddenly became aware of the figure of a lone man standing there, wrapped in a rich cloak and gazing directly into her hiding place, she caught her breath in fear. Then she summoned up her courage and, with no trace of recognition in her eyes, demanded, "Are you a soldier?"

"No, my lady." And the young man opened his hands, showing them empty of weapons. Indeed he wore no belt or armor, and his tone was so humble that it set fear at rest.

But the wearer of such a fine cloak, standing idle in such a commanding attitude, could hardly be a slave or menial. "A landowner, then?" Ariadne demanded. "Or the priest of some local god? If you have no weapons, and no soldiers at your bidding, you'd better take shelter while you can."

"Why?"

"Why? You fool, pirates are ravaging the land! One shipload of them have run away like cowards, but others may still be here. More ships may be landing. If you don't care for your own safety, at least try not to give my hiding place away."

"That's the very last thing I'd want to do." Appearing concerned, he moved forward with alacrity, and slipped in among the rocks to stand beside her. There wasn't much room in her hiding place, and he had to stand very close to Ariadne.

Ariadne, her nerves already drawn to breaking point, had to fight to stifle a scream; but a second look assured her that the man was only standing there, calmly, being a perfect gentleman. Despite his fine clothes, there was still something humble about his attitude, and with an effort she controlled herself. "I don't suppose you know where I could get my hands on a boat?"

"No, my lady. Do you think you would be safer in a boat?"

Why had the fates sent this idiot to pester her? "I don't know, but I've got to do something. I can't just hide among these rocks until I rot!"

"Certainly not. Would it please you to have some food? Something to eat and drink?"

"Yes! Please. I'm very thirsty. And hungry too."

Her mysterious visitor made a little bow, the best he could do in the constricted space, and took his leave. "I'll be back shortly."

He started away, then turned to call over his shoulder. "And I'll see what I can arrange in the way of transportation."

And when he had gone apart from her by thirty or forty yards, getting himself just out of her sight, Dionysus began getting his chariot mobilized, calling up out of its usual state of invisibility his whole exotic entourage.

"Should I send a sprite to her with wine and water?" Alex asked himself, muttering aloud. "No, those things I will bring to her with my own hands—in a minute. And—what an idiot I am!—food, too, of course. She said that she was hungry."

Critically he studied the display that was now being presented for his approval. Six or eight varieties of fruit, of course; that was good. He tasted a morsel of the presented cake. Not the very best he, Dionysus, had ever enjoyed, but—definitely satisfactory. There was no time just now to strive for absolute perfection.

Then he addressed his permanent escort. "And now, show me, how are you going to display yourselves?"

The entourage exploded suddenly into visibility, making an impressive array. Even the satyrs, commanded to appear more or less fully clothed, in suitable raiment, could achieve a kind of nobility. Alex would have been dazzled, but now, equipped with the mind of Dionysus, able to recall many occasions when the team had done much better, he was forced to judge it an inadequate, shambling sort of show.

"No, that is not good enough," he demanded of his inhuman servitors. "It's plain you haven't practiced this kind of thing for a long time. I have seen and heard better than that at a merely human court. Improve your costumes, and your manners, quickly. As for music, let us have first a fanfare, suitable for a great lady, and then a kind of serenade. But softly! Let her not hear until I have given my approval."

And now there seemed to be a greater variety of instruments tuning up to play. Strings and horns, flutes and timpani. And stuff for the eyes to feast upon: a whole panoply of lights and colors, gold and silver, scarlet and purple, was borne in the seeming substances of gems and fabrics. The whole scene was lighted by flames that burned coldly in the air, or with no heat greater than that of human bodies fired with passion.

"No, it must not turn into an orgy this time. *No,* it certainly shall not." Alex paused, trying to find the exactly proper words and thoughts with which to instruct his helpers, to produce exactly the effect he wanted. "Let the style of madness with which we approach the princess be of quite a different sort."

After the third or fourth revision of the whole display, all accomplished in accordance with the god's instructions, even the Dionysian memory at last found it acceptable. Besides, the princess must be growing impatient, and it would hardly do to let her faint from hunger.

And, besides that, Alex was reluctant to prolong their separation for even another minute. "That's more like it. Forward!"

$\mathcal{O}$he slender, huddled figure stirred. Ariadne began to say, "Sir, I feared you were not coming back. If I could have only a cup of fresh water . . ."

Then, at the sudden crash of timpani and horns, she lifted her head, so all the colors of the flames of the procession were reflected in her heart-shaped face, between her hanging strings of grimy hair.

A moment later the princess had sprung to her feet in utter wonder at the leaping, marching music, at once sweeter and stronger than anything most mortal ears had ever heard. As the procession came fully into her view, swaggering and dancing past the entrance to her rude shelter, she remained motionless, getting a good look at every part of the parade. Spreading her hands in a gesture of unconscious grace, she stood there marveling.

Alex/Dionysus had made no effort to disguise himself, or to conceal his new nature. Still there was no sign as yet that the princess had recognized either the god who now stood before her, or the young soldier who had once pledged his undying loyalty.

But when the parade had passed, and turned, and was coming back again, her wondering eyes became fixed on Alex. As he approached she could see that he was carrying in his right hand a crystal flagon of what appeared to be clear, sparkling water, and in his left, a delicate dark bottle of what must be wine. Beside him and a little to the rear, a silver tray of choice dishes floated waist-high in the air, pastries and cheese and fruit borne by invisible hands. Mechanically she took the water from his hand and drank.

Never in her young life had the Princess Ariadne looked upon any god but the cruel Shiva; but now she understood at last that she stood in the presence of some very different deity.

The proud neck of the princess, that in the course of her

young life must seldom have been bent to anyone, bowed low, but only for a moment. Then she raised her head again. "You are—you must be—the Lord Dionysus." Somewhere in the back of her mind passed the thought that this was the form Theseus had been planning to put on. But evidently that effort had miscarried—the young man now standing before her was certainly not Theseus.

"Whatever I am, my lady, I owe to you," the noble-looking youth said now. And to Ariadne's amazement, she now beheld what seemed the enormity of a god going down on one knee, offering obeisance to a mere mortal woman.

But her wonder at the gesture was overwhelmed in a new mystification. At last her attention was fully concentrated on the one who stood beside her.

She said, "But . . . it seems to me that I have known you. Your face is almost the same as that of a young soldier I remember, the one named Alex. How can that be?"

In sober fact it was hardly strange that the princess should remember him—only a few days had passed since they were engaged in planning desperate deeds together—but still Alex felt a rush of joy at the acknowledgment.

"My name was Alex then," he said. "And it still is."

"I don't understand," she breathed.

"Don't you? Princess, I think you must be well aware of how I came into possession of this Face."

Her cracked lips made a perfect O. "I? How should I know?"

"Don't you?"

"Great Dionysus! I have no idea what my lord is talking about. You are the second god that I have ever seen. The first was more a devil. Never in my life have I laid eyes on the unworn Face of any god."

Wondering, Alex raised a hand to touch the medallion that still hung around his neck. "You gave this to me, when I was no more than a young soldier."

"Yes. Yes, so I did." A sharp sound made the princess turn her head. Around them, the surfaces of barren seaside rocks were cracking, green shoots peeping forth, the tendrils of vines beginning to make progress.

Again she faced the man before her. "You?"

He wondered if the troubles she had endured had left her mind confused. "Yes, my lady. My name is Alex," he repeated. "I am the new avatar of Dionysus. Here, sit down." On a rock behind the princess, soft green moss had already grown thick enough to make a cushion.

"Yes," said Ariadne, nodding her head slowly. "Thank you." She sat down. But her face indicated that what she had just heard explained nothing for her. "Yes, I did give my medallion to—to the young soldier. But what of it?"

"The Face of Dionysus was concealed inside it." And Alex snapped the two halves of silver and gold apart, displaying the empty compartment. Then he sighed; obviously the princess was as surprised as he had been at the revelation.

Dionysian memory suggested . . . if not an explanation, then a likely place in which to seek one. Whenever the god's affairs took a turn that he himself found particularly mystifying, the solution was usually found to have some connection with his inhuman associates.

With one of them in particular.

As the result of a silent summons, Silenus once more appeared as their spokesman.

Dionysus posed the question in a godly voice. "Can you explain this business of the medallion, Silenus?"

Everything has worked out in a most satisfactory way, Lord Dionysus. Again Your Divinity is united with a congenial mind, in a suitable host body.

"I begin to understand," said Alex after a pause. "It was you who put the treasure where I found it."

Evidently the satyr took that comment as approval. *My lord is perspicacious as always. I ask no special reward. But would it not be a good thing, lord, to begin a celebration at once? The lady appears to be in a receptive, congenial mood.*

"It would *not* be a good thing," Alex rebuked his servant

sharply. "Not what I suppose you mean when you say 'celebration.' Certainly not with this lady. Do not suggest it again."

Of course not, lord! Silenus seemed aghast at the possibility.

"Do not suggest what?" the princess queried, obviously mystified, and Alex understood that her mortal ears had heard nothing of what Silenus said to him.

"Never mind," the god continued sternly. "We can speak of all that later." The last remark was addressed to his entourage; he had more questions that he meant to ask of them, especially of Silenus.

But for the moment he focused on Ariadne once more. "I would be pleased if you would allow my servants to minister to you."

There were suddenly in the air clouds of fragrant steam, and gauzy curtains, enveloping the princess. Now her wide eyes, along with the rest of her, disappeared from the view of the man-god who watched.

A sprite, taking the form of a nearly invisible blur in the air beside his head, whispered a suggestion to him.

"Oh yes, her clothes," Alex responded, in a whisper too faint for the lady herself to hear. "Of course. What to do? Yes, good idea. See to it, I command you!"

Foreseeing that there would now be a time of waiting, Alex sat down on a handy rock. "Here, I have brought you food and drink," he called into the clouds of steam, and clapped his hands.

There came trickling sounds, as invisible hands poured wine and water into crystal cups. A chorus of singing, dancing satyrs and maenads, beginning on schedule the next phase of their performance, as their master had commanded, took form out of nowhere to surround their master, and the princess, who was still lost from view inside her improvised bathchamber of steam and gauze.

Meanwhile, the revamping of the princess's dress proceeded quickly. Coarse dirty cloth, only briefly visible as it emerged from the chamber of the bath, appeared to be consumed in a white flame, fire that burned or heated nothing but the stuff that it destroyed. Replacing the discarded rags came gauzy fabrics, silk from somewhere past the edge of the known world, gold thread and fine embroidery. In the traditional high fashion of the queenly women of Corycus, the style left her breasts bare.

As always, the entourage of Dionysus managed to convey, even in their dullest routine actions, a hint of frenzy. For a moment Alex could feel the turmoil strongly and he cringed inwardly. But this time the onslaught was not overwhelming. Something—something that even the god found strange and unfamiliar—tempered the impulse toward madness, turned it away from the mania that sought blood, and even from lustful coupling, toward a less fleshy and more inward ecstasy.

Now, with his beloved for the time being out of earshot, Alex took the opportunity to call Silenus to a full accounting.

As soon as the goatish figure stood before him, he demanded of it, "Explain the matter of the Face."

Which Face does my lord mean?

"Which Face do I—? How many Faces are we talking about? You know what I mean." Alex tapped his own forehead. "How it came to be in the medallion."

While we were still on Corycus, lord, one of us who now make up your loyal entourage—one of us observed the work of clever Daedalus, a man who in my opinion, lord, is himself most worthy of apotheosis. Indeed, we might have left your Face where he would find it, had I not been fearful that instead of putting it on, he would have wasted much time in a useless attempt to cut it open, looking for its secrets.

" 'One of us' meaning yourself, I suppose. Stop these damned circumlocutions and get on with it. Why didn't you simply tell me, the first time you dragged me into the chariot, that the treasure I sought was hanging around my own neck . . . ?" Alex's voice died before he had finished the question. Now, with the experience of a god to draw upon, he could find a reasonable answer for himself, even before the ready voice of the satyr furnished one.

Great lord, had you been reborn while still on Corycus, your new avatar would inevitably have been exposed to great peril.

There could have been no time of accommodation, of the necessary development of your new avatar, before you had to face your enemies again.

"That might make sense," the Twice-Born admitted. "Especially if Shiva were taking an interest in what happened on the island. It *might*, I say. Any other reason?"

The satyr briefly hung his head. *Also it is possible—remotely possible, I must admit—that your poor servant Silenus was experiencing the joys of wine when he hid the Face.*

"Yes? Go on."

And when . . .

"Yes?"

When sober again, had forgotten where he put it.

There was a silence.

"Ah, Silenus," Dionysus whispered at last. For once it seemed the god had been shocked into solemnity.

Evidently mortified by that stunned whisper, the satyr remained silent, eyes lowered, shuffling the goat-hooves that he used for feet.

Presently Dionysus sighed. "I see. We must let that pass, for now. Now wait, don't go darting away. I have another question for you."

Yes, lord?

"A moment ago, you seemed genuinely uncertain as to which Face I was talking about."

Alex was vaguely surprised as Dionysus moved forward two long strides on Alex's legs, reached out an arm, Alex's right arm, and with the power of a god closed the fingers of his right hand upon Silenus's throat, now held by the same power in a tangible and bruisable form. The voice of the Lord of Frenzy roared, with sudden power, *"Tell me, ancient villain, what do you know of the Face of Zeus? And be sure that this time you speak the truth."*

Ariadne's eyes were filled with wonder, some minutes later, when the clouds of steam and walls of gauze were dissipated, and she emerged from her bath already wearing her new clothing.

Her eyes were wide with wonder as she brushed her fingers,

newly clean, over the fabric. "But—but this is—I have never had a dress as fine as this. Nor have I even seen one, I believe." And with a distinctive motion of her head, she tossed back her coil of light brown hair, almost the color of fine Corycan honey, that had never been so lustrous.

When the princess had slaked her thirst from crystal goblets, and nibbled at some food, she again looked closely at her rescuer.

"So, you were—are—Alex the Half-Nameless, who once served me. And now you have become a god, and I, a werely mortal—merely wortal—woman—must serve you. Even if I am a princess. That is the way of the world," she pronounced wisely, and finished with a light hiccup.

"One cup of strong wine has been too much for your empty stomach," Dionysus mused. "And my very presence brings on in many folk a touch of lunacy. There are important things I must discuss with you, an important discovery I have just made. But I see that for the moment they must wait. Ariadne," he added softly. "Now I have the right to call you Ariadne."

"Indeed you—*hic*—indeed you may. And I may call you . . ."

"Call me Alex. Please."

It was soon obvious that what the princess needed most of all just now, more than additional finery, reassurance, celebration, or even a declaration of undying love, was rest. And for a time the God of Joy considered causing his beloved to fall into a deep sleep that should last for many hours. There appeared a couch, as finely appointed and as temporary as her bath had been. Surrounding the princess where she slept, his powers could construct a wall, an encirclement, of protective greenery. He might hope by such means to keep her safe, until he had concluded his business back on Corycus, and could return here for her.

But as Alex thought it over, he doubted they had many hours to spare for the luxury of rest. And neither he nor Dionysus was convinced that it would be safer to leave his beloved here than to carry her along—there was not time to construct a stronghold of safety. Nor, indeed, had Alex any reason to believe that anything Dionysus could build would protect her against Shiva.

*   *   *

Events precluded any chance of the princess being allowed a long time in which to recruit her strength. Ariadne had been napping for only a few minutes when one of the sprites alerted Alex to the fact that a couple of men were watching him, from behind some rocks about a hundred feet away.

He turned and studied them with the augmented power of his divine vision. The taller, younger observer, standing with folded arms, looked military, capable, and stoic, not as nervous as most people would be, confronting divinity at close range; the older man looked fretful and nervous and so out of shape that he had to be civilian, though he had brought along a spear that now stood leaning against a nearby rock.

"Pirates?" Alex softly inquired of his entourage.

Not so, lord, whispered the nearest sprite in her soft voice. *Quite the opposite.*

Gently Alex reached out a hand and touched the dozing princess on the arm. He had to touch her twice before she stirred on her silken couch and opened her eyes.

"We are being watched," her guardian informed her. "Do you know either of those men?"

Ariadne stretched luxuriously, frowned, and then turned on the two watching men a gaze still mellowed by that single cup of Dionysian wine.

She said, "I believe—yes, I'm sure—the one wearing the sword is the same man who got me off the ship when it was burning. Nestor, the others called him."

"And did he treat you well?"

"He did. Actually he did. You see, he and his men were fighting against, against Thes—*hic*—Theseus. And I was sick of it all, sicker than you would believe, my lord—my Alex—sick of all the things men do—and all I wanted was to get away. Do you know, my head is still a little light?"

*N*estor and his former employer continued to observe, in awe, and from some distance, the meeting between Dionysus and Ariadne.

"He's seen us," the civilian was whispering, shivering in a kind of agony of anxiety. "Let's get out of here."

"Of course he's seen us, that's why we're standing here. Withdraw if you like," said Nestor, making no attempt to keep his voice down.

The older man twisted his body, the tense writhing of one struggling to control his bowels. "But—but *he* may be angry if I turn my back on him and walk away!"

"Walk backwards, then." Nestor was irritated. "I don't know, chief. You've said that you're displeased with my methods, that you'll need my services no more. So naturally I must try to find another client."

The civilian did not seem to be listening. "What does it mean?" he pleaded, in a near-frenzy of doubt and worry. "What is a god doing on our island? No one living can remember the last time that happened."

"So now it's come to pass. I assume there's some connection with the raid we just fought off. Or it might be simple coincidence—though I don't believe that. I'd surely like to find out."

"Oh gods! *The god is beckoning to us to approach.*" Nestor's companion moaned the words, and was practically paralyzed at the prospect. "What shall we do? I can't walk. I can't move!"

Nestor shook his head. "Then why don't you just stay here, chief? Sit where you are. I suspect I'm the one he's interested in." He lowered his voice to a mere whisper. "Won't be the first immortal I've ever talked to face to face; and this one doesn't look as scary as some I've seen."

Once more the male figure standing in the rocky recess raised one hand in a gentle beckoning motion, and Nestor moved forward slowly, the chief still groaning at his back.

He came to a stop, and bowed, two or three yards from the couple in their stony niche. "Lord Dionysus? My name is Nestor." It was easy to feel confident of this deity's identity, with fronds of greenery bursting out of the rocks on every side of him, and strains of wild music half-heard in the background.

"So I have been told," the figure in the purple cloak responded. "This is the Princess Ariadne, of Corycus. How she comes to be here is a long story."

"I have already met the princess," said the soldier, bowing again. "Though I was not aware of her exalted rank."

Ariadne responded with a distant, mellow smile. The god beside her nodded. "She tells me that you treated her well, and brought her to safety from a burning ship. For which we are both grateful."

"It seemed the least I could do, lord."

"How do you come to be here, Nestor? Surely you are not a native, your speech has not the Dian sound."

"That's quickly explained, my lord. Some months ago, certain members of the Dian ruling council got together and decided they were tired of being harassed by pirates. They sent a delegation to the mainland to hire some help, and after interviewing several candidates, made me a good offer to come here and take charge of the island's defense."

"And now they are dissatisfied with your work?"

"So it would seem." Nestor glanced back in the direction of the chief. The chubby man was lying so still, curled up against the base of a rock, that he might have fainted. "Would you like to talk to a council representative?"

"Not necessarily. But I would like to talk to *you*. My powers tell me that you have discouraged the raiders pretty effectively."

A few hours later Alex, walking now with a somewhat revived Ariadne on his arm, and accompanied also by Nestor who said he had urgent military matters to discuss with him, strolled in sight of the recently defiled temple on the Dian shore. The only images of

Apollo that he could find recorded in the Dionysian memory were fragmentary, and they were also of an extreme age. So frighteningly old that Alex made no attempt to compute the gap in years. The avatars who had then worn the Face of the Far-Worker, and that of Dionysus, must have ceased to walk the earth long ages hence.

Suddenly the sharp senses of the Twice-Born were recording something—odd. Faint, and odd, and interesting. Dionysus said, "Let us walk a little closer to Apollo's temple."

"As my lord wishes," said the princess demurely.

Alex had in mind the need to discover some kind of sanctuary where the woman he loved might stay safely for a few hours or days. In the present situation, he was afraid to leave her alone and unprotected, even for a few minutes. Not that he was at all confident of his ability to protect her from an angry Shiva.

Now they were steadily approaching the defiled temple. There was a strange glow in the tall, marble structure, subtle lights that did not seem to come from any natural flame, and corresponding shadows. And Dionysus, if not the mortals with him, could, if he chose to harken in a certain way, detect a series of tones, unearthly music. Very different from the tunes of sprites and satyrs, but strains of ineffable rightness, sounding more in the mind than in the ears.

There is someone in the temple now, lord, said a low, disembodied voice, in which a note of stress was evident.

"Yes, no doubt about it."

Nestor's footsteps had been gradually slowing, and now they stopped. When Alex turned to look at him, the mercenary said, "Lord Dionysus, in my life I have encountered several gods."

"Yes?" Alex prodded.

"I have even achieved a certain—I might even call it friendship—with one or two divinities. As I would like to do with you." Nestor paused and swallowed. With a nod he indicated the temple ahead of them. "I'm not sure why this case is different. But . . ."

Alex was nodding. "But Apollo is something else again. Lord of Terror, Death, and Distance, among his other attributes. I understand. It's all right, most of the gods themselves are uneasy in his presence. Without necessarily knowing why." Alex was try-ing to avoid being too sharply aware of the usual attitude of Dionysus in that regard. By comparison with the one who waited just ahead, he himself felt more completely human than he had for several days. He said, "So wait here, Nestor, if you like." He turned. "Ariadne?"

The woman beside him laid her hand upon his arm. "I will come with you." Her voice was warm and confident.

Slowly the couple moved forward. This time it was Diony-sus, even more than Alex, who was reluctant to advance. Alex's own feet felt leaden, though he could not have said precisely what he was afraid of. He knew that the being he was about to encounter was no friend of the Destroyer. And it was necessary to go forward.

He had advanced only a couple of additional steps when he realized that his usual escort of inhuman hangers-on had suddenly left him. Even Silenus for once was silent, offering no jests or jab-bering. The sprites and satyrs had withdrawn in awe, or were hanging back, desperately reluctant to draw any closer to the Far-Worker. Their absence produced an unaccustomed sense of emptiness in the space around him, and that further fed his own uneasiness.

Somehow Alex, the mere mortal, continued to be less affected than the god whose nature he now shared. And on entering the temple, there was nothing intrinsically frightening to be seen, though in his left eye, the figure before him shimmered mightily.

Alex with his right and merely human eye, and Ariadne, beheld only the figure of a beardless youth, perhaps not quite fully grown, his athletic body partially wrapped in a belted robe of snowy white. A lyre hung at his belt, and a great bow, improbably silver in its color, was slung over one shoulder. The youth was standing straight, cradling weightlessly in his arms a burden of pale flesh that had once been a boy. At his feet lay the butchered corpse of a priest, still laurel-crowned like the god himself.

When the Far-Worker saw the couple approach, he gently set

down the body he was holding, and stood up straight again, several inches taller than Alex.

"I am Apollo." The voice was mild, nothing like Shiva's commanding tones; still, it had a resonance. Seen at close range, the figure in the white robe was of striking appearance, rendered odd by the fact that his hair of glossy black contained a strong admixture of red curls. Had it not been for a certain dignity in the face, a shadow of divinity tinged with sadness, Alex would have assumed the other to be a year or two younger than himself.

Even though Ariadne stood with her hand resting on the arm of one deity, in a touch that claimed the beginning of familiarity, that name was enough to silence her. But Alex, aware of the powers of a god in his own blood, managed to answer steadily enough.

"We join our lamentations to yours, Lord Apollo, on the death of your worshipers here. I am now Dionysus—as I have no doubt you can see. My human name was—is—Alex," he added on an impulse. Then with a touch of defiance he supplemented, "No family name. And this lady with me is Ariadne, princess of Corycus."

The youth before them nodded his odd shock of hair. "Not exactly of a famous ancestry myself. I grew up in a village. I'm Jeremy Redthorn." He extended a hand, and Alex immediately took it. It felt completely human. Apollo was looking at him searchingly. "Alex, then, if I may."

"Of course."

"And I am pleased to meet you, princess."

Exactly what protocol demanded of a princess, on being introduced to one of the mightiest of gods, was a question that Ariadne's early lessons in deportment had never covered. But she took Apollo's hand, and did the best she could under the circumstances.

Having greeted her casually, Apollo turned back to her companion. "If you don't mind my asking—I have good reason—have you been very long involved in this god-business?"

Dionysus remained awed and wary. But Alex was conscious of the beginning of a feeling of considerable relief, at having encountered another deity who was willing to make a simple confession of humanity. "Not very." Then Alex impulsively decided to trust the other. "Actually only a few days."

The tall youth nodded sympathetically. "I thought so. It took me much longer than that before the thing began to feel at all natural. I've had more than a year now to get used to it."

Alex let out a sigh. "Lord Apollo—"

"Jeremy, if you prefer."

"Jeremy, then. There are about a hundred questions I would like to ask you. But I expect most of them can wait."

"I expect you are right," Apollo said. "But I have a few that had best be answered quickly. Tell me where you are from. And how you got your Face."

The Sun-God listened attentively, and when the story was finished, he advised the neophyte deity to take the Princess Ariadne back to Corycus with him.

"It could be more dangerous for her there than here," Alex suggested.

"Possibly. But in my opinion, even riskier to leave her here, unprotected. Understand that whatever you do, I can offer no help as bodyguard; I'm going to be very busy."

"I understand."

"Besides, there is another reason why she ought to go on with you to Corycus. From what you tell me, it might be possible to see this lady here—or more likely her sister, Phaedra—installed on that island as the true queen."

Alex shook his head. "Realistically, I can't believe that I am strong enough to overthrow the usurper. Not if he has the help of Shiva."

"I wanted to be sure you understood that point."

"I do. And to make matters worse, I fear Shiva may have assistance from the Underworld."

"No one would expect you to overcome such an alliance— without substantial help."

The two had many things to discuss.

Especially Alex wanted to pass on to Apollo the information he'd recently had from Silenus, that the satyr had in fact been spreading the rumor that the Face of Zeus was really hidden in the Labyrinth.

"There is no truth to that rumor, then?"

"Ah, there, Jeremy, we run into complications. Truth and lies and guesses are so entangled in what passes for the satyr's mind that I doubt he could give us a straight accounting if he tried. Ages of debauchery, of celebration without thought, have warped his—"

"I see. I believe I understand. We can't afford to deny the possibility that the Face of Zeus is really there."

"I think that's it." And Alex heaved a sigh of relief.

When the recent developments involving Corycus had been explained to him, Apollo reiterated, "I think the people of that island might rise to overthrow this usurper Perses, and support a decent human ruler, if you could find a way to offer them such a choice."

"Many people would find it hard to believe that whatever happens in the lives of a few mere mortals, on one small island, could matter much to Apollo."

"It could matter to Jeremy Redthorn."

"I'm glad to hear that."

"And Apollo, at least in my avatar, is very reluctant to see Hades increase his power."

When the chariot and the leopards arrived, Alex and Ariadne left the Far-Worker in his temple and went out to meet Silenus, who lingered in the vicinity long enough to turn the reins over to Alex.

And with her first ride in the chariot of Dionysus, Ariadne lost the last trace of any longing for the Prince of Pirates. Beside her now was not only a god, but, and this was foremost in her thoughts, the man whom she had once thought to embrace in the person of Theseus. She took his strong arm in both her hands, and he turned his head to smile at her.

"Princess Ariadne." It was his human nature rather than divinity that gave him the strength to say the next few words. "I love you."

For a long moment she did not respond. Then she said, "Once—how long ago it seems!—once I dared to ask my . . ." She paused, and started over. "I prayed and sacrificed to great Zeus, to send me the man who above all men I could love, and who would love me, and marry me."

"And what happened?" Alex prompted when she fell silent.

"I thought I had found that man in Theseus, but I was wrong. Terribly wrong."

"Do you want to tell me more about it?"

"No. Except that there was a moment—only a few hours ago, how strange!—when I came near throwing myself into the sea."

"My dear—!"

"But I could not see drowning as an improvement, and that impulse did not last long."

"Let it never come near you again."

Whether he himself or the princess was the first to raise the subject of marriage, Alex could not afterward remember. Spontaneously the princess admitted (or perhaps it was more of a complaint) that she and Theseus had never gone through any kind of ceremony.

"Princess Ariadne. Will you be my wife?" Alex drew a deep breath. Somehow the moment he had thought might require all of his strength was past before he had time to dread it.

"I will," said the princess at once. Then her eyes grew wide. "Oh, I will, I will!" After a moment she added in a small voice, "At this point, were I at home, and had I just become engaged to some prince from a neighboring kingdom, there would be required official testimony on the subject of my virginity."

"When the world knows that the Lord Dionysus has proposed marriage, I believe it will also know that the time is long past for any such tests or testimony."

Her eyes were miracles of joy, of promise. "I will gladly do whatever my Lord Dionysus asks of me. But I am only a mortal woman."

"My Ariadne. Mortal or not, you are the only one that I have ever asked to marry me." And the immortal memory of Dionysus assured Alex that it was so.

And Alex took Ariadne in his arms and kissed her tenderly.

It was obvious, even without discussion, that any more formal ceremony was going to have to be postponed indefinitely, until certain great obstacles to true happiness should have been removed. But it would not be forgotten, and they could only hope that the delay would not be great. "One must make an effort to do these things properly," said the god who had fallen in love. But Alex could feel that Dionysus could never make more than a half-hearted effort at propriety.

The god's memory held numerous examples of marriage between gods and mortals. The rate of success, both in terms of happiness and progeny, had been as varied as it was in unmixed human unions. Children born to such mixed unions were not gods—no Faces issued from their heads when they died. Nor did their identities survive death, in any form that could be passed on—but as humans they tended to be extraordinary in ways that were unpredictable, Asterion being a rather extreme example. Alex supposed it would be surprising if they were not.

Ariadne protested the presence of the sprites and satyrs, who had quickly returned to close attendance on their lord, as soon as the Far-Worker's overpowering presence had been removed. "They make me feel faint."

"Sometimes they have a similar effect on me," sighed Alex. "I will see to it that they stay farther away." And with a gesture Dionysus banished his escort to a greater distance. In his left ear he could still hear them, but by now he knew from experience that not even he could banish them entirely.

One thing this avatar of Dionysus knew that he would never do with Ariadne—and that was to subject her to, or induce her to take part in, one of the rawer episodes of madness that now and then afflicted him, and especially afflicted his followers.

With vague distaste Alex recalled his orgy of sex on the Isle of Refuge, and the later one of blood and death aboard the pirate ship.

"Some call you the god of madness. Frenzy. Ecstasy." The young woman sounded frightened and fascinated at the same time.

"Many do. And I call you my lady—my princess. Ariadne, I think that as long as you are with me, my madness will be only of the most welcome and creative kind."

"My love and my lord!"

he young soldier Sarpedon was asleep in his bunk, dreaming that he had to perform some incomprehensible military exercise under the Butcher's eye. General Scamander was glaring at him, shouting orders in some language that Sarpedon had never heard before, and in another moment the general's temper was going to snap, and he was going to order some horrible punishment, worse than flogging.

In the dream the executioner had Sarpedon in his grasp, but at the last moment whipped off his hood, revealing a great bull's head on a tall man's broad-shouldered body. And suddenly all the military trappings of the dream were gone, as was the dread scaffold of punishment.

"My name is Asterion," said the bull's mouth in an odd voice. "Seek in the Labyrinth if you would find a friend."

A moment after that, Sarpedon woke up gasping, relieved beyond measure to find himself amid the sights and smells and sounds of the familiar barracks, much as he had come to dislike the place in waking life. And as for the Minotaur . . . he had never dreamt or imagined a monster yet as terrible as the Butcher could be in his wrath.

He had had the same dream, or one very like it, for several nights in a row. He could no longer try to convince himself that it was only an accident.

After another morning of waking life, having worked his way through routine duties, including a weekly inspection that required polishing of weapons and uniform metal, Sarpedon was off duty for the next half-day. He changed into a civilian tunic and made ready to set out as if for an ordinary foray into town.

Lurid rumors continued to circulate in the barracks, concerning the aborted ceremony of the Tribute, and what had really happened in the Labyrinth on that occasion. Sarpedon, as one of those who had actually been there when Theseus got away and their comrade Alex disappeared, told the truth as he had seen it. But soldiers, like people everywhere, tended to believe what they wanted to believe.

As he left the palace complex behind, he felt the ground quiver faintly beneath his feet. Sometimes strange minor tremors passed underfoot, and the breeze brought a sulphuric smell. Now and then in the air there hung a sound so deep it might have been the whole earth groaning. Other parts of the island were said to be shuddering with a volcanic oozing, in which Cerberus, dread three-headed guardian of the nether regions, was said to be crafting a new opening to the Underworld, somewhere in the mountains. No one on the island had ever seen Cerberus, but almost everyone claimed to know someone who had done so recently.

Sarpedon looked back over his shoulder. A wisp of cloud was indeed hanging over the high country, wisps of ashes in the air that city-dwellers breathed.

There was griping in the barracks, but then there was always griping. Sarpedon wondered how many of the others were nursing ideas as rebellious as his own. So far as he knew, none of those thoughts had yet broken out into barracks conversation, even among close friends. Units had recently been reorganized, people shifted around. There were strangers everywhere, and probably informers were among them.

One thing the men of the guard did talk about was the increasing presence on the island of mercenary troops.

"Who're they going to fight? Not a hell of a lot of doubt about that. The plan has to be to use them against us. The king must think we're unreliable."

"If the king's bringing in people like that, he already *knows* he doesn't want to trust us."

The official announcement from the palace had said that new mercenary troops were being imported, as a precaution against a threatened invasion, and against terrorism by unspecified foreign troublemakers.

The mercenary units were some which had a bad reputation, even among their kind.

On the day of the aborted ceremony, when Alex had run after Theseus, Sarpedon had followed Alex for a short distance into the Maze. But as soon as Sarpedon had lost sight of the man he was chasing, he stopped and turned back in fear of getting lost.

For a few hours, he had nursed hopes that some kind of coup was in progress, that a glorious conclusion of the day would see the usurper deposed, and, ideally, one of the princesses on the throne. Maybe their father hadn't been the greatest king who'd ever ruled anywhere. But he'd been a hell of a lot better than his replacement.

But then Sarpedon, along with many others, had been plunged into gloom when it very quickly became obvious that nothing remotely resembling a coup was taking place. And when you thought about it, it was hard to see any way that could have happened. A Palace Guard might manage to depose a king, especially an unpopular one, but how could any combination of mere humans overthrow a god? At the last minute, old Minos had tried to enlist some divine help to save his throne, but the best he'd been able to come up with was Dionysus, in an avatar who looked almost dead when he arrived—such were the facts, as Sarpedon had heard them, from one of the few people who'd actually been present in the great hall on that momentous night. You could hardly do better than recruiting Dionysus if your objective was to have a party, but winning a civil war against the God of Destruction was quite a different proposition.

When a quick roll call was taken, shortly after the debacle of the Tribute, and Alex still didn't show up, Sarpedon had been eighty percent convinced that his friend was dead.

But now he wasn't at all sure. Day after day had passed, with no announcement made of the discovery of any of the escapees, living or dead. Shiva made an appearance now and then, in the palace or flying over the city, often enough to squelch any germinating hope that he was gone for good. As for the Princess Ariadne, the official story put out soon after the event was that she had been kidnapped—again "troublemakers" and foreign agents were to blame.

When questioned by officers on the very afternoon of the great escape, and in several sessions after that, Sarpedon had stoutly denied having caught sight of Alex doing anything out of the ordinary on that day, or anything disloyal at any time. Nor had Sarpedon heard or seen anything else that might help in the search for the fugitives now.

He could tell his questioners truthfully, and with impressive conviction in his voice, that he had been as much surprised by that day's events as anyone else.

So far he had managed to divert suspicion from himself.

"I don't know what happened to Alex. Maybe he was kidnapped, like the princess, and Daedalus."

But the officers and Shivan priests who did the questioning were not so easily put off. They had fastened on the fact that Sarpedon and Alex were known to be friends. "I understand you went to town together fairly often?"

"Once in a while, sir."

"Did his girlfriend live in town?"

"I don't know that he had any particular girl, sir. When he had some money he went to the houses, just like most of us."

"Which house did he prefer? The one where men lie with each other, or with boys?"

"No sir, not that I ever noticed. Just the regular ones."

"The one for those who enjoy being beaten with whips?"

Sarpedon hadn't heard of any such establishment in Kandak, and had serious doubts that one existed. But he wasn't going to debate the point. "No sir."

They would stick with one line of questioning for a while, then switch abruptly to another, as if they expected to shatter his whole structure of lies by confusing him. Or maybe they were just doing it for practice.

"Maybe his girlfriend worked in the palace?"

"Sir, I don't know that he had any particular—"

"Tell me what you know about a slave-girl named Clara, personal attendant of the Princess Ariadne."

No official announcement had ever listed all the missing. But by now, everyone knew the names, and Clara's was on the list. "I've seen her around the palace. Everyone's seen her. Before the day when—"

"Ever speak to her?"

"No sir, not that I can remember—no sir."

"Take her to bed?"

"I—no sir."

"What about your good friend Alex the Half-Nameless? How close was he with Clara?"

"As far as I know, sir, no closer than I am. Was. Knew her by sight, and that was all. Never said anything to me about her. I can't remember ever seeing them together."

"Who else was a particular friend of Clara's?"

"Sir, I can't remember anyone. As I say, I hardly knew—"

"One of the men in your barracks, maybe?"

The interrogation sessions tended to run in a pattern. Eventually, after going over and over the same territory until Sarpedon thought he would go mad, they had told him to return to duty.

"Keep thinking about it, soldier. Maybe something will come to you. Wait, don't be in such a hurry to leave. Before you do, let's go over again what happened on the day of the insurrection, and the kidnapping."

And of course there still hadn't really been anything like insurrection on Corycus. The way things were going, though, it might not take much to start one. You could smell it in the air.

Sarpedon thought there would be no use trying to get aboard a ship and leave the island altogether—everyone knew the harbor was being closely watched. Maybe if you had a friend with a ship, or even a small boat, departing from somewhere else along the coast could be managed readily enough. But Sarpedon was out of luck in that regard.

Having made up his mind as to what he was going to do, he

had gone into town, alone, taking care not to deviate from what he commonly did on his day off—except that today he was wondering if some agent of the Butcher's was following him. Once, only once, he looked back, casually, and could see no one.

For several blocks after leaving the palace complex he stayed on the route he regularly took on the way to his usual taverns and houses. But on reaching a certain point he suddenly turned aside, careful to maintain the same steady walking pace. He was now headed straight for one of the entrances to the Labyrinth, that as he remembered always stood open.

The few passersby seemed to be paying him no attention, and he ignored them as well. The opening ahead, drawing nearer with every stride, looked in fact quite ordinary, like an archway in the outer wall of the dwelling of any solid citizen. And it was still unblocked and unguarded. Evidently Shiva and his pet king had decided that if disaffected elements of the population wanted to lose themselves in the Labyrinth, they were welcome to it. There was nothing easier than to plunge inside . . . legend had it that once you got deep into the Labyrinth, there were fountains everywhere. You might be hunted down and eaten by the Minotaur, but you weren't going to die of thirst.

My name is Asterion. Seek in the Labyrinth if you would find a friend.

Shiva, getting a report from some creature of the Underworld, now knew with certainty that his informant had been wrong about the location of the Face of Dionysus. There could no longer be any doubt that a man who was not Shiva's preferred candidate had picked up the essence of the Twice-Born somewhere and put it on.

Shiva looked forward to imposing a punishment on Creon, for allowing himself to fall victim to this deception. More than likely it was all a part of the great plot against Shiva. He could not decide whether to have Creon arrested at once, and interrogate him under torture, or wait a little longer, until the details of the plot became clearer, and he could be certain of everyone involved.

Another chronic, major concern was the Face of Zeus. Was it

really possible that the most valuable and powerful object in the universe was lying about somewhere, waiting for any human who stumbled on it to pick it up? Creon had suggested that too; more false information, very likely.

If it was indeed hidden in the Maze, who had put it there, and when? Certainly it hadn't been Zeus himself—even the most powerful deity in the universe could not remove his own Face from his head, and set it aside somewhere. Unless he did so in the accidental way that the previous avatar of Dionysus had accomplished exactly that feat: by crawling into a hole somewhere and dying.

Suppose some other god had come into possession of the Thunderer's Face—in that case, of course, the finder would be unable to put it on himself, and might well seek a hiding place. Or find a human ally to give it to. But, to what human being would this hypothetical deity be willing to entrust a power so much greater than his own?

There are certain regions within the Labyrinth that I, Asterion, consider unlikely ever to be penetrated by even the best-organized searchers from outside. I had taken myself to one of these zones in search of rest, but even there, I no longer felt entirely secure. When Shiva came looking for me, he would come by air, and at an altitude from which whole sections of the Maze would be simultaneously exposed to his penetrating gaze; and probably he would be able to muster additional powers that I had not yet even imagined. Dreams had shown me all too clearly that if the Destroyer made a determined effort to locate me, he would succeed.

Still, I needed sleep. It afforded me a kind of rest, even though I could not afford to be idle in my dreams. There was now a task before me that I feared and disliked, but yet I felt compelled to undertake it. It was now required that I try to spy on Hades himself.

Oddly enough I thought it helped my approach to Hades when I deliberately thought of myself as the Minotaur. That slavering monster was daring enough to try to interfere with the dreams even of a god like Hades.

Before I began to play that game, I viewed the feat as comparable to that of trying to find and enter the dreams of Zeus himself—which was one exploit the Minotaur had never quite managed to nerve himself to attempt.

Ever since I had been old enough to think at all, I had known an inner conviction, doubtless based on little more than a few hints and clues received in earliest childhood, that made me certain that Zeus was, or had been, my true father.

All the evidence indicated that Minos, my stepfather, had been a moral and reasonable man—as kings go. In contrast, my true father, the most powerful being in the universe, was generally acknowledged to be quite a lecherous monster, and traditionally his offspring over the centuries were legion.

There was every reason to believe that Ariadne shared the same parentage, and was indeed my full, true sister.

Though one might observe that there is not much family resemblance between my sister and myself.

The affair of Zeus with the mortal queen of Corycus had ended only with her death in childbirth.

Sometimes, as I grew older, I wondered whether the Thunderer had ever been able to feel grief. There were days when I wanted to meet him, face to Face, and demand from him an answer to that question. But lately I had grown uncertain of his very existence. Somewhere, of course, his Face must still exist; but quite possibly no one was wearing it.

But my latest dreams (besides allowing me to give Sarpedon directions to find me) had led me to an intriguing discovery, that I thought might be connected with Zeus. Actually finding him was not my immediate goal. My objective was much more modest and practical. What I needed was a messenger, to convey a certain item of urgent news unambiguously, and in waking life.

And at last I succeeded in intruding upon one of the visions that marked the slumber of the Dark God, Hades.

But very quickly my psychic surroundings grew so terrible that I was forced to withdraw, unable to endure that overwhelming presence even for a few minutes. The dream that engulfed me, defying all my efforts to control it, was almost sightless, filled with heat and the smell of sulphur, as well as with fear and discontent. And almost the only sounds in it were what seemed to be the sobs and screams of human torment.

When I awoke, I saw a human figure standing at a little distance, and I feared for a moment that my nightmare had somehow trapped me.

But when I sat up, and my mind cleared, I discovered to my relief that the truth was much simpler: I once more had a human companion. He stood before me a weaponless, weary, bedraggled youth, still wearing the uniform of the Palace Guard.

His voice was tired, and not so much afraid as filled with resignation. "Lord Asterion? My name is Sarpedon."

Slowly I got to my feet. "Yes, I see. I recognize you now."

"I am glad to hear that . . . sir." The young man took a deep breath and drew himself up. "Yesterday I deserted from the barracks. Last night I slept in the Labyrinth. I've had strange dreams, last night and before . . ."

I nodded. "And I have visited you in some of them. Otherwise you could not have found your way in here to me."

Gradually my visitor allowed himself to relax, and told me his story in some detail.

I in turn was grateful for any friendly human presence, and after we had talked for a while, I tried to relieve myself of my own most recent dream by telling it aloud. "I dreamt I stood on the brink of a black and empty nothingness. And what made it unendurable, was the fact that it was dark and empty by its own deliberate will."

The dreams of Hades, if one could call those sickly nightmares dreams, were profitless for an intruder, and I suspected they could be deadly.

"But enough about nightmares," I told my new ally. "I have good news for you as well."

The last time I had tried to penetrate the dreams of Dionysus, a surprise awaited me. I found myself in close contact with the mind of the young man I had known only as Alex; and what the mind of that youth had now become astonished me.

I was vastly cheered to discover that Alex, who was certainly no ally of Shiva, had now put on the Face of Dionysus. The fledgling immortal now stood in mortal danger, but at least Alex seemed to be aware of the fact.

And I came upon hints, obscure indications, that there was, after all, something of overwhelming importance in the Maze—in or near the center, where Daedalus had spent his fruitless months in search of something he could understand well enough to be able to investigate.

"I can try to communicate this discovery to Alex/Dionysus at a distance, in a dream. But we cannot wait to see if this attempt at communication succeeds. I badly need a messenger."

It was just sunset when the magic chariot of Dionysus, drawn by twin panthers through the high wind above the sea, arrived on Corycus. Nestor was in the chariot with the god, and so was Ariadne, who throughout most of the long flight had been clinging to her lover. The mercenary captain had stood most of the time with his eyes closed, keeping a white-knuckled grip on the chariot rail; meanwhile Ariadne seemed less affected by the experience of the ride. As long as Alex's arm was around her, and her eyes fixed on his, speed and altitude appeared not to bother her at all.

Alex had timed the flight from Dia so as much of it as possible took place in daylight, the vast memory of Dionysus containing evidence that the considerable dangers would thus be minimized. The influence of Hades was diminished when the sun itself, the Eye of Apollo, dominated the sky.

With the island only a thousand feet or so beneath them, Alex directed the leopards to land in some place where he was not likely to be forced into an immediate confrontation with his chief enemy. He left it up to Silenus, who as usual was on hand with the rest of the inhuman entourage, to make the final choice: a rocky glen, through which a small stream trickled, high up in the rugged hills that were locally called mountains. No human habitations were in sight, save for the roofs of a small village a quarter of a mile down the slope.

The chariot of Dionysus came down to earth as silently as a falling leaf. Still, a pair of owls, sacred to Athena, flew up in alarm as the chariot came down. It had left a very faintly luminous streak behind it in the dimming sky, which Alex supposed must have been noticed by numbers of people on the ground. He tried to brace himself for a sudden attack by Shiva, but so far the evening remained peaceful.

Nestor hopped out even before the vehicle had quite come to a stop, and stood with hand on his sword-hilt, slowly regaining his composure, and trying to look as if a long flight was only part of the day's work. The two leopards licked their paws and took their ease. Now, on the ground, they might almost have been mistaken for ordinary animals.

Dionysus looked out, frowning. "It seems we were expected," he told his companions in a low voice, and nodded toward a lone figure that had emerged from among some trees to greet them.

Alex gazed, frowning in surprise. "Sarp?"

"Alex?" called Sarpedon, tentatively. There was a pause, while the two old friends looked each other over.

"You look like nothing very bad has happened to you," Alex said after a moment.

"I've been lucky." Sarpedon swallowed. He refrained from saying anything about how Alex looked. "I bring a message to Dionysus from the Lord Asterion. He saw in a dream that your chariot was coming, where and when you were going to land."

Ariadne said, "What my brother sees in his dreams is generally true."

Alex performed introductions. Sarpedon bowed low to the princess, whom he had seen many times before, but never spoken to. He said, "The burden of my urgent message is that Master Daedalus must be brought to the Labyrinth as quickly as possible."

"Daedalus? Why?" the princess wondered.

"I don't know why, my lady. If your brother knows, he thought it wise not to risk the knowledge in my care."

"Perhaps I can find out," Ariadne murmured. "My lord Dionysus, Alex, you must excuse me for a few minutes." Stepping gracefully over the railing of the chariot, she moved a few yards away. There she stood with eyes closed, hands folded before her, as if deep in meditation.

Alex looked at her, then at the leopards and the chariot, then back at her again, undecided. "If that's what Asterion wants, we must try to do it. But I don't want to leave you here while I fetch Daedalus."

"Now that I have come home," said Ariadne, eyes still closed, "I must stay."

"Very well. Sarpedon, old friend."

"Yes?"

"Will you recognize Daedalus, if you see him? Yes, of course you will. Therefore I want to lend you my chariot. You must catch up with the Artisan—he must be still aboard ship en route to Megara—and bring him back here."

"But if he's at sea—can I find him?"

"My helpers will locate him for you. All you need do is speak to him."

Sarpedon, after hearing some further explanation, accepted the task willingly. "I'll rout him out of his snug mainland cottage, if I have to."

"Ask him courteously, at least at first. But convince him that he must come back to Corycus."

"And if he still declines that honor?"

Alex heaved a sigh. "Tell him that at last there is a promise that the secret of the Labyrinth may be solved. Tell him anything you think may help, but bring him here. If all goes well, it shouldn't take you more than a few hours."

The soldier started toward the chariot, then stopped, gesturing helplessly. "Lord Dionysus—Alex—how do I control the leopards?"

Alex thought. "You don't—you won't be able to. They'll locate the Artisan on their own, once I have given them their orders, and bring him back when he's aboard. But they can't talk to him. That's your job."

And in another moment Sarpedon had climbed aboard the chariot and was on his way.

Nestor's sufferings during the long flight had been considerably greater than he had allowed to show. Not that either of his fellow passengers had paid him much attention en route; indeed he thought he might have fallen out of the chariot and not been missed.

To occupy his mind, he had speculated privately as to how many human bodies the chariot might be able to accommodate. It seemed that a pair of human passengers, in addition to Alex/Dionysus himself, posed no problem. Nestor thought that the space inside the chariot's enclosing rail had expanded modestly, just enough to give them all comfortable elbow room. And as far as a mere mortal could tell, the leopards betrayed no signs of weariness or strain from coping with the unaccustomed load.

Nestor had also been distracted from his fears by the rowdy chorus of maenads and satyrs, almost always invisible, that kept near-perpetual attendance on the Twice-Born God. Occasionally during the flight Alex had encouraged his sprites and satyrs to manifest themselves quite openly. Traveling airborne as easily as smoke, they went rushing and capering along in a lively torrent beside the chariot, doing their best to entertain the passengers with song and dance. Nestor was grateful for their efforts, though he was unable to enjoy them to the full.

Ariadne had already assured Nestor he would be welcome in her homeland, where the faction loyal to the princesses would soon be organizing in an effort to overthrow the usurper. And she also promised him that he would be well paid, when she or her sister, or some ruler sympathetic to their cause, should be restored to power.

And Dionysus had also pledged a substantial reward. "Provided of course that we both survive until this matter has been settled."

"I could ask no more than that, lord. What do you want me to do?"

As the sun went down, and night began to well up out of the valleys and creep over the lower foothills, the lights of the city of Kandak were plainly visible from the hills, a thin scattering of orange sparks of hearth fires and wall sconces. Larger fires marked the two great lighthouse fires bracketing the entrance to the harbor from the sea. Also conspicuous, by contrast, was the adjoining patch of absolute, unbroken darkness where the Labyrinth sprawled over its square miles.

The princess, having for the time being learned all she could from her visionary web, emerged again from meditation, looked around at her homeland and asked, "And are we really now in Corycus again? Or is this all another vision?"

"We are here, my love." Alex took a long look around as well. "All that you see is grimly real and solid. I'm afraid I've brought you to a place of greater danger."

"I'm not worried. I have a god to protect me."

"A very new and inexperienced god. And not much of a warrior, as gods go."

The princess murmured something loving, expressing great confidence in his abilities.

"My love," Alex murmured in return, kissing her again.

"My sweet love," she murmured back. "*You* are the one I have been looking for."

Nestor recalled them to their current situation. "Look. People with torches, coming up the hill."

"Someone must have got a good look at us, when we were landing, and spread the word about what they saw."

The torches in the hands of people climbing burned brighter as twilight thickened.

Soon the god and his entourage of divers beings were surrounded, at a little distance, by a small murmuring crowd. The mood seemed to be one of eagerness, only slightly tinged by apprehension. Gradually the curved line, marking the farthest advance of the less timid, was edging closer, and again a little closer still.

Obviously some of the people of Corycus had observed the chariot's landing, and had correctly interpreted it as a welcome sign of divine interference. Some of the braver folk, or those who were more desperate, had started climbing toward the place to see what was happening, but maybe it took them an hour or more to reach the remote spot.

Some had already recognized the princess, for her name was being spoken in hushed tones.

Close on the heels of the first climbers came a steady trickle of others. Humble people, peasants and workers of the island, who saw the princess shortly after her arrival, recognized her at once, and greeted her joyfully.

The torchlit circle of welcomers grew, and thickened, and the happy murmuring grew louder. Alex thought that the village below, or several villages, must have emptied out completely.

As it became obvious how fervently she was being welcomed, and by a great number of people, Ariadne responded to the demonstration with tears of joy, and impulsive gestures.

"Oh Alex! I never realized how much I missed my good Corycan people until now, when I see them around me again. I feel as if I've been away for a year."

"Let's show them we appreciate their attitude," said Alex.

"How shall we do that?"

"Probably a little refreshment is in order." With a minimum of thought and effort the god, making himself relatively inconspicuous, created samples of magic fruit, grapes of a dazzling perfection and incredible taste. These he handed to his betrothed who passed them out to the people who were bold enough to come to get them. Emboldened, the crowd soon lost almost all of its timidity, and was pressing closer.

One of the young Corycans cried, "We thank all the gods, princess, that you have come back! We will burn rich grain and fat meat upon the altars of Dionysus and Apollo!"

"The temples of all the good gods have been destroyed," another onlooker mourned aloud.

A third chimed in. "But the stones of altar and hearth were taken away and hidden, and I know where."

And Alex had a little speech to make. "My friends, my people, you had better go home now, before our gathering here becomes so big and noisy that it draws unwelcome attention."

"According to what the people here are saying, the island is swarming with mercenaries. More have landed even in the few days since we left."

Alex and the princess wanted Nestor to go into the city and

scout. Other mercenaries by the hundreds, hired by Perses and his ruthless god, had begun arriving on the island shortly before the great escape. More were still coming in now. So anyone Nestor encountered in the city or in the countryside would almost certainly assume that he was there at the invitation of the new rulers, the supporters of Shiva.

"Find out all you can about the mercenaries," Alex instructed him. "If you can, get some of them to change sides."

Nestor nodded thoughtfully. "I'll see what I can do. I may very well see one or two colleagues who know me fairly well, and I them. Of course it's bad for a soldier's professional standing to get a reputation for changing sides. But that doesn't mean it's never done."

"It would be a big help if you could persuade some of them to do it this time."

Speeding over the sea, in silent obedience to the orders of their divine master, the twin leopards soon located the ship that was carrying Daedalus, and brought Sarpedon in the chariot alongside in the moonlight, wheels spinning gently as it hovered in the air, the chariot's rail just a little higher than the deck.

The crew goggled and yelled in terror, and Daedalus emerged from somewhere below to stare in frank amazement.

On hearing in whose name he was summoned, and for what purpose, the Artisan grumbled, but finally grabbed up his bag with a few small tools, reached up boldly enough to grab the chariot's rail, and swung himself aboard with Sarpedon.

Clara and Icarus remained on deck, wailing their sorrow that he was leaving them.

"Goodbye, husband! I fear I will never see you again!"

"If I'm not back before you reach Megara, tell the king there you are my true wife—Captain Ottho can testify he's married us." Daedalus quickly explained to Sarpedon that he had planned to arrive at his new home in the character of a married man with a family. He wanted his time free to concentrate upon whatever work his new patron might assign him.

Leaning over the chariot rail, cupping his hands to yell, the

Artisan had a few last instructions for Clara. "And tell our new master the king that I will be back as soon as possible. Promise him . . ."

"Promise him," suggested Sarpedon, "that he may name his own compensation for your absence—within reason, of course—from Dionysus himself."

The chariot rose higher over the moonlit waves, turned in the air, and gained speed rapidly. Daedalus seemed already to have forgotten wife and child, in the sheer fascination of having a god's odylic chariot at hand for close inspection. He stood upright, gripping the railing, obviously enthralled. "How does it work?"

When Daedalus arrived back on Corycus, the time was almost midnight. Some of the local people had gone home, but many were still in attendance on the god and princess. The sight of the returning leopards had a powerful restraining impulse on their tendency to crowd forward.

Alex/Dionysus greeted the Artisan warmly, and said to him, "Since divine Hephaestus is currently not available, you are our next choice for this task, of all the gods and humans we know." A little flattery wouldn't hurt.

Daedalus accepted the flattery absently; his main concern was the job for which he had been summoned. "Princess, it seems to me wonderful that you moved about inside the Labyrinth for years, and yet only now have your powers revealed to you that the Face of Zeus may lie hidden there."

"Not so wonderful. I think, Prince of Artisans, that you may have forgotten how vast the great Maze is. Also, I have never till now thought of trying to find my father's Face."

Now there was a murmur from the remaining crowd as a little girl came forward with a gift of wildflowers. The leopards only yawned benevolently as she passed close in front of them. Dionysus accepted the bouquet gravely, and passed it on to Ariadne.

There had been many moments during the past few hours when Alex could hardly resist the impulse to insist on having some time as absolutely alone with his bride-to-be as it was possible to be.

But too much was at stake, including Ariadne's safety, for them to be able to shut themselves off from the world.

Alex said to Ariadne, "Our wedding is going to have to wait." Then he added, only half in jest, "I fear that if we were to hold a ceremony now, Shiva and your uncle might insist on being invited."

She emerged from the laborious interpretation of her web-images long enough to kiss him lovingly, perhaps to eat and sleep a little, and hold brief conversation—then she had to plunge back into the effort that haunted and consumed her.

Alex considered offering the gathering a hint or two that any effort to overthrow Perses could expect to be blessed with strong support from Apollo himself. But on second thought he decided to save that cheering news for some time when it was really needed. Also he had to assume that whatever was said or done in public now would be known to his enemies in a day or two.

Some in the crowd impulsively pledged themselves to fight for the princess and her sister. They had come armed with pitchforks, sickles, and scythes, to be ready for attack or defense as seemed to be required, and now waved their weapons in the air.

When Ariadne assured them that neither she nor her husband had any personal interest in crowns or thrones, the denial was quite credible: Why should any god be interested in ruling a merely mortal realm? Support for Ariadne's sister grew more vociferous and open. In the estimation of most of the people of Corycus, Princess Phaedra had become the rightful ruler of the island on the death of her father, Minos.

Judging by what the welcoming committee had to say, everyone on the island seemed ready to believe that the two younger children born to Pasiphae had been fathered on her by the god Zeus in one of his mysterious manifestations; Pasiphae's affair with Zeus had endured for years, ending only when the birth of their youngest child, Asterion, had resulted in the queen's death.

One of the villagers cried, "Better even the bull-man for a king than what we have now!"

Many of the people would be more comfortable if their human ruler was entirely human.

Nestor said, "In my experience, most folk are of two minds as to whether they want their ruler to be entirely human or not."

Tonight the joyous welcome extended, with growing enthusiasm, to Ariadne's high companion, who was standing back a little so as not to interfere with her reunion with her people. Apparently everyone on the island had long since learned that the earlier Minos, the father (at least by adoption) of Ariadne, had shortly before his death concluded an alliance with the God of Revelry.

The newly returned princess, when it was obvious that everyone wanted her to make a longer speech, said something gracious in return. Once more she explained that she had no personal ambitions for the throne.

"My new husband probably would not want me to assume such a burden." There was a murmur of applause, and faces turned toward Alex, who smiled and did not contradict her.

Then, when it seemed to him that some direct comment was called for, he said, "My dear, you would make a lovely queen. But the memory of Dionysus assures me that gods do not make good kings, as a rule; and he has no wish to try."

Ariadne assured everyone that she fully supported the claim of her older sister, Phaedra, who was really deserving of the crown.

Now certain people, who had close relatives in the military, assured the returned princess that there was still a faction in the army and the navy who would be ready to support her, and even more readily her sister, in a power struggle with her uncle—especially if they believed there would be a good chance of winning. None of the current senior officers, all chosen or vetted by the Butcher, had such an attitude.

Alex and his divine partner both kept hoping that Apollo would show up soon. The Sun-God had pledged his help in the coming battle, but had warned Dionysus not to expect to see him on Corycus immediately.

Ariadne suggested to her bridegroom that one of their first moves should be to find Phaedra, and offer her half-sister protection against the forces of darkness. It would also be necessary to sound her out on her willingness to lead a rebellion against their usurping uncle.

"I don't want to alarm you, dear one. But first we must make sure that she's still alive. She has not the protection of being thought a child of Zeus."

"She will be. Shiva still hopes to be able to use her as a figurehead, if Perses proves unsatisfactory. And Perses would not dare go against the wishes of his god."

"I don't know your sister at all. When I was a soldier, everyone in the barracks wished her well, but we never saw much of her. How do you think she'll respond?"

"We have never been truly close, as some sisters are. Phaedra's usually the quiet one, but I think not easily frightened. I know she loved her father, and that she loves the people of the island. I anticipate that she will be ready to be a queen."

Now there was a bustle among the local people. A messenger coming up from the village had just brought word that Perses the usurper had placed the Princess Phaedra under house arrest. There were rumors that he had ordered her to be killed.

"Then show me to the place where they are holding her."

Ariadne was clinging to his arm. The sprites had given her new garments again, including the simple tunic of a warrior woman that covered her body almost completely. At her belt hung a short sword of mainly symbolic value; Silenus had obtained it somewhere and presented it as a gift.

Now the princess was saying to Dionysus, "I fear no danger when you are with me."

"If only I could tell you truthfully that you need fear none!"

But the princess was already busy with her web.

Alex thought to himself that Theseus might well be on his way back to Corycus also.

"Shiva might very well go to fetch him, if he wants him here to receive the Face as soon as it's removed from my own shattered head."

Also Alex could not keep from wondering what would happen when Ariadne saw that man again. So far, the subject of her previous lover had never come up between them.

---

*W*hen Dionysus took the leopards' reins again, Ariadne, Daedalus, Sarpedon, and Nestor were aboard the chariot with him. Alex held the vehicle at or near ground level on their swift foray into the city, only going airborne when fences, walls, or the occasional building presented obstacles in the most direct route.

Ariadne repeated her web-spinning search at intervals as they drew closer and closer to the city of Kandak, and the adjoining Maze and palace. Her findings steadily confirmed what Asterion had told Sarpedon—the place they sought lay somewhere near the center of the Labyrinth.

The Artisan's ride in the chariot, and the prospect of being able to come to grips with a supremely challenging problem, freed him from the last traces of shyness in the presence of the god. Daedalus grumbled briefly about the stresses of the flight that he had just endured. But actually he did not seem displeased by his near-kidnapping. He told the princess that in a way he had been sorry when they had left Corycus several days ago, feeling that he was abandoning puzzles unsolved, secrets undiscovered, some-where in the monstrous Maze.

Princess Ariadne was reluctant to try to use her powers to probe into the affairs of Zeus. Perhaps, she thought, she was afraid to be brought closer to the man who had been wearing that Face when she and Asterion were conceived.

But she dared not ignore the possibility that the overwhelm-ing power of the Thunderer was almost within reach, ready to be taken. With gods and a king against her, help of that magnitude was desperately needed, to save her own life, and her sister's, and above all the life of the god she had so suddenly come to love.

When Ariadne in secret silence, in the privacy behind her

closed eyelids, asked the oracle of her webs to show her the best way to keep the love of Dionysus, she received no answer at all.

This upset her so much that she could not keep from blurting it out to Alex. "What does Dionysus have to say about that?" she concluded.

He took her in his arms and answered immediately. "That only means that there is no way you can lose my love. As long as my spirit lives, it will be yours."

The chariot had covered a mile or more before either of them was ready to speak again. Then Alex whispered in her ear, so close that the other passengers could not hear. "There is something we should decide now, my love. If we do discover the Face of Zeus, who is going to put it on?"

And she whispered back, "There is at least one man with us who I think can be trusted."

Daedalus, when he was offered the chance, declined—Alex was not surprised, having already heard the Artisan express his reluctance ever to be a god.

Ariadne knew the moment might come when she herself would have to put on the Thunderer's Face, if that should prove to be the only way to deprive the enemy of its powers. She feared such a transformation would cost her the love of Alex/Dionysus— but she would make that sacrifice, if necessary to save his life. Again she and Dionysus conversed in low whispers.

The princess said, "Perhaps, if and when Daedalus is confronted with the reality, he will change his mind."

"Perhaps. In any case, we must find the Face before any of us can put it on."

Meanwhile, Alex continued to wonder what had become of Shiva. He kept turning his head, searching the night sky with Dionysian vision. What was distracting the Destroyer, keeping him occupied with other matters? Could he possibly be waiting simply until he had all of his chief enemies in one place, subject to one blast of destruction?

A journey that would have taken many hours of steady travel by wagon or cameloid, from the high hills to near the center of the

Labyrinth, was accomplished in less than half an hour. The time could have been much less had Alex not stopped several times to observe conditions, and once to drop off Nestor in a deserted alley near the waterfront, where he assumed that when daylight came he would find it easy to mingle with imported mercenaries.

The observations en route revealed evidence of military repression in several portions of the island. It seemed that numbers of people had been arrested. Alex saw bodies hanging at a crossroads; the dead wore placards accusing them of treason to the great god Shiva. If anything like a rebellion had actually been attempted, so far it was evidently going badly for the rebels.

When at last the chariot began to skim low over the Maze's twisting walls and narrow passages, Ariadne kept a sharp eye open for her brother. But she saw nothing of Asterion before they began to descend, guided by her private visions, to land near the center of the Labyrinth.

They found a squad of soldiers present, men of the Palace Guard gathered nervously in torchlight, who, after a moment's shocked retreat, came forward again to unanimously welcome the princess and pledge her their loyalty. The presence of Sarpedon, whom they all knew, helped put the men at ease. Some of them recognized Alex, despite his apotheosis, and he propped one foot up on the chariot rail and made them a little speech.

"When I joined the Guard, my friends, I remember the recruiter told me I had a great future ahead of me. Well . . ." With a gesture he indicated the chariot, and the princess at his side. After a moment's silence, the men burst into a roar of laughter.

Disembarking from the chariot, leaving it waiting in the space that had been cleared for Shiva's sacrifice, Alex and Daedalus advanced on foot under the guidance of the princess, with most of the squad of soldiers following.

The time was now a little after midnight, and Dionysus called upon his invisible entourage to provide some light. Bright flames that gave no heat were soon dancing erratically across the pavement and along the enclosing walls.

Ariadne's web-spinning vision brought her party closer and closer to the spot she sought.

It was on a lower level, almost below the central space where Shiva's stage of sacrifice had been erected, certainly one of the most-traveled sections of the Labyrinth. And at first glance there seemed nothing to distinguish this spot from any other, though the eye of Dionysus, when he looked at it steadily, noted certain subtle peculiarities.

The soldiers were set to digging, moving earth. Busy hands were excavating a cavity that had been filled with rubble, deeply saucer-shaped and perhaps twelve feet across.

As the underlying basin of solid rock was cleared, gradually a strange configuration was revealed.

Getting his first good look at the mystery, Daedalus said nothing for what seemed, to his nervous companions, a long time indeed.

Curtly he dispatched one of the squad of loyal soldiers to his old quarters to look for a certain bag of small tools, telling the man where he thought it could be found. Everything he'd left behind had been ransacked and scattered by the new king's agents, in a fruitless search for clues to where he might have fled, but his small tools would have been meaningless to those angry searchers, and though they had been scattered most of them were still there.

Then, gesturing at the problem before them, the Artisan invited comment by his associates. "How would you describe this?"

The center of the revealed pit was a round concavity about two yards in diameter, a series of concentric rings, like the design on an archer's target, with the innermost circle the lowest. At the very center was what seemed obviously a door, a circular panel no more than about two feet wide, set in the lowest spot of the floor. A single massive hinge was visible, as was a handle of bronze with which to lift it open.

"The door must swing up, not down," said Alex, stating the obvious.

"Of course," the princess agreed. "Look at the hinge."

"But the lock keeps it from opening," the god observed.

Daedalus gave him a look that was far from worshipful. "To prevent a door from opening is generally what the designer has in mind when he creates a lock."

The solid rock near the hinge had been carved with the lightning-symbol that was sometimes used to represent Zeus.

Looking over the door and its intricate lock, Alex's left eye, armed with the vision of Dionysus, showed him some meaningless color variations, but nothing special that he could interpret in any useful way.

But Ariadne could see more. Now, standing near the locked door, she reported a vision of a thread of her imaginary web-stuff, weaving its way through the intricacies of the lock.

She frowned, squeezing her eyes more tightly shut. "It is as if the thread were attached to some invisible, impalpable needle. And as soon as it has been pulled all the way through, the trapdoor swings up and open . . . I can see no more beyond that."

And of course the door in the real world remained solidly closed and locked.

Somewhere under the earth, quite nearby, a murmur of unseen water could be heard. To the Artisan it was obvious that the nearby streams must be channeled past this spot in conduits, or even wholly contained in round copper pipes, as if here, over a kind of fissure in the earth, they might otherwise be in danger of plunging all the way to the Underworld, never to be seen again by mortal eyes.

Daedalus muttered to himself, "And of course there may well be—there probably is—more to the trick than appears on the surface."

To Alex, what appeared on the surface certainly seemed challenging enough.

The lightning-symbol of Zeus was not the only carving in the rock. Around the circular rim of the broad depression ran a lengthy inscription. The seven lines of symbols, each seemingly in a different tongue, reminded Alex of the words carved in the wall of the ruined temple on the Isle of Refuge.

When he looked at these letters through the eye of Dionysus, he could read what amounted to the same verse seven times. Alex recited:

> "'Who would hold in his hand what lies below
> Must subtly plan and gently go.
> The key required is a supple strand
> One might think only a thread of sand—'

"—and there it breaks off."

The Artisan nodded slowly. "Then the inscription confirms the princess's vision. To solve this puzzle we must thread a string, or length of fine yarn, or some equivalent, all the way through the shell. That is the only kind of key that is meant to fit this lock."

"And I doubt that even you can make a thread out of loose sand, or a key either."

"So it would seem. But let me think about it for a bit."

Dionysus was the first to admit that cleverness in problem-solving was not his own strong point. It might be within his power to transform the vault and all that it contained into a mass of living growth—but he feared that would blur and probably destroy whatever secrets it might now contain.

His residence within the Labyrinth had allowed him to begin to appreciate its strangeness. Therefore he was not surprised that a marvel like this locked door had lain almost under his feet for several months, without his ever suspecting its existence.

"We can try digging down here beside the door," Sarpedon suggested tentatively.

Bigger tools were soon brought from the Artisan's old workshop. But digging in the hard and solid rock was going to be difficult at best. And the very first attempt along that line ended in frightening failure.

Daedalus himself tried first, hitting the shell-like structure with a sharp steel chisel, driven by a hammer of moderate weight. The chisel slipped away, and sudden tremors went coursing through all the surrounding earth.

Someone let out an involuntary cry, and clutched the rough

stones of a shortened wall for support. But the wall was swaying noticeably too.

"Hold up, no more of that!"

The lock itself was not even scratched; the unknown material from which it had been made was extremely hard and tough.

By now one of the loyal soldiers had brought the Artisan his bag of small tools, or such of them as could be found, and he tried one of them against the mechanism, and then another. But this preliminary poking and probing accomplished nothing either.

"The entry passage, where our key of sand must enter, is no thicker than a baby's finger, and intricately curved."

Daedalus found it simply too hard to see clearly, to get a good look at the problem. "I must have some air to breathe in here, and room to turn around. And give me some light!"

The Artisan ordered the low overhead to be broken away, opening the tunnel-like passage to the plaza above it. The soldiers set to energetically, fracturing ancient stonework and tossing away the fragments. *If anyone takes notice of our noise*, thought Alex, *well, let them.* Dionysus feared no opponent except Shiva or some other malignant god—and he expected, fatalistically, that the ones he truly feared would come when they were ready, noise or not.

A couple of the upper walls in the immediate vicinity were also knocked down, and the ivy and laurel growing on them cleared away. The loyal guardsmen, eager to serve the princesses, broke and slashed and heaved with a good will. The moon, almost full, shone down on the secret door from the western sky, an hour or so after midnight.

Now, with steadier, better light available, the mysterious encircling inscriptions became a more insistent presence.

Now the Artisan gave the impression of settling in comfortably, to do a job.

"We must hurry!" the princess burst out impulsively.

Such urgings made no impression on him. "Did you ever see a lock like that? I've never seen one in my life before." Coming from Daedalus, that was an impressive statement indeed.

Now it could be clearly seen that the key part of the puzzle was shaped like a shell of the many-chambered nautilus, or some very similar seashell. It might have been a real shell of some obviously mutant creature, heavily bioengineered in ages past.

No one could forget that a single hammer-blow, directly on the lock, had provoked a serious shaking of the earth beneath them.

"Open it by gentle means, I pray you, Daedalus!"

"It seems I must use subtle means, or none at all." And Daedalus growled at his would-be helpers to stop standing in his light, keep quiet, and let him work.

Transparent forms came whispering in the air, and then Silenus took solid shape, as real as a cameloid and almost as odorous as a goat. Sometimes Alex thought it would be an excellent idea to rid himself of Silenus permanently, but such Dionysan memories as were readily available offered no encouragement for such a hope. The satyr murmured a warning that the Princess Phaedra had just been placed under house arrest, confined to her apartment in the palace.

Leaving Daedalus to begin his task, with Sarpedon and the squad of loyal soldiers as protection, Alex set out with Ariadne to rescue her sister.

At first he hesitated. "You might be safer if I left you here—"

"But nowhere will be safe until we win. Come, and I will find my sister." And once more the princess assumed the role of guide, deviating from the marked route to take an even shorter pathway to the right side of the palace.

Alex was also quite familiar with the interior of the palace, having pulled interior guard duty many times within that rambling structure. Certainly he could find his way without difficulty to the private quarters of the princesses, though he had never actually been inside those rooms.

Now when he approached and entered those corridors and rooms, exerting his power to clear a path, they underwent a transformation similar to that which had happened aboard the pirate ship, when the powers of Dionysus had it in their grip. Around the advancing god, stone columns sprouted branches and green leaves. What had been an iron grillwork, recently installed, had become a screen of gentle branches, easily brushed aside.

Some of the soldiers and servants here greeted Dionysus as their savior, while others fled in terror. Alex could hear one of the mercenaries cry out, "No one's paying me enough to battle a god. Let them fight it out among themselves."

haedra started up in wonder when Dionysus suddenly appeared at the door of her apartment. Joyfully she recognized Ariadne at the god's side. "Sister, is it you? Thank all the gods!"

"Not all of them are against us, Phaedra. You are free, for the time being at least." The two young women fell into each other's arms.

"Praise be to the good gods!" Phaedra cried.

"I promise I will offer a worthy sacrifice," her sister said. "To one of them, at least." She looked over her shoulder toward Alex, who had withdrawn a few paces and was keeping watch.

The older sister said, "My life was about to be sacrificed for nothing, and I thank you for returning it to me."

"You are entirely welcome. Now we must be on our way."

"Where?"

"Back into the Labyrinth. I have much to tell you as we walk, and much I want to hear from you as well."

Dionysus had transported Nestor into the city in the chariot, and dropped him off in an alley near the waterfront, where it seemed likely he would soon be able to make contact with some of the mercenaries imported by King Perses.

Nestor found this chariot ride mercifully much shorter than the previous one. It also helped that the trip was conducted over land, practically at ground level. Observing the countryside as well as he could by night, Nestor saw that the state of roads and fences showed that it was, or recently had been, a prosperous land—even if the prosperity had been founded, over generations, on tribute and taxes extracted from other kingdoms on the shores of the Great Sea, mostly by the powerful Corycan navy. What he could see of the land had the lush, innocent look of a country that had forgotten, if it had ever known, what it was to be invaded and despoiled.

Well, if civil war erupted here, as now seemed practically inevitable, there were plenty of lessons in horror soon to be taught.

Nestor's biggest personal worry at the moment was that among the villagers welcoming the returning princess might have been one or more secret supporters of Shiva and Perses. That would mean his own arrival on the island would soon be reported, and much increased the odds that as soon as he showed his face in the city he was going to be arrested.

The locals had warned him that a curfew had been declared in Kandak, and though he arrived a little after midnight, he was forced to lie low until sunup. At least this enabled him to get a few hours' sleep.

Once the sky brightened with morning, and the streets began to be busy again, Nestor emerged from hiding and bought some fresh melon and fried cakes from a vendor. The man seemed surprised that this hard-looking foreigner paid without dispute. He was willing enough to vent his displeasure with foreign mercenaries in general—present company of course excepted—but he could provide little in the way of specific information.

Munching a fried cake, Nestor strolled around, getting his bearings. It would be an interesting city to return to someday, as a man of peace.

He walked with a touch of arrogance, nothing furtive in his manner. And he saw, here and there on the streets and in the markets, other men with the air of self-confident strangers. Some of these were simply merchants and sailors, as might be expected in any busy seaport; but some had a definitely military look.

Nestor sat for a while on the quay, chewing a wad of the leaf favored by many seafaring men, and at intervals thoughtfully spitting the yellow juice, observing the traffic in the harbor. Only those people attempting to board ships were being stopped and questioned. Among the many vessels visible, he was able to spot a familiar ship or two, belonging to colleagues, with some of whom he was on good terms.

An hour or two after sunrise, on one of the streets adjacent to the waterfront, Nestor recognized one or two of the men he saw on shore as colleagues with whom he'd had dealings in the past.

He had parted with one of these on particularly good terms, and he chose this one to approach now.

"Hello, Rafe."

The man turned and looked at him in mild surprise. "Nestor. I see Perses is really working at this business of beefing up his army."

What more natural than that they'd turn almost automatically into a tavern to share a drink and exchange ideas about their new jobs. It was a little early in the day for serious drinking, but Rafe said he'd discovered yesterday that the beer in this establishment was not too bad.

"Glad you came to Corycus?" Nestor inquired cheerfully.

The other shrugged. "It's a job. What about you?"

Nestor naturally had to remain closemouthed about his own supposed job here on Corycus.

His companion was not surprised. "Can't talk much about it, hey? That's all right."

"What about you? I've not seen anything of this King Perses yet, have you?" Rather leaving the implication that the god Shiva might have hired him.

"Not much, one quick meeting in the palace. But so far he's paid on schedule, and I'm content."

But Rafe was pessimistic about the prospects for success. "When a king must hire foreign troops to keep down his own people, my thought is he's not long for this world."

"Who else is here?"

On leaving the tavern, half an hour later, the two men went their separate ways.

Nestor thought that if his mission in Kandak went sour, he might want to seek out the Labyrinth as a place of refuge. In there he might have a powerful friend in the person of the Minotaur.

Alex had cautioned him, "Don't be, ah, put off by his appearance."

Thinking about that, Nestor could not repress a slight inward shudder. But he'd certainly run to embrace a monster rather than face Shiva or interrogation in a dungeon.

Alex/Dionysus had been introduced to Phaedra, and he and the princesses were threading their way back into the Labyrinth, when the sprites, who seemed to live almost always on the verge of one kind of frenzy or another, brought Alex word that Shiva was approaching.

Lord, thy enemy approaches with the speed of the whirlwind, and in terrible wrath. He cries that he will burn to a cinder this body you now wear, and recover thy immortal Face!

"We must see to it that he does nothing of the kind," said Dionysus.

Alex's chief concern now, when a deadly battle with Shiva seemed only minutes away at most, was to arrange some kind of protection for Princess Ariadne, and for her sister. The best expedient currently available seemed to be to send Phaedra and Ariadne into the Maze, to rejoin Daedalus. The Artisan might profit from the younger sister's help once more, and whatever powers were guarding him would protect the princesses as well.

And, even as Ariadne and Phaedra entered the Labyrinth once more, they felt the earth quiver and lurch beneath their feet.

Ariadne, frightened as she was, was still very confident of her own ability to locate some safe hiding place for herself and her sister within the Maze. Finding her way in the predawn darkness was no problem, not with the strands of her web always ready, behind her eyelids, to offer guidance.

Not many days ago, she had guided Theseus through these windings. Then she had imagined that she was escaping to freedom and adventure. The idea that the Face of Zeus might be nearby had never entered her mind—nor had many other things of great importance. Like a child, like a fool, she had believed with all her heart in her great true love, that brave and handsome Theseus was devoted to her, that in his arms she might find everything that she would ever need. . . .

What an idiot she had been! And she was really frightened now.

But it would not do to show that fright. Grabbing her older sister by the hand, she tugged her ever onward, deeper and deeper into the engulfing Labyrinth.

Phaedra had lived near the Maze almost all her life, and yet had seldom set foot in any part of it. Now she found its high, curving walls and constricted spaces frightening and unfamiliar. She hesitated briefly, protesting, "May we not become hopelessly lost?"

"That, at least, will not happen." The younger sister was calmly certain.

"Why not? We've made so many turns already, that for all I can tell, we might round the next corner and find ourselves right back in the grounds of the palace, with Shiva waiting, and Uncle Perses grinning at us."

Ariadne paused in her flight, giving both of them a chance to catch their breath. She decided that it was time at last that she explained a few things to her half-sister. "We haven't talked about this for a long time. But you must remember that I have a talent for finding things—and, which may not be so obvious, for hiding them. So we can be reasonably confident of being on the right track."

"What are we looking for, besides a place of safety? You strongly implied that there was something else."

"Something I never thought to look for, in all the years I traveled through these passageways."

"And that is?"

"It might be dangerous for you to know."

At this point Phaedra was not going to insist. "You were always good at finding, Ariadne. I remember having one or two long talks with you about that. But that you were good at concealment as well—that is something I never noticed."

"Perhaps because I concealed the fact." It was a sober answer, and the half-smile died from Phaedra's face. "Now watch, and I will do my best to conceal us both." Closing her eyes, the younger sister took the older by the hand and led her forward.

"You are walking with your eyes closed," the elder whispered.

Ariadne nodded silently, not breaking the rhythm of her stride.

I, Asterion, had been asleep most of the night; in my case, of course, sleeping does not mean I was inactive. I hoped that Sarpedon had accomplished the mission I had entrusted to him; but my dreams had brought me no reassurance on that point, and therefore I could not be sure.

To say that I had devoted that night's precious dream-time to a continued search for Edith would be exaggerating. But while roaming the visionary corridors of night I kept my eyes open for any sign of her, and I nursed hopes. It was perfectly possible that she might still be somewhere nearby. There were certainly convolutions within the Maze that I had never seen. There were whole sections, acres in extent, where for years, for centuries perhaps, no human feet, not even mine, had ever trod. As a child I had often thought that some day, if I could live long enough, I would have memorized every room and space and passageway. I suppose I might possibly have achieved that end had I made it my life's work. But the world of dreams was an even vaster puzzle, and also more intriguing, and most of my hopes and plans were invested there.

Waiting for his enemy to attack, trying to concentrate on matters of life and death, Alex/Dionysus could not banish from his thoughts hopeful visions of the time when he would at last possess his bride. At that moment, he was thinking now, all the sprites and satyrs were going to be shut out, kept at a distance. He did not want them intruding upon that holy time, any more than he would have wanted other humans present.

He doubted it would ever be possible to rid himself of his entourage completely, but at least he could banish them to the middle distance, where he could still hear them singing.

Earlier, when he had tried to discuss these matters with Ariadne, in one of the brief periods when they seemed to be quite alone, she had felt sure enough of her divine companion to gently tease him about it. "Some would think it strange to meet an avatar of Dionysus who is opposed to orgies, or at least chooses to avoid them. How will the world change next?"

"Orgies . . . have their place. Or so says Dionysus, who ought to know all there is to know about the subject. But I am also Alex, who was once half-nameless, and I say that I no longer want anything to do with such events. Certainly not when I am with my love."

And somewhere in the background he had heard a murmur from invisible Silenus: *We will see if the Twice-Born can be content with such a monogamous relationship.*

Loyal soldiers patrolling near the center of the Maze raised a sudden alarm: a new version of the monster Cerberus had burst up out of the earth, at some unknown location on the island, and was approaching swiftly.

Alex, mounting into the air in the chariot of Dionysus, soon caught sight of the thing. He could not tell where it had come from, but it seemed to be following the path the sisters had taken into the Maze, tracking one or both of them like a hound on the scent. Driving in pursuit now, urging the leopards to greater speed, he closed in rapidly on Cerberus: big as an elephant and with three fanged heads, stalking and striding on long legs through the Maze, stepping right over walls at places where they were no more than ten feet high.

Cerberus was not a human, nor a god, nor yet a normal beast of any kind. In part, at least, it was no more than a machine; and yet his Dionysian memory assured Alex that earlier versions of the monster had possessed enough of life to render them subject to madness and to frenzy.

Had there been an open volcano nearby, he might have tried to plunge it in. Still, Dionysus had doubts about the beast's susceptibility to that kind of damage, coming from the Underworld as it did. Prolonged sunlight might wear it down, but that was not a helpful hint now in the middle of the night.

Anyway, there was no volcano handy at the moment.

Alex shouted, "After it, you sprites and satyrs! Goad it, tempt it, turn it from its course!"

And his crew of invisible, inhuman helpers soon afflicted the machine with madness. It turned away from the center of the Maze, bursting through walls at random, stopping and retracing its steps, wandering off course.

Meanwhile, Alex had driven his chariot closer and closer to Cerberus. The influence of Dionysus was strong enough to cause its lifeless surface to break out in plant growth. Gradually, whatever power it was that steered and energized the machine was disrupted, weakened, confused into chaos and helplessness.

The thing staggered on its long legs, and at last crashed down in a heap. The stalks and tendrils of new life, springing from its flanks, finding themselves now with motionless ground to grow in, turned to grope toward the sun.

Nestor, as he made his way across the troubled city of Kandak, could feel some of the earthquakes that Hades had now begun to induce, sending minor temblors rumbling clear across the island. Such disturbances were usually interpreted as evidence of the displeasure of some god. The God of the Underworld could bring houses and shops and palaces tumbling down, if that was what he chose to do.

Nestor, having learned from Rafe that his old acquaintance Captain Yilmaz was quartered in this section with his troops, had come looking for him. Yilmaz would not be Nestor's choice for a bosom companion, but his reputation for venality and untrustworthiness was great enough to raise Nestor's hopes of getting him to defect.

Among the beautiful older buildings in the city of Kandak, there stood one in particular that had once served as a gathering place for worshipers of Apollo. It had been repeatedly desecrated, profaned, by the new Minos and the fanatical devotees of Shiva. Maybe some of Hades's earthquakes had begun to crumble it.

While in the process of tracking the captain down, Nestor happened to look in through an open doorway of the former temple of Apollo. High windows filled the interior with cheerful morning sunlight, showing him a band of four or five priests of Shiva, identifiable by their skull-necklaces, who had stripped a young girl of her garments and were stretching her out between them on the floor; the victim seemed to have given up struggling, but she was obviously still alive. A couple of irons were heating in a small fire in a brazier nearby.

Adopting his best sergeant-of-the-watch voice, Nestor called in through the open door, "Anyone know where Captain Yilmaz is? And what do you think you're doing there?"

To these men the sergeant of the watch was apparently not an impressive figure. "Yilmaz is not here, outlander, nor any of his company. I am Creon, high priest of Shiva."

"Whatever you think you're doing, looks to me like you'd better stop." Nestor wasn't sure, when he said the words, if he was only bluffing or not.

Maybe they were just the wrong words to have used to a high priest of Shiva—or maybe there were no words that could have made a difference.

It turned out that Nestor wasn't bluffing, and a savage swordfight quickly ensued. None of the skull-wearers had looked to Nestor like men who really felt at home with weapons in their hands, but he knew better than to trust to first impressions in such matters.

If he had underestimated his opposition to begin with, they had made the same mistake. In the space of a few heartbeats, Nestor had killed one of his opponents, going after the most aggressive first.

Then he cut down a second.

There must have been one more opponent than he had mentally accounted for, because the blow that struck him down came from behind, and was totally unexpected. It allowed him only an instant to feel regret, or anything else, before the world went glimmering away.

Regaining his senses, slowly and painfully, Nestor at first was uncertain whether he was truly dying or only felt that way. His head ached fiercely, and pain in his upper chest told him that he had been stabbed there also—his shirt was wet with blood. His enemies had not bothered either to tie him or to finish him off— that would have been good news, if he could move. As matters actually stood, it didn't seem to be good news at all.

In the middle distance he had a good view of the one who had called himself Creon, and two or three others, gathered within reach of a small fire in the middle of the temple, preparing to get on with the business at which Nestor had interrupted them. The young girl was stretched out on the paved floor while four men each held one of her limbs. It seemed that only a minute or two had passed, and Nestor could not have been unconscious long. Not long enough.

But the proceedings were not going to proceed, not just yet anyway. A tall young man had just appeared in one of the doorways leading to the street, and stood there surveying the scene inside. The newcomer wore a white robe or cape, and nothing else, suggesting that he too was one of Apollo's acolytes. Now he stepped inside, advancing with steady strides.

"Who in all the hells are you?" The priest of Shiva who had just picked up a hot iron from the brazier, causing the girl to scream and faint, now waved it in the newcomer's direction. "You want a taste of this too?"

The tall youth came right up to him, and spoke in a tone of gentle remonstrance. "This is not your house, after all." And he put out his hand and gently caught the wrist of the arm that held the iron, guiding it even closer to his own calm face; and then with a gentle puff of breath, like a man extinguishing a small candle, he cleansed the metal of its fiery heat. The one breath drenched and quenched the orange glow and its radiance, in an icy cold that might have come from the dark side of the moon; even Nestor at the distance where he was lying could feel a faint chill spreading through the air.

"Rather this house is mine," the newcomer added quietly.

For a long moment, the girl's tormenters gazed unbelievingly at what had happened to the iron. Then, with Creon in the lead, they jumped to their feet and fled in screaming panic, the necklaces of toy skulls rattling madly. Terror himself came under their new enemy's dominion.

Apollo only watched them go, allowing them to leave his presence unharmed. But as the last pair of running legs vanished through the doorway he shouted after them, in a voice that might have been heard half a mile away, "*Let me never see you again under the sun!*"

A moment later he was bending over the unconscious girl, touching her so that she roused from her faint. Nestor heard him murmur, "More than enough blood has already been shed inside my house."

Then the Lord of Light came to Nestor, and with another touch sent renewed life flowing into him, body and mind. Nestor thought that he could feel, could almost see, the black wave of death receding.

"You will tell me your story later," said the voice of Apollo, which seemed to reach him from a great distance; and that was the last thing he was aware of for a time.

Nestor slept briefly, lying as he was on the floor, and when he awoke he felt almost entirely restored. The back of his head was still sore when his fingers pressed it, but that was all. Of the stab wound he thought he had discovered earlier, there was now no trace, though his shirt was caked with dried blood.

The sunlight in the temple was even brighter now, a clear and steady illumination that seemed not to depend entirely on the windows for its source. The thought crossed his mind that Shiva and Hades might someday succeed in tearing down Apollo's temple, but they were never going to put out the sun.

The girl was gone. And now Nestor saw, with no capacity for surprise left, that his recent acquaintance Dionysus had come to join Apollo. At the moment, Alex was indicating with a gesture the bones and offal that had been burnt for Apollo on the nearby altar. "Some of them mean well," he observed.

Jeremy Redthorn nodded. "People most often do mean well, while they are praying to Apollo; they would rather turn toward the sun than to the darkness. But why even well-meaning folk should think I crave burnt guts and bones . . . ?" He shook his head. "So it has been for ages."

Alex agreed. "I don't care for sacrifices either." He paused, looking inward and considering. "I speak for Dionysus as well as for—me."

"If it makes people happy to slaughter a few animals in my name—well, let them. They could be doing worse; and wisely they keep the good meat to eat themselves, while putting the gristle and guts and bones in the fire as my share. Fortunately I need not depend on them for nourishment."

"I understand." Alex drew a deep breath. "What are we going to do now?"

"I am going to seek out Hades, as soon as the sun comes up," Apollo said quietly. "There's no use waiting longer. I see no reason to think that I'll be stronger tomorrow, or the next day, or that he will be weaker."

"Are you strong enough to stand against him?"

"In daylight I think I will be. But there is no certainty about the outcome. He has hurt me badly in the past. You must do all you can to see to it that he gets no help from his allies."

"I will do all I can. I am—I was—a soldier. But Dionysus isn't . . ."

"I understand."

"Can we count on help from anyone else?"

"Hephaestus is my friend, and would stand with us if he were here. I know of no other Olympians willing to risk their necks." Apollo paused, then added, "I think that we can win, but I will need all the help that you can give."

"You can count on that."

"Let me tell you, my colleague," said Apollo, "that I have

sworn a great oath to foil Hades wherever and whenever I can, in this great game that we and others play."

"I see it as no game, but war."

"It can be both. A war whose first battles were fought so long ago, that the gods themselves can scarce remember. A game, with the whole world at stake."

*A*t dawn on the morning following the arrival of Dionysus, Shiva returned to Corycus, with Theseus riding behind him on his flying bull.

Nestor had climbed to the roof of the temple of Apollo, intending to get a view over the city as the sun came up. He observed what appeared to be a mob of angry citizens, more or less spontaneously marching on the palace.

Nestor was about to report this to his two divine allies, when his eye was caught by a startling image in the sky. Looking up, he saw in the distance Nandi, with two man-shaped figures on his back, air-trotting downward as if intending to land. Nearly as Nestor could tell, the creature was coming down close to the edge of the Labyrinth opposite the palace.

The mob dispersed in panic, and the mercenary captain ran to tell the gods who had now become his companions.

Grumbling and discontent had been gradually becoming more and more open among the officers and men of the Palace Guard, and most of them were now ready to join the revolt. Unfortunately much of the Guard's strength had been dispersed to distant regions of the island, as Perses became doubtful of its loyalty.

Wild rumors had been flying regarding Shiva's whereabouts. There had been speculation that the God of Destruction was really a coward, and had fled the island altogether at the first hint of serious opposition.

Others feared that Shiva was only standing back a little, to encourage all his enemies, mortal and divine, to raise their heads, that they might be more readily and thoroughly cut down.

And still others feared, with good reason, that an even stronger and more terrible god than Shiva might now appear on Shiva's side.

*   *   *

When Nestor had reported Shiva's arrival to Apollo and Dionysus, Apollo took leave of his two allies, saying he had to try to find
out what Hades was up to. He hoped he would be able to rejoin
them soon.

Dionysus and Nestor rode the chariot back into the Labyrinth,
there to join Sarpedon and the other loyal soldiers in defending
Daedalus.

On the way, they wondered who the second rider might have
been, on Nandi's back.

Alex observed, "Well, I don't like him or her, whoever it was.
Shiva is very powerful indeed. But Shiva can only be in one place
at a time."

Also Shiva tended to treat people with an arrogance that quickly
made enemies, if only secret ones, out of the majority of those
he met.

The bull Nandi had come down to land inside the Maze, only
a few hundred yards from its very center. "The Face of Dionysus
will yet be yours," said the God of Destruction to his human
client, nudging him unceremoniously to the ground, so unexpectedly that Theseus failed to get his feet under him in time, and sat
down hard. "Stay right here, so I can find you quickly when I
need you. I will kill this God of Many Names, this Great Party-
Goer, again, and as soon as he is dead you shall have the Face he
wears."

As soon as Theseus regained his feet, he forced himself to
make a deep obeisance. It had been a long time, but with a little
effort he remembered how.

He might have saved himself the trouble and humiliation, for
Shiva totally ignored him. Nandi bounded into the air again, and a
moment later the god was gone.

Theseus, right hand on his sword hilt, stood staring after the
divine figure, which had already vanished over the surrounding
Labyrinthine walls. The man was thinking dark thoughts, and

wondering to himself. "Do I really want to be a god of wine, madness, and lechery?" All amusing things in which to dabble—but are such matters really the important part of a man's life, after all?

Besides which, he was already tired of being carried along like a child, or a mere woman, on a god's magic steed.

His sword had been ready at his side, and now it was ready in his hand. He decided that what he really wanted to do now was to slay the Minotaur. Shiva would be angry—but when he, Theseus, started worrying about who might or might not be angry at him, it would be time to retire. Or to die.

He said to himself now, "It never does a man any good to be furious with a god. You can of course defy him." In the legends, that course was likely to lead to some eternal and truly heroic punishment.

He moved on.

Somewhere in the Labyrinth ahead of him he could hear the shouting of men's voices. He could not make out any of the words clearly, yet somehow he felt sure that they were soldiers. He set out to investigate.

The true rebellion had broken out first in the city of Kandak, only hours after the first rumors of the return of Dionysus. From Kandak it spread rapidly across the island. People in the hinterland had always resented Perses's usurpation, and away from the capital there was little support for Shiva and his puppet.

Even in the big city their support, apart from the mercenary troops, was very thin. Nestor in his reconnaissance of the city had seen that in the narrow streets of the old quarter, citizens were constructing barricades, tearing up cobblestones, as if they planned to stop a cavalry charge. On observing this activity Nestor judged it a total waste of time, as no good cavalry officer would launch a charge down a narrow, winding street like this. But he supposed it gave the people a feeling that they were doing something useful.

In the wealthier quarter of the town, some houses and other

buildings owned by people suspected of being especially close to Perses and his imported, bloodthirsty god were set on fire.

Strong factions of the army and navy were ready to join in the revolt. The Butcher remained loyal to Perses, but the Palace Guard he commanded had largely been already transferred out from under his supervision. He really had no choice but to stay with Perses; the Princess Phaedra would have nothing to do with the man who had connived at her father's murder.

As was usually the case at any given time, more of the navy's ships and sailors were out to sea than were in home port; but the royal sisters and their allies were confident that most sailors would approve of the revolt when the news reached them. But by then, of course, the matter would have been pretty well settled, one way or the other,

People loyal to "our true queen, Phaedra" were determined to put her on the throne, and to depose the usurper and his gang.

I, Asterion, with the help of Sarpedon and a squad of guardsmen, continued to do my best to stand guard over Daedalus, as the Artisan concentrated on his investigation of the locked door.

As dawn approached, I had withdrawn from the area where Daedalus was working. Feeling a weight of weariness, I withdrew to one of the remoter fastnesses of my domain. There I lay down on a couch of stone, well-padded with moss, and was soon asleep. Almost immediately I plunged into a kind of nightmare, in which Theseus had captured Edith again and was trying to wring secrets out of her.

Other people and gods well known to me were taking part in the dream as well, but I was encountering only their images, not their minds. Some of them, I knew, were dead. There were Shiva and Dionysus, the old King Minos and the new—

There was Theseus, again, shouting a challenge and waving from some elevated place quite near the Labyrinth—

The dream changed abruptly, and I was alone with Daedalus.

The Artisan was talking earnestly, trying to reveal some great secret; but with all the noise and shouting, I could not make out a word of what he said.

Presently I dreamt of my sisters too—and realized suddenly that what was happening was something more than a dream.

Out of sleep I fell, cold and disoriented, into the world of wakefulness, where as always I was immediately bothered by the lack of control. Even before my eyes were open, I was aware that Ariadne and Phaedra were nearby, calling my name, beseeching me to come and help them. There was shouting in the distance, and the sounds of fighting.

I rose to my feet, stumbling clumsily for once, as dreams became entangled with reality, and lumbered away.

I dashed around a corner and there they were. Ariadne immediately ran forward and threw herself into my arms.

When my gaze fell directly on Phaedra, she shrank back involuntarily. It had been many years since she had laid eyes on her brother.

All she could get out in her confusion was, "You were much, much smaller when I saw you last."

Then slowly, while Ariadne and I embraced in greeting, our older sister moved forward, obviously in awe of the gigantic, bull-headed and beardless figure dressed in kilt and sandals. But she took the hand that I stretched out to her.

I made sure that the pressure of my fingers was very gentle. She did not seem startled by my odd voice when I said, "My sister. Now you shall be my queen."

"My brother."

"I suppose," said Ariadne, "that you two have never actually seen each other before."

"Not strictly true," her sister said.

"Not true?" Ariadne was amazed.

"No." The elder sister's gaze remained fixed on my face. "In fact you are one of my earliest memories. I remember feeling so— so terribly *sorry* for you."

She told the story to us then. Phaedra had been about four years old when I was born, and had only the haziest and most fragmentary memories of that time. She had not, of course, actually witnessed her mother's death.

Ariadne would have been only two, unable to remember anything at all.

Phaedra as a small girl had had at least one long look at the horned and monstrous infant. In the realm of fact and logic, that horror was of course intimately entwined with the fact of her mother's death. But in the memory of the four-year-old, the two events had nothing directly to do with each other.

Princess Phaedra would not have chosen to bring up that subject now, but there seemed no way to avoid it. And maybe a direct confrontation was really for the best.

"After that we were kept apart," she said to the bull-man.

His huge head nodded slowly. "Yes. Sometimes I wonder that our father on earth, King Minos, did not kill me on the spot, when mother died. But I suppose he had received some omen, some warning against that."

"Minos was not a ruthless man. And I believe he loved his queen. Even as she loved all her children."

Ariadne, as she grew older, had not been prevented from seeking out her brother and spending time with him.

The visits had started early, with the connivance of a nurse, who had been the early wet-nurse of the monstrous infant, who thought that siblings ought to know each other.

Naturally both girls had been forbidden to wander in the Labyrinth, as children in general would be, by their parents. But Ariadne's special talent had enabled her to find ways around the prohibition, while her older sister, naturally more inclined to follow rules, had stayed in the palace grounds like a good girl.

When King Minos eventually learned that Ariadne had made several visits to her brother, he had been shocked at first. But then he had not forbidden the meetings.

I doubt that my foster father Minos ever laid eyes on me.

Whether he did or not, he could never bring himself to acknowledge that such a creature might be one of his family, or bring it into the palace.

Ariadne had to leave us, to go on with the all-important business of her visions and her web. But Phaedra stayed with me for a time, and for the first time in our lives we could begin to know each other.

$\mathcal{A}$lex was intimately aware of Dionysus's chronic reluctance to engage in battle. The God of Many Forms had been a hunter, in the past, and might someday hunt again—but being a warrior was something else again. When, as now, the god faced unavoidable armed conflict, his overwhelming reaction was not so much fear as a sense of his own total incompetence. His instinctive preference was to enter combat, if he must, moving at high speed aboard his chariot. On the other hand, Alex the simple soldier, considering the situation as unemotionally as possible, quickly decided that such a conspicuous presence in the sky would only make him a better target for Shiva's lancing rays of death. Staying close to the ground, where he could at least try to shroud himself with greenery, might make the enemy's task a little harder.

In this question it seemed that Dionysus readily yielded to the superior experience of his human component.

As to what direct action the God of Joy—the Great Party-Goer, as some irreverently called him—might be able to take against Shiva, or any other divine opponent, his Dionysian memory was anything but reassuring. He was no better at fighting than he was at puzzle-solving. Alex's divine partner could command no armament to match the Third Eye. His chances of being able to turn the God of Destruction into a dolphin, or working any similar transformation on him, were practically zero. On the other hand, driving Shiva into a frenzy might be all too easy to accomplish, and might require no effort at all. But Alex was not at all sure that that was the result he should be trying to achieve.

Now the young man could better understand the behavior of his predecessor on that cold night, half a year ago. As soon as Shiva had shown his face in the great hall, the previous avatar of

Dionysus had simply turned and fled for his life. It hadn't done him a bit of good, of course—save that it had prevented the Face of Dionysus from immediately falling into Shiva's hands.

The only effective weapon he could use against Shiva must be his wits; but the sharpest wits in the world could be quite helpless unless provided with something material in the way of tools.

The twin leopards could be deadly fighters against any ordinary opponent. Unfortunately Alex could find no memories to suggest that the magical beasts would be able to stand long against Shiva, let alone kill him.

Reluctantly he summoned his inhuman auxiliaries, intending to give them instructions on what to do if he, the present avatar of Dionysus, should fall in battle. His predecessor seemed to have decreed certain behavior along that line, if only indirectly.

If Fate granted him the chance to pick his own successor, whom should he choose?

It would not be Ariadne, even though Faces seemed almost indifferent to the gender of those who wore them. Alex could not give her to satyrs and maenads, who were always beckoning their lord to dances and orgies. His soul recoiled from the image of Ariadne in that role. Nor could he hand over to her the Face of Zeus, if that should fall into his hands. To enter into such intimate union with the Ruler of the Universe, to become the Thunderer, must change her, or any human being, beyond all recognition; somehow, even her death would be more bearable than that.

When Silenus appeared, in his usual role as spokesman for the entourage, Alex issued his own orders. "If I am killed, I command you to pick up the Face I now wear, and carry it to the soldier, Sarpedon. If that proves impossible, bring it to Daedalus. If you cannot do that either—to one of the princesses." He added those last words with great reluctance. Still he could not bring himself to consent to Ariadne's melding herself, body and mind, with anyone, human or divine, besides himself. As for Phaedra, Alex still thought the elder sister should be queen of Corycus, not a goddess.

But who else was there worthy of being trusted with such power? Asterion came to mind. But Dionysus found it hard to believe that Asterion's bull head would ever be able to wear a Face. Asterion was too much the son of Zeus to partake of the nature of any other deity.

We will not desert you in the battle, Lord! Silenus managed to infuse his wheezing protest with tones of deep sincerity. He even sounded vaguely offended, as if Alex had suggested that the satyr might value his own personal safety higher than his god's.

Dionysian anger flared. "Whether you might desert me is not the question. Why do you persist in misunderstanding? What I am talking about is the need to prevent Shiva or Hades from gaining control of *this*." And Alex raised a hand to touch his forehead. Then he added, "If you do run away, don't go too far."

The ancient satyr looked sadder than ever. *If any of us survive the battle, master, we will do then what we must do.*

Neither Alex nor Dionysus found that very reassuring, but it seemed to be the best that either human nature or divinity could hope for.

Memory assured Alex that it was undoubtedly a very long time since any sprite or satyr had been killed by violence, but they were certainly not immune to such an attack. Not when it came on the scale employed by Shiva.

Trying to make war against Shiva might be hopeless, but against merely human opponents the Twice-Born had every reason to expect success. In the memory of Dionysus Alex discovered that one effective method consisted in the god's driving opposing soldiers mad, causing them to kill each other.

This scanning of the past evoked certain related memories, including scenes of cannibalism, which so revolted the young man that he turned his thoughts quickly away from them.

His main task continued to be the defense of the princesses, and of Daedalus, who must be protected from interruption as he worked.

Anxious to know what success Daedalus was having, Alex went to look, and found him still hard at work upon the puzzle-lock. At the moment the investigator had his ear pressed against the shell-like surface, face scowling in concentration, while his fingers tapped and probed at various places on the mechanism.

Watching the Artisan now, Alex got the impression of a man who was making progress on a job, though Alex would not have been able to say exactly what made him think so.

If the enemy did not yet know that Daedalus was present, and in what kind of task he was engaged, then it was worth some considerable effort to keep Hades and Shiva and their creatures from finding out.

On the plus side, Alex again had the chariot and leopards available for his own tactical use. But he wanted to keep them hidden as long as possible.

Alex had not yet called forth the chariot when he found himself facing a company of mercenaries, the really bad ones from the company of Captain Yilmaz, men who, as Sarpedon informed him, had been used by Perses to interrogate people suspected of disloyalty. They were following the marked pathway leading to the center of the Maze, and in the process getting uncomfortably close to the site where Daedalus still labored. Of course it was still possible that they would never reach it, but it was dangerously exposed to discovery.

Nestor, who knew these men professionally, saw them approaching, and came running up, out of breath, to deliver a warning about them.

Drawing on his own experience as a soldier, his familiarity with the men in the ranks, Alex understood that most of the men in any fighting unit would be terrified at the prospect of face-to-face combat with any god. The only ones not terrified would be the berserk, some of whom were likely to show up in any fight.

Taking a cue from Apollo, he did not pursue the soldiers who ran away from him. But he could not ignore those who were brave enough, well-disciplined enough, or simply vicious enough, to try to stand and fight. Also any orderly retreat would be difficult in the Maze, and the troops might well feel that they were cornered.

He knew he must do all he could to weaken the usurper's human army, before he had to meet Shiva, an encounter that would more than likely result in his own death.

Reacting with professional instinct, the mercenaries sent a

concentrated hail of projectiles at him, arrows and slung stones, and it was not beyond the bounds of possibility that one such missile might do his human body injury. Sprites and satyrs, virtually immune to such gross physical attacks, formed a defensive screen before their god, and his own powers, almost without conscious effort on his part, could deflect stones, turning them into ripe fruit even as they flew.

Turning his human opponents permanently into animals would take more time and effort than he could spare just now, with much greater demands upon his powers looming in the near future. Recalling commands from some of the Twice-Born's earlier memories, Alex inflicted on some of his opponents a temporary transformation. Hogs grunted and squealed and ran. Even when those men returned to human form, they would remain out of action, in shock, for some time.

But he must not become too absorbed in this business to watch for Shiva. Turning away, Alex left his company of sprites and satyrs to conclude the skirmish. Capering phantoms immune to sword and spear and arrow, they first distracted the remaining enemy troops, then maddened them into frenzy.

The satyrs especially took on martial forms, brandishing illusory weapons.

As Alex turned away, Silenus began blustering in a position of assumed leadership—waving a broken wine bottle, as if it were a sword. Alex knew that he would be perfectly willing enough to relinquish what he thought of as his command, as soon as it began to appear genuinely dangerous—but that was hardly likely to happen until Shiva or Hades came on the scene.

Soldiers infected with new frenzy began trying to catch and rape and kill the phantom females, or come to grips with taunting, leaping, chanting goat-men. Instead the mortals only crashed into each other, and in the growing madness of their rage, took out their frustrations upon each other's solid flesh.

What had been a squad of working professionals quickly fragmented into a swarm of individuals—but instead of separating, those individuals quickly came together again, in an orgy of mutual destruction.

Alex took note especially of one pair, locked in a desperate death-grapple.

The voices of the struggling mob rose in a cacophony of screams, threats, howls and insane laughter.

Alex/Dionysus stalked away. His mind was quivering, thoughts jumping, with the burden of his own divine madness. Resolutely he refused to think about the horror he was leaving behind him. He had to struggle hard to free his own mind of the craziness he had invoked, and part of him remained revolted at his own nature.

Alex closed his eyes and leaned against a wall. The God of Madness must not be undone, defeated, by his own nature. *I am more than a God of Madness. I was a human being before I became a god, and a human being I still remain. And I always will.*

When Alex opened his eyes, the world was reasonably steady once again.

His invisible escort swirled around him again. They were highly excited with the results of the just-concluded skirmish, exulting in the bloody deeds they had provoked. To these inhuman servants the only thing that seemed to matter in the war was the degree of frenzy to which the participants could be driven.

Alex, and for a moment even Dionysus, was repelled by this attitude.

Dionysus, like any other god, could not long hold any emotion, any wish, unless it was shared by his human avatar.

Alex hurried to catch up with Ariadne. He called her name, but received no answer. She was nowhere in sight, and sprites and satyrs reported anxiously that they had lost contact with the princess.

He also wanted to make sure that Daedalus was still on the job, and see if he was any closer to success.

There came a distant shouting, as of the enemy in triumph. Shiva had paused to visit destruction upon some rebel formation.

Alex could only hope that Ariadne and Phaedra, and Daedalus as well, might find some place of safety with Asterion.

Because now at last Shiva was in sight, airborne astride the great bull Nandi, gripping in both hands indeterminate shapes that must be weapons. The mouth of his death's-head face was open in a howl of rage. The necklace of skulls was swirling with the speed of the Destroyer's motion through the air.

Alex turned at bay to face his deadly enemy. At all costs he must avoid leading the killer to the woman he loved.

His soldier's instinct urged him to pick up a spear that had been dropped by one of the squad of scattered and slaughtered mercenaries. Alex the soldier felt a shade less terrified, with hilted metal in his hand. But he might as well have saved himself the trouble. The world seemed to dissolve in a burst of white light, eating into his eyes and brain like acid.

The first lance-thrust of light from the Third Eye hit the chariot directly and knocked it out of the air, spilling its divine occupant rudely on the ground.

Alex lay stunned, god-powers at an ebb, waiting for the next blast to sear away his life.

---

lex lay sprawled on the ground, shrinking in expectation of the death blow that must fall on him at any moment. But heartbeat after heartbeat passed, and he was spared. In the background, he thought he could hear one of the princesses screaming.

Granted another moment of life, he tried to move his body, to go to her aid. But all of Alex's half-formed plans for survival in combat had been shattered instantly by Shiva. There was no use deceiving himself; Dionysus was helpless before the Destroyer's deadly power.

And in the back of his mind, as he waited for the searing bolt of death to strike, Alex realized that the entourage of Dionysus had suddenly and finally deserted him. Only an hour ago, he would have sworn that when this moment came, his sprites and satyrs would stand by their master to the death. But now they had all fled in panic . . . not that either Alex or Dionysus could blame them, with Shiva already triumphant and Hades no doubt looming near. Only once before, in recent memory, had his creatures ever forsaken him. That had happened when . . .

. . . when they found themselves suddenly in the presence of . . . but no, that hadn't been Shiva. Someone else.

Groggily Alex, his flesh still cringing in anticipation of a fatal stroke, turned over and tried to focus on the sky. His vision cleared.

Nandi was prancing strangely in the air; Shiva had reined his great mount around, as if preparing to make a charge. Or maybe in an attempt to flee. It was hard to determine which, and suddenly it did not matter. The bull's body had just been transfixed front to back by a Silver Arrow, a shaft so long that a portion protruded on each side. Nandi let out a long bellow, a sound seemingly pure animal and almost deafeningly loud, and at the same time lost the power of flight, fell like a stone, all four limbs frozen in position.

Before Nandi's lifeless shape could hit the ground, Shiva had vaulted nimbly from the dead beast's back, coming down catlike on his feet in the space cleared days ago for the Tribute, not far from the silken chair where he had once reclined at ease, intending to enjoy a sacrifice of blood. Now the God of Destruction, brought to bay, crouched facing his new foe.

Apollo, embodied in the straight-lined, youthful body of Jeremy Redthorn, Silver Bow in hand, was standing atop one of the high walls of the surrounding Labyrinth. The Far-Worker had drawn a second Arrow from the quiver on his back, and was nocking it to his Bow.

Alex/Dionysus, looking over his shoulder as he tried to crawl to safety across the broken pavement of the Labyrinth, had the scene in clear view before him.

First Alex could only crawl, and then he found that he could get one foot under him, though he could not yet stand. But still his thoughts were chiefly for the princess. *If I am dying*, he thought, *let it be for Ariadne. All good gods, protect her!*

In the next instant, Alex winced in sympathy, squinting his eyes shut, as the silver lance of Shiva struck home on its mighty target. His eyes were open again in time to see how Apollo almost lost his footing atop the wall, as he staggered in the act of fitting his next Arrow to his Bow.

When the beam from the Third Eye struck the body of the Far-Worker, obviously it inflicted pain, as Dionysus supposed it must have done even on Zeus himself. But even the Third Eye could not kill a god of Apollo's stature. He whom the legends credited with mastery of the Sun itself, seemed immune to mortal damage by any lesser fire. Few opponents indeed could ever claim victory over the being who held authority over Terror, Death, and Distance.

Apollo's weapons had remained firmly in his hands, and now the Bow was drawn again. In the split second before it was released, Alex had the impression that the whole world was tilting sideways around that arc-segment of metallic silver. Echoes of a deep sound, so low-pitched as to be almost beyond the range of human ears, like movement in the world's foundation, went chasing themselves around the sky.

This time Alex attempted to follow the Arrow in flight, but there was no hope of that, not even for an eye of godly power. Missile and target seemed to have come together even before the Bow had thrummed.

Shiva was down on the ground now, gut-pierced and spouting blood though not yet dead. Some immense reserve of vitality kept the God of Destruction moving. Howling like a demon, laboring and scrambling in a crawling progress on all fours, he was trying to reach one of the newly created chasms in the earth. But just as he gained the brink of one of them, another of Apollo's shafts struck like a lightning bolt before him, blasting up chunks of stone and soil, hurling fragments of wall foundation, sending the Destroyer reeling and rolling backward, still mortally exposed.

At the last moment Shiva, with the Arrow still protruding on each side of his body, got his feet under him and stood erect again, bravely turning his face and his own terrible weapon back toward Apollo.

Only an eyeblink later, Alex saw the head of the Destroyer's avatar explode in a great blur of blood and fragments. He had a clear, momentary look at the glassy Face of Shiva leaping free undamaged, with Apollo's final Arrow perfectly centered in the eye that marked the center of its forehead.

The Face, still transfixed by the Arrow, was only briefly visible before it slid into the new hole in the ground.

One of the soldiers who had been crouched down nearby, seeking shelter, went scrambling in an effort to catch the Face before it disappeared. But the young man was too late, and had to scramble back to keep from falling into the hole himself.

The only visible remnant of the God of Destruction was a headless human corpse, scrawny and nearly naked. The pitiful remnant of the avatar's human body seemed suddenly only a symbol of itself, no more than one of the tawdry emblems of death with which it was still adorned.

*   *   *

In another moment, Apollo was kneeling beside Alex, helping him to regain his feet. Dionysus must have exerted some protective power over the body that they shared, for Alex felt jarred and bruised by his fall, but no part of him had been burned or broken.

Ignoring Alex's outpouring of thanks, Apollo was already talking about the evidence of the locked door, which he had just seen for the first time, and speculating on what might lie beneath it.

When Alex mentioned the Face of Zeus, even Apollo seemed taken momentarily aback. He looked at Daedalus, and the delicate investigation the Artisan had now resumed, and declined to interfere.

Alex asked, "Do you think the story is true?"

"When Zeus is involved—" began Jeremy Redthorn, then stopped, shaking his head. Then he added, "There was an hour, not too long ago, when I was standing atop a mountain that might once have been Olympus—then I thought I might be about to encounter Zeus. But he turned out to be a tree stump."

"*What?*" Alex and Dionysus were about equally astonished.

"It's a long story, and not very helpful for our present purposes. I'll tell it to you someday."

While the fight had been taking place almost over his head, Daedalus, like all the other humans in sight, had crouched down trembling. Now he was already back at work. It seemed he was in a dangerous position now, for the solid rock surrounding the puzzle-door had been rayed with fine cracks by the impact of Apollo's Arrow on the earth.

Jeremy Redthorn was saying to him, "Find the answer for us, Artisan. No one will attack you while you work." Daedalus looked up, nodding abstractedly, perhaps hardly aware of who had just saved his life and was speaking to him now.

Apollo discussed with Alex the next move that he was contemplating: a raid on what he thought was probably enemy headquarters—the huge temple newly dedicated to Shiva, adjoining the royal palace, a couple of miles straight from the center of the Labyrinth.

Apollo told Dionysus that he preferred to do most of his aerial travel with a pair of winged Sandals; the story of how they had come into his possession would have to wait until another day.

Dionysus offered his colleague the use of his chariot. "The leopards seem to tolerate your presence if my other servitors do not."

But the Lord of Light declined. On his Sandals, he thought he could probably move as fast as any other being in the universe.

Another round of combat seemed inevitable. Everyone knew that a little more than a year ago, Hades and the Sun-God had fought a bitter and inconclusive duel, from which both had retreated with serious injuries.

"It's very fortunate that you were able to kill Shiva as quickly as you did."

Testing the string of his great Bow, Apollo confided to Dionysus that he wasn't entirely sure that he wanted to kill Hades. "Assuming that it's even possible."

"But why shouldn't you, if you can?"

"If he dies, it is inevitable that another human will find that Face and put it on. Thus a new Hades will be created, who will be perhaps even more of a curse to the world than this one."

"Possible, but unlikely. We would at least have something of a breathing space, while the new avatar began to feel at home with the Underworld and its powers."

"That may be the best outcome that we can hope for."

"No, the best would be to have a decent human assume the rule of the Underworld. And if we are gentle with Hades, what about Shiva? Was it a mistake to slay him too?"

Apollo had come to understand that no god is truly good, or bad, except by the will of the person who wears the divine Face at the moment.

"Not even Shiva?"

"Not Shiva, or even Hades. Destruction and death have their place in the universe."

Apollo confessed that he knew nothing of what might be under the secret door. "It's true that, as far as I know, years have passed since the Thunderer was last seen by either gods or mortals. I have certainly not laid eyes on him for many years; and it may be that his last contact with anyone was shortly before the death of Pasiphae, and the birth of Asterion."

"What did he look like?"

For a moment Apollo only stared at his questioner. Then he gave a short burst of laughter that seemed to have nothing to do with Jeremy Redthorn. "What does the lightning look like? Or the thunder?" Then the Far-Worker condescended to explain. "At one time or another, my eyes have seen Zeus as an eagle, as a bull, as a shower of gold, among other manifestations. The possibilities are unlimited."

"But underneath it all, behind it all, there must always be a man. A man like you or me."

Jeremy's personality seemed in full control again. "I suppose. Or, for all I know, a woman."

Apollo shrugged. "I see no reason why not."

"But could a woman have fathered two children on Queen Pasiphae? That's what some Jovian avatar did, almost twenty years ago."

"A woman who wore the Face of Zeus, or Jupiter—in some lands they call him by that name—might be capable of that, or almost anything. The powers inherent in Zeus are as far above those of an ordinary god, as your abilities and mine are above the merely human."

"Would we, gods and humans in general, somehow be aware, would anyone necessarily know, if Zeus was dead? Would the universe be any different than it is? We see the lightning flash as it always has, we hear the thunder sound, as it must have sounded a thousand years ago."

"The world seems to be able to keep itself going without the immediate supervision of gods and goddesses."

"How many avatars have worn the Face of Zeus, since the beginning of the world?"

It would be a wise deity indeed who knew the answer to that one.

Alex/Dionysus, seizing the opportunity to make sure that Ariadne was still safe, paused to take a close look at the woman he loved. Some of the things he had learned about her during the last few days were surprising. He thought her beauty had not been damaged by rough treatment, and exposure to the sun and wind, but only made more real. Her wit, and energy, and the fierce devotion she had now begun to show to him, seemed greater marvels even than the mysterious and special powers she had inherited from her father. Even though he himself had attained godhood, he still stood somewhat in awe of the Princess Ariadne.

When Ariadne stood in front of the locked door in the floor of rock, she reported seeing in her vision a thread of her imaginary web-stuff weaving its way through the intricacies of the lock, as if the thread were attached to some invisible, impalpable needle. And as soon as the thread had completed its progress, the trapdoor in her vision swung up and open.

But the vision refused to show her what might lie beyond the seal.

Visions were all very well, and poetic ideas of a thread of sand, but a real strand of some tough fiber seemed to be needed to solve the puzzle and open the lock.

Alex, now watching the Artisan closely, got the impression that Daedalus, incredible as it seemed, was far from being ready to give up. Instead, his look of quiet satisfaction suggested that he might be on the point of succeeding in his seemingly impossible task. Alex thought that the Artisan possessed formidable qualities that in a soldier would have swept the enemy from the battlefield.

Some of the watchers kept silent, but others could not. Phaedra at last cried, "Hurry, hurry!"

The Artisan, with magisterial calm, ignored all efforts to hurry him. When people had specific advice to give, he listened, but so far had quickly dismissed every suggestion as to what he should do next.

At the moment he was lying sprawled on his belly, head lower than his feet, contemplating the mystery that lay a little below his nose. His position looked painfully awkward, but somehow he was managing to ignore the resulting discomfort, as he did the sweat dripping from the tip of his nose. He appeared to be ignoring, also, the ominous rumblings and tremblings of the earth.

Alex, returning to the scene after a short absence, heard a little murmur, as of wonder and appreciation, go up from the small group surrounding the Artisan.

Approaching more closely, Alex noted with surprise that Daedalus was now sitting back, hands clasped, watching the lock with an expression of satisfaction. Alex in astonishment beheld a moving thread of gossamer fineness being gradually pulled into the windings of the shell. This filament was so like one of the gossamer threads of Ariadne's web, as she described them, that for a moment Alex wondered whether her powers might have objectified it into solid reality. But that was not the case.

He could not at first imagine what agency was doing the pulling. With a shock he saw that the thread was moving, progressing into the miniature maze in little fits and starts, a quarter of an inch now, half an inch more a moment later. About two feet of the thread remained outside the lock, and its visible end had been tied, or glued, to a slightly larger and stronger filament.

"But—what magic is this?"

"No magic," said Daedalus. "Watch." And pointed with one gnarled finger to the tiny hole that formed the exit of the passage through the lock.

A tiny creature emerged from the hole, and the mystery was solved. The Artisan had somehow glued his slender filament to the back of an ant, which he had then somehow induced to go crawling through the many-chambered nautilus, dragging the thread through after it.

With a gesture Daedalus indicated the other side of the concavity, where dozens of similar insects, large, red, and active,
were darting about over the rock. Dirt had spilled through a crack
in the rock there, and doubtless their nest had been disrupted,
when the earth moved in its most recent tremor.

"In the past," said the Artisan, "I have found them to be excellent helpers, for certain very special jobs."

And now he leaned forward, taking in his strong fingers the
end of the fine thread that had already been pulled through the
windings of the lock. Delicately pulling, Daedalus gently tugged
the heavier strand, to which it was connected, into place after it.

There came a sharp click, to Alex unmistakable as the sound
of a fine mechanism peacefully yielding. A moment later the Artisan reached for the handle of the door, and started to lift it open.
The door began to open, for whatever bolts had been holding it in
place had smoothly and suddenly been withdrawn.

But the motion of the opening door was interrupted. As swiftly as
a sprung trap, the fine cracks in the surrounding rock split open
and yawned wide. A crash, like a great explosion, sounded from
underground. In the next instant the round door and the whole of
the broad depression surrounding it disappeared as if by magic,
vanishing down into the earth.

Thunderous noise accompanied the disappearance, a roar that
went trailing away below, muffling itself at last in distance and
interior gloom. Belatedly a light cloud of dust rode up out of the
hole on a faint air current. When someone looked over the brink,
his line of sight went down and down, disappearing at last into a
vertiginous darkness, relieved near the bottom only by a sullen red
glow as of heated rock.

The collapse was so sudden that the Artisan and several soldiers came very near to falling in. Daedalus was only saved by the
prompt action of Dionysus, who sprang forward to grasp him by
the collar. In the next moment Alex had hurled the Artisan backward, away from the new hole, saving him from being badly
burned by the hot gases that came belching up from below, a sul-
phurous exhalation of the Underworld.

As he recovered from being thrown yards away, Daedalus was a little dazed, though basically uninjured. He muttered, "The door—the door was just starting to swing open. I almost had it in my grasp."

"But what was under the door?"

The Artisan gasped and coughed, exhaling dust. "All I can say is that there was certainly—something there. I mean a structure, a vault, a room. Stone walls and a floor. But whatever was inside it fell clean away, in a cloud of dust, before I could get a decent look."

"*But what was in the vault?*"

He shook his head disconsolately. "I tell you I couldn't see."

"Then if the Face of Zeus was in there, it's now tumbled into the Underworld."

"Or simply into a crevice in the earth." Dionysus, though he had never entered the domain of Hades, understood that it did not extend everywhere beneath the surface of the ground. He tried to explain this to his comrades.

"Hades may be setting a trap for Apollo, trying to lure him underground."

The huge cavity shocked the eye.

A funnel-shaped volume of soil and rock, some five or six yards in diameter at the top, had gone sliding and collapsing down into the bowels of the earth. The whole apparatus of nested rings had completely disappeared, along with whatever might have been immediately beneath it.

The great, gaping hole, as seen by some observer who found himself hanging precariously over it when the pavement broke, indeed looked as if it might open a passage into the very Underworld.

"In fact—" Apollo began to say. But he stopped abruptly, and after standing frozen for a moment, peering down into the pit, quickly jumped back.

Dionysus stood close enough to see a little of what was going on. Darkness was moving down there, as if a negation of sunlight, of all light, had taken on a solid, objective form. And it was hurtling toward the surface, at the speed of a slung stone.

Hades came erupting out of the earth, a boiling cloud of

shadow. The Cap of Invisibility concealed his precise form, even from the other gods nearby, but everyone could feel his presence.

One Silver Arrow, and then another, went flying into the heart of the darkness; and in return, there came back a shaking and rending of the earth beneath the Sun-God's feet, a hurling of chunks of solid rock.

And then another Silver Arrow, this time drawing blood. Darkness flecked with red burst open, like pus from a boil, and seemed about to engulf the entire Labyrinth. Alex felt the need to brace his feet, straining against what seemed a combination of wind and gravity, that threatened to suck him down into the earth.

Gradually, irresistibly, the sunlight seemed to be eating away the billowing darkness.

The awesome weapons of Hades and Apollo shook the rock beneath the feet of all the humans unlucky enough to be caught nearby. Those who were able went scrambling to find some kind of shelter.

The earth was trembling again.

Now Alex/Dionysus saw, with a chill of horror, another figure emerging from the newly enlarged pit.

Dionysus recognized the new shape, superficially quite human. It was that of the God of Death. The lower half of his ugly face was covered by a ragged growth of dark beard, and the eye of Dionysus could make out the red and ghostly wings sprouting from his shoulders.

Thanatos struck at him, a staggering blow whose force was borne by no visible weapon or movement of the arm; and in another moment, a four-way fight was in progress.

The weapon of Thanatos was a subtle extraction of life; but it was hard to extract life entirely from anyone when Dionysus was defending.

Neither Alex nor Dionysus had thought ahead of time how the God of Joy might be able to fight the embodiment of Death. Laughter to shake him to pieces? That would not work. But if Dionysus could not strike back at Death directly, he could maintain his own life against the onslaught, and spread it as far as possible into the world around him.

How long their silent struggle lasted, neither Alex nor Dionysus could have said. But a time came at last when he realized, with a kind of desperate relief, that Thanatos was in full retreat.

Death fled close on the heels of Hades, who had been wounded, perhaps mortally, by a barrage of Silver Arrows, and had gone tumbling down through the opening from which he had emerged.

For hours, Theseus had been prowling the Labyrinth, sometimes with sword in hand. When he heard human voices somewhere ahead, he followed the sound as best he could, until the voices faded away, to be followed by the crashing noises of divine combat. In a few minutes, that too had faded.

Still he kept going, trusting to the luck that almost never failed him; and after several hours he emerged in the central open space, the very spot from which he had escaped, some days ago, by bounding over a wall. He looked around him warily, but the plaza with its central tiers of seats, and torture-cages, was now deserted. But for the seats and cages, he might not have recognized the place, so drastically had it been transformed, with some of the surrounding walls torn down and a great ragged cavity hollowed in the earth.

But still there was no sign of the Minotaur.

In frustrated anger he turned round, glaring at the walls, and shouted, "Come out and fight, damn you, Cow-head. Where have you got to now?"

Only silence answered.

And suddenly, for the first time since returning to the Maze, Theseus knew fear—fear that he was dreaming again, and that he would not be allowed to recognize the fact that he was dreaming—not until something truly horrible had happened to him.

But Theseus would rather die than allow his life to be ruled by fear. Moving on, a moment later he almost stumbled over the blasted, headless, shriveled-looking body of Shiva's most recent avatar. The necklace of skulls made it impossible to mistake—though for just a moment he had almost taken it for some fallen priest of Shiva's service.

Theseus raised his head, and looked around him, and listened carefully. For a moment, a moment only, he thought of Ariadne. "Time to go home," he said aloud at last. He was speaking to no one but himself.

No, it was not a dream this time. He was not going to allow it to be a dream.

That evening, an irregular string of mercenaries' ships were putting out to sea from the harbor of Kandak, oars working the water in a steady rhythm. Captain Yilmaz, like many of his colleagues, had not waited to hoist sail; Theseus, leaning on the rail beside his friend, remarked that it was easy enough to tell when a fight had been lost, when there was no longer any prospect of getting paid.

Dionysus understood that the killing of Hades would have more far-reaching implications than the deaths of Shiva or the God of Death. But was the Lord of the Underworld truly dead as a coffin-nail, his Face lost somewhere down a fissure in the earth? Neither gods nor humans could be sure.

No one really depended on the Destroyer for anything, but the Underworld had widespread and far-reaching business—some said that the soul or shade of everyone wound up sooner or later in that dark domain.

Apollo, though once more victorious over the Lord of the Underworld, had been weakened by the conflict, and had withdrawn to rest and try to restore himself; and not even Dionysus knew where his great ally had gone. He had promised to return in time for the wedding.

Gazing down into the pit, as well as he could while keeping at a safe distance, Daedalus said, "Not easy to see how any object that falls down there will ever be brought back within reach of a human hand. Yet I must believe that it will."

But the satyr Silenus, who had launched, or at least helped to spread, the rumor concerning the Face of Zeus, had already confessed the fact to his master Dionysus.

Princess Phaedra asked, "Then whether or not there was any truth in the story of the face of Zeus being there . . ."

"Is something that we simply do not know," said the Twice-Born.

The current avatar of Dionysus, he who had once been Alex the Half-Nameless, could only hesitate as to whether to punish his servant, who was now prostrate before him and putting on a show of great repentance. The god said sternly, "Whatever effect you intended, the result was to sow great confusion among our ene-mies—and among ourselves as well."

It was easy to bewilder the foolish Creon. He had already befuddled himself, with much seeking after exotic wisdom. Next time we will be more careful, lord. Oh great lord, is it time yet for another celebration?

It would be time, and very soon, for a great wedding feast. But the Twice-Born was not ready to allow his erratic servant the joy of making such a plan—not just yet. Instead, Dionysus told him, "We will be lucky, you ancient fool, if any of us live long enough to see another celebration. Hades will always be waiting somewhere."